LASTING TREASURE

ANDREW ROTH

ELK LAKE PUBLISHING INC

PUBLISHING THE POSITIVE
Plymouth, Massachusetts

COPYRIGHT NOTICE

Cover and Interior Design: Derinda Babcock

Editor(s): Cristel Phelps, Deb Haggerty

PUBLISHED BY: Elk Lake Publishing, Inc., 35 Dogwood Drive, Plymouth, MA 02360, 2022

Library Cataloging Data

Names: Roth, Andrew (Andrew Roth)

Lasting Treasure / Andrew Roth

360 p. 23cm × 15cm (9in × 6 in.)

ISBN-13: 978-1-64949-510-5 (paperback) | 978-1-64949-511-2 (trade paperback) | 978-1-64949-512-9 (e-book)

Key Words: Western, Frontier, Romance, Cowboys, Treasure, Friendship, 1860s

Library of Congress Control Number: 2022932105 Fiction

DEDICATION

To my wife Laurie, my children David and Kate, Cameron and Sara, and my grandchildren Levi and Emma. Thanks for being the treasures of my life.

CHAPTER ONE

Wendy Moylan stared at the dark forest beyond the fallow fields, longing niggling at the edges of her mind as rain dribbled down the long windowpane. Around her, the library felt cold as a tomb. Despite the inclement weather, she yearned to be in her beloved woods, concealed from everyone. Absently, she smoothed her dress, the black taffeta rustling beneath her touch.

Tiny rivulets streamed lazily down the glass, and she shifted in the high-backed chair, wishing the servants had started a blaze in the library fireplace. No doubt they'd believed the spacious room would remain vacant during the funeral. But Wendy craved the retreat the chilled room offered. Disappointment stirred as the comfortable chairs and high windows did not provide the relief she sought, the countless colorful books normally affording peace and solitude when she could not be outdoors.

She leaned forward, and the stiff, tight dress rustled again. The unusual sound grated on Wendy's taut nerves, reminding her how much she preferred the comfort of her riding breeches. Besides, Wendy hated the worn black dress that reminded her there was no money for new clothes.

The library door opened behind her, the sound of distant conversations and the clinking of glass drifting in with the intruder to Wendy's refuge. The door closed softly, and she relaxed when she recognized Aunt Lil's soft tread.

"I thought I'd find you here." Her aunt's accusing tone rang hollow as she halted beside the chair and rested a hand on Wendy's shoulder.

The young woman leaned her cheek against her aunt's knuckles, closing her eyes briefly against her disturbing feelings. What would she do now? Certainly, Aunt Lil's situation was tied to her own. Wendy opened her eyes and gazed toward the high ceiling, beseeching answers from above. Would God guide her?

Lil gestured to the scattered buggies and horses tethered at the edge of the trees, wet saddles gleaming dully in the wan afternoon light. "Your father certainly knew a lot of people."

"They probably knew him better than I did," Wendy murmured bitterly.

Aunt Lil clucked her tongue and squeezed Wendy's shoulder. "He should've spent more time here—with you—but after your mother died—"

"After Mother died," Wendy cut in. "Father wanted nothing to do with Moylan Plantation or me," Wendy finished for her aunt, unable to conceal the hurt in her words.

An awkward silence hung in the dreary room until Wendy sighed. "I'm sorry, Aunt Lil, but I can't take any more sympathy wishers. Besides, the war is as good as over in Arkansas. Why do so many of the men wear the gray uniform here? Haven't they had enough of fighting?"

Lil said nothing for a long moment while the pair stared out the window at the sodden grounds. Dark woods stretched to the horizon, the unseen Arkansas River beyond, as water dripped endlessly from naked branches. Thunder rumbled as they watched the storm that had pelted the region for the past two days, turning the roads into soggy, muddy paths. The forest would be saturated, yet Wendy preferred their gloomy game trails to the faded finery of the ramshackle plantation they lived in.

The older woman drew a sharp breath, drawing Wendy's attention once more. "You know why they're here," Lil remarked crisply. "They need to know the Moylan business will go on, despite Tad's death. And the war is not over yet, not to them."

Wendy nodded. "I know. But I wish I could escape to the woods, ride my horse in the rain, and possibly jump a sleeping deer from the brush. Mary said we need meat. Besides, no doubt Mr. Whitmore will continue Father's affairs."

Lil glanced at her with narrowed eyes. "Did he say so? Have you spoken to him about it?"

"No." Wendy bit her lip, not wanting to think more about Father's unsavory business partner, his inappropriate attentions of a year ago still fresh in her mind. "No, and I won't. He looks at me ... like a tasty morsel. I don't trust him."

"Nor should you," Lil agreed as she turned to lead the way toward the door. "And no more talk of forays into the forest. Act like a lady, with no mention of rifles and riding and hunting. Don't forget you are mistress here. Now, on your feet. We have guests to attend to."

Lil paused by the door, her hand on the knob as Wendy lifted reluctantly from the chair and joined her. "And put a smile on your pretty face," Aunt Lil ordered. "You might catch the eye of a suitor, funeral or not."

Wendy rolled her eyes, unable to stomach her aunt's constant jibes to pursue a husband. She had no intentions of finding a mate.

A scowl settled on Wendy's smooth features as Lil opened the door and stepped into the dark hallway. She followed Lil, squinting into the passageway, overwhelmed with a sense of responsibility and duty she didn't want to face. Her heart ached with the grief the recent funeral had brought to her, filling Wendy with memories of her dear mother's passing eleven years before. Pursing her lips, she plunged into the murky hallway.

Their feet made little sound on the worn carpet as the pair trod softly down the long corridor toward the great front hall. But grief and sorrow accompanied her as she followed Lil, determined to do her part despite her reserve. She felt shocked at the number of strangers who attended her father's funeral, so many men who spoke knowingly of the man she knew so little about.

Her steps faltered as they neared the door to Tad Moylan's office, and Wendy hesitated, sagging against the door frame, ignoring the impatient look on her aunt's face. She glanced out the tall window at the gray day beyond before allowing her gaze to sweep the lavishly furnished room where a thick layer of dust lay over everything.

"I rarely saw him here, although the office holds a memory of him. A hint of cigar smoke lingers," Wendy whispered. Deep shadows filled every corner of the small room, and again, her eyes sought the familiarity of the distant woods through the long window behind her father's oak desk.

Lil huffed as she peered into the little room. "He was my brother, yet so different than when we grew up here. He became so driven after your mother's death." Her gaze shifted to Wendy. "I remember her funeral when I came to live with you. You were only twelve then."

Wendy nodded, a sad smile lifting the corners of her mouth. "You've been a mother to me, you and Mary. Father never liked coming home after that."

"He loved you, Wendy," Lil said in a reassuring tone. "But when the sickness took your mother, he wanted nothing around to remind him of the grief he suffered."

"Not even me?" Wendy felt the tear slide down her cheek, chilling her.

"No, dear, especially you. You're the spitting image of your mother, a constant reminder of his loss." Lil paused and then smiled. "You are like her in looks but also in temperament and spirit. Tad couldn't control her, and he couldn't control you."

"He didn't even try. I wish he had tried." Wendy crossed her arms over her chest. "My own grief became more than I could bear."

"Enough," Lil said, patting Wendy's arm. "Everyone deals with grief in their own way." Her smile fled and Lil squared her shoulders. "And now you roam the wilds with a rifle like any backwoodsman. No decent gentleman will look at you, despite your trim figure and glowing skin. But a lady should not have tanned cheeks," she reproved, giving Wendy a sharp study before turning and leading the way down the hall once again. "I feel I've let your mother down somehow," she called over her shoulder.

Wendy pursed her lips, not completely understanding. She wanted to shout about her loss, her sorrow, but bit her tongue. Now Father was dead, and she didn't have to understand. Despite Lil's nearness, Wendy felt alone, lost, wondering which way to turn. And God had been no help, silent, leaving Wendy feeling pensive and weary. Did Jesus know her anguish?

Lil drew a deep breath, drawing Wendy again from her self-absorbed reverie. "There are people here you must greet and thank for coming. The officers are eager to be off before the Yankees learn they're here. You are the mistress of the house. Many difficult tasks will fall to you now, the heir of your father's property and business." Her aunt's voice was stern but laced with a touch of kindness Wendy appreciated. "Responsibility calls, Wendy, and you must meet it head on. You're not a little girl anymore."

Wendy nodded absently as she trailed Lil through the shadowed corridor, the sound of voices rising as they neared the great hall. Another rumble of thunder pealed in the distance, reminding Wendy the storm had not yet passed. She couldn't just ride horses in the hills and pretend difficult times had not rained all around her. Lil would need her assistance.

And her father? Wendy's thoughts darted to the reason for the day's event, and her palms grew moist. What would he wish

Wendy to do? She couldn't guess what he wanted for his only child. He'd been so elusive since Mother died, visiting his land holdings in Little Rock only when absolutely necessary. Yet his supportive funds had arrived every month like clockwork, even if their amount had dwindled the past few years.

Although she'd turned to the Lord as Lil and Mary instructed, Wendy had found an uneasy solace from her heartache, as if Jesus wanted something different from her. Doggedly, she persisted in wandering the lonely hills of the Moylan property. Surely this cold winter storm could not keep her from her roving if not for Father's unexpected funeral. Not even the advent of the war nearly four years ago could keep her from riding and exploring the woods and waterways of her father's extensive estate. But as Lil pointed out, she wasn't a little girl anymore. Things were sure to change now.

Located just west of the city, the Moylan house could not be called a proper plantation. There were no slaves and only a few hired servants, who managed the big house. The hemp and cotton fields of many years ago had been let go after Mrs. Moylan determined the injustice of slavery. Weeds had taken over some of the fields, others leased to nearby farmers to manage. Father had been consumed with his shipping business in far off New Orleans, and when Mother died of pneumonia a month after Wendy's twelfth birthday, things had only become more desolate on the Moylan place.

Wendy shivered as she peered farther down the hallway and glimpsed the tall doors of the great hall, her thoughts turning to the throng of strangers gathered just beyond. She had a responsibility to greet each of them and thank them for their condolences. They had all conducted business with her father in some capacity or another, even the army officers that were present. Yet an undertone of curiosity hovered above the crowd, filling the old house like the stench of a rotted carcass. Duty and respect had brought these many mourners, but Wendy sensed something deeper. They wondered if their business arrangements would continue now that Tad Moylan had died.

Wendy understood, for she also wondered about her own future.

Restless voices sounded behind the thick doors of the great hall and Lil halted, hand on the doorknob as she turned to Wendy.

The older woman's features were shrouded in the darkened passageway, but Wendy heard the anxiety in her aunt's voice as Lil spoke. "Remember ... grace, poise, decorum. Ignore any doubtful comments regarding your father's business enterprises."

Wendy nodded and forced a shaky smile as the pair of women pushed the heavy doors open and entered the huge room.

CHAPTER TWO

Aunt Lil marched into the great hall with her head held high, shooting Wendy another sharp glance before she merged into the milling crowd. Wendy hesitated only an instant before circulating among the throng, shaking hands, and nodding courteously to everyone she met. Tables laden with platters of food were surrounded by men in business suits or the gray uniforms of the Confederacy, and Wendy spoke with many of them, ignoring the countless inquiries about her future. And not just regarding her father's business. At twenty-three, Wendy was far too old not to be married, or at least engaged, to a serious suitor. But these days, women sometimes waited for men fighting the distant war, the conflict in Arkansas already decided after the Union Navy controlled the Mississippi River. Grant's capture of Vicksburg effectively isolated Texas, Louisiana, and Arkansas from the rest of the rebellious southern states.

Wendy paused before a trio of gray clad soldiers as they bowed to her, all three smelling of rum. Small clusters of guests whispered in hushed tones around them.

"Thank you, gentlemen, for coming to my father's funeral. I know how difficult this must be for you to attend with the Yankee occupation only a stone's throw away."

"Little Rock has fallen," one man agreed. "But the South is far from defeated in Arkansas."

Wendy arched an eyebrow at his fanciful claim. Even she knew the last of the Confederacy's great armies were hemmed in around Richmond, the Confederate capital, or on the run in the Shenandoah Valley. Surely the war could not last much longer.

"Besides," another soldier offered. "A patriot such as your father deserves the respect of other loyal men. His shipping deals have helped supply the Confederacy through many challenging days."

He paused and allowed his gaze to roam over Wendy's lithe form. She blushed, the heat rising to her cheeks, but she lifted her chin. *The smuggler's daughter,* she mused, her gaze locked on each man who addressed her, refusing to crumble before their brazen glances.

The officer continued, his gaze darting to his comrades as he did so. "Although your father did not join the military, his efforts cannot go unappreciated."

"True enough," the last soldier added. "When New Orleans fell in '62, it was only through the tireless work of men like Tad Moylan that our boys in gray still received food and weapons. He is responsible for saving countless lives."

The three men nodded, but Wendy sensed the discordant hints in their praise. Although smuggling was extremely profitable, it was not respectable, not even by the desperate Confederate officers. They would praise her father to her face, but their ill-mannered looks proved her suspicions. Her father had been a scoundrel.

Despite the difficulty of the ongoing war, Moylan had maintained his business. Shipping was still lucrative, even though now it was the Union Army that controlled the ports of New Orleans. Union gunboats patrolled the waters of the lengthy Mississippi River. Had her father dealt with the Yankees too? Wendy bit her lip, deciding she didn't really want to know the truth.

"I'd heard your father had taken a partner," one of the officer's said, tilting his head as he studied Wendy. What could she say? Randall Whitmore had become her father's partner, but Wendy had met the man only last year, the rogue not bothering to conceal his interest in her. Since then, she'd always gone riding when the business partners met at the estate, which was seldom.

"He's from Mobile, I understand," the officer persisted. Wendy nodded, remembering the same information, although she couldn't understand the interest in Randall Whitmore.

"Of course, he will continue your father's business?"

Wendy squinted at the three men, finally comprehending. These men still needed supplies from the blockade runners and the smugglers. The war wasn't over yet, despite the ever-tightening noose of the Union blockade around southern ports.

Should she warn these men? Surely Randall Whitmore was not a trustworthy man. Then she nodded agreeably. They could make their own assessment in good time.

"Speak of the devil," an officer hissed as a form glided nearby, stepping closer to Wendy than necessary.

Twenty years her senior, Randall Whitmore still appeared very handsome. His short, cropped hair showed silver at the temples, but his manner reflected strength and vitality. His perfectly tailored suit looked out of place among the other guests in their worn, threadbare costumes and uniforms. Whitmore's watery blue eyes darted restlessly, roving around the gathering. He reminded Wendy of a rat searching for some forgotten or overlooked crumb. His piercing gaze settled upon her, and he smiled, the corners of his mouth tipping as if he'd discovered a tasty tidbit. A shiver ran down her back, but she straightened and kept her place beside the trio of officers.

Before Whitmore could speak or address the quartet around him, a distinguished, tall soldier halted before Wendy, bowing slightly. The other officers shifted, and Wendy saw the golden epaulets on the newcomer's shoulders. The general wanted to pay his respects.

"Miss Moylan, I am General Stafford. I worked repeatedly with your father to procure supplies. He smuggled goods through the Yankee lines on more than one occasion. I can tell you your father was a true patriot."

She bowed in return and shook the general's outstretched hand. "Thank you, sir. I know my father did all he could for the war effort," she quipped woodenly, unsure if she should be proud of her father's contribution to the Confederacy.

The general's glance took in Whitmore, and Wendy saw a scowl pucker the senior officer's features. "Well, Whitmore, I've been informed you employ deserters and river pirates. Will you continue Tad Moylan's business?"

"Of course, General," Whitmore replied easily, shooting a quick look at Wendy. She tensed, wondering at his meaning. Certainly, his business dealings didn't include her. She wanted nothing to do with her father's illicit occupation.

"And your disreputable agents?" The general took a step forward, pressuring Whitmore to respond to his charge.

Randall shrugged. "Whatever it takes, General. We all serve the Confederacy in our own way."

"But some receive a profit," General Stafford growled.

"Excuse me," Wendy muttered and moved away, annoyed at Whitmore's presence and connection with her family. She didn't trust him and wanted nothing further to do with the rascal. Perhaps she would never see him again after today.

Brushing her annoyance aside, she continued to mingle with the guests and to thank them for their attendance. For the remainder of the afternoon, Wendy made herself agreeable to the many strangers who made kind remarks regarding her father while she stole impatient glances through the windows to the darkening forest beyond. She felt as if she were in a play where she acted the role of a dutiful, loving daughter. But she yearned for the day's end.

LASTING TREASURE

Wendy felt a sour grin tug at the corner of her lips. Dutiful? Hardly. Hadn't she hidden these many years from reality herself? After her mother passed away, hadn't Wendy disappeared into the woods and swamps of the family estate just as Tad Moylan had disappeared into the business dens of New Orleans and Mobile?

She recalled Aunt Lil's words—everyone dealt with grief differently.

Across the crowded room, she caught her aunt's eye, a strained smile passing between them. The spinster sister of Tad Moylan, her aunt had come to be all the family Wendy knew or cared about. But the older woman had indulged Wendy's fancy to ride the countryside, only occasionally forcing her to meet with the few suitors who'd unsuccessfully tried to win her hand in marriage. Rumors circulated of the wild girl Wendy had developed into, and only those men determined to gain the Moylan money were tempted to approach the shy, isolated young woman. Secretly, Wendy delighted in her reputation, avoiding as much contact with others as Lil allowed. Yet her self-imposed exile was lonely.

Aunt Lil worked her way through the thinning throng and sidled next to Wendy. "See anyone that takes your fancy?"

Wendy's eyes widened at her aunt's whispered insinuation. "This is hardly the time to find a beau," she hissed through clenched teeth.

"Take advantage of every opportunity, girl, or you'll end up alone like me," Lil warned as Wendy moved among the attendees and out of earshot.

The afternoon wore on, most people departing before sunset. Only a few holdouts remained, reluctant to leave while food was still available. Many had experienced the deprivation the war had brought. Only after removing the food trays from the scattered tables did the last of the crowd disappear, a somber quiet descending upon the darkening house.

Gratefully, Wendy escorted the final guests to the door, sighing as she closed the heavy oak panel behind them. She leaned against the door and listened to the steady rain outside as she studied the lengthening shadows across the hardwood floor of the great hall. Exhausted after the day's events, she waved to her aunt and headed down the hall toward the sanctuary of the library.

"Wendy," Lil called after her, the older woman managing the servants as they cleaned up while Wendy made her escape. "We need to talk."

But Wendy only waved again and stole down the dark passageway, a sense of hurry propelling her. She needed to get away, to be alone. She wasn't used to crowds and parties and lots of people demanding her attention.

She entered the library and closed the door behind her with a satisfying click. She closed her eyes, soaking in the comforting scent of dusty books and old furniture. Her shoulders slumped.

"Well, it's about time," a familiar voice snarled. Wendy opened her eyes, staring at Randall Whitmore where he stood beside the tall window, the final rays of the setting sun revealing the crooked smile on his handsome face.

CHAPTER THREE

Wendy tensed anew, and blinked. "Mr. Whitmore," she stammered as she straightened. "What are you doing here?"

Something about his poised stance warned her, and Wendy drew a deep breath, steadying herself for a new ordeal. Apparently the trying events of the long day were not over yet.

His initial impatience melted away and he grinned. "Hello, Miss Wendy," he drawled, fixing a piercing gaze upon her like a snake staring down its prey.

Should she be frightened by this business associate of her late father? She chewed her lip, wondering at his presence.

"Come over here by the window where I can get a good look at you," he insisted with a ring of authority that nettled her. Still, he'd been her father's partner, and Wendy found herself moving toward the far end of the room. She halted before him, a subtle glow of the muted sunset casting dark shadows in the lines of his face. He reminded her a little of her father, austere and formidable, but there was something different too. A hungry look glinted in his pale blue eyes Wendy didn't like.

She shot a worried glance toward the door, wishing she hadn't been so hasty to leave the great hall. Randall must've sensed her disquiet, for he moved to block any escape, assuming an innocent looking position between her and the door.

"There," he purred as he leaned on the wing-backed chair, Wendy's favorite. "Your figure stands out better with the light behind you." He paused, leering openly. "You're a right handsome girl, Wendy Moylan."

"And you are no gentleman, Mr. Whitmore." Wendy bristled and glanced again at the door. Would Lil come check on her?

Whitmore chuckled as he slid a hand inside his suit coat and withdrew a thin cigar. He bit the end and retrieved a match from another pocket. A quick flick of his wrist against the back of the corduroy chair and the match flared.

With his gleaming eyes upon Wendy, Randall bent to meet the flaming stick, drawing deeply as the end of the cigar glowed. A cloud of smoke obscured his face for a moment.

"I've been your father's partner for almost two years and have learned many things," the businessman began. His manner seemed relaxed while Wendy felt the anxiety mount within her. She crossed her arms protectively over her chest.

"What things?" She hoped he didn't hear the tremor in her voice.

He smiled an unpleasant smile, almost a sneer. "I have learned that the Confederacy cannot win this war, and your father was a horrible businessman."

Wendy could not refute his declaration about the Confederacy. Surely, she'd tried hard to ignore the war that tore the country apart. She'd always suspected her father's business dealings but didn't like to think of them, either. It had been enough that he sent money to Aunt Lil regularly, allowing Wendy to wander the dark paths of the forest and remember her mother.

"Father made lots of money," Wendy countered, choosing her way carefully. "This estate and the extensive property seem to affirm rather than disprove his business abilities."

Whitmore snorted. "This estate? They freed the slaves almost twenty years ago and only a few servants keep up the big house, the garden, and the stables. The other buildings have fallen to ruin and the fields are choked with weeds or leased to other farmers. Yes, I'm well aware of the land's worth. Smuggling various goods has provided a nice income for your family, but now that is over."

"Over?" Wendy felt her chest tighten as her heart thudded slowly. She didn't think things could get worse.

He drew on his cigar again and patted his coat pocket. "I have letters confirming I possess all of your father's lucrative holdings including this estate."

His words struck Wendy like a fist. Now she guessed his game. He owned her house, the woods along the river, and the distant hills where she loved to race her horses to feel the wind in her hair.

"He owes me a great deal of money," Whitmore went on, a cloud of blue smoke lingering around him in the darkening room. He took a step toward her, and she backed against the cold windowpane.

"His dealings were losing money. More than one of his cargoes was seized by the Yankees, and I lent him the capital to continue." He took another step closer, and Wendy's gaze darted past him, looking over his shoulder, gauging her chances at making a run for the door.

He chuckled again, his mirthless laugh laced with anticipation. "I already own everything he had … except you."

Wendy glared at him. "What does that mean?"

Instead of replying, he merely smiled. She could barely make out his features in the fading light, but his eyes gleamed with malice. A final vestige of courage crept into her, and she lifted her chin. "Whatever your deals with Father, they don't include me."

"They do now," he barked. "I already own everything. This plantation is mine. If you want to stay in your little kingdom with your aunt and horses and servants, I have a proposition for you."

The thought of Lil and her being set adrift into the unknown unnerved Wendy. Where would they go? She didn't even know if they had sufficient funds to make such a move. Wendy narrowed her eyes. "Proposition?"

Whitmore nodded, his smile spreading across his shadowed face. "Marry me."

Wendy gasped, her eyes widening. "But ... but I don't love you," she spluttered.

He laughed so loudly, she almost stomped her foot.

"I don't love you either, Wendy. But you'll be able to stay here and provide a home for your aunt. My business keeps me very busy, so I'll only come here rarely for, uh, marital visits. You'll keep the life you've become accustomed to, and I will be away often. Ideal for both of us."

"Preposterous," Wendy whispered. The tightness around her chest made it difficult to breathe, and she felt as if she might pass out. "I'm a lady, a Christian. I would never enter into such an arrangement. Your suggestion disgusts me. You disgust me."

"You need to climb down from that ivory tower you've created in your mind," Randall snapped. "Everyone knows your grandfather, old Sean Moylan, came here from the old country with nothing. It was his hard work and sweat that earned your family's fortune. There's not a drop of aristocratic blood in your veins. You're as Irish as Paddy's pig, no more a lady than I am. If it weren't for your father's ill-gotten gain, you'd be nobody."

"Get out," Wendy hissed, unable to keep the quaver from her voice now as his slur cut her to the quick.

He shrugged and took a step backward, then another. "Your father owes me forty thousand dollars. He can't pay me dead, and I know you haven't the funds, but if you marry me, the debt is forgotten. Otherwise, you will have sixty days to vacate these premises. I intend to clean the place up and put free labor on here. The war is as good as over, slavery is dead, but cotton will bring high prices after the war. I will become a respectable landowner, but you will be homeless, penniless, with nothing. You see, Wendy, you need me."

LASTING TREASURE

Wendy couldn't speak. She realized her constricting chest was from squeezing herself tightly, her arms still crossed before her, but she couldn't reply to the ludicrous demands of this vile man. He made no attempt to disguise his crude appraisal as his gaze traveled slowly down her slim form, like a horse buyer evaluating a young filly, making Wendy blush with shame and anger.

With a nod, he turned and walked to the door. He hesitated, and Wendy could barely see him now, the room cast entirely in darkness except for the dull opaque light of twilight through the tall window behind her. "Remember, you have sixty days to either marry me or leave this house. Either way, I will develop the land as I see fit. This place has a lot of potential. The choice is yours."

The door closed behind him, leaving Wendy alone with her troubles.

CHAPTER FOUR

Wendy slumped into her favorite chair and choked. Her lungs strained to draw enough breath, and she straightened, inhaling deeply as she clenched the arms of the chair, her thoughts whirling. Marry Randall Whitmore? She wanted to laugh at the ridiculous notion, but fear gripped her, unwilling to release its icy hold on her heart.

Without Father's money, could she maintain the house and stables? Financial affairs had been left to Lil, and Wendy knew nothing of the expenses of the dilapidated plantation. Her self-absorbed existence had allowed her to ignore the raging war beyond the borders of the estate, but now things had changed in the twinkling of an eye. As if by magic, her situation had altered, her free lifestyle thrown aside for one of expectation and responsibility. She couldn't stay here any longer, and she wouldn't marry Randall Whitmore.

She tilted her head, staring out the tall window into the darkness. She couldn't marry him, could she? He'd promised not to visit often, to allow her continued freedom. Should she consider the wicked man's sideways proposal and maintain the big house, a home for her and Lil? Surely her decision would impact her aunt's future as well as her own. Lil had been more than an aunt, filling a mother's role Wendy desperately needed.

She shook her head and drew another deep breath, crossing her hands in her lap as she considered her options. Aunt Lil said to always bring concerns before the Lord. God did not want his children to struggle alone. The Holy Spirit had been given as a guide and counselor. Surely the Lord would give her a direction, an answer to her dilemma.

"Father," Wendy breathed into the gloom, her heart lifting as she turned toward the Lord. "I know I can trust you, but I don't know what to do. I hate the idea of marrying Mr. Whitmore. He's not a believer, and I know what the Bible says about marrying unbelievers. But I'm frightened. Where will we go if I don't marry him? Lil is not a young woman, and I have no skills, no trade to fall back on."

The word "useless" flashed across her mind, and Wendy winced. What abilities did she possess that might help her and Lil find work or a new place to live?

A sense of panic welled within her, and she felt the despair threaten to swallow her like the fish that swallowed Jonah. "No, Lord, I will not allow the devil to trick me with his negativity. You are with me. I can do all things through Christ who strengthens me. Please don't let me despair."

Lil's favorite passage glowed in her heart and Wendy recited the familiar words. "Be joyful in hope, patient in affliction, and faithful in prayer." She pressed into the chair's soft backing, surrendering to Jesus, allowing his spirit to speak to her heart. "I know you are with me," she repeated, and the heavy blackness of night seemed to fade away. "Tell me what to do."

She shifted as her eyes roamed the unseen bookshelves. Only a dim outline hovered around the edges of the tall window as the steady rain continued outside, the storm obscuring any hint of stars or moon. Yet anticipation seeped into Wendy. She was not alone, and a smile crept to her and pushed her cheeks higher.

"I am not defeated," she whispered into the murky room, and she felt bolstered by an unseen presence. "Together, we can handle this."

Despite the sudden support, fear persisted, and she craved the company of her housemates. Grasping the arms of the chair, she pulled herself erect. Wendy lifted her chin, attempting strength. "Onward, Christian soldier," she whispered, unable to ignore the doubts in her own words.

She marched from the room, leaving the library door open behind her as she made her way toward the kitchen. She navigated the darkened passages until a soft glow beneath a doorway revealed her destination. Behind the door, tired voices told her Lil helped Mary and Jasmine with cleanup. She pushed the kitchen door wide and blinked in the glare from several lanterns clustered on the table, gathered together for oil refills. Jasmine and her mother, Mary, bustled around the room as Lil managed the water pots boiling on the stove.

"Hello, child," Mary greeted as she gestured to Jasmine for assistance. The former slave woman had been freed two decades earlier by Wendy's mother but still served the family faithfully. "Help me lift these pots, Jasmine."

Mary's daughter moved hastily to grasp the heavy cauldron and pour streaming water into the sink. They replaced the empty pot on the stove where Lil filled the vessel again from the hand pump on the counter, water sizzling as the stream splashed into the hot metal container.

"Dry for me, Wendy." Jasmine handed her a dish towel, and Wendy sagged against the counter while the servant girl scrubbed dishes.

"How are you, dear?" Lil smiled at Wendy from beside the stove, but Wendy read the fatigue and concern in her aunt's eyes. Did she guess the new calamity that had fallen on her since Father's recent death?

Wendy steeled herself, trying hard to lean into the Lord. He was with her, right? "You'll never believe what just happened in the library. On the eve of my father's funeral, I received a marriage proposal."

She wanted to laugh at how outrageous her words sounded, but the severity of her situation overwhelmed her, and Wendy's shoulders slumped as she took a plate from Jasmine and started drying.

"Mercy." Lil clucked. "What next?"

"Men," Mary huffed from the table as she trimmed a wick and filled a lamp with oil. "It never surprise me how stupid men can be. How is proposing marriage at a funeral ever a good idea?" She cackled and shook her head, the oil jug shaking unsteadily in her arms.

"Mama, you're going to spill that lamp oil and we don't have no more," Jasmine cautioned as she handed another plate to Wendy.

"Who?" Lil's direct query drew Wendy's gaze to her aunt, the dish towel stilling in her hands.

"Randall Whitmore," Wendy whispered. Her eyes dropped to the worn boards of the plank floor as Lil gasped.

"That man is a bigger pirate than my brother and not fit to wipe the dirt off your boots," Lil declared from between clenched teeth as she waved her stirring spoon like a saber above her head. "What is this world coming to when disreputable men feel they can propose to decent women, even girls half their age?"

"He is handsome," Jasmine put in dreamily. "And rich."

"He's a no account." Lil parried quickly and plunged her spoon into the simmering pot.

"And not worthy of Miss Wendy, no matter how rich the rascal is," put in Mary as she shot Jasmine a disapproving glare before her gaze shifted back to Wendy.

"What did you say?" Lil's stirring slowed as another pot began to boil.

Wendy hesitated. "Well, I said no. But he told me Father owes him a great deal of money."

"Did he tell you that before or after he proposed?" Mary tilted her head while she rested the jug of lamp oil on the edge of the table.

A scowl played across Wendy's face as she tried to recall the details of the unexpected proposition, more like a business deal than a heartfelt appeal. She sighed. "I don't know. What does it matter? He told me to marry him or Aunt Lil and I are out of the house."

Lil gasped again and her eyes widened as she stared at Wendy. "The no account," she hissed, eyes blazing.

The room stilled and everyone grew silent as Wendy's words settled around them like an unexpected storm blowing an ill wind. Abruptly, Jasmine lifted her chin, scrubbed another plate, and handed the dish to Wendy. "So what?"

"What do you mean?" Wendy accepted the clean plate.

"I mean, so what? Who cares how old he is or what he wants? He's offering you a good home, plenty of money, a comfortable living. I'll bet his business will keep him from Little Rock like it did Mr. Moylan."

"He said it would," Wendy corroborated.

"There you go," Jasmine said with a sly grin. "Marry the rascal and live good. I don't know that you have any choice."

"Hush, girl," Mary snapped as she rose and took a step toward the younger women. "You have no business giving Miss Wendy marriage advice or guidance. She is a lady who—"

"Who has nothing else but a pretty face." Jasmine's cold assessment quieted the room once more, and Wendy flinched, hating the serving girl's callous estimation of her sum worth. But surely Jasmine was right. Besides a firm seat in the saddle and a true aim, Wendy possessed little to recommend her to eligible suitors. Even the pretense of owning land had now been stripped from her.

"Nonsense," Lil put in with a sharp glance at Wendy. "You are a lady, with a good name and, uh, a good name, I say."

Wendy sighed loudly. "A good name is not enough," she said softly and tried to smile at Jasmine as she took another dish to dry. "Jasmine is right. I have nothing now. No money, no wealthy father, no estate. If I don't marry Mr. Whitmore, you and I will have even less."

Lil shook her head. "We have our faith. We will trust in the Lord."

"Faith don't put food on the table," Jasmine said quickly.

"Girl, you're not too old for me to take a switch to your backside if you don't stop being so contrary." Mary glowered at her daughter as she crossed her arms over her chest. "And faith does put food on the table, as I can swear. There must be something else Miss Wendy can do."

"Too bad she don't have a rich uncle or a secret treasure her daddy buried long ago," Jasmine offered with an apologetic look at Wendy.

Wendy narrowed her eyes when she saw the furtive glance exchanged between Mary and Lil. "What?" Her hurried demand reflected her growing anxiety. Would nothing present itself as an alternative to marrying Mr. Whitmore? Surely the Lord would not have her joined to an unbeliever just to provide a home for her and Lil. But the war had destroyed many of Wendy's neighbors and the roads were choked with the ruined refugees moving northward or to the far west. Where would Lil and she go if she refused to marry Mr. Whitmore?

"What?" Wendy asked again when Mary hesitated, and Lil shifted beside the stove. Mary pursed her lips as she put out the light from all of the lamps but one, casting the room in a dim glow.

"I was remembering when Miss Lil and Mr. Tad used to pour over your Grandfather Moylan's old journals of his travels out west. They would play for hours, drawing treasure maps and discussing battles with bandits or wild Indians."

Wendy peered intently at her aunt, searching for answers. "Journals?"

After a moment, Lil nodded. "Funny you should remember that, Mary. I thought the same thing." She frowned when Wendy pressed, squinting at her aunt while tapping her toe impatiently.

"There's nothing much to tell. Tad and I heard someone mention Daddy's travel journals and we tore the attic apart finding them. Two leather-bound ledgers of his days along the Santa Fe Trail and business deals with Spanish merchants. There was a vague account of an attack on a mule train loaded with trade goods."

She paused and lowered her spoon as Mary helped lift the hot pan and refresh the dish water in the sink. Jasmine added soap and plunged her hands into the steaming water.

"Aunt Lil, you're killing me. What about the attack on the mule train?"

Lil placed the empty pot beneath the hand pump and briskly worked the handle, water gushing with a hiss as the heated pan filled. "I don't recall the details. Something about sacks of gold."

"Gold?" Wendy rolled the magical word in her mouth, savoring the thrill that raced along her spine as Jasmine handed her another plate.

Lil waved a hand in the air. "I'm sure I don't remember any of the particulars now. That was decades ago. Tad and I were children. Something about an attack and some of the gold from mountain mines was hidden in a ravine or a canyon or in a secret crevice. I can't recall."

Wendy glanced at Mary as the servant nodded. "Yes, I remember something about a man visiting old Mr. Moylan one night, years later, and discussing plans to return to the place again. I don't remember anything coming of the idea."

Lil tilted her head, her lips puckering. "No, I don't either."

"You mean the treasure might still be there," Jasmine whispered as her eyes gleamed in the glow of the single lantern on the kitchen table. Mary had completed filling the lamps and screwed the lid on the oil jug. With a rag, she polished each glass chimney.

Lil laughed. "There was no treasure." She shot Mary a sharp scrutiny. "I don't recall a man coming to make plans with Father to return west. When was that?"

Mary waved her rag. "Sometime later, I think. Or maybe it was to join Crockett in Texas. Or Houston. I don't know. So many things have taken place with Texas and then the war with Mexico. Who can keep it all straight?"

Wendy tensed as she placed a dried dish in the cupboard. Was there any merit to the tale of lost treasure? Frustrated with Aunt Lil's and Mary's disjointed memories, Wendy tossed her towel on the table and looked at her aunt. "Where are those journals?"

CHAPTER FIVE

"Surely those reports weren't real, Wendy," Lil mused as she leaned back in her chair, eyes studying the kitchen ceiling thoughtfully. "Too bad, because we could use that gold right about now. Your father's money will be sorely missed."

Wendy brushed her aunt's comment aside like a pesky fly. "What did Father think of them?"

Lil smiled, her gaze darting to Wendy before drifting to the ceiling again, remembering. "Tad believed the journal entry was real. Even Pa said they were, his eyes glowing as he told us of the Indian attack that resulted in the gold being hastily hidden away, waiting for him to come claim the buried loot. I didn't learn until later that he wasn't actually there. When Father died before the Mexican War, Tad wanted to go after the treasure, but then he married, and you came along. I haven't thought of the journals since then."

Lil shot Mary a glance. "You remember our talks? We always included you in our plans."

Mary nodded as she finished wiping the base of each extinguished lamp, the polished globes glinting in the dull light of the single lamp, casting the corners of the room into shadows. "How could I forget? A lost treasure, any treasure, would consume the dreams of a young slave. I wondered how I could accompany you and Mr. Tad on the journey west."

Mary and Lil laughed. "Well, we would've taken you with us, Mary, have no doubt. We were an inseparable trio back then."

Mary wiped at her eyes with her apron. "Oh, the mischief we'd get into. I surely forgot those wild days before the war, and not this horrible one that has divided the country. No, I mean the war to spread our lands into the far west."

"You were a slave back then?" Wendy's question drew Mary's gaze and the servant woman sighed.

"Your sweet mama seen to it that there'd be no more slaves on Moylan Plantation. Mr. Tad was furious when he found out, yelling about the money he'd lost. He always valued money more than people. The good Lord called her home soon after that, but I stayed on. This place is my home."

Wendy touched the older woman's shoulder. "I'm glad you did, Mary. You're family."

Mary smiled and patted Wendy's hand. "Now, child, what you going to do about that gold? You need money to pay off that devil Mr. Whitmore."

Jasmine looked over her shoulder as she lifted a dripping dish from the suds. "Or you can forget this fancy story about lost treasure and marry Mr. Whitmore. That sounds the most sensible to me."

"No," Mary said as her smile fled. "Miss Wendy will not marry that scoundrel. The Lord would not wish such a joining. He has someone special for you, child, have no fear."

Lil stood and stretched, stifling a yawn. "I agree with Mary. Pray about your predicament, Wendy. There's nothing you can do about the treasure tonight. I daresay this has been a trying day and we're all tired."

Wendy lifted her discarded towel from the table and accepted another dish from Jasmine and rubbed briskly as she shook her head, recalling Whitmore's time limit. "I couldn't sleep, Aunt Lil. Tell me where the ledgers are, and I'll be going to the attic after dishes are done."

Mary took the towel and dish from Wendy. "Go now, before it gets any later. As you pray, the Lord will guide you. Maybe the journals will come to nothing, but then you'll know for sure. Search, knock, and the Lord will open a door."

Lil moved toward the hallway. "Grab a candle and let's go up there. I know precisely where the ledgers are, if memory serves me well. This will be a quick visit to the attic," she promised as she led the way along the dark passage.

Mary pressed a candle to the lamp and then handed the glowing tallow stick to Wendy. She smiled at the servant woman and hurried to catch Lil.

Thunder rumbled in the distance, reminding Wendy the storm continued outside. Boards creaked as they ascended the wide staircase to the second floor where bedrooms lined the long hallway. Wendy paused as they halted before the attic door. She lifted the candle high, squinting at the door. What answers lie just beyond the barrier?

Lil studied her in the half light of the glowing candle. "What's wrong, dear? There's nothing to be afraid of here. This attic is messy and stuffy, but no monsters live here."

Wendy shifted. "I know that. It's just ... well, I wonder what awaits me. Jasmine is right. I have nothing else, no talents to recommend me. What will I do if I can't find the money to pay Mr. Whitmore? I don't want to marry him."

"Nor should you even consider doing so." Lil huffed in exasperation. "A wicked man, to be sure. But I put no stock in the lost treasure of Sean Moylan. I don't believe it's real, and I don't think Tad did either or he'd surely have gone after the gold, money hungry as he was. The foolish dreams of his youth faded with the responsibilities of adulthood."

"You mean Mother and me," Wendy said softly, hanging her head. Oh, she missed her vivacious mother. Unlike Wendy, Mother's faith in Jesus had been so alive, so personal. Her relationship with Christ had been the wedge between Wendy's parents, but all of that didn't matter anymore, with both dead and gone.

Wendy's mother had been more than her mama. She'd been a real friend Wendy valued, just as the turmoil of womanhood had blossomed within her. Just when she truly needed a mother, Wendy found herself alone, wandering the dark woods for the peace her isolation afforded. Besides, Father didn't seem to mind her absence. Thank God Lil had come to stay, but the austere woman wasn't the same as Mother.

"Your father needed to grow up," Lil went on. "He avoided real responsibility and Pa allowed his tomfoolery. Tad married a beautiful woman and was given a working plantation, but he didn't want to settle down and work hard. He'd rather hobnob with those disreputable river pirates on the docks than socialize with honest people."

Aunt Lil's stinging words wounded Wendy because she knew they were true, but they hurt, nonetheless.

Grief weighed her down, and Wendy tilted her head. "But what am I going to do?" Her question sounded like a whimper in her ears, and Wendy hoped Lil wouldn't chide her for complaining.

"You're going to trust the Lord, like your mama did after she found Jesus. Oh, your daddy was mad as a hornet when she freed the slaves, but she had courage." She patted Wendy's arm. "You do too, dear."

Her kind words lacked conviction, and Wendy frowned. Without another word, Lil pushed the door open. Wendy leaned through the opening, the musty odor of the ancient chamber assailing her nostrils, the undisturbed air laced with dust. She followed Lil up the steep stairs, the rhythmic sound of dripping water growing louder as they climbed.

At the head of the stairs, Wendy peered past Lil to see the space littered with old trunks and racks of antique clothing, discarded furniture, and boxes of memorabilia. The leaky roof dribbled ceaselessly into strategically placed tin wash basins, proof someone visited the attic occasionally. Perhaps Mary or Jasmine dumped these receptacles after each storm, Wendy wondered as she moved past her aunt and studied the vintage luggage. Were the leather ledgers in there?

"Here," Lil directed as she led the way to a scarred and rotting bureau. She indicated Wendy should lift the light and Lil pulled the top drawer on the old dresser.

"Ah, here they are, just like I remembered." She drew the two leather volumes from the drawer and glanced at them briefly before handing them to Wendy.

"Which one has the story of the gold?" Wendy placed the candle atop the bureau and rifled the journal pages, glancing at the unfamiliar handwriting. Black ink had smudged some places, detailed maps filled others. Curiosity filled Wendy as she peered at the journals, wondering if the yellowed pages held a clue to her future. She stared at them, hope warring with reality within her. Her heart thudded and she glanced at Lil as her aunt watched her over the top of the books.

"Trust not in your own understanding, Wendy," Lil quoted. "Lean on the Lord. I don't know what his intentions are in this situation but allow him to work. Trust he has something for you that you cannot even imagine. Something better than you can even hope for. God longs to shower you with his goodness, but his guidance often doesn't look like what we expect. Sometimes you have to cross a desert to find the streams on the other side. Be patient and wait on the Lord."

Wendy tilted her head. "But I thought you didn't believe the gold is real."

"I'm not talking about the gold," Lil replied as she reached for the candle and led the way to the narrow staircase. Their footsteps made little sound in the halls as they walked, but Wendy's thoughts were far away, dreaming of wealth and the opportunity to stay at the old plantation, the buildings crumbling into ruination. But the trails along the river called to her, beckoning her to frequent her favorite haunts where she'd been left alone these many years since her mother's death. Like the abandoned things in the attic, Wendy had fallen into a pattern of uselessness, wasting time in idle recreation and isolation. Jasmine's stinging words came back to her, and she shivered, admitting her lack of abilities would force limited options. Her head whirled as she knew she must hope in lost treasure or marry Randall Whitmore. To leave the plantation and migrate elsewhere was out of the question. Especially for two single women during a great war. She and Lil had no funds for such a journey and certainly no talents for employment.

A third option whispered into her ear, and Wendy remembered the Lord. She could trust God had something in mind for her, something she couldn't envision. But did he?

She bumped into Lil in the darkness, her troubled thoughts unnerving her as Lil halted before a door. Wendy was startled to recognize her own chambers.

"Sorry, Aunt Lil," Wendy whispered, afraid to disturb the eerie solitude of the inky blackness around her. She glanced at her door, not sure how they'd arrived here so quickly.

"I will help Jasmine and Mary finish. You go to bed," Lil suggested, lifting the candle as Wendy opened her bedroom door. "Look over the journals, but don't get your hopes up. Better to spend time in prayer and petition the Lord."

Wendy nodded as her brow furrowed. "I know, but what if Jasmine is right. Perhaps I should just marry Mr. Whitmore, put aside what I want, and think of what is best for both you and me. This is our home. I wouldn't have any idea where to go if we were forced to leave Moylan Plantation."

Aunt Lil narrowed her eyes, her face setting in stern lines in the dim candlelight. "Now you listen to me, Wendy Moylan. You don't need to worry about me. The Lord is my shepherd, and I am the sheep of his hand. He will take care of me, whatever happens. But you are young, and the Lord wants to grow your faith. Perhaps Jasmine is right that you have few choices, but do not underestimate the Lord. He can part the Red Sea and strengthen shepherd boys to vanquish giants, and he can deliver forgiveness for sins through a man nailed on a cross. The Lord can handle any situation, including this one you find yourself in now. Only be patient, wait, and watch what God can do when we allow him to work. He promises to never leave or forsake you. He is with you now and wants to do a great thing in your life. Trust him."

Wendy shrugged and squinted in the gloom. "I guess so. But I only have sixty days to come up with something. Can I put such time constraints on God? Will he do something for me so quickly?"

Lil placed a hand on Wendy's arm and squeezed. "Wait on the Lord. Trust him," she repeated.

Wendy sighed. "I'll try," she mumbled.

Aunt Lil turned to go, talking over her shoulder as she moved down the murky hallway. "Besides, your father's lawyer is supposed to speak with us tomorrow, tell us the facts of your father's estate. Let's see what we can learn from Mr. Johannes. Perhaps Mr. Whitmore is speaking prematurely. Goodnight, dear."

Wendy leaned against her door as the dim halo of candlelight faded around the corner of the hallway, leaving her alone in the darkness, weighted down with her nagging problems.

CHAPTER SIX

Wendy opened the door and entered her chilled bedroom. Despite the late hour, she wanted a fire to chase the cold from the room but also to keep her company. She hated being alone with her troubling concerns. Perhaps a fire would cheer her on this cheerless day.

She stumbled toward the fireplace in the total darkness, arms outstretched. Her fingers fumbled along the edge of the mantel until she located the box of matches. The hissing flame fluttered and glowed, slicing the gloom with welcome light. Wendy bent to thrust the burning stick into the prepared kindling and her eyes fixed on the hungry little flames as they licked at the pyramid of splinters and dried pinecones.

Tomorrow the lawyer would meet with her and give confirmation of the true state of her father's business affairs. Tad Moylan had never been much of a father to her, but Wendy loved him and hoped he'd been wise in preparing for this unexpected yet inevitable day.

Wendy collapsed in a chair, sagging into the soft fabric as if her strength had failed. She clutched the two leather-bound books in her lap and watched the fire swell and dispel the inky night. Light revealed the phantoms that lurked around her, and Wendy found herself muttering prayers, long remembered Bible verses that came to her mind unbidden, repelling a sense of foreboding that threatened to overtake her.

She must trust God. Her worries consumed her and drove her to despair, but the light of the crackling fire reminded her that Jesus, the light of the world, was with her. He was faithful and she could trust him. He would help her, and he would conquer the darkness that swirled within her heart.

"Oh, Jesus," she whispered into the lonely room, and suddenly she didn't feel so lonely anymore. "You are with me, aren't you? You'll tell me what to do, right?"

Jasmine's sharp critique darted into her mind, and then Aunt Lil's sound caution pushed the servant girl's accusing words aside. Give in or fight? The warring ideas battled until Wendy held up a hand.

"I will gather information. That's wisdom. I will look at the journals and listen to what the lawyer has to say tomorrow. And I will shelf Mr. Whitmore's scandalous proposal for now as a final consideration, keeping all my options open."

She knew she was wrong to go against the mandates of Scripture regarding matrimony, but fear made her consider the sinful proposal anyway, at least for a while.

She lifted the first journal and scanned the beginning of the book. Page after page told of merchandise purchased, from whom for how much, and the anticipated return on the investment. Rifles, linen goods, bolts of colored cloth, steel traps, and hard to obtain glassware were listed and catalogued.

She leafed through the pages more rapidly, searching for the particular entry of the attacked mule train. Her examination was interrupted a few times to feed the fire, but after an hour, she felt satisfied the tale of the hidden gold was not in the first journal. She set the book aside and hefted the second book.

Wendy wished she had briefly glanced over both books before taking the time to read mundane information about purchases and sales, for the dog-eared page of the second journal led her immediately to what she sought.

Her blood raced when she found the correct entry, the margins marred with dirty smudges from other viewers. She thought of her young father and aunt peering over these same pages so long ago as she did now. Her eyes moved across the written lines of black ink, drinking in the information, hoping for clues to the lost gold.

Sean Moylan had been a teamster on the Santa Fe Trail and learned both the lands of the vast American plains and the deserts of northern Mexico. He'd left the business after marrying, settling on a plantation in Little Rock with his young family—virgin farmland for the expanding cotton empire sweeping the South—when the war for Texas independence broke out. Not willing to sit out the conflict, he raced to Texas and joined Sam Houston's army on the Brazos River. There he learned the fate of the defenders of the Alamo, the Spanish mission turned fort in San Antonio.

After the ensuing battle was won and Texas independence secured, Moylan was approached by a captured Mexican colonel named Gomez and offered an interesting proposition. For the loan of a fast horse and for agreeing to turn a blind eye, the colonel would share valuable information regarding a hidden treasure in the mountains northeast of Santa Fe.

Moylan knew Houston planned on releasing the Mexican prisoners but decided to play along and see if Gomez really had information about lost gold. His escape from the Texas camp was promised, and the colonel relayed a fantastic tale.

Wendy hesitated and looked up from her reading, a sense of anticipation washing over her. She wondered if the account of lost gold would have any significance on her life. Something whispered to her soul that these next few pages held great importance to her. A thrill raced up her arms, and she gripped the book tighter as she eagerly studied the journal again, her gaze locked on the dark scribbles of her grandfather's record.

Years before, as a young captain, Gomez had been commissioned to escort a government mule train from the gold mines in northern Mexico along the Rio Grande to Santa Fe.

His Indian scouts told him a large number of Apache were following the mule train, looking for an opportunity to raid the valuable cavalcade, more likely for the rifles and mule flesh the caravan offered rather than the gold. In an attempt to evade his pursuers, Captain Gomez led the mule train east into the mountains, crossing over the summit and down the Mora River, attempting to strike the Canadian River and approach Santa Fe from the east.

But the relentless Apache could not be shaken from the Mexican's trail, and the Indians attacked the mule train as the caravan wound along the smaller river, hurrying to reach the Canadian River, far from Apache territory.

The sudden attack took the guards of the cavalcade by surprise. A few mule skinners and soldiers died immediately as the others organized return fire. One mule driver, Ornelas, chased a frightened mule into a notch in the hills from which a narrow stream poured into the Mora. Gomez stressed this stream lay on the north side of the Mora. The captain pursued Ornelas, trying to protect both his men and the precious gold packs.

The frantic mule ran a short distance into the steep-sided ravine before the beast broke a leg on the rocks. Without waiting for instructions, Ornelas removed the heavy gold packs and stowed them in a crevice in the wall of the little canyon. Gomez helped conceal the canvas packs with stones before putting a bullet in the hapless mule, allaying its suffering.

Returning to the caravan, Ornelas and Gomez pushed the remaining men and mules down the mountain, returning fire upon the Apache as they trailed along. No more mules were downed, although three more soldiers and Ornelas lost their lives. Now, Gomez alone knew the whereabouts of the hidden gold.

As night descended, the caravan pushed on, refusing to halt, knowing the Apache hated to fight at night.

They passed two more small streams flowing into the Mora

before finally reaching the Canadian River. Turning south, the cavalcade lost the pursuing Apache and eventually returned to Santa Fe. Gomez received a medal for valor under fire and was sent immediately to a better posting near Mexico City. But he never forgot the hidden gold along the Mora River. With no opportunity to ever return to the region, Gomez was willing to trade his freedom for the information of the lost gold.

Wendy leaned back in her chair, pensive and nerves taut. Her cheeks ached and she realized her jaw clenched into a tight scowl. Working her jaw, she forced herself to relax.

She peered at the dark ceiling, wondering about God's intent, and then her gaze shifted to the faded pages once more. Sean Moylan released the Mexican colonel. The next few pages were filled with details of the emerging Texas government and Houston becoming president of the Lone Star Republic. There was no more mention of the gold.

Despite her efforts, Wendy felt the tension return, her shoulders hunching tightly against the chair back. What should she do? Could it be true that her father had signed papers giving Randall Whitmore a ruling voice in their partnership? How could her father do that to Wendy and his sister Lil?

Her fingers gripped the journal, squeezing the leather binding. Was the tale of lost gold true? Did this ledger contain the power of her escape from Whitmore's hold on her?

The fire had died down and suddenly Wendy felt too weary to replenish the fuel. She must get some sleep, if she could. The morrow promised to be challenging with the visit to her father's lawyer.

Still dressed in her black dress, she crawled into bed, pulling the covers after her. She lay on her back, staring into the dim surroundings of her silent room as the flames dwindled and went out, only a faint glow of embers casting a ruddy radiance near the fireplace. Even the rain had stopped, and the entire earth fell quiet, watchful, as if waiting to hear Wendy's decision.

What would she do? She drew a deep breath, attempting to fill her laboring lungs with refreshing air, but to no avail, as if unable to catch her breath. The panic lingered and she doubted she'd sleep.

"Help me, Jesus," she whispered into the blackness.

CHAPTER SEVEN

"What if it's all true, and Mr. Whitmore legally owns the house?"

Wendy's question sounded heavy to her own ears, and she wondered what Aunt Lil thought of leaving Moylan Plantation. Forever.

They walked the long lane, avoiding puddles as they made their way to the main road that led to Little Rock. Mr. Johannes expected them at ten o'clock, and Aunt Lil was very prompt about scheduled events. Wendy preferred to be a little late, to melt into a crowd, to avoid detection if possible. But today's meeting would not allow such a clandestine presence. This meeting would very likely define her future.

"We will not despair until despair cannot be avoided," Lil said brusquely. But Wendy could tell her aunt was merely trying to keep a stiff upper lip. No doubt she worried as much as Wendy at the imminent proceedings.

"Did you find the entry in the journal? The one of the gold hidden in the rocks?" Lil's quiet question did not conceal her deeper fears, and Wendy bit her lip, reluctant to share she had little hope of ever finding hidden treasure. But she hated to see the anxiety in Lil's eyes.

"I found the proper entry. Farfetched, at best. A tale for children, little else. I can't believe Grandfather fell for the trick to give a horse and allow the Mexican colonel to flee." She shuddered with a skeptical eye surveying the cold winter sky, and she drew her shawl tighter around her. "There's no gold."

Lil chuckled as she hunched her shoulders against the chill wind. "I think Tad and I came to the same conclusion, but the fanciful tale occupied our dreams and thirst for adventure. If the account were true, I'm sure Tad would have gone west."

They left the lane and turned into the main road, moving quickly to one side as a column of mounted soldiers trotted past, their blue uniforms looking so regal against the bleak background of leafless bushes and skeletal trees that lined the side of the road. They seemed such a well-fed lot, sitting tall in their cavalry saddles with gleaming black boots while the Confederate boys marched barefoot to battle.

Did any of them have sweethearts or wives back home? Wendy wondered at her loneliness as she watched the troopers ride from view. She had no husband or brother or boyfriend. Certainly, she'd avoided any suitor that made bold to call upon her, making sure they understood she had no interest in their unsolicited attentions.

Yet now an unfavorable marriage loomed before her. Wendy knew Lil didn't want her to accept Mr. Whitmore, surely even the Good Book frowned on such alliances between unbelievers and Christians. But a fear smoldered within Wendy's chest. She might be thrown out of her home soon and Lil along with her. Maybe Randall Whitmore offered more than marriage. Perhaps the security and protection that came with marriage would save both her and Lil.

She shot a sidelong glance at her aunt. The rigid lines of determination she read there spoke of Lil's strength, but Wendy still detected the soft contours of former youth, fading but still present. She wondered why Lil had never married and then glanced past her to the foliage beyond, washed clean from the previous night's rain.

Birds called to them from the thickets, the bare dogwood branches waving from beneath the towering elms and cottonwoods across the ditch. Deep woods filled the sodden lands beyond the river, waiting to be cleared for the inevitable cotton fields that had spread across the countryside since Wendy's childhood. Cotton was king around here, promoting not only the wealthy plantation owners, but the countless businesses that thrived because of the rich agricultural environment of Little Rock. Merchants, blacksmith shops, farriers, freighters, and river boats all benefitted by the exploding cotton prices that powered the Southern economy.

She glanced over her shoulder to see if the Yankee cavalry riders were still within sight, but they'd passed a corner of the road and disappeared. Only a single man followed at a distance, a red bandana tied around his head. She couldn't make out his features at this distance, but she imagined he was a pirate, her fanciful mind triggered by the wild tale of hidden gold she'd read the night before.

She turned to continue beside Lil. Things would be different now the Northern soldiers had conquered Arkansas. Maybe this was a time for things to change for Wendy too. Perhaps her father's untimely death was the catapult that would take her in an unknown direction, heading somewhere she couldn't even guess.

Outbuildings loomed as Wendy walked on, uncertain of the welcome she would receive today in the familiar town. Neighbors thought she was odd, never wanting to marry. And surely her riding the woods and hills made her a target of speculation and idle gossip, if not outright disdain from those who thought a young lady should behave properly. Yet she'd heard more than one matronly woman give allowance for Wendy's behavior due to her lack of suitable parenting.

Wendy smiled to herself, remembering how Aunt Lil always took offense at such accusations.

A cold wind buffeted her back, and Wendy shivered. The New Year had just passed last month—the war was in its fourth year. How much longer could the Confederacy hold out? President Lincoln just won reelection, but the southern Democrats hadn't voted. Wendy heard whispers they had voted in their own election, those states in rebellion not retaining political power in the United States. They instead had their own government, a new government, with Jefferson Davis as president.

Wendy vaguely wondered what would become of the former Mississippi senator if the South lost the war.

The ring of a hammer on anvil brought Wendy from her reverie, and she looked up, surprised to find herself nearing Mr. Johannes's office. Lil picked up her pace and hastened from the vicinity of the noisy blacksmith shop, forcing Wendy to keep up.

Lil waved to friends and familiar acquaintances, but they avoided eye contact with the Yankee sentries that patrolled the main street and stood on street corners, hawk-like gazes following every passerby.

"Buzzards," Aunt Lil whispered accusingly as she halted before Mr. Johannes's door and knocked. Not waiting for admittance, she pushed the door open and stepped into the dim room, Wendy fast on her heels, eager to get off the crowded, noisy street.

"Good morning, ladies," Mr. Johannes greeted as he met them in the office entry, bowing slightly. His threadbare frock coat had seen better days, but then so had their dresses, Wendy mused. She hadn't seen a woman wearing the latest fashions from London or Paris or even New Orleans since the war began.

"Ten o'clock, prompt," Lil remarked as she took the seat the lawyer indicated as the big clock on the wall chimed.

"Indeed. I would expect nothing less from Lilian Moylan," Mr. Johannes replied as he gestured to a chair for Wendy before seating himself behind his huge oak desk. The top gleamed from recent polish.

Lil seemed pleased the lawyer knew her full name and praised her punctuality, all in one breath. Wendy rarely heard anyone use Lil's proper name, and she tilted her head, studying the lawyer. Surely this day would be full of surprises.

A tingle tripped down her back, and she wondered anew if the lawyer's news would be glad tidings or spell doom for the remaining Moylan family.

Mr. Johannes reached for a small stack of papers, glancing at the pair of ladies over the top of the documents as he bounced them on edge, lining them perfectly between his hands. His balding head shone dully in the bleak morning sun that struggled through the tall window behind the desk. Wendy felt herself tense as he peered down at the papers, his lips thinning as he read aloud.

"Last will and testament of Thaddeus Moylan, son of Sean Moylan." He glanced up quickly. "Where is old Sean buried? Is he in the family plot on the plantation?"

His unexpected query caught Wendy unprepared, and she shifted impatiently, eager for news regarding *her*, not her grandfather's final resting place. She reprimanded herself for her lack of dignity and tried to smile. "Yes, Grandfather is buried beside my mother and father in the family plot."

He narrowed his eyes and glanced at Lil before his gaze rested again on Wendy. "There will be room there for the two of you, in due time, if you—well, I mean, if you, uh ..."

He peered down at his papers again and shook them briskly. "I'm getting ahead of myself," he muttered, shooting Aunt Lil another sharp glance.

"Get on with it, Mr. Johannes. What does Tad's will say?" Aunt Lil shook her head and huffed.

"Yes, yes, of course," he mumbled as he studied the papers before him once more. "Well, I have gone over these documents time and again, and I don't see any way around it. Plain and simple, everything Tad Moylan owned has been transferred to Mr. Randall Whitmore, his business partner."

"Everything?" Lil echoed, squinting at the lawyer.

Wendy felt her heart drop in her chest, her last hope dashed upon the rocks of fate. She was poor and Lil was poor along with her. And they had nowhere to go. To depart for the North was not to be considered. They would receive little sympathy for their plight if they moved north. The Yankees had suffered too. The war had lasted far too long.

Mr. Johannes cleared his throat. "You are allowed personal belongings, clothing, and jewelry, but the furniture is to stay with the estate. Apparently, Mr. Moylan needed cash and signed his entire estate over to his partner."

Lil scowled as her hand snaked to Wendy's. "We sold anything of value long ago, and I'm not much for jewels and baubles. And certainly, Wendy isn't either. We have nothing."

He drew a deep breath and leaned back in his leather chair, his gaze resting on Wendy. "Well, there is another way." He placed his elbows on the arms of his chair and laced his fingers together, forming a steeple. "Mr. Whitmore called on me and informed me of the proposition he offered Miss Wendy. If there is no other way to stay in the house, perhaps you should consider his offer."

"He's not a Christian," Lil scoffed.

"No," he said quickly. Too quickly. "No, he's a scoundrel to be sure, but he will allow the two of you to remain at Moylan Plantation."

A heavy somberness filled the room, and Wendy squirmed beneath the weight, wanting to hear another possible solution. This couldn't be all there was to it. Marry Randall Whitmore or move out? It seemed too barbaric to consider.

Despite the cold day, heat roiled in her belly, and she felt a trickle of sweat roll down her back. A longing for her woods and the shaded paths of the forest filled her, and Wendy had to grip the arms of her chair to remain seated. She wanted to flee and to hide, but there was nowhere to go. They were not her woods anymore.

"Be reasonable, Lilian," Mr. Johannes pleaded, glowering at the older woman. "The war has changed a great many things. Nothing has remained the same. Scoundrel or not, perhaps his offer of marriage is the best one Wendy may receive. Everyone has lost so much. This may be your best option."

"Jesus Christ is the same yesterday, today, and forever. The Lord doesn't change and neither does his Word," she whispered as the room quieted once more. Lil stood abruptly. "Thank you for your time, Mr. Johannes."

The lawyer stood and held up a hand. "Wait, Lilian."

Aunt Lil hesitated as she stared at the door, her back ramrod stiff. Mr. Johannes looked at Wendy, still seated, still too stunned to move.

"Life has been tough on you." His eyes softened as he spoke, and Wendy arched her eyebrows, startled by his solicitous voice. "I know you were very close to your mother. After she passed, I ran into you down by the river. I was fishing, and you came along, carrying a rifle. Folks say you've become a good shot."

He peered at her closely, and Wendy nodded, although she didn't recall the incident. But back then, Wendy couldn't recall much of what happened. Mother was gone, and only sorrow walked beside her in the forest.

Mr. Johannes smiled. "It's probably been a good thing that you can hunt, there being little food for decent folks anymore. But there will be little need for a marksman if you marry Mr. Whitmore. He could provide—"

"Good day, sir," Aunt Lil interrupted and flung the door open. "We will not listen to another word," she bellowed over her shoulder as Wendy hurried to catch up. She shot an apologetic glance at the scowling lawyer, but turned to follow her aunt out of the office.

CHAPTER EIGHT

Wendy scurried after Aunt Lil, her questions drowned out by the nearby blacksmith's ringing hammer. Near the smithy's, a swarthy man with a red bandana tied around his head stared at Wendy as she strode along the boardwalk. A hoop earring dangled from his one good ear, half the other missing. He turned aside when she caught his eye. She vaguely recalled seeing him before but didn't give the stranger another thought. She was intent on speaking with Lil.

She caught up to her aunt as the hammer strikes fell behind, matching her aunt's frantic pace. "Lil? What do you think? Is there anything that can be done?"

Wendy frowned at the obvious panic in her voice. Despite her resolve to trust in the Lord, she wanted answers now. She *needed* answers now.

Lil halted and spun around, pointing a shaking finger toward Mr. Johannes's office. "The nerve of the man," she rasped out before whirling and continuing down the main street.

Wendy arched an eyebrow. "Well, he didn't say anything I haven't thought of myself," she admitted as they left Little Rock, the busy town falling behind them.

A bitter wind blew from the north and Wendy glanced skyward, wondering if yesterday's rain would return. Dark clouds lowered without a hint of blue sky anywhere.

"Well, God forgive me, I've thought of the easy way out as well. Marrying Mr. Whitmore would solve our immediate problems but would create long lasting difficulties. I doubt if he'll live out the war. The smuggling business is getting far too dangerous, the Union blockade tightening its noose around the South. I've heard rumors that your father did not simply die of sickness, as we were informed. There's whispers his competitors had him killed and covered up the evidence. I wouldn't be surprised if even Mr. Whitmore had something to do with it."

Wendy gasped and huddled deeper into her shawl. "I can't believe Father would associate with such men." She hesitated and then glanced at her aunt. "Would he?"

"He would and he has," Aunt Lil spat as she maneuvered around a large puddle.

The short hairs prickled on Wendy's neck, and she peered over her shoulder. She pursed her lips when she saw the man with the red bandana following a short distance behind.

"There's a man behind us," she whispered to Lil as if the man were near enough to hear.

"I know. He followed us from home. No doubt a spy for Mr. Whitmore." Aunt Lil huffed as if nothing would surprise her further.

"A spy? Why?" Wendy glanced back and took another, longer look at the stranger. "Whatever reason would a man have for following us?"

Her thoughts tumbled over one another as scenarios, each one worse than the previous, darted across her mind. There was a war going on, for God's sake, and anything could happen to two women walking along a quiet road. These were desperate times with desperate men. Wendy blamed her naivety and inexperience for her foolhardy, innocent thoughts. Surely, she would have to sharpen her senses, be more alert now that she would not have the protection of her remote plantation. In some ways, her father's clandestine affairs had shielded her from the tragedy that now shook the country. Until now, the war had not much effect on Moylan Plantation except the occasional hard to obtain food materials. They had simply expanded the extensive garden, and Wendy had hunted for meat along the river. She remembered Mr. Johannes mentioning the time he'd met her near the river. He specifically mentioned her rifle, but she still couldn't recall the encounter. She'd known how to use a gun since she was a child.

Up ahead, Wendy spied two men in a buggy, parked at the end of their lane. "Aunt Lil?"

Lil nodded. "I see them, I'm sure they have something to do with this rascal behind us. Oh, I wish you'd brought your rifle," she muttered as they neared the motionless buggy.

Wendy blinked when she recognized Randall Whitmore in the vehicle, his handsome features somehow stark and chiseled in the gray, dreary day.

"Good morning, ladies," he greeted as the two women approached. "How did your visit to Mr. Johannes go?"

"You know where we went?" Wendy could not hide her amazement. This man was more than merely her father's business partner. He seemed to have information and resources beyond her understanding.

"Of course. I make it my business to know everything I can about people that concern me. Information is power." Whitmore nodded as the man with the red bandana halted a dozen yards distant. "That's Kincaid. This is Brewer," he added, indicating the roughly dressed man beside him in the buggy. "They're watching you for the next two months, to let me know your whereabouts. I think it's important I keep an eye on you." He chuckled without humor. "Don't want you getting into any danger."

Wendy tensed when Kincaid took a step nearer. She looked back to Whitmore, fear bubbling within her like cold water coursing sluggishly through her veins.

"Kincaid," Whitmore called. "You keep an eye on Miss Wendy for me and send word by Brewer if need be. Don't let her out of your sight."

"I'll keep two eyes on her tempting figure, boss," Kincaid said in a slow drawl that dripped with menace.

Wendy shivered as her eyebrows arched. She knew then she could not marry Mr. Whitmore no matter how the decision might affect her and Lil. She'd been used to solitude, but her father's funeral and the impending expulsion from Moylan Plantation had thrust her into a world of upheaval she'd tried to avoid. Now, despite her best efforts, she had to face reality, filling her with anxiety.

"Shut your dirty mouth," Whitmore shouted at the lout. "This is my future wife you're talking about."

"There is some doubt as to that, now isn't there?" Lil's sudden intervention caused all eyes to turn on her, Wendy's included. But Aunt Lil stood straight, head high, and stared Randall Whitmore in the eye. "I mean, if you need these two rogues to watch Wendy, you must be worried about the outcome of your proposal."

Whitmore scowled, the slightly amused look he'd held fading with Lil's accusation. He lifted the leather reins. "Call them insurance. I always get what I want. Besides, what else can she do? I know you have nothing and nowhere to go." He paused and stared at Wendy. "I'm already planning the honeymoon."

He pointed with his chin for Brewer to climb down. As the two spies moved to the side of the road, Whitmore nodded once more and slapped the reins. With a jolt, the buggy moved down the road away from Little Rock.

Wendy wondered if he were going to the docks where the river boats loaded and unloaded freight, the shore lined with disreputable businesses that catered to the rough river boatmen. She'd heard rumors her father was well known among the notorious bunch that frequented the waterfront.

Kincaid laughed, and Wendy peered at him. His eyes gleamed wickedly, and she noticed the gap of two missing teeth in his leering grin. Aunt Lil huffed and led the way into the long lane, the two women leaving the dirty watchmen behind.

Wendy felt her shoulders sag as the two men behind her snickered ominously. How much longer would the decrepit plantation be her home?

Dead, stunted weeds littered the dirt road, a testimony of neglect. But on either side, twin columns of young oaks lined the avenue to the house, planted long ago by Sean Moylan when he first settled the land. The trees towered thirty feet above the women, shaking in the chilled breeze. Wendy lamented the far-off summer, when the green leaves of the trees would glimmer and flutter in the humid, sultry air. She wondered where she'd be this summer as the branches quivered above her. Despair threatened, but Wendy tried to think of Christ and the idea of a soldier for the Lord flitted across her mind and then vanished as quickly as it had appeared.

"Aunt Lil, what am I going to do?" The question sounded almost like a wail, and Wendy cringed, ashamed of her dismay and unpreparedness for what the future might hold. *Her* future.

Lil turned to face her, spreading her arms wide for Wendy to collapse into. They embraced in the cold, the oaks murmuring overhead like observant sentries as Lil patted Wendy's back. Wendy squeezed her aunt and wanted to cry, but something told her to stay strong. *Don't cry yet.*

"I know I'm different, but I always thought I'd marry one day for love, not necessity."

Lil pulled Wendy away and stared at her. "What do you mean you're different?"

Wendy shrugged and wiped a hand across her moist eyelids. She blinked, holding back the tears and telling herself to be strong.

"You know. I like to ride horses in the woods, and hunt, and wear men's breeches. I'm not really like other girls, but I still wanted to marry for love."

She hesitated and then squinted at Aunt Lil. "Do you think good things are for me? I mean, I know I have you and Mary and Jasmine, but sometimes I feel so lonely. Can God have something special for me? *Someone* special? Does God have a plan just for me?"

Lil nodded, her own eyes glistening in the gray morning. She drew a deep breath and then something flitted across her features, and she nodded again, as if coming to a decision. "You will marry for love, dear, if I have anything to do with it. I feel the Lord is asking us to trust him. He already knows what's going to happen, so let's walk with him and not let worry have a hold. I think I know what we're going to do."

Wendy's eyes widened and she gripped Lil's arm. "What?"

Lil tugged her shawl tighter around her shoulders. Turning, she walked on, talking as if putting her thoughts in order. "First, I'll put tea on while you change out of your nice dress. I don't want to explain twice what I'm thinking, and I want Mary to help with details."

"Mary?" Wendy almost had to run to keep pace with Aunt Lil.

"Mary is wise in the ways of the Lord, and I value her insight and counsel. I've been up all night, praying and seeking the Lord. I wanted to hear what Mr. Johannes had to say, but I think I already knew what we're going to do. I just wanted to make sure of all our options. We'll eat and then discuss my idea. Scoot now and hurry," Lil concluded as they neared the front porch of the big house.

A tingle of excitement ignited within Wendy and then exploded. Lil sounded like she had a direction for her, and Wendy felt relieved to have someone give her guidance. Not even glancing at the derelict old house with its sagging shutters or weathered walls, she bounded up the stairs and left the door open as she raced across the entry and into the great hall to the wide staircase, taking the steps two at a time to the second floor. She sat on the top step and removed her dirty shoes, wishing she'd done so outside. Padding down the hallway in her stockings, she heard voices coming from Aunt Lil's room. Slowing, she recognized Mary and Jasmine in hushed conversation. She tiptoed closer and pressed her back against the wall, listening through the open door.

"I love Miss Wendy," Jasmine said as shaken sheets crackled in the air. "But she's off center somehow. You know what I mean, Mama. I wonder if she should just marry Mr. Whitmore. He'll take care of her. She just has to give him a few children and smile when he visits, but she'll have nothing to worry about, never have to wonder where her next meal is coming from."

"Mr. Whitmore is not to be trusted," Mary countered. Wendy leaned closer to the door as the two women stretched the sheets and tucked in the corners. "There's no promise he'll take care of Miss Wendy. After he gets what he wants, he might decide to leave and never return. She'll be worse off then, for certain."

"Maybe," Jasmine agreed. "But she might not have a choice. Lord knows the number of eligible men has been whittled to nothing, and I wonder how many will return. Not many men want a wife who can ride a horse better than she can cook. She may never get another offer of marriage."

"I don't believe that," Mary said as the sound of blankets tumbling across the sheets came to Wendy's ears. "And marriage is not for everyone. I say obey the Lord and follow the Good Book. She can't marry a man who doesn't fear the Lord. Besides, she don't love him. A woman should marry for love, like your daddy and me."

"But she's been so spoiled, living an easy life of riding and wandering the woods. Mayhap she isn't cut out for real hard things. Ever since Mrs. Moylan's death, Miss Wendy has hidden away in the forest." Wendy listened as Jasmine moved around the bed and lifted the blankets.

"You have no idea the grief she felt, the loss she suffered. There's no accounting some folks' way of grieving," Mary remarked as she helped spread the blankets, tucking them into place. "Miss Wendy has been protected from more hardship until now. The Lord knows when to give a person a trial, usually unexpected but always with deep purpose. He must have a plan for her, to grow her faith, to teach her something important."

"But things have always been hard for us, Mama," Jasmine grumbled.

"And look at what we've learned," Mary went on quickly, not giving Jasmine time to complain further. "We've learned God's faithfulness, we've learned to be patient, and we've learned to be satisfied. Didn't Mrs. Moylan give me my freedom? Don't we eat every day? Oh, yes, the Lord provides."

"I know," Jasmine said. Wendy could picture the servant girl nodding her head. "But sometimes I want more. I want good things for us, Mama. A future more than just tending the garden and waiting for Miss Wendy to bring home some meat she shot down by the river."

"She has her road to walk as we have ours." Mary paused before going on, her voice dropping to just a whisper and Wendy strained to catch. "Maybe one day, maybe the Lord will bring us an opportunity—"

Wendy shifted in the hallway and a board creaked beneath her.

"Miss Wendy?" Mary's call made Wendy jump.

"Yes, I'm changing clothes. Aunt Lil wants you to help with lunch and then she wants to discuss something with you."

Mary came to the door and peered at Wendy. "Discuss what?"

"My future, I think," Wendy said as she stepped across the hallway to her room, undoing dress buttons as she went.

CHAPTER NINE

Wendy nudged the door open with her stockinged foot and entered her room. Jasmine's words hurt, but they were nothing Wendy had not considered herself. Aunt Lil always said Wendy was unique, made special by God, but Wendy wondered. She tossed the dress over the back of a chair and walked to the window, scanning the bleak landscape. The vast estate extended farther than Wendy could discern, the borders of the Moylan land concealed by woods and watercourses that hadn't been cleared for farming. Many of the fields that once produced cotton or hemp or rice now lay fallow, slowly filling in with weeds and foliage as the land returned to a wild state.

Wendy loved the land, the wildness of the rotting plantation. She did not love Little Rock or the gossipy neighbors or the wicked war that raged around her, tearing the nation apart. And she certainly didn't love Randall Whitmore. Yet a part of her considered accepting the protection his offer of marriage would provide. But she didn't like to think about disobeying God. She wanted to always be among the trees and watch the great river and imagine the far away mountains where the source of the river formed.

She drew a deep breath as she looked out her window, studying the patchwork of brown fields and the dense undergrowth of forest between and beyond the cleared grounds. A deep ache filled her heart and again she wondered why God wouldn't release her from her sorrow. Didn't he care about her pain and loneliness and lack of direction? She longed for the Lord's guidance, yet nothing came to her.

Wendy sighed and hoped Aunt Lil had some ideas. Her head throbbed and she rubbed her temples, the tumultuous whirl that consumed her mind making her reel. Wendy gripped the windowsill, attempting to steady herself and slow her troubled thoughts.

She peered up at the gray clouds, pregnant with more rain. "Lord, I need you. Guide me as Aunt Lil shares her notion. I need direction, but I want to do your will. Forgive my selfish heart when I consider tempting ideas that I know will not please you. But I'm so afraid. Don't let me put my fears before your wisdom."

She glanced over her shoulder and eyed her britches in the closet. Perhaps she could get in a short ride before the storm continued. She slipped into her riding breeches and boots.

Thumping down the stairs, Wendy felt better than when she'd first come home from the visit with Mr. Johannes. She would trust in the Lord, trust that the Holy Spirit guided Aunt Lil. Wendy could not make up her mind what to do, but Lil suggested she had an idea and Wendy hastened to the kitchen, eager to hear the details.

A wave of heat blasted as she shoved the kitchen door open—the one room they kept warm all day. Firewood was too precious to heat the entire house. She tossed her hunting jacket over the back of a chair and accepted the steaming cup of tea from her aunt.

"Thank you," Wendy murmured as she sat at the table, sipping the hot drink. Jasmine and Mary were already there, and Mary stood beside the stove, stirring meat in a skillet. She glanced at Wendy. "This is the last of that little deer you shot, Miss Wendy. You'll have to go hunting again."

Wendy narrowed her eyes, remembering Jasmine's stinging appraisal from upstairs. Was her only purpose to supply meat? Had she truly lived a safe, sheltered life devoid of hardship? What about her inner struggles? She'd surely suffered from loss and anguish.

Wendy stewed as Lil took her seat and Jasmine delivered the potatoes to the table. The other women took their seats, and everyone bowed their heads.

Lil cleared her throat. "Lord, you know what's going on here, and I'm asking your forgiveness that I was afraid to think big. Sure, it took your Spirit a day to kick me in the backside, but I know what you want us to do now. Give us strength to trust in you. And thanks for this food. Amen."

Wendy contained her impatience and studied her companions covertly as they ate, detecting a tension etched in all their faces. No one spoke, unwilling to break the somber silence.

Thunder rumbled and Wendy glanced out the window, seeing the rain had started again. She wouldn't be riding in the woods today.

Lil wiped her mouth with a napkin and pushed back her plate. Mary and Jasmine followed suit, but Wendy squinted and held her fork, refusing to end the meal. What her aunt had to share likely would impact her more than the others, and she felt both eager and reluctant to begin the proceedings. But at a sharp glance from Aunt Lil, Wendy sighed and dropped her fork.

"All right then," Lil began, making eye contact with each of the women. "I have to start by telling you how excited I am at this amazing idea. It's like it was made for us, as if it'd been holding itself in time for this very moment. A true adventure." She pointed at her arm and chuckled. "Look, I have goosebumps."

"Well, we don't have an idea what you're talking about," Mary said and rose to retrieve the tea kettle from the stove. She poured refills and removed dirty plates as she went on. "I declare, you'd think we were children the way we're huddled around this table, listening to plans about Miss Wendy's future. Will she get married or not? Will you run away or not? Where will you go?"

Mary sat down again and lifted her steaming cup. "I just need to know *something*. What are you going to do?"

Wendy nodded and stared expectantly at her aunt, but Lil only smiled. "I'm on pins and needles. Tell me," Wendy whispered as a fresh wave of fear assailed her.

Lil squirmed in her seat, eyes glowing above flushed cheeks. "Well, it just came to me this very morning when Wendy and I returned from town. Of course, I prayed for guidance all night. I feel God told me what to do, but I wasn't sure. I wanted to hear from the lawyer to make sure. Now, I'm convinced this is the way to go, at least for now. If not, the Lord will tell us. Step out in faith, I say, and seek God's will."

"I still don't know anything," Jasmine muttered and hid behind her mug as she sipped her tea.

Rain splashed against the window and Wendy stared at the shower, feeling her doubts and anxieties flutter higher still. The pain in her head surged and she felt almost dizzy as she turned from the winter storm and glowered at her aunt, willing the older woman to spill the beans.

Lil waved a hand. "I know, I know. Oh, I'm getting ahead of myself, but I'm that excited. I said it was an adventure, didn't I?"

"Spit it out," Wendy prodded in frustration as she squeezed her teacup, her knuckles whitening.

Aunt Lil's grin faded as she grew serious. She leaned forward as if sharing a priceless secret. "I say we go west and search for the hidden gold."

Wendy gasped and Mary dropped her mug. "You said the gold wasn't true," Mary accused as she reached for a towel to wipe her spill.

"Aunt Lil, I thought you had a real suggestion, something to actually help me," Wendy groaned. "Do I have to marry that pirate Mr. Whitmore?"

"No," Lil said and placed a hand on Wendy's trembling arm. "Hear me out." She leaned back in her chair, suspending her teacup in midair. "We all agree you can't marry Mr. Whitmore."

"I don't agree," Jasmine interjected quickly. "He still might be your best chance."

"Hold your tongue, daughter," Mary snapped, shooting Jasmine with a piercing glare. "Go on," she urged Lil.

"Well, I used to dream of that gold when I was a girl, almost as much as Tad did, I'm sure. But we never had the nerve or the need to go after the prize. We grew up and life got in the way and now, near thirty years later, I feel the time is right."

"But you said it wasn't real," Wendy repeated.

"I did, that's true. But the fact is we simply don't know if this tale is real or not. And that might not be the reason for this journey."

"If the gold isn't real, why go west?" Wendy massaged her temples. Was her headache getting worse?

"The purpose of the journey might be the adventure itself. So, what if we go out there and find nothing? We might discover what the Lord wants you to find. The purpose of the trip might not be what we expect, but what God wants to do through the adventure. We have sixty days before we need to make a decision, go or stay, but we're foolish to wait here for the axe to fall. Better to walk through the only open door the Lord has provided. Let's see what God does with a faithful, trusting heart."

"A fool's errand," Jasmine blurted. "You can't be serious. The trip would be dangerous, and anything could happen to you. Better to stay here and be safe."

Wendy scowled at the word "safe," and she wondered if there was something to Lil's plan. Jasmine had accused her of playing it safe all of her life. Now, an opportunity appeared for Wendy to step out and experience life's unpredictability. Perhaps Lil's unorthodox notion held merit.

Mary raised a hand and Wendy looked at her, surprised at the intensity in the older woman's features as she peered out the window. "No, no, I see what you mean," Mary breathed, her eyes shining as if she looked at something amazing. "Plenty of the doors are closed. Miss Wendy can't marry Mr. Whitmore, she can't move north without money or a trade, and she can't stay here where things are only getting worse. The only way open is the lost gold." She shifted her gaze to Wendy. "Did you read the book about the treasure's location?"

Wendy bobbed as she chewed her lip. "I did. I'm not sure if there's enough details to find the place or if the Mexican colonel was telling the truth. It could all be a wild goose chase."

"Don't you see?" Lil lifted her cup and took a sip. "The trip might be the way the Lord wants to bless you. Walk through the only open door and see what God has in store for you."

"The adventure, the not knowing, is more important than the gold," Mary muttered as a smile creased her face. "I see what you mean. Walk in faith and see what God does. Believe he is with you and has something good for you."

"He might have a murderer's knife for you," Jasmine warned. "Or worse. There's deserters from both sides wandering the dark trails of the countryside. It's not safe for a woman to travel these days."

"The Lord will protect us if this is what he wants us to do," Lil declared.

"Or he'll let you suffer if this is not what he wants you to do," Jasmine added as Mary lifted a hand.

"I told you to hold your tongue. Your negative words will only scare an already frightened girl." She glanced at Wendy and smiled again. "An adventure, Miss Wendy. I think this is right. Watch what the Lord will do with a trusting heart."

Jasmine shook her head and scowled, pressing her lips tight as she crossed her arms over her chest. Although she didn't say anything more, Wendy read the cautious counsel in her eyes.

"Let me get this straight." Wendy tried to clear her mind of muddled and alarming thoughts. She pushed her doubts aside and grasped Lil's plan with hopeful desire. What did she have to lose? "We are going west to search for hidden gold, right?"

Lil leaned forward and grinned. "Are you ready for an adventure with the Lord?"

Mary laughed and her eyes glittered with excitement. "An adventure of a lifetime," she said, and Wendy felt her heart beat faster.

CHAPTER TEN

Wendy pulled her canvas bag open and stuffed a clean blouse in. "We'll not be able to take much," Aunt Lil called from her room across the hall as she chose a valise from under her bed. "Only take what is necessary, Wendy, but pack something nice for a special occasion."

"What special occasion will we have out west?" Wendy replied as she threw clothes into the durable bag. She already wore her riding breeches and boots and felt suddenly pleased she was dressed for their twilight departure. They would need to slip past Kincaid and Brewer to truly escape Whitmore's spying attention.

She paused and glanced out the window, the late afternoon sun concealed behind a thick layer of dark clouds. Rain dribbled steadily, and Wendy knew this would be the perfect night to flee undetected. With a grin, she peered up at the black clouds and wondered if this was the Lord's first sign he was helping her in this wild scheme.

"I pray this is from you, Father, allowing us to get away without Mr. Whitmore's men seeing us go. Are you with us, Lord? Is this the best course of action for me? Will I truly find something out west?"

The glowering clouds didn't reply, but Wendy nodded anyway, feeling the excitement build as she turned to complete her packing. This was a quest, and come what may, she hoped to honor God in her travels, trusting him, waiting on him, turning to him for leadership.

"What do you think?" Lil's voice made Wendy turn, a smile wreathing her face when she saw her aunt's getup. Lil preened as Wendy surveyed the worn britches and heavy coat. "Some of my brother's old togs," Lil explained as she stuffed her bunched hair beneath a slouch hat that she pulled low as to almost hide her eyes.

"Looks great." A twinge of doubt tugged at her heart at sight of her father's old clothes. Then Wendy shook her head. She needed to keep focused on current events. Everything rode on this last chance to discover treasure, and Wendy resolved to give her best.

Later, as Mary and Jasmine prepared a small dinner, Mary talked. "Jasmine will take you to the river where old Jimmy will take you upriver. He'll know of other men who will help you travel without being seen. I believe you can catch the stage at Fort Smith. Remember, it'll be easier if you don't look like women, to discourage talk. Two men traveling will excite no undue attention. God willing, in a few days, you'll be long gone before Mr. Whitmore discovers your absence."

"What about you two?" Lil's question mirrored Wendy's own concerns.

Mary exchanged glances with Jasmine. "We all have our own roads to travel," she said in a low tone. Wendy recalled Mary speaking these same words from earlier when she'd listened from the hallway. Funny how her aunt's freshly made bed would not be slept in for a long while.

Mary shrugged when her gaze returned to Lil. "We'll go to my sisters. We have friends on other plantations where we can blend in and hide for as long as we need."

"Which will not be longer than sixty days," Aunt Lil said decidedly. "Whatever happens, we'll be back to face the music when the time is up. Count on us, Mary, we'll see you in a couple months."

Wendy tried to smile at her lifelong friends, but she couldn't conjure the confidence Lil must've felt. Anxiety dogged her heels, making Wendy wonder if they were doing the right thing. Safety and food concerns made her doubt their choice, but Lil's self-assured look bolstered Wendy's flagging spirits. She reminded herself that an adventure would not be an adventure without some misgivings. A certain amount of risk was probably to be expected, she mused, not sure all of the particulars of a true adventure. Although she didn't know what to expect, she would try to trust the Lord.

Mary shot Jasmine another quick look and then shook her head. "No, ma'am. This will be goodbye. With you two gone, we'll have a hard time getting supplies. I've been wanting to go north for some time but didn't want to leave you. So, as the Lord has led you west, I feel he is leading us north."

Lil blanched, and Wendy read the disappointment and loss in her aunt's features. With clarity and understanding, Wendy knew they were never to see Mary and Jasmine again. Things were changing too quickly.

"This war is about over," Mary went on. "Arkansas is already liberated by the Yankees, and now is the right time for us to get out. Even though we're free, I hear things are better up north. I'm ready for my own adventure."

Aunt Lil stumbled to her feet and embraced Mary. Wendy couldn't look as the two friends hugged, her world crumbling a little bit more as every hour passed. First, her father's death and then Mr. Whitmore's proposition and now this, Mary and Jasmine leaving them forever. Wendy wondered if she could endure much more.

She stood and embraced first Mary and then Jasmine. "I'll miss you both. You've been my family, but I wish you luck. Wherever you go, I hope you find peace and joy."

Jasmine wiped the tears from her cheeks. "We'll need to go soon if we want to catch old Jimmy. He likes to move about, even in the rain, and I saw his boat earlier today down near the big sycamore."

The invisible sun had set, and darkness stretched across the plantation, shadows filling the folds in the land and beneath the trees in the thick woods. The lantern glowed on the table, revealing all the women were crying. But Wendy wiped her eyes. She must be strong as she and Lil would be leaving soon. As everything she'd known came crashing down, she vowed to embrace the wild spirit of the journey that yawned before her. Misgivings buffeted her from every side, despite her resolution to lean into the Lord and hope for good things. God was with her, right? Surely, he would not lead her into the wilderness to abandon her.

"Better get your packs," Jasmine said as she carried plates to the sink. "After you're gone, we'll wait a few hours before we douse the lantern and make our way to friends. With any luck, it'll take a day or two before they realize you've gone."

Wendy gave Mary a final goodbye and gathered her pack before following Jasmine to the back door. Wendy glanced at her rifle where the weapon leaned in a corner, but she would not take the long gun, not wanting to be encumbered with more weight. She heard Mary and Lil whisper their final words, and then, Aunt Lil joined her in the dark hallway, and they slipped out the back door into the rain, close upon Jasmine's heels.

Water dripped from the old hat Wendy had found in the attic, and she hunched her shoulders in her hunter's jacket. Despite her sorrow at leaving Mary, she almost grinned at Lil in breeches, the unfamiliar men's garb fitting poorly on her aunt.

Jasmine walked swiftly until she reached the protection of the nearby forest and then halted, allowing her two followers to gather close. "We could take the trail through the woods and work our way around to the river, but I fear old Jimmy might be gone if we go too slow. I think we should take the quicker route down the lane until we can cut off and make our way to the river. It'll be faster but a little more dangerous if those men at the end of the lane see us."

Wendy leaned closer. "Go the quicker way. We can't afford to miss Jimmy. This is our night to flee, while the rain hides us. If the Lord is with us, we'll soon know. And I only have fifty-nine more days to discover something to help me. Lead on, Jasmine."

Without another word, Jasmine left the protection of the murky woods and hurried down the dark lane, deep shadows from the columns of oaks masking their passage. No one spoke and Wendy moved as quietly as she could, although her boots squished in the mud. A few minutes later, she saw a glow ahead, and discerned a low fire beneath a tarp stretched between two trees near the main road. Figures loomed around the tiny blaze, and Wendy knew these were Kincaid and Brewer, guarding her and monitoring her movements. She smiled slightly as she thought of their surprise when they discovered her gone.

Jasmine left the dim road and led the way into the darker woods, reaching behind her and grasping Lil's hand before she melted into the blackness of the forest. Lil laced fingers with Wendy, and the three women plunged into the dense woods. But Wendy paused, tugging on Lil's hand as she turned around and peered down the long lane to the big house. She couldn't help but feel like Lot's wife who turned to glance longingly at her home. Wendy wondered if she'd ever see the huge house again. Lil pulled impatiently on her hand, and she shuffled through the blackness, her feet slipping in the muddy path.

Eagerness wrestled with anxiety, and Wendy worried about her heavy heart. But the adventure had begun, and she chose to embrace the apprehension that filled her. Despite her fears, she felt resolved.

For a long while, Wendy stayed busy keeping her pack balanced on her shoulder and not letting go of Aunt Lil. The silent trio wended through the thick foliage until a dull ribbon of water gleamed through the thinning trees, and Wendy knew they neared the river.

As if from a great distance, Wendy heard singing. Deep, melodic notes drifted through the rain.

"Swing low, sweet chariot, coming for to carry me home."

Wendy heard another line about the Jordan River and then they were upon the singer, an old man huddled beneath the wide branches of a giant sycamore tree that leaned out over the wide river. He rose to his feet as the women stumbled into his camp.

"Jimmy," Jasmine panted as she wiped rain from her face. Wendy stared at the young servant girl and noticed the nervous look in her eyes. "Thank the Lord you're still here."

"Sure, I'm still here," Old Jimmy beamed in the dull glow of the tiny blaze. "I'd be a fool to try and move about in this weather. It's a bad night to be on the river, Jasmine, and I'm wondering what brings you to this lonely place in the woods on such a night."

His glance took in Aunt Lil and Wendy, and he took a step backward, as if unsure at strangers so near.

Jasmine hooked a thumb toward her companions. "These two need passage upriver. Tonight. They make for Fort Smith, Jimmy. Can you help us out?"

The elderly river man hesitated, and Lil stepped forward. "We can pay ... a little."

He rubbed his whiskered chin and scowled as his gaze darted between the women and finally settled on his campfire. "Well, sure, if I get paid. Surely need the pay. But the river—"

"No time to lose," Jasmine cut him off as she shoved Wendy toward the little boat moored beneath the spreading tree branches. But Wendy turned and drew Jasmine into her arms. "Thanks again—and good luck."

Jasmine stepped back and tilted her head as she squinted at Wendy. "Good luck to you, Miss Wendy. Something tells me you have to do this thing. I sense goings on I can't explain. I guess everyone needs to step out into danger before their faith is really tested."

"Yours too?" Wendy peered sharply at her friend. A distance had always stretched between her and Jasmine, although Wendy didn't think it was her fault. Something had kept Jasmine from accepting her as an equal—someone the servant girl could truly trust or understand.

A quick grin leaped to Jasmine's face. "Mama's right. We each have our own roads to travel. I wish you luck as I learn the lessons the good Lord has for me."

Wendy nodded and then hurried to climb into the little boat.

"Goodbye, Jasmine," Lil called quietly to the figure alone by the little blaze as Jimmy slid the coins she'd given him into his pocket before pushing the skiff off from the riverbank. Jasmine's reply was muffled by the plunging oars as Jimmy steered the craft into deeper water. Wendy knew there was no going back now.

CHAPTER ELEVEN

Old Jimmy maneuvered the little boat around and pointed the bow upstream. Then, with tremendous pulls at the oars, he moved the craft through the water.

Wendy could see very little as the rain showered all around. She huddled beside Aunt Lil and shivered, her clothes soaked through. Would she freeze to death before they ever arrived out west?

"Here, put this over you," Jimmy said as he let go an oar and reached for a wide oilskin. Lil helped Wendy hoist the tarp over their heads and they sat quaking in their wet clothes as they watched Jimmy row.

"Aren't you cold?" Wendy's teeth chattered, making the words difficult to say.

Jimmy huffed and made a great pull on the oars, shooting the craft ahead. "Sure I'm cold, but I'll warm soon enough with this work." He paused and then went on. "Jasmine said you want for Fort Smith. That'll take me weeks to get you there."

Wendy felt her shoulders slump at the disheartening news. She didn't have weeks.

"We need to remain unseen," Lil insisted.

Jimmy nodded and took another pull. "Figured as much, us moving in this storm. But if it's the stage you want, I can get you to Morrilton real quick, and you can catch the stage there, if you have a mind to."

"We need to hurry, Jimmy," Wendy added. She didn't have time to travel slowly. The two-month limit would pass far too quickly. From under the tarp, she glanced at the few dim lights glowing from windows of houses along the river as the three travelers passed. A few boats appeared to be tied to private docks, and she worried they might be seen. On shore, a dog barked, but the darkness and the rainstorm would surely hide their flight. Little Rock would be behind them soon enough.

Jimmy chuckled. "Well, the only way I know to go fast is tie up to Percy's steamer. 'Course it ain't really his steamer. Boss Branson caught fever and died, and Percy just never told anyone. He took over when the river captain passed, and now he takes the money and runs the ship. With the war on and everyone desperate for supplies the boats bring, no one's asked about Boss Branson."

He grinned, and through the faint glow of a muted moon, Wendy saw the gaps where teeth should have been. "Percy's my son," Jimmy added proudly.

"How do we find him?"

Lil's question reminded Wendy that time was of the essence. They needed to be far from Little Rock before Mr. Whitmore discovered she was gone. And to reach the far western lands where she hoped the gold still lay hidden would take time she was unable to calculate. She patted her canvas bag where the journal nestled between her spare clothing.

"He should be along tomorrow night or the next day." Jimmy took another pull on the oars. "I'll get you two hidden farther upriver before dawn and then we can wait for Percy if you want to. He'll tow us all the way to Morrilton where you can catch the stage."

Hours later, as the eastern sky lightened, Jimmy rowed into a screen of Spanish moss hanging from low branches and halted the little boat beneath towering oaks. The old man leaned on his oars and panted. "I haven't had a workout like that in a long time."

"We appreciate your efforts, Jimmy," Lil said as she scrambled out of the boat and onto the bare shelf of land beside the tall trees. Without being told, she went to a small stack of dry wood bundled beneath wide strips of covering bark and began to build a fire.

"Keep the flames low," Jimmy warned, still not moving from the boat. But Wendy clambered out and stretched, her stiff muscles protesting in pain.

"Make breakfast and get some sleep," the river man suggested as he stretched out in his boat and covered himself with the oilskin tarp. A moment later, Wendy heard his steady snores.

"We've tired him out," she commented as Lil put a large tin can full of water on the fire to boil. A bucket and a few camp utensils were stored beneath the tree, and Lil whooped when she discovered a small stash of tea.

Wendy watched curiously as her aunt puttered around the fire. Lil had always been a stoic, serious woman. Rarely laughing, she now seemed lighthearted and eager for the journey ahead. Wendy marveled at how she seemed to be thoroughly enjoying herself, despite her bedraggled appearance and sodden clothes. Hair usually tucked neatly in place now hung below the rim of her wide brimmed hat and Wendy suddenly realized Lil hadn't complained even once. Could she be relishing the rough journey?

The downpour had abated by sunrise, and Wendy and Lil rolled in blankets ashore while Jimmy slept on the boat. Although they rarely spoke, afraid their voices might carry to some nearby passerby, chaotic thoughts pestered Wendy. Were they safe? How long must they wait for Percy? Would they ever reach the far west?

But soon a blue sky replaced the gray clouds that had persisted for the past five days. Winter days passed slowly, with cold rain rather than snow, yet Wendy knew that February

1865 would end too quickly. Or was it March already? The recent days blurred together. Her limited time would fly by, and she wondered what mid-April would bring, for herself and for the United States. Would the war ever end? The Confederacy hung on by a thread. Surely they couldn't hold out much longer.

Her thoughts turned from her own concerns and those of the nation to her silent companions. Afternoon had arrived, and Wendy peered at her aunt—still asleep—before her glance took in the little boat and the motionless tarp. No doubt they'd worn the old man out with the night escape from Little Rock.

Far out on the river, a shrill whistle sounded, and Jimmy threw the oilskin tarp back with a lunge as he scrambled to his feet. His eyes gleamed and his broken smile flashed when he caught Wendy's eyes upon him.

"It's Percy. He whistles like that to find me. Hurry, missy, and gather your gear. We haven't a moment to lose or he'll pass us, and we'll never catch him."

Aunt Lil rose and busied herself folding blankets and tossing their packs into the little boat. Without even a greeting, she'd completed her tasks and leaped aboard the small craft. After Wendy boarded but before she found her seat, Jimmy had shoved off and rowed out into the river, heedless of observers.

"Will we be seen?" Wendy scanned the forest-lined banks as the small craft sped toward the chugging paddleboat. Plumes of dark smolder rose above the twin smoke stacks and a man waved at Jimmy as they neared. Wendy heard the paddles slow and could tell the ship had cut their speed to intercept the small boat. Pale sunlight glittered upon the ripples, and Wendy glanced at the gray water, wondering anew at how far they must travel. Was she a fool? Certainly, the journey would hold dangers at every turn. Fear threatened, but she shoved it down, hoping she and Lil were doing the right thing.

Aunt Lil stood in the bow and tossed a rope to the passing steamer. A deck hand caught the flying line and tied the end fast.

LASTING TREASURE

With a jerk, the little boat swung aside the larger paddleboat and the steamer started chugging faster as the engines worked.

Wendy frowned at her aunt, almost not recognizing this new person, and then glanced at Jimmy. The old man grinned. "Percy will do the work now." His eyes gleamed brighter and he nodded. "He's my son, you know."

CHAPTER TWELVE

Wendy swayed to the rocking of the stagecoach and bumped roughly into Aunt Lil's shoulder. She held Grandfather's journal and studied the faded words as Lil dozed beside her, the older woman's head jostling drunkenly. A one-legged peddler, his crutches leaning beside him, occupied the coach with them, his flowered vest and long frock giving away his profession. The portly man had promptly ignored them when he took his seat, pulling his hat down over his eyes as he slouched on the forward bench. Wendy discovered her increasing body odor kept curious people away from them, and not for the first time in her life, she appreciated the ability to quell interest.

Percy had delivered them safely to the docks in Morrilton, and the stage quickly carried them on to Russellville and then Fort Smith. Traveling night and day, it hadn't taken long to cross into Indian Territory and then the Kansas plains, still following the Arkansas River. Soon, they should arrive in Buffalo Wallow where the driver had informed them, they would join the Santa Fe Trail. Then they'd travel up the Purgatory River to Trinidad, the final town before the pass through the mountains and into New Mexico Territory.

Wendy glanced out at the bleak landscape as the wagon bumped along. What was she doing here on a stagecoach speeding across the prairie? She felt a great sense of relief they'd left the war behind them, but also despair of leaving everything else she'd ever known. Had she gone crazy? Surely some might believe so. But Lil had spoken so persuasively. God had a plan for her, right? Surely the plan was not to marry a man who didn't love the Lord as Wendy did. Yet ... hidden treasure? The thought of the gold wore heavily on her thoughts. She didn't want great wealth, but how could she make her way in the world without means? Albeit reluctantly, she'd been raised a lady, without skills except in the arts of dancing and wearing party gowns. Her life up until now seemed so empty.

She dropped the window covering and scowled into the dark interior of the stage. Why did God have to drag her from her comfortable surroundings to this desolate, unfamiliar setting? Comfortable? Well, perhaps her home wasn't truly grand or nice or even well off—the old place was falling down after all—but she'd been comfortable, certainly.

She bit her lip and her shoulders sagged. Who was she kidding? She'd been in a rut for years, comfortably complacent with how things were going. Did Jesus want something different for her? Is that why she was on this fantastic quest? Mary had claimed the Lord knew when to stretch a person's faith with trials. Was this one of those times?

Wendy squinted as she moved the canvas window covering aside once more and peered out over the frozen prairie. Kansas in early March was locked in cold, the stems of the frozen grass unmoving in the relentless wind. But they could not afford to wait for more favorable weather. Time was ticking.

She counted the days since Father's funeral in her mind. Only five days ago? She felt pleased at their progress. But another glance out the window made her shiver, and Wendy let the canvas fall back into place and tucked the buffalo skin the driver had lent them into place.

Fatigue weighed upon her—they'd barely slept in those five days—and she thought of her father. There was no way to escape the ravages of the war, yet Tad Moylan had avoided wearing a gray uniform by becoming essential to the troops receiving contraband supplies through the Yankee blockade that choked southern ports. His small shipping company could better be used as a means of gathering much needed medicines and armaments than pressing Moylan's swift ships into the Confederate navy. Suddenly, pirating had become acceptable, if not respectable.

Wendy lifted her chin and drew a deep breath. She would also make her way forward despite the hardships. Not as her father did. She would trust the Lord to lead her. But her faith had been shaken, and the indecent proposal still lurked in the shadows of her mind. Knots coiled in her stomach at the memory.

"Please, Father, don't let me consider a sinful path," she whispered into the gloomy stagecoach. "One you don't sanction. Let me trust you have something else for me, something better." She bit her lip again and gripped the buffalo robe that spread across her lap. "But I'm so afraid."

Something stirred within her, and Wendy narrowed her eyes at the unexpected sensation. Resignation? Resolve? A feeling of determination? Tenacity surged, and Wendy knew she would go on with the ridiculous plan Aunt Lil had hatched. She sat up straighter as strength coursed through her.

Wendy nodded and reached for the leather-bound journal once more, lifting the book to the faint light streaming through the slim gap of the window covering. She'd read Colonel Gomez's directions to the gold more than a dozen times but still wondered at the precise location. Turning the page, she studied the faded map Sean Moylan had drawn based on his extensive knowledge of the region. Here, his experiences on the Santa Fe Trail held him in good stead. He knew the land, and his idea to return one day and claim the hidden gold didn't seem farfetched to him as it did to Wendy.

Could the treasure still be there? She tapped the journal with one finger as she pondered. Had Colonel Gomez shared this secret with others? Decades had passed since the attack on the mule train. Surely the secret had gotten out in that time.

But what if it hadn't? Could the gold still be there, waiting for her to find it? And what then?

Wendy chewed the inside of her cheek, her musings growing clear as she wondered about her future. She'd grown tired of the fundraising dances to support the Confederacy, such weak shadows of the once grand and elaborate balls she used to attend. They had lost their luster, and not only because of the war. She wasn't interested in finery and nice clothes, nor a grand house. Wendy had learned she thirsted for more out of life. She craved purpose and something to do, something that mattered and filled her with a satisfaction she lacked. Her roams in the woods had helped her learn she didn't want to always be alone with her grief.

She'd been surprised how easily Lil had convinced her to run away on a wild hunt for lost gold. She felt like a coward now, the way she'd retreated into the safety and isolation of her house after Mother died. Mary had said there was no accounting for how folks grieved, but now Wendy wanted to be busy and to have substantial tasks to complete.

She nodded again. Yes, purpose. If she found the gold, she would pay Mr. Whitmore the money she owed him, and then she would ... what? She scratched her long hair piled beneath her slouch hat and glanced at the journal again. She didn't want to simply be wealthy and buy things. Somehow, the prospect of great wealth seemed so empty and without meaning. Purpose, she decided. Wendy wanted purpose.

Father's untimely death on the docks of New Orleans reeked of more than an accident, but nothing could be proven. Many savage and desperate gangs of men roamed the waterfront in New Orleans, searching for any possible way to make some money or steal something of value. It was said that Tad Moylan had been attacked by such a gang. Tragedy could be found everywhere these days.

Certainly not an uncommon story in these terrible times, Wendy well knew. Hadn't she been in town just a few weeks ago when the list of the dead from the most recent battles were read aloud? Hadn't she seen the strain on her neighbors as they waited to hear their son's names called?

Wendy had felt relieved she had no brothers in the war. Foolishly, she'd believed her father would be safe from injury while he performed his shipping duties. She'd been so naïve. And now she was alone to find her way in the world, the country torn apart by war and poverty and inability.

She glanced covertly at the man in the frock, but she could not tell if he slept or not. He rocked gently on the front bench, his one leg seeming to not have an effect on his balance as his body swayed with the jostling coach.

Her gaze shifted to her sleeping aunt, her head bobbing with each jolt of the stage. Lil would attempt to help and give counsel, but ultimately Wendy would be responsible for herself. Now at twenty-three, there were no suitors knocking at her door. Most eligible men had gone to war, and Mr. Whitmore's proposition made her feel ill. What options did she have?

Heat stole up her neck, and Wendy frowned at her embarrassment. Until recently, she hadn't considered marriage for herself. Although lonely, men hadn't interested her. Now after Whitmore's proposal, she thought of marriage more than she had in her entire life. But surely not to just any man. Was it possible to be friends with a husband?

Her gaze returned to the journal, and she studied the map once more. Trinidad was on the Purgatory River, close to Raton Pass that breached the mountains. Over the summit lay New Mexico Territory. Perhaps, with a guide, Wendy could follow the Santa Fe Trail south, past Fort Union, and onto the Canadian River where she could locate the smaller Mora River. Traveling up the Mora and finding the third stream that flowed into the watercourse, she should be able to locate the hidden gold. According to Colonel Gomez, the Apache Indians usually roamed far to the west of the Canadian River. With luck, she could hire a guide, find the gold, and return to Little Rock within the allotted time.

Abruptly, Mary's prophetic words rang in Wendy's mind. "Sometimes God puts us into difficult situations to move us to the next level, to grow our faith. If we become too comfortable, he often pushes us out of the nest and forces us to spread our wings. Flying high, we can see with a new perspective."

Was God pushing Wendy to make a change? To make a decision? She frowned and closed the journal, packing the leather book carefully into the canvas bag at her feet.

The wagon rocked violently, and Wendy was thrown against her aunt. Lil's hat tumbled to the coach floor, revealing her thick hair pinned like a crown atop her head. Lil snorted and leaned back against the cushions, eyes still shut as Wendy cringed and scrambled to shove the hat over her aunt's hair.

"Well, now," the trader said from his front seat. Wendy pressed Lil's hat on and glanced at the salesman, hoping he hadn't seen the revealing tresses. But his wide grin said much.

CHAPTER THIRTEEN

"I wondered why you fellows were so quiet and kept to yourselves," the peddler said. "Nowadays, everyone has an opinion on the war and is eager to share their views. I'm Albert Levine. I lost this leg at Bull Run almost four years ago, and I enjoy telling the tale." He patted his stump and then wiped his whiskered face with a handkerchief. "We've all suffered from the war, and I'd enjoy hearing your story, for surely women dressed as men have an interesting story."

Wendy wondered at his desire to hear others' calamity, but perhaps misery loved company.

Mr. Levine grinned as Lil's eyes fluttered wide, and the two women stared at him in the shadowed coach. Wendy reached for her aunt's hand and squeezed. They'd been discovered, and now she considered what the implications might be for them. She glanced quickly out the window and hoped they would arrive in Buffalo Wallow soon, allowing them to disembark from the confining stagecoach. But the dealer only chuckled at their silence and crossed his arms over his chest.

"I'm used to traveling the roads of the west, and my curiosity always gets the better of me. I have to wonder why a woman is disguised as a man. Is your companion a woman as well?" He peered intently at Wendy and then chuckled again. "Well, the boy is a handsome lad, I'll say that."

"I'm twenty-three," Wendy snapped, trying to mask her voice with a deep baritone.

Mr. Levine narrowed his eyes. "At twenty-three, you'd at least have some peach fuzz on your chin, sonny. Or should I say, lass?"

Wendy scowled at his shrewd observation, but Lil leaned forward, wide awake now. "So what? We want to avoid inquisitive people. Is that a crime?"

"No," Levine admitted.

"It is none of your affair," Lil replied stiffly as she shifted on the bench. "And haven't you heard that curiosity killed the cat?"

"Yes, yes, I have heard that. Yet, I am only a lonely traveler, seeking a fiction. Amuse me, ma'am, and tell me a little about yourselves. Why the disguise?"

Wendy pursed her lips, determined not to share their secret. But Lil shifted again, glanced at Wendy, and settled back on the bench. "We are fleeing the South. Refugees, I think we're called. We've lost everything and wish only to relocate out west. We believed it best to travel as men, keeping interest in us to a minimum."

Wendy pressed into the seat cushion as Aunt Lil spoke, trying to disappear. They were hunted women. How much would Lil reveal to this stranger?

"Well, any woman out west will draw attention," the salesman agreed. "There seems to be a shortage of women on the frontier, but I suspect that will change as more refugees move west."

"Then we are not the first?"

Again, Levine nodded at Lil's query. "No, ma'am. There are lots of folks moving these days. The war has taken a toll on everyone. But the west draws people, gives the hard-working souls a new lease on life. There's resources yonder. Coal and timber and even precious minerals. Not to mention the vast lands available to the brave and the determined. Lincoln's Homestead

Act gives a hundred and sixty acres to anyone who can live on it for five years. And then there is cattle and farming, operating a business or mining. Coal was just discovered in Trinidad a couple of years ago. Blacksmiths and store owners or hostlers will find ready work out here," he said as he hooked a thumb over his shoulder, indicating the lands across the plains.

Lil nodded and relaxed further. "And you, sir? What do you do on the frontier?"

"Very little, I'm afraid. After the army discharged me with this"—he gestured at his missing limb—"I accepted my sister's offer to fill her late husband's role of gathering orders for fine dresses. With the war, there've been few orders for fine dresses, but I have evolved into the go-between for supplies from distant markets. Before, shopkeepers would write letters to my sister and request specific materials. Now, I go west to represent our company personally, allowing me to guide the storeowners in making their purchases and placing orders. Perhaps, with a little encouragement from me, they purchase more than they intended."

He laughed, and Wendy marveled how the one-legged man could be so cheerful.

"You see, ladies, despite my missing leg, I have reinvented myself, and it brings me much satisfaction. A body needs purpose. But if things change as I believe they will, then I will change also, hopefully a step ahead of the devil and the debt collectors."

He rubbed his hands together briskly, and Wendy tilted her head. Purpose. There was that idea again, the concept seeming to taunt her. The seller had found his, would she? She glanced at Lil beside her and narrowed her eyes. Would *they*?

"But surely your services will be required for many years to come," Lil said.

"I doubt that." Mr. Levine shifted his stump. "Already the telegraph wire has crossed the plains north of here. In time, Western Union will stretch to my most distant markets."

"Certainly not for years to come," Lil protested with a supportive smile.

"I fear it will happen sooner than later. And then the twin rails will arrive, carrying passengers and goods quickly to every frontier store."

The two women laughed at the preposterous suggestion. "A railroad? Out here? Whatever for?" Wendy couldn't keep her silence any longer. Was Mr. Levine teasing them because they were women? Or did he truly believe train tracks would one day stretch across the vast plains of America? The war had brought many changes to Wendy's life, but perhaps there was more to consider. Many more changes were coming to the battered country if Mr. Levine's predictions could be believed. Were changes coming her way as well? A sense of anticipation welled within her, and Wendy wondered what the next few weeks might hold for her.

The peddler shrugged. "To ship cattle to eastern markets. To deliver farm produce to the big cities. To carry lumber east. And to bring settlers west. The Oregon Trail and the Santa Fe Trail will not last forever."

He paused and wiped a hand across his face. "Yes, I see my time as a traveling salesman will pass sooner than I wish. But perhaps it is for the best, for I am forever tired of riding the stage. When the mighty winds of change blow me about, I hope I can bend and sway in the storm and not break. Maybe I will become a lawyer or a ticket man on the railroad, whatever the west demands of me."

Wendy nodded and chewed her lip, understanding washing over her. To not break, that was the real point, right? To find something fulfilling, something that serves the Lord and brings satisfaction to her soul. Could she find such happiness in the west?

"How far along the line do you travel, Mr. Levine?" Aunt Lil's question brought Wendy back to the stagecoach. She listened, speculating at the length of the Santa Fe Trail in proximity to her own mission.

The portly salesman straightened, and his features took on a serious air. "I have much to do in Buffalo Wallow. There are a few trading posts and mercantile establishments. Also, a large number of saloons. I wish to discover some way to provide supplies to the drinking halls, perhaps in glassware. I will be there at least a week, perhaps two."

"And then?" Wendy leaned forward and considered his profession. She didn't want to sell dresses or goods to frontier stores or glass to saloons, but what was she fitted for? This one-legged man had shown determination and flexibility, and he'd found a place for himself. Could she do as much?

"I follow the route of the postal system, on to Trinidad, the last town before crossing the pass into New Mexico. There's a cutoff that takes a shorter route to Fort Union, but it's more dangerous and there's no town out there. Fort Union is on the Cimarron River but has little need of my services, although I will make a stopover at the General Store there. Then onto Santa Fe, my most lucrative stop."

"So, we will leave you at Buffalo Wallow?" Wendy could hear the disappointment in Aunt Lil's query. Surely the seller would've been a wealth of information for them as they hurried west.

"Afraid so," Mr. Levine agreed as he reached for his crutches at the driver's call from above.

"Buffalo Wallow!" The driver banged on the coach below him and shouted again. "Buffalo Wallow!"

CHAPTER FOURTEEN

Wendy leaped from the stagecoach and helped Aunt Lil to the ground as her gaze drifted up and down the long, dusty avenue. A row of mismatched buildings lined both sides of the main street, some made of stacked prairie turf, others of false-front clapboard. A few curious bystanders looked on as she turned to give the peddler a hand.

"I've got it. I've got it," Mr. Levine muttered as he hopped to the ground and positioned the crutches below his shoulders. He gripped his valise in one hand and tipped his hat with the other. "Ladies, I wish you well. May I suggest the Range Rider Cafe?" He pointed at a wooden house farther down the street. "Best food in town."

Without waiting for a reply, he hobbled to the boardwalk and merged with the watching crowd.

Lil stretched. "Let's hurry," she whispered as she tugged on her hat and started toward the indicated eating house. Wendy had to hurry to keep pace with her aunt. "I don't want to miss the stage when it continues."

Wendy felt reluctant to hasten the delicious meal, the best they'd enjoyed in days. But they kept one eye on the stage and watched the tired teams replaced with fresh horses. Soon, they'd be on their way again.

"Trinidad," Lil whispered and glanced over her shoulder as she spoke.

"What?" Wendy buttered a biscuit, surprised to find such luxuries on the frontier.

"Mr. Levine said Trinidad is the last place before the New Mexico land. There's Fort Union farther on, but I think we'd best avoid the Yankees. They might not allow two southern women to explore into the wilderness."

"Two southern men," Wendy corrected. "And you're not exploring the wilderness with me. I will hire a guide and locate the gold using the maps Grandfather Moylan drew. With luck, it should only take a few weeks and then we can return to Little Rock."

"And how do you propose to locate a trustworthy guide? We know no one out here," Lil snapped. "You will need me along for help."

Wendy rolled her eyes. "You can't even ride a horse. No offense, Aunt Lil, but I don't think this will be a trip for you." She narrowed her eyes as she studied her aunt. "Although I must admit, you have shown tremendous courage and fortitude so far."

Lil lifted her chin and glowered at Wendy. "What did you expect? This is a lifelong dream come true for me. I have thought of this gold as mine and Tad's long before you were even born. This is not only your adventure."

Wendy waved a hand. "Back to the problem at hand. You think we should take the stage to Trinidad and hire a guide?" Her gaze roamed the simple yet comfortable eating house, and then she studied the stagecoach again as two men pushed the final horse into the harness. They would be leaving soon.

"Can we afford all this?" Wendy gestured to their surroundings and indicated the coach in the street outside. "Can we afford another stage ride and to eat in nice places and hire a guide?"

Lil shifted before lifting her coffee mug to her lips, eyeing Wendy over the rim. "We can afford such niceties for a short time. I've always put a little aside when your father sent us money occasionally. I knew we would need the funds for a rainy day. But we are almost out of cash."

Wendy blinked. "Out of cash? How do you propose to hire a guide and pay for our return trip?"

Lil shrugged. "Have a little faith. I trust the Lord will provide."

Wendy squinted, not liking what she heard. They both looked out the window when a gust of wind lifted a sheet of dust from the wide avenue and naked tree branches swayed in the distant grove along the Arkansas River. Gray and brown and tan blended into the bleak landscape and Wendy shivered, feeling spring was far off. Suddenly, she felt small on the vast Kansas prairie as their precarious situation overwhelmed her once more. They had nothing, or almost nothing. And surely their meager funds would not last long. What would she and Aunt Lil do if they didn't find the gold?

Wendy shivered again, and not only from the cold that covered the land. She glanced at the plank ceiling and aimed a hurried prayer skyward. She shifted on her seat and lifted her own mug. "Well, this is about as much of a rainy day as you could ask for. I don't know how much worse things can get."

Lil chuckled and popped the last bite of her biscuit into her mouth. "Oh, Wendy, you're young. Things can always get worse. But that's not our concern. Don't look at the problem, look at the solution. Let God worry about the problem as he guides us to the solution. For now, we have enough funds for this adventure. Focus on now. Let God work as we trust in him. He has a plan, and we are to wait on him, not get ahead of him."

"If you say so," she mumbled and then hastily wiped her napkin across her lips as the stage driver waved from the street. "We'd better get out there." Wendy stood and led the way to the door.

Three soldiers in blue coats lounged beside the coach as the women approached. Wendy glanced hurriedly to Lil, making sure her aunt's hair was concealed beneath her hat. Wendy's own hair lay coiled in two tight braids wound around her head, the black slouch hat pulled low to cover any hint of her long, brown hair. She slouched and dragged her boot in the dust, attempting a casual strut as they neared the somber soldiers. The trio of Yankees eyed the two disguised women as they hesitated beside the wagon.

A cold wind buffeted Wendy's back and she thrust her hands into her pockets as she snuggled deeper into her hunter's jacket, the garment too big for her slender form. Gratefully, she remembered the thick woolen sweater she wore beneath the big coat.

One of the soldiers gestured at their packs of gear. "There won't be enough room for all five of us in the coach. Someone will have to ride on top with the driver."

Wendy felt her eyes widen as the three soldiers stared at her. "You look young and strong, boy," one of the bluecoats said as he moved toward the stagecoach door. "You ride up top first, and then we'll take turns."

The other two soldiers snickered and followed their companion, the wagon lurching as they loaded their packs within.

Wendy frowned and turned to Lil. "Will you be all right in there?"

"Don't worry about me. Stay warm, and when you need a break, bang on the side of the coach. We'll make do as best we can." Aunt Lil eyed the jostling soldiers as they found seats in the coach. "They must be bound for Fort Union. I will see what information I can glean from them. I don't fancy them being Yankees, but we'd best get used to it. I think the war is almost over."

Wendy scowled. "I've heard that before, and now it's been four years. Be careful," she warned as her aunt moved to take her seat in the coach.

"Climb up here, sonny," the driver yelled above the wind and gathered the long leather reins. "We need to get moving."

Wendy climbed to the place beside the driver. His face was masked by a red scarf pulled high, and he wore gloves. Only his eyes peeked from beneath his wide brimmed hat. She glanced over her shoulder and noticed the space atop the stage where luggage would be tied down. "Why didn't the soldiers put their packs up here?"

The driver chuckled and looked at her from the corner of his eyes. "Because you let them throw their gear inside where it won't get wet if it rains or snows. Your fault, sonny."

With a slap of the reins, the horses leaped forward, the stage rumbling into motion.

Wendy wrapped a scarf over her hat and across her face before lashing the ends beneath her chin. Despite the cold, she relaxed beside the driver, knowing he couldn't tell she wasn't a man.

"The soldiers are going to Fort Union," he yelled above the wind as the stagecoach rolled swiftly over the rutted road, the powerful teams of horses straining against the harness as they left the small frontier town behind. "Where are you and your friend heading?"

Wendy stuffed her hands deeper into her pockets and tried to adopt her baritone voice as she leaned closer to the driver. "Trinidad."

The driver nodded. "Things have sure changed. Trinidad didn't exist a couple years ago. Coal was discovered, made the town boom."

He gestured to the Arkansas River on their left, and Wendy glanced at the placid, wide waterway as a pair of antelope watched the wagon pass from the riverbank. Small ripples bounced over the gray surface, and Wendy shuddered as she considered how cold the water must be.

He pointed at the river with his chin and slapped the reins again. "That river used to be the border between Spain's land in Mexico and the United States after President Jefferson bought this land from Napoleon. This trail has been a trade route with other countries for decades. Now, after the war with Mexico"—he gestured off to the southwest—"all this land is ours. And I mean the United States, all of it, for the rebels sure don't have a chance of winning anymore. I think Lincoln will hold the Union together."

Wendy squirmed, not sure where she stood on such matters. She'd been pleased to learn Mary and Jasmine were free and not slaves, but the economy of the south was dependent on vast acreage of crops that demanded much labor. Could they successfully transfer to a free labor system, like the northern states employed? The northern states did not have the huge farms of the South, but she'd heard the stories of the long days and low pay factory workers endured up north.

Wendy recalled Mr. Levine's words, and she knew it was time for America to change. They must embrace freedom for all people, and perhaps even the poor immigrants of the overcrowded cities would receive fair jobs. As America changed, Wendy hoped she might change too.

She felt ashamed she'd never thought much about the social and political issues that surrounded her. Wendy had been so absorbed with her own grief. Now she realized isolation had been wrong, selfish, not caring. Perhaps this journey was her opportunity to grow.

"Where you from, sonny?" The driver pulled on the left reins, maneuvering the lead team around a deep rut in the road.

"Arkansas," Wendy admitted with a little shame.

He glanced at her sharply. "Oh, I didn't mean to offend."

Wendy nodded. "No, that's all right. I know slavery is wrong. The war is wrong. But now America needs to adjust, for the better, and so do I."

"Well, you're coming to the right place. The west is big, and a man can do anything he sets himself to do out here. You can work cattle or be a miner, or work in a store, or farm." He paused and then looked at Wendy, his eyes twinkling. "Or you can drive a stagecoach. Do you want my job, sonny?"

Wendy shook her head, smiling behind her scarf. "No, sir."

The driver nodded and slapped the reins again. "When I was a lad, I went to California, eager to find gold."

At the word, Wendy's interest pricked. "Gold?" The word sounded like music to her ears, honey on her lips. Was she destined to find gold out west? A thrill raced through her veins.

"Did you—did you find any?" Her voice faltered, almost whipped away by the wind, but she desperately wanted to hear his response. Perhaps she would find gold. Perhaps she wouldn't have to marry Mr. Whitmore and could return to a life of safe routine, a life she felt comfortable with.

"I stood for hours every day in a frozen stream. Never found enough dust to make me rich, but I had the time of my life. I'll never forget those times in the California gold camps." He laughed, and Wendy imagined his excited memories as he remembered his glory days. Would she find such fond memories after this trip to the frontier?

Her gaze drifted to the wide plains around them. In the distance, a small herd of buffalo stood, heads down, backs to the wind. She felt her back was to the wall, forced into a corner with few options. What would happen to her?

"We're making good time," the driver remarked, bringing Wendy from her anxious thoughts. "If you want, climb onto the top behind us here and wrap up in that canvas tarp. We won't stop for hours, not until we swap horses at the stage station on Wildcat Creek. Get some rest."

Wendy scrambled over the back of the seat and wrestled the tarp against the wind. Slipping between the folded canvas, she curled tightly, teeth chattering as she slowly warmed. Days and nights of travel had exhausted her. The anxiety of escape from Little Rock and the long hours aboard the stagecoach had worn her out. Despite the chill and the jolting stagecoach, Wendy felt a sense of exhilaration at her prospects, looming like a great adventure on the horizon. She felt she was learning and growing as she met interesting people of the west. Was her quest for more than just gold? As if a curtain had been pulled aside, Wendy felt she was seeing things for the first time, thinking of things she hadn't considered before. Perhaps Lil's idea of going west was indeed for more than just hidden wealth.

Wendy yawned and tucked her head deeper into the tarp. As every mile passed, she worried less and less about Randall Whitmore and Brewer and Kincaid. She felt something exciting awaited her farther west, and she blinked, wondering what the Lord had in store for her.

What treasure would she find on her expedition to the distant lands?

CHAPTER FIFTEEN

When they alighted from the stagecoach in Trinidad, the sun had slipped behind the Rockies, and shadows stretched across the dusty street of the little town. Lantern lights glowed through windows of the businesses still open at this hour, and Wendy assumed they were the saloons or eating halls of the young mining town. Lil had hurried Wendy to the dark boardwalk, out of the street and into the deeper shadows along the silent, dark buildings which had obviously closed for the day.

"What now?" Wendy peered farther down the street, pulling her collar higher as a breeze from the nearby high mountains tugged at her hat. She desperately wanted a bath and to change into clean clothes, but the disguise had worked so far—except with Mr. Levine—and Wendy felt loathe to return to women's garb. She must keep her eye on the prize. They were here to search for hidden gold, not to be comfortable.

Before Aunt Lil could reply, a figure stepped from a nearby building and closed the door behind him. Vaguely, the women watched the man lock the door and turn, his face gleaming dully in the wash of the distant lights.

He was a tall man, probably around Lil's age, with a clean-shaven face. There seemed to be a peacefulness about his eyes that drew Wendy's notice. Enviously, she stared at him.

"Excuse me, sir," Lil said as she stepped from the shadows.

The man stepped back quickly and then chuckled. "You startled me, stranger. What can I do for you?"

Wendy picked up their small bags and followed Lil into the splash of lantern light on the mud-covered boardwalk. A banjo played from down the street and Wendy glanced in that direction, worried about their proximity to the lively saloon. Yet the warmth of the drinking hall beckoned to her, and she shivered again, wondering where they would sleep tonight. Wearily, she squinted toward the noisy part of the dark town. Were there rooms to let above the saloon? Could they afford the cost? How much money did Lil carry?

"We've just arrived in town on the stagecoach," Lil explained, and Wendy edged nearer her aunt. "Can you direct us to a hotel or are there rooms available elsewhere?"

The man shook his head. "I'm Hanson." He pointed to the sign over the dark building behind him and Wendy made out the dim lettering above the door. Hanson's Mercantile.

"There are rooms above the saloons," he admitted, and Wendy wondered if Lil caught the dubious tone in his words. Hanson shifted and drew a deep breath. "But I don't recommend them. If you're not too particular and just need a warm bed out of the wind, I can let you stay in my stockroom out behind the store. There's a bed and a woodstove, and all of my supplies. Sometimes I rent the room to the stage driver or to traveling mining men sent here from the east to inspect the coal diggings."

Lil nodded eagerly. "Show us the way."

Mr. Hanson walked into the deeper shadows behind the mercantile and Wendy burrowed her chin behind her coat collar, the mountain wind chilling her to her core. Even her bones felt frozen, and she hoped the stockroom would meet with Lil's usually high standards.

Keys jangled as Mr. Hanson approached a small building in the alley. He wrestled the lock and then pushed the door open. "Wait here," he ordered as he stumbled into the gloomy room.

Wendy sagged against Aunt Lil as they listened to Mr. Hanson move about the interior, and then a soft glow illuminated the room, glass tinkling as he replaced the globe to a small oil lamp.

Aunt Lil leaned into the stockroom as Wendy's gaze roamed the crowded space. She saw the bed tucked between barrels and wooden crates stacked to the ceiling. Large sacks of flour and sugar lined each wall. Only a single tiny window peeked between piles of dried goods. Wendy thought the charming room perfect for their needs. She narrowed her eyes as she glanced at Lil, knowing her aunt would have the final say. They stepped into the room and Wendy felt grateful for the break from the wind.

"Appears adequate," Lil announced noncommittedly. "How much?"

Mr. Hanson smiled. "Two dollars a week. There's plenty of work in the mines, if you're such inclined. A few small ranches out of town, and some lumbering at the new mill on the road to the pass."

"We are not looking for work," Lil said crisply as she indicated an open place on the plank floor for their luggage. Wendy dropped the bags as Mr. Hanson placed a key in Aunt Lil's hand and stepped toward the door.

"What do you boys do, if you're not looking for work?"

Lil glanced at Wendy and then straightened. "We are looking for a guide to take us to the New Mexico Territory, across the pass and south of Fort Union."

"What do you want out there?" Mr. Hanson pulled the door closed and leaned against the wall, apparently in no hurry to depart. He thrust his hands into his pockets and then hurriedly pulled them out when his glance took in the lifeless potbellied stove.

"Forgive me," he said as he reached for kindling from the stacked woodpile and struck a match. Flames sputtered and then glowed as the fire blossomed. He slammed the metal grate and turned back to the women, tilting his head as he studied them in the lamp light.

"What's out there?" He repeated the question slowly, as if not sure he wanted to know.

"We're searching for a marker a relative of ours left there years ago. Do you know of a good, trustworthy man who would guide us?"

Hanson scratched his chin and stared at Lil. "There's nothing out there but barren land and Indians between Fort Union and Santa Fe, except the small town of Las Vegas. And the only fellow who knows that land has vowed never to return."

"Why is that?" Wendy stepped forward, awake now and eager for information. Had God led them to this place because a local man knew the land where the hidden gold was located? Gratefully, Wendy smiled at Mr. Hanson, quietly thanking the Lord for guiding them to this kind storekeeper.

Mr. Hanson shook his head. "Kurt doesn't like to talk about it."

"Kurt?" Wendy pressed.

Hanson scowled. "Kurt Jordan. He was hunting stray cattle from a ranch near Las Vegas and ran into a bunch of Apache. Somehow, he gave them the slip and found his way back. Almost died. Very rare for a man to enter Apache country and live to tell about it."

"If he can do it once, he can do it again," Wendy challenged, unwilling to accept opposition to her plan. She'd already spent more than a week getting to Trinidad, and she needed to hurry to the Mora River and locate the gold.

Aunt Lil shot her a sharp glance, and Mr. Hanson shifted, his boots scraping loudly on the rough plank floor.

"Well, there's nothing to do about it tonight." The storekeeper reached for the doorknob. "Get some sleep and we'll talk in the morning. I can introduce you to Kurt, but don't get your hopes up."

Lil gave him some coins, and Mr. Hanson disappeared into the darkness. Wendy took the bucket he provided and followed his directions to the pump behind the livery barn. The muffled roar of a river drifted to her ears, and she guessed the Purgatory River ran close by. As she worked the handle, a pistol shot rang out from the direction of the saloons, then another. She pumped faster until the bucket brimmed, and then hurried back down the alley. When she returned, Lil sat on a cracker barrel near the stove, her hands stretched to the heat as she stared into the flames.

"He seems kind," Wendy ventured as she placed the bucket near the bed.

Lil gave a noncommittal grunt and didn't move, her gaze riveted on the little stove. An upturned crate held the small lamp and revealed Lil's open satchel upon the bed. Wendy glanced longingly at the thick blankets before joining her aunt beside the little stove.

Lil said nothing, and a full minute passed in silence before Wendy turned around, allowing the heat to warm her back as she gazed again about the storeroom. For the first time in a week, they were alone, and Wendy allowed her thoughts to wander over the recent trip to Trinidad.

"Did you see that herd of buffalo we passed today? The stage driver worried they might cross the trail and slow us down. I loved watching them and the tan colored calves that scampered near their mothers."

She paused and unbuttoned her coat. With a fling, she tossed her slouch hat on a wooden box and loosened her braids, her ice-cold fingers fumbling where they used to be so nimble. "I saw a pair of antelope near the Arkansas River and another small group of them when we passed that old burned down little fort, Bent's trading post, the driver called the place."

Wendy kicked off her boots and wiggled her chilled toes. The heat from the stove filtered to the far reaches of the crowded stockroom, and she could feel herself begin to thaw. She felt so tired but relished getting out of her travel-stained, rumpled clothes.

She studied her soft hands, now red and rough from wind and cold. Several of her fingernails had broken into jagged lines. Suddenly, a deep weariness weighed on her, and she wondered how much more she could endure. The plan to go west and find gold to save her and Aunt Lil had only just begun, and already she worried if she'd made a mistake.

"I've fled my home at night," she muttered as her gaze penetrated the deep shadows of the quiet storeroom. "I took a tiny boat in the rain to a steamer on the river and rode a stagecoach across the plains. I've never been colder in my life while three Yankees rode inside. Now we're in Trinidad, staying in a drafty stockroom with no idea where to turn next."

She glanced over her shoulder at her silent aunt, then stomped to the bed and rummaged through her canvas bag, pulling out clean clothes.

"Didn't you hear me?" she grumbled and spun around, facing Aunt Lil.

Lil lifted her face, eyes shining as she smiled at Wendy. "Yes. Isn't it delicious?"

CHAPTER SIXTEEN

Sunlight streamed through the small window, and Wendy knew she'd slept late. With a yawn, she pushed the covers back and stretched.

Aunt Lil stirred beside her, eyelids fluttering before she stared at Wendy. "Sun's been up for an hour," she mumbled and closed her eyes again as she snuggled deeper into the warm blankets. "I haven't slept this late in years."

"Well, except for naps while sitting up, we haven't slept in a week." Wendy looked around the still storeroom and smiled. "I can't remember when I've slept so well."

Lil opened her eyes and peered at Wendy. "You sound happy."

Wendy scowled. "Hardly. But I'm rested. We need to get dressed and find something to eat and find a guide. Time is ticking." She swung her legs out from under the covers and sat up, the cold bracing her as she reached for clothes. "Do you think we can find a decent meal in this town?" she asked between chattering teeth.

Lil laughed and started dressing. "I haven't had decent food in a week, except that nice place in Buffalo Wallow." She glanced down at her figure. "I'll bet I've lost five pounds."

Wendy shoved her feet into her boots and stood, her eyes widening when she saw Lil's dress. "Are you sure?" Wendy gestured to her aunt's feminine attire.

Lil shrugged. "Why not? We've given Mr. Whitmore the slip and I certainly don't need to hide as a man anymore." She pulled a brush through her hair and eyed Wendy. "You'd better stay in breeches. No one will guide us to the Mora River if they know we're both women."

"We?" Wendy squinted and shook her head. "You're not going. We'll need to ride horses and move quickly. There will be no time to train you in horseback riding. There isn't time."

"I'm afraid you're right," Lil admitted a little too quickly as they left the stockroom and ventured into the alley. Frozen mud ridged ruts in the road, making it difficult to navigate the path around Hanson's mercantile to the main street. A bitter wind whistled from the high peaks and Wendy glanced to the nearby mountains, marveling at the white capped peaks to the west. She'd never seen the Rocky Mountains, and Wendy pulled her hunter's coat tighter about her.

Their feet thudded on the boardwalk as they rounded the corner. Only a few horses lined the short street, heads hanging at hitch rails. A buckboard stood before Hanson's store, and Wendy hurried behind Lil, eager to get inside and out of the cold. A bell sounded above their heads as they entered the warm room.

Wendy stared at the crowded emporium filled with stacks of wooden boxes, shelves lined with canned foods, and piles of dried goods. The fragrant smell of tobacco, coffee, and leather permeated the air, and Wendy inhaled deeply, impressed with the volume of merchandise the store boasted.

A stranger in hat and boots stood near the front counter where Mr. Hanson waited on him. The storekeeper looked up when the two women entered, then he tilted his head as he looked at Lil. "Good morning, uh, ma'am."

Aunt Lil laughed, and Wendy felt surprised at her aunt's easy manner. "Good morning, Mr. Hanson. I can tell you're startled to see me in a dress. I wore breeches only for travel, trying to discourage unwanted attention."

The stranger turned, eyeing Lil appreciatively. "Wise choice, ma'am," he said as he tipped his hat to Lil. "A woman as handsome as you should be careful."

Lil curtsied, and Wendy felt her eyebrows reach for the ceiling. "Why, thank you sir," Lil murmured. "I haven't had the pleasure of making your acquaintance."

Mr. Hanson scowled and gestured at the stranger. "This is Jeremy Bloomberg. He has a ranch east of town."

"The biggest ranch hereabouts," Mr. Bloomberg bragged as he took Lil's hand. Wendy stared at the pink that stained her aunt's cheeks at the rancher's greeting.

"Ralph Peterson might disagree with you on that score, Jeremy," Mr. Hanson remarked.

"I am Lilian Moylan. It's a pleasure meeting you, Mr. Bloomberg," Lil gushed and glanced at Mr. Hanson from the corner of her eyes. "Perhaps you gentleman could refer me to a guide, a man willing to take us to the Mora River country down south."

Hanson snorted. "I told them about Kurt Jordan. He won't go again."

Bloomberg squinted and then nodded once. "He's busy. I tried to give him a job riding for me, even offered to hire that Indian that tags along with him, but he refused. Said he had to build his own ranch." He chuckled. "There's no men available for anything, let alone guide a boy and a woman to Indian lands. Everyone's busy, off to the war or the coal mine yonder. I can't find enough men to work my own ranch, let alone hire one to wander the wilderness."

Lil frowned and shrugged a shoulder. "Then perhaps a recommendation for a dining hall."

Bloomberg glanced at Hanson. "The only place is Bill's. The other big cafe is only for the mine employees."

Mr. Hanson nodded and pointed down the street. "Bill serves good food. Right down the main street here, toward the livery."

Lil smiled as Bloomberg picked up his packages and moved toward the door. "Right nice to meet you, ma'am, and I hope I see you again."

Lil waved. "I'm sure you will." She turned to face Mr. Hanson as the bell rang again, signaling Bloomberg's departure.

"So? Nothing has come to you? Other than the man who has been there before, you know nobody who would take us south?"

Mr. Hanson stared at Aunt Lil and then glanced thoughtfully at Wendy. She tilted her head, hiding behind her hat brim, and he cleared his throat. "Well, Kurt Jordan certainly will not guide you to the Mora River. His interests lie elsewhere at the present."

"What does that mean?" At Lil's query, Wendy lifted her eyes to the storekeeper once more.

"He's after money, fast money, if I understand correctly." His gentle demeanor settled into stern lines, puckering as if he'd tasted a pickle. "He's intent on getting married."

"Nothing wrong with marriage," Lil countered as she lifted her chin. Wendy sensed a change in her aunt that surprised her, and she stared at Lil curiously.

"No, no," Mr. Hanson agreed hastily, waving a hand. "I mean he needs money to secure the young lady's hand."

Aunt Lil shifted and frowned, exchanging glances with Wendy. "I don't understand."

Mr. Hanson drew a deep breath. "I will say no more."

Lil turned and led the way to the door. "We will see you later, Mr. Hanson, and I hope you will find someone to guide us."

"Don't hold your breath," he called after them as the bell tinkled and the door closed behind them, a cold wind buffeting the two women as they stepped onto the boardwalk.

They tugged collars higher against the cold as they walked toward Bill's place, Wendy's stomach growling loudly.

"I declare, Wendy, you have the manners of a dock worker," Lil grumbled under her breath.

"I can't help my stomach from being noisy. I'm starving," Wendy protested and placed a hand over her belly.

A tuft of dust rose and scuttled along the road, like a floating veil or a fleeing ghost. Wendy watched the dirt settle once more, and her gaze strayed to the eating hall where men stepped on the stoop, buttoning coats as they sauntered toward the mine at the east end of town. A few gave Lil and Wendy curious glances, but the men moved on, keeping their thoughts to themselves.

The food was good, and Wendy lifted her mug for seconds of the strong coffee. Bill filled her cup and loitered beside the table. Wendy smiled when she caught the cook attempting to study her aunt from the corners of his eyes. He wiped a hand down his stained apron and faced the women's table.

"A guide?" Bill rubbed his chin while he glanced at Lil again. "The only man I know who's been that way is Kurt Jordan, although word has it he won't go again."

"Mr. Hanson said the same thing," Aunt Lil grumbled with a hint of scorn. "I can't see what could be more important than a job where he stands to make a great deal of money."

Bill shook his head. "Money ain't worth a thing if you're not alive to enjoy it."

"Is it really that dangerous in the Indian lands?" Wendy raised her mug to her lips and watched the cook over the rim.

"You can't think of anything as bad as what the Apache can do. They're more dangerous than a rattlesnake in your shirt, begging your pardon, Miss Lil." Bill's neck reddened and he looked away.

"Not to worry, Bill. We're just anxious to find a guide," Lil explained.

"Well, Kurt Jordan is having problems finding men himself. He's rounding up loose stock down on the Purgatory and can't hire anyone to help. Of course, he's got no money, and a man would have to work on a promise of pay. He's got that Indian that follows him around, but that's not enough to push cattle from the brush and brand them. They need, at least, one more rider."

Wendy straightened and leaned her elbows on the table. She could ride, and Kurt Jordan knew the way to the Mora River in New Mexico Territory. He'd been there once before and somehow evaded the Indians. Perhaps they could make a deal.

Wendy looked up at Bill. "How do I find Kurt Jordan's camp?"

CHAPTER SEVENTEEN

As they hurried to the stockroom to gather gear, Wendy explained her plan to Aunt Lil. "He needs me, I need him," she concluded as they entered the little storeroom behind Hanson's store. She folded blankets into a tight roll and then hesitated as she glanced at the leather journal beside the bed. On impulse, she stuffed the book into her bedroll and scrambled to her feet.

"I'll miss this warm bed," Wendy said as she closed the door behind them and led the way down the main street toward the livery. The roar of the nearby river drifted on the morning breeze and Wendy glanced up at the towering peaks of the Rockies, looming so close she felt she could reach out and touch them. There were no mountains as majestic as these in Arkansas, and Wendy thrilled anew at seeing new lands, new places. Her journey had begun, and except for being nowhere closer to her goal, she'd appreciated the unfamiliar scenery.

A young woman in a buckboard pulled into the livery barn as Wendy and Lil stepped inside the wide avenue of the enormous structure. Stalls filled with horses lined both sides of the barn, and Wendy glanced lovingly at each of the animals, missing her horses from home more than ever.

"Boy, hold my horse while I climb out," the young woman in the buckboard ordered, and it took Wendy a moment to realize the stylishly dressed girl was yelling at her. Scurrying to obey, Wendy shot Aunt Lil a sidelong glance before grasping the harness and steadying the spirited horse while the woman stepped down.

She brushed imaginary dust or straw from her fine overcoat as she glared at Wendy. "When I come to this livery, you must always be prepared to help me from the buggy. I should not have to explain this to the hired help."

Wendy only stared at the girl, probably a couple of years younger than Wendy herself.

An older man appeared and hurriedly pushed Wendy aside. "I'm sorry, Miss Peterson. I didn't hear you come in."

The young woman's glower shifted to the hostler. "Mr. Edmonds, I was telling this boy to be prompt when I come to town."

Edmonds turned on Wendy, his eyebrows arching. "Who are you, young man?"

Before Wendy could answer, the girl stepped closer, peering intently at Wendy. "He doesn't work for you? I thought he was a stable boy."

Without an apology, the girl moved away, strolling from the livery as if nothing had happened.

Edmonds stared after her, shook his head, and looked at Wendy and Lil. "Howdy, I'm Edmonds. How can I help you?"

"I will need a horse," Wendy said, stepping forward. She wondered how Lil would introduce her, so she took the lead. "This is my aunt, Lil Moylan."

Lil smiled and extended a hand. "Lilian Moylan. Pleased to meet you."

The hostler gripped her hand hurriedly, a startled look on his face giving way to a wide grin. "Well, now, Miss Moylan, the pleasure's all mine."

He held her hand a moment longer than necessary, and Wendy frowned before she cleared her throat, reminding the pair of her presence. "I will need a horse," she repeated.

Mr. Edmonds released Lil's hand and faced Wendy. "Sure, I have plenty. The miners don't use their mounts and I often have to ride them to keep them fit. How long do you need the horse for?"

"I'm riding down river to Kurt Jordan's camp. I hope to be there only a day or two, but that will depend on how stubborn he is."

Edmonds laughed. "Yes, Kurt is stubborn. Impulsive too, if you ask me," he said in a lower tone as his gaze drifted to where Miss Peterson was stepping into Bill's café farther down the street.

He tucked his thumbs into his belt and looked at Wendy again. "But he's rounding up stock along the brakes of the river. What do you need with him?"

"We're looking for a guide to lead us to the Mora River country, down south," Lil interjected.

Edmonds squinted. "Not a good idea. Apache lands. Kurt's been there and said he'd never go back."

Wendy stomped her foot. "Do you know of anyone else who would lead us to that country?"

"Well, no—"

"Then rent us a horse and allow me to discuss this matter with Mr. Jordan myself."

Lil patted her bonnet and shot Wendy a disapproving glance before she inhaled deeply and looked away. Wendy frowned and regretted her outburst, but she needed to keep moving forward with the plan. She didn't have time to waste when a possible guide might be located right outside of town. It was worth a chance.

A few minutes later, Wendy swung into the saddle, enjoying the familiar feel of a horse beneath her. She accepted the worn leather gloves Mr. Edmonds loaned her and slipped her slim hands into them.

The hostler corroborated Bill's directions to the cowboy's camp, and Wendy smiled down at her aunt. "I'll see you when

I see you. I might be gone a few days, but don't worry about me if it's a little longer. I'll do my best to persuade Mr. Jordan to join us. But you keep searching for a guide here in town."

Lil stepped closer and rested a hand on the horse's neck. A glance over her shoulder confirmed Mr. Edmonds had moved away, but Lil lowered her voice anyway. "We need Mr. Jordan, Wendy. Time is against us, the winter is against us, but we need to go south and find that gold."

Wendy tilted her head, studying her aunt and her sudden seriousness. "I know."

Lil's scowl deepened and she licked her lips. "What you don't know is we're almost out of money. I have a little put aside, but we need to hurry and find that treasure."

Wendy felt her chest tighten at Lil's disclosure. "But we have enough to outfit an expedition and return to Little Rock, right?"

Lil shrugged and stepped back. "No, but we will trust in the Lord. Do your best and be safe," she replied noncommittally.

Wendy pursed her lips as she pulled her slouch hat low and gathered the reins. A gentle breeze blew frigidly from the high mountains, but the sun shone brightly, and Wendy felt excited as she nodded and kicked her mount in the ribs. She trotted down the main street, peering into Bill's café when she passed. An odd sensation assailed her when she saw Miss Peterson sitting at the window table, looking out, and their eyes met. For a brief instant, Wendy thought of stopping and giving the young girl a piece of her mind. Wendy was no stable boy. She was a lady like Miss Peterson and should not be spoken to in such a manner.

But the sensation passed, and Wendy kicked her mount into a gallop, leaving the little town behind. She had other business to attend to. Her personal feelings were not important. Miss Peterson was not important. Only finding the gold and returning to Little Rock mattered.

She rode past the row of disreputable-looking saloons before turning north, passing the coal mine at the edge of town and taking the trail that followed the Purgatory toward the Arkansas River far ahead in the distance.

The rocky trail proved challenging for her horse to continue such a quick gait, and she slowed, allowing the animal to find its own pace. Only the wind kept her company. Not even a bird called to her from the nearby brush that bordered the fast-moving water of the Purgatory River. Wendy craned her neck for a better look at the river. White capped waves revealed where the current divided around submerged rocks, and gray pools suggested deep places where the flow eddied. In the summer, these pools would make ideal fishing holes. Wendy tried to imagine the dry land in summer. Probably hotter than Arkansas, but maybe not any humidity at this higher elevation, so near the mountains. Prickly pear mingled with manzanita, and scrub oaks scattered across the hills. Cedar trees and an occasional pine tree cast a dark green to the bleak landscape. Wendy had to admit the scenery wasn't ugly, only different from the woods she knew along the river in Little Rock.

Her gaze drifted to the high peaks, and she caught her breath. Nothing she knew could compare to this glorious sight. The ridges were frosted with glistening white snow, and large patches of pine trees flanked the shoulders of the mountains, coloring them darkly. The word beautiful lacked the true depth of her appreciation. Wendy breathed in the crisp air and filled her lungs with the fragrant, pine-scented aroma.

"They're awesome, Father," she whispered as she studied the huge mountains where they stretched as far to the northern horizon as she could see. Magnificent, amazing, and remarkable, the tall peaks called to her and demanded praise to their creator.

"Your handiwork speaks to my soul," Wendy breathed as the horse plodded through the scant grass and around rocks. "I love the signs you give me, pointing to your presence and creativity. Help me trust you. I know this journey is from you. Only one door opened to me, and I hope I chose correctly. Guide me where you wish to take me, and help me find the treasure you desire."

She traveled on for another hour before she came to the first of the series of meadows Bill and Mr. Edmonds had mentioned. Sage brush and occasional outcroppings of speckled granite dotted the wide, grassy plateau. Even Wendy's inexperienced eye could read the ideal pastureland for cattle or horses.

Crossing the grass-covered expanse, the trail led near the river again for a short distance before dipping into a swale. Out of the wind, Wendy realized the sun felt warm on her shoulders despite the time of year.

Another hour passed, and then another, and yet Wendy continued on, the babbling waterway providing an incessant melody that she grew to enjoy.

Finally, about twenty miles from Trinidad, Wendy heard the bawling of cattle. A thin veil of dust hovered above a grassy plain, and she saw two men riding horses as they moved about a cluster of a dozen cattle. A tendril of smoke rose from a fire at the edge of the meadow. Near the small blaze, packs and gear lay strewn below a monarch pine tree that stood sentinel over the surrounding region. Wendy recognized the ideal camp location when she sighted a little rivulet of clear water flowing beneath the knoll where the pine towered.

When she looked back to the men, the pair watched her approach with obvious curiosity. She licked her lips and nudged her horse forward, picking up her pace.

"Help me, Lord, and may this be part of your plan," Wendy whispered as she rode to meet the two strangers.

CHAPTER EIGHTEEN

Wendy could feel herself tense as she neared the two men sitting their horses watching her draw closer. The small bunch of cattle bawled loudly as they stood stiff legged, staring at the two men on horseback, and Wendy wondered if they were sending her some kind of warning.

"Too late now," she muttered as she drew rein a dozen yards from the staring pair of cowboys. Although both men wore the chaps and boots of the range cattleman, one had flowing black hair that blew in the wind beneath the brim of a battered cavalry hat. Wendy stared at the Indian, but his dark eyes told her nothing. She shifted her gaze to the other man, probably a couple of years older than herself. His chaps were smudged with dirt, and he wore a sheepskin coat. His square, unshaven jaw jutted below high cheekbones, and Wendy felt her stomach flutter when she peered into his piercing eyes. He looked at her as if he could see through her, and she worried. Could he guess her deception?

No matter now, she realized as she leaned back and squinted at the cowboy. "Kurt Jordan?"

The man in the faded sheepskin coat narrowed his eyes. "I'm Jordan. Who's asking?"

Wendy blinked. She hadn't counted on giving her proper name, not yet. "Wen—Wen—Wen Moylan," she stammered.

Jordan and the Indian snickered at her faltering speech. "Well, I haven't seen a boy around who stutters. You must be a stranger hereabouts." He glanced at his companion. "Miguel, do we know a Wen Moylan?"

Miguel shook his head and replied in Spanish. Kurt rested his forearms on his pommel and studied Wendy. "Well, Wen Moylan, you found me. What can I do for you?"

She knew he wasn't impressed with her and wanted to give him a sharp retort, but Wendy choked back her fiery reply. She cleared her throat and adopted her most baritone voice. "Mr. Hanson told me you've been to the Mora River country. He said you're not afraid of the Apache, and you've been there and come back."

Jordan shifted in his saddle. "Anyone who says they're not afraid of the Apache is a fool. I've been there, and I know I'll never go again. Only by the Lord's protection did I escape the first time. I've learned my lesson."

Wendy scowled, wishing the interview would move faster. She'd expected Kurt Jordan to refuse to take her and she wanted to move ahead to the part where she explained why he should guide her. She'd also expected him to be a tough-looking older man with an air of experience about him, not this young, handsome cowboy who seemed amused at her presence. She drew a deep breath and plunged on.

"Look, you know the area. I need a guide to take me there. My grandfather knew of a special place on the Mora River, and I want to find it."

"What special place?" Kurt's interruption surprised Wendy and she sagged in her saddle. Would they argue about the trip and get nowhere? She needed to find the gold hidden in the rock crevice. Surely the gold bags would contain enough money for her to pay her father's debts and provide a good living for her and Aunt Lil. Time was passing far too quickly, and Wendy knew that even if she procured Jordan as her guide, it may take weeks to gather the essential supplies she needed for an expedition into Indian lands.

"I am not prepared to share the specifics of the place," Wendy said with an icy tone. "Let it suffice to know it is along the Mora River, above where it pours into the Canadian River. I will share more details when we are on our way south."

Jordan glanced at Miguel and the two cowboys laughed loudly. "Boy, you are a bold one," he said as he wiped his eyes with a gloved hand. "I'm not going to the Mora River country again, with or without you. And I've got more important things to worry about."

He gestured toward the small cluster of bawling cattle. "I'm working to gather lost stock. I need the makings of a ranch, my own ranch, to win the heart of my lady love."

Wendy tilted her head, eyeing Kurt before shifting her gaze to Miguel. The Indian sat silent, but a muscle twitched in his jaw at Kurt's blunt declaration.

"Your lady love? You need money? That's what I'm trying to tell you. I can pay you to accompany me south. We'll both get what we want."

"Show me this money." Kurt nudged his horse and took a step nearer.

Wendy shook her head. "Well, I don't have the money right now. That's what we're looking for. But I can pay you when we find it."

Kurt pushed his hat back on his head and puckered his brow. "Let me get this straight. You want me to guide you into Apache lands and hope we find money hidden there? You don't actually have any money to pay me with. I'm to just trust you and then *maybe* I'll get paid, if we survive and you find what you're looking for."

The way he put it sounded ridiculous, and Wendy frowned. Was she crazy? Was there any chance they could find Grandfather Sean's hidden gold? The treasure might not even be real.

Wendy gazed up to the high mountains and sent a silent prayer skyward. What was she doing out here?

"I'm not interested," Kurt said, drawing Wendy's attention back to the cowboy. "Like I said, I'm in love. I learned a valuable lesson down there in Apache country, and now I'm going to live a good life. No more working for another man and waiting for things to come my way. I'm going to shape my own future. I'm going to build my own ranch and marry a good woman, settle down and raise a family. I'm not afraid of hard work, and I'm willing to build slowly, but it's time to start laying the foundation and stop wandering."

The lengthy speech startled Wendy, and she found herself respecting the young man's determination. Hadn't she come to the same conclusion?

"Purpose," she said softly.

"Huh?" Saddle leather creaked as Kurt straightened.

"Purpose," Wendy said again. "I understand. Time to grow up. Time to do something good with your life. Don't waste any more time. Make your life count."

Kurt stared at her. "Yes. That's what I mean." He pulled his hat brim low and narrowed his eyes as he studied her. Then he made a wide sweep with his hand, encompassing the big meadow, the nearby river, and the small bunch of noisy cattle. "And I'm beginning right here. These are loose stock, some lost on the Santa Fe Trail, some by local ranchers. I intend to round them up and return the ones I can and keep the rest to start my own ranch. I need a place of my own, for me and my wife."

"You're married?"

"No, no," Kurt shook his head at Wendy's query. "No, I'm trying to build a ranch so I *can* marry. No lady wants to come to a man who has nothing."

He looked at the surrounding country, and Wendy watched his shoulders sag. "Problem is, I can't find enough riders to help me round up the stock. Then, I need help building my ranch. I have a house, but little else."

"I can ride," Wendy said. The words were out of her mouth before she could consider the implications. He seemed so sincere, and she sensed a connection between them, a similar desire to make life count. She felt as weary as he seemed about wasting the days the Lord had given them.

A scowl creased his features, and Kurt cocked an eyebrow. "I thought you were off to find hidden treasure."

She ignored the sarcasm in his words and smiled anyway. "I need a guide. Mr. Hanson and Bill at the café and Mr. Edmonds at the livery are all looking for one. I'll work for you in the meantime, if you won't take me. I can use the money."

"No money until I sell the stock," he said hurriedly. "And then I need to pay Mr. Hanson for the supplies he loaned me. I hope to return some of the stock to rightful owners, but the rest I'll sell in town or keep the young stuff to build my own herd."

Wendy nodded, anticipation mingling with eagerness as she realized she'd just accepted her first job. "So, I'm hired?"

Kurt smiled. "You just got a job with the Slash J, Wen Moylan."

They determined Wendy was too inadequately outfitted to ride the brush and drive cattle into the open. "You don't even have chaps to protect your legs from the thickets," Kurt lamented. "Besides, you're too small and wet behind the ears to wrestle these big steers."

Wendy stiffened and sat as straight in her saddle as she could. "I'm twenty-three," she reported, chin rising.

"Twenty-three?" Kurt shot a doubtful look at his partner, but Miguel only shrugged. "You don't even have peach fuzz on your chin yet. I figured you for about sixteen."

"Well, I'm not," Wendy snapped. "Now, tell me what to do."

Kurt gestured at the handful of cattle that milled in the center of the meadow. A hillock to the west protected the swale from the coldest winds coming from the nearby mountains. "We don't have much work for you yet. We need to gather more cattle before you'll have your work cut out for you, keeping this mob in the meadow and not allowing them to drift back into the brush." He tilted his head and eyed her doubtfully. "Can you shoot?"

"Of course," Wendy said without hiding her disappointment. She wanted to work, to earn her way. But more importantly, she wanted to show Kurt Jordan that she could ride and wasn't just a charity case he took on out of desperation.

"Go to camp and get my rifle. Find us a buck, if you can. With me and Miguel beating the brush, we're bound to flush a few deer."

He nodded at Miguel and the two cowboys turned away to ride back toward the river. "Just don't shoot us," Kurt added over his shoulder.

Wendy sat her horse, listening to the two men laugh as they rode away. She thought about shouting a sharp retort after them but bit her tongue. Excitement bubbled within her and Wendy grinned. She had a job. The overwhelming worry that assailed her since her father's death had not dissipated, but now she had something concrete to concentrate on. She would help these cowboys gather loose stock as Aunt Lil hounded the men back in Trinidad to locate a guide. With a little luck, Wendy would eventually impress Kurt Jordan and he would accept the guide position, or Lil will locate one in town. Either way, she would go south to search for the hidden treasure. In the meantime, she would work hard and be diligent with what the Lord had provided. The task before her allowed Wendy to focus on simpler things, and she relished the idea that she could do something she was fitted to accomplish.

With a nudge, she guided her horse toward the tall pine

where the cowboy's gear lay scattered. She squinted at the dirty dishes piled beside the dying fire and promised herself to return and clean up the campsite after she shot a deer.

Picketing her horse on a long rope, she reached for the rifle that leaned against the tree and then stopped, eyeing the three horses that grazed outside of camp. Two of them were powerfully built geldings with scratches across their shoulders, showing they'd been used to chase cattle from the brush. The smaller horse peered at Wendy, as if taking her measure. She smiled at the friendly looking horse, but the animal bent her head and went back to cropping the brown meadow grass. Perhaps the mare wasn't as friendly as Wendy hoped.

"Well, Jesus, I still have you, right?" she whispered as she tossed fresh fuel on the fire. She took up the rifle and strode toward the river, making sure she was far from the two riders who rode among the thickets. "No matter where I go and no matter who I meet, you are always with me." Wendy cast a final look at the small cluster of cattle before she plunged into the dense foliage along the river. "Who would've thought I'd be hunting deer along the Purgatory River only a week after my father's funeral? You knew, didn't you, Lord? You know when I rise and when I sit down. You know everything about me. Let me trust you. Let me rest in your constant presence."

She slowed when she could no longer hear the bawling cattle behind her. She tried to make little sound as she navigated the thickets and boulders beside the roaring river. Occasionally, Wendy caught a glimpse of the white capped waters of the Purgatory as the raucous river raced to join the Arkansas River farther to the north.

At a small clearing beside the river, Wendy stared at the noisy water. This same water would pass her home back in Little Rock. A pang pierced her heart and she frowned. Would she ever see her home again?

A branch crackled, and Wendy crouched as she studied the place where the sound came from. Three deer walked toward the river and the two does bent to drink as the buck peered around, head held high as he watched for danger. Wendy brought the gun to her shoulder and took careful aim.

At the sharp explosion of the rifle, the three deer leaped for the protection of the brush, but the buck stumbled and fell while the two does disappeared among the trees, white tails flashing as they fled.

Within no time, Wendy had skinned the buck and piled the choice cuts within the hide. A gray, skulking coyote caught her eye, and she knew the bloody deer carcass would not last long. Taking up the rifle, she hefted her heavy load over one shoulder and marched back toward camp, resting a few times on the return trip.

Fifteen cattle now stood watching her as she entered the big meadow, but there was no sign of the two cowboys. She butchered the venison and put some meat on the fire to broil as she washed the dishes and gathered firewood. The sun perched atop the mountains, threatening to depart soon, when the two grimy cowboys rode into camp on weary mounts.

Miguel dismounted and led the horses away as Kurt Jordan approached the fire, his eyes locked on the prepared dinner. He took off his hat and slapped it against his leg as he looked up at Wendy. "Well, Moylan, you sure did the right thing," he said, gesturing to the steaming pots on the cheerful blaze. Coffee bubbled and the smell of roasting meat filled the air. "I wanted to fire you after I hired you, but Miguel told me to wait and see. He's always advising patience when I want to just jump in and make a decision."

Wendy felt her brow furrow beneath her slouch hat. "Why would you fire me after hiring me?"

"I don't want to share my profits. You can see how many cattle we've rounded up after a week of work. I thought there were more stock hiding in the brakes, but we sure can't find them now."

"Miguel sounds like a wise man," Wendy said as the Indian walked into camp. Shadows stretched across the meadow, and the cry of a nighthawk pierced the twilight. The cattle lowed while the horses grazed, and Wendy tugged on her coat collar, the wind rising as the sun dropped behind the mountains. She shoved her hands into her pockets and scanned the surrounding land as darkness descended. Small patches of snow glimmered along the north side of rocks and thickets, proof of a recent storm, but the sky seemed clear, with bright stars shining above in a canopy of lights that glittered like diamonds.

"He's that, all right," Jordan agreed and slapped the Indian on the shoulder as Miguel went to the fire and filled a cup with coffee. "Don't be fooled by his quiet ways. He understands everything we're saying, but it takes a long time for him to trust folks."

Wendy caught Miguel's eye and smiled, feeling as if the stoic Indian might be a confidant, or at least someone on her side. "He does sound smart." Her gaze shifted to Kurt. "Do I still have a job?"

Jordan shrugged, then reached for the meat. The two men ate in silence while Wendy watched. Finally, Kurt looked up. "We need someone to cook and keep the cattle bunched while we drive the thickets. These cows keep wanting to stray back to familiar places, and we need them to stay in the open while we gather our herd. I need another rider and you're all I can get."

"What does that mean?" Wendy crossed her arms over her chest.

Kurt inhaled deeply. "It means I wish I could get a real cowboy, or someone used to working stock, but I'm stuck with you, Wen Moylan. With the war on, there's few men out here to choose from."

He paused and then pointed at Wendy with his coffee cup. "You're going to run into the same problem. You'll have a hard time finding men willing to guide you into Apache country."

Miguel said something in Spanish and Kurt chuckled.

"What'd he say?" Wendy looked at the two men and wondered if she'd made a mistake joining them.

Kurt kicked at the burning logs in the fire and refilled his mug. "He said I'm not very smart, and going into Apache country after lost stock was foolish. But the Lord protects me and has something special for me to do."

"And what is that?" Wendy leaned forward. Was he supposed to be her guide into the Indian lands south and west of Fort Union? Did her adventure include this cowboy?

Kurt chuckled again and looked at his silent companion. "He says my impatience gets me into trouble, and I need to wait and see what the Lord will do with me. In other words, Miguel and I disagree about what God's plan is for me."

CHAPTER NINETEEN

Wendy rose early and fed sticks to the tiny glowing embers nestled among the gray ashes. While water boiled for coffee, she returned to her bedding in the darkness and worked her long hair with clumsy, numb fingers. Teeth chattering, she washed her face and hands in the little stream before cutting venison into thin strips and heating them with sliced potatoes in a skillet.

When the coffee and meat were ready, Wendy kicked Kurt and Miguel's boots, waking the sleeping cowboys. Kurt grunted and they rose, shrugging into coats and putting on their hats while Wendy pretended to tend the fire. A single star lingered overhead in a canopy of deep blue. In the east, a hint of gray hovered.

Wendy shivered and held her hands to the flames. The cold had surprised her, and she felt grateful for her thick woolen blankets, helping her ward off the bitter March chill. Was she crazy to be working with these cowboys while winter still plagued the plains? Was she crazy to be out here at all?

She dished plates of food for the cowboys and poured steaming coffee into mugs. The three of them ate in silence while the sun slowly tipped the eastern horizon.

"I'm no nurse maid for the two of you," Wendy complained as Kurt and Miguel dropped their dirty plates beside the fire.

"You'll clean your own plates and cups, or we can take turns making food."

Kurt grumbled, but they complied, and Wendy smiled as she cleaned her dishes and stacked them near the fire.

"Your old nag will be of no use out here," Kurt said as he led the way to the picketed horses.

Wendy held her saddle and watched as the two men saddled their horses. "What am I going to ride?"

Kurt tightened his cinch and then faced Wendy. "That horse is not fit for hard riding. Better throw your saddle on one of our mounts. They're good cutting horses and will help you round up stock we push from the brush."

Wendy eyed the pair of big geldings and then her gaze shifted to the smaller mare. "How about her?"

Kurt glanced at Miguel and the Indian shook his head, but Kurt raised a hand. "She's a good cutting horse, no doubt about that. We call her Shannon for short."

"She looks more my size," Wendy said as she walked to the mare and pulled the picket rope toward her. The bay mare came easily to her, and Wendy scratched the horse's nose and long ears. "I think she likes me."

Kurt nodded. "She does that to everyone, makes them think she's real sweet."

Wendy tossed her blanket across Shannon's back and smoothed the material before throwing her saddle. She cinched the girth tight and stepped into the saddle just as the sun sent glowing rays across the grassy meadow, the brown grass shimmering dully in the morning light.

Shannon looked at Wendy over her shoulder and then took a step toward her tail, moving in a tight circle. Wendy tried to pull the reins the other direction, but Shannon kept moving, going faster until Wendy was forced to pull on the reins and grab the pommel. With a sudden bow, Shannon lowered her head and lifted her hind quarters. Wendy sailed through the air and piled into a heap on a grassy mound.

Her eyes rolled in her head. Vaguely, she heard laughter coming from the two men, but she struggled to her feet, her legs wobbling beneath her. She didn't feel like anything was broken or seriously injured, except her pride. She'd been riding since she was young, and now she'd been thrown like any tenderfoot.

Shaking her head to clear her vision, Wendy stalked back to the horse and grabbed the reins in one gloved hand. She shoved a boot into the stirrup and mounted in one fluid motion. She sat straight, steadying her position while she gripped the reins and glared at Kurt. "The little devil thinks she can throw me," Wendy growled, trying to hide her shame.

Kurt and Miguel said nothing, the cowboys watching her silently, as if waiting for more.

Shannon turned in the opposite direction she'd twirled before, spinning faster until she bowed again, throwing Wendy once more. Again, Wendy crumpled into a heap, her eyes brimming with tears as she staggered to her feet, arms, legs, and shoulders aching.

Glowering at Kurt, she walked to the mare and mounted again. "I can ride this horse," she panted between clenched teeth.

"You show her who's boss, Moylan," Kurt shouted as the mare walked forward, bowed, walked backward, and then lifted her hind quarters again. Wendy sailed up high and could see the cowboys watching her as she made a slow arc before tumbling once more to the frozen turf.

The men didn't laugh at her this time as she marched to the horse and gathered the reins. She put a foot in the stirrup and then hesitated, glancing toward the cowboys. "Why do you call her Shannon?"

"Short for shenanigans. That mare has a bag of tricks to toss riders. Miguel won't even ride her anymore, and I only use her when the others are played out." Kurt shifted on his saddle. "You don't have to ride her again, Moylan. Throw your saddle on one of the geldings."

Miguel put the heel of his palms together and made a fluttering motion as he said something in Spanish. Kurt nodded.

"What'd he say?"

Kurt pressed his lips into a thin line. "He said you're Wren Moylan, not Wen. Said you fly like a bird."

Wendy scowled at the Indian and Miguel grinned, putting his palms together and fluttering his hands again.

With a bounce, she threw herself into the saddle, but this time, she kicked the mare in the ribs. Shannon grunted and moved out, startled by the swift kick. Wendy kicked more, nudging the horse into a trot and then into a run.

The mare ran to the far end of the meadow, and Wendy turned her around and ran her back to the watching cowboys. She raced past them and guided the mare to turn at the end of the meadow once more, leaped the smaller horse over a log, and dragged her by the reins to turn on a dime and race back to the cowboys.

Wendy leaned back in the saddle and stretched her legs in the stirrups as she tugged on the reins. Shannon almost went to her haunches, but she reined in and stood panting as Wendy glared at the two cowboys.

"I'll ride Shannon. I like her," Wendy said. Kurt and Miguel exchanged glances and turned their mounts and rode into the brush.

For the remainder of the day, Wendy rode the edge of the big meadow, bunching the tiny herd of cattle and relieving the cowboys of any stock they drove from the brush. Shannon would dart behind the bawling cattle and nip at their flanks, pushing them into the growing herd. By the end of the day, they'd rounded up an additional nineteen head of stock.

"Maybe you're good luck," Kurt commented as the three weary riders walked toward the campfire glowing beneath the pine tree. Throughout the day, Wendy had replenished the blaze, and now, fresh coffee bubbled on the coals.

LASTING TREASURE

Wendy hurt all over, but she straightened proudly under Kurt's praise as they trooped up the small knoll to their camp. Already, the evening star hung low on the horizon, and shadows filled the folds in the land. The brisk wind off the nearby mountains cooled her heated cheeks, but Wendy barely felt the cold. The day had flown by in a blur while the two cowboys scoured the brakes of the river and drove loose stock from the thickets. They'd roamed miles downstream and had more than doubled the small herd in a single day.

Miguel said something as he slipped from his horse and unsaddled. Firelight played on their ruddy faces as the cowboys stripped the gear from their mounts and picketed the tired horses.

"He says you saved us a lot of work today," Kurt said as he carried his saddle to the fire and dropped his tack beside his bedroll.

"Thank you, Miguel," Wendy murmured, but inside, she felt her stomach flutter. She'd been helpful and the cowboys knew it. She'd proven her worth, and a sense of joy filled her, saturating her with a happiness she hadn't felt in ages.

Kurt fetched water as Miguel searched for more firewood. Soon, dinner simmered on the fire and the exhausted riders ate in silence. The small herd of cattle bawled occasionally, never letting Wendy forget they were out there in the darkness. She tossed another log on the blaze, stretched her boots toward the flames, and eyed Kurt over the rim of her third cup of coffee. "What made you go into the Apache lands? I mean, why go there if you hate it so much?"

Kurt shook his head as he refilled his cup and settled back against his saddle. The flames leaped for the fresh fuel, making his unshaven face appear as if in shadows. "I don't hate that land. No, not at all. It's a beautiful land, full of mountains and rivers and desert and woods high up."

He paused and took a sip from his mug. "Miguel and I worked for a rancher near Las Vegas, on the trail to Santa Fe.

We lost some stock, those dumb cows going into Apache lands to find better grass. I just took out after them and tried to bring them back." He smiled, and Wendy noticed his white, even teeth. "Only I found Indians instead."

Miguel said something, and Kurt grinned. "Yes, I'm stubborn. And impulsive. But the good Lord rides with me. He's always got my back. And it's hard for me to wait for help or take the time to go ask for permission. So, I rode into the Apache land after those lost cattle."

"What happened?" Wendy leaned forward, eager for the story.

"I never did find those cows. Maybe the Indians ate them. Whatever happened, I trailed their tracks and come up on a bunch of braves. They started yelling and shooting, and I kicked my horse into action and took out of there. Only problem, I was riding west, deeper into their lands. A bullet caught my horse, and I went down, flying over him like you did this morning."

Kurt and Miguel chuckled. Bruises had formed inside her pants and coat, and Wendy felt the smart reminder of the morning toss from Shannon. She frowned and hid behind her mug as she took another sip.

"I'll miss that horse. He was a good one," Kurt said softly.

"How'd you get away from the Apache?" Wendy could tell he was holding back, not wanting to brag about himself, and she felt pleased at his self-restraint. Suddenly, she thought better of him.

The cowboy shrugged and then yawned. "I just hid from them, gave them the slip, and eventually walked back to the ranch. I never found the cows and it ate at me, urging me to think about my life. I realized I wasn't getting any younger. Here I am, twenty-five, and nothing to show for all of my work. Work for another man."

The night quieted, and even the fire seemed to still as Kurt stared into the flames. He seemed so far away, and Wendy wondered what he thought. When he continued, his voice had dropped to barely a whisper.

"I was alone out there with only the Lord for company. I felt Jesus spoke to me. He told me to make something of myself, to pursue life with an intention. He made me think about what I really want out of life and make a plan on how to chase it."

He sipped his coffee and Wendy couldn't help but wonder if the Lord were asking her the same things. Even if she found the hidden gold, did she wish to simply return to Little Rock and ride in the woods of the Moylan estate? It all seemed so hollow now when she thought of it clearly.

"What do you want from life?"

Kurt looked up at her words, and Wendy felt surprised she'd spoken, as if the words had been wrenched from her without her effort.

"First, I want to serve the Lord. Jesus and me got real close out there in the desert. If he allows, and if it's his will, I want a family, a wife and kids. A nice little ranch where I can build and work, raise Christian children and love a godly woman."

Miguel said something, and even Wendy caught the discordant tone of rebuke. Kurt lifted a hand and waved at his friend as if waving at a pesky fly.

"What? Tell me what Miguel said." Wendy could sense the undercurrent of an argument.

"Oh, he's worse that a mother hen. I came from the desert and we took off up here, the two of us, 'cause I wouldn't wait another minute to begin my quest for what the Lord had in store for me. I prayed and fasted, hungering for a sign, and he led me here to Trinidad. But only two local girls are unmarried. Jenny Blair, who's kind of engaged to Bloomberg's son, and my lady love. Sure, it didn't take me long to acquaint her of my intentions."

Wendy almost laughed at his ridiculous claim. "I don't understand. If the Lord led you here and there's only one girl available, it seems clear to me who is to be your betrothed."

Kurt missed her intended sarcasm and reached for the pot, filling Miguel's cup before topping off his own. Wendy placed a hand over her mug and shook her head. "Sure, I told Miguel the same thing, but he's always telling me to wait on the Lord, to be patient. How clear does the Lord's involvement need to be before you believe? Where's your faith?" The cowboy eyed Miguel skeptically and sipped his coffee.

Wendy glanced at Miguel where the Indian sat brooding in the shadows. "Perhaps Miguel has a point. You can never tell the Lord what your plans are and expect him to follow. He leads his children like a shepherd leads his flock. We listen to his voice and trust he knows what's best for us."

Miguel nodded and gestured at Wendy, saying something very rapidly. Kurt snorted and shook his head.

"What? What?" Wendy gripped her cup expectantly.

"He says you're the wise one now, Moylan, as if a young kid could tell me spiritual truths or insight into love." Kurt hung his head while Wendy shot Miguel a conspirator's grin. The Indian nodded and Wendy thought she detected a faint grin in return.

She lifted her chin. "And why not? From the mouth of babes, you know."

Kurt looked up and scowled at Miguel and then at Wendy. "I know what I know. No matter how the two of you fight me, I know I'm to marry Marigold Peterson."

CHAPTER TWENTY

Wendy blinked and stared at Kurt. Marigold Peterson? Could that be the same snippy young woman she'd met at the livery barn in Trinidad? Sure, the girl had style, but she seemed almost severe and without kindness. Wendy remembered how Miss Marigold had been so rude to her.

Kurt must've noticed the dazed look on Wendy's face, for he narrowed his eyes. "Do you know Miss Marigold?"

Wendy's jaw tensed. "I met someone named Miss Peterson in Trinidad, but perhaps there's more than one."

Kurt shook his head, a wide grin on his unshaven face. "Nope. There's only one Marigold Peterson. Isn't she a beauty? Yes, sir, I'm getting quite a catch."

Wendy shot Miguel an inquisitive glance, but the stoic Indian wouldn't lift his eyes from the flickering flames, a deep scowl lining his bronzed face.

"Well, maybe I met her on a bad day," Wendy said softly.

"What's that mean?" Kurt shifted and kicked a log deeper into the fire. Sparks fluttered, drifting heavenward and into the night sky.

Wendy hesitated. "I only mean that maybe she was preoccupied when we met. She seemed a bit snobbish."

Miguel chuckled, and Kurt glowered at the two of them. "So? Maybe she is a little snooty. Why not? Her pa owns one of the biggest ranches in the area. And I'm not the only man after her, I can tell you. Webb Larson is foreman at the Peterson ranch, and he's made it no secret he's after Miss Marigold. And he's a handsome cuss to boot."

Wendy said nothing, and Miguel only watched the fire for a little while longer before going to his blankets. She yawned and rose to her feet. "Goodnight, Kurt."

Kurt refused to look up from the flames. With an unfamiliar ache in her chest, Wendy went to her bed. For a long time, she studied the bright stars overhead as she shivered, waiting for her blankets to warm. Was she where the Lord wanted her? Was this truly the place he'd led her to?

She thought of Kurt and his assertion that God had brought him here and to Marigold Peterson. Could she feel so assured of God's intentions for her? She envied Kurt's confidence but then remembered Miguel's skepticism. The Lord could be so quiet sometimes, not speaking while her heart searched for answers. Why wouldn't Jesus just tell her what to do?

She glanced once more at the dying fire where Kurt still sat huddled beside his saddle. Would God ever bring someone special to her the way he had for Kurt?

The next day, Miguel helped Wendy push the herd south along the river's edge while Kurt continued to drive cattle from the brush. They moved camp another three miles downstream where another large meadow offered sufficient grazing. Another nine cattle were added to the growing herd.

They stayed there one more day as Miguel helped search for loose stock, pushing them toward the big meadow where Wendy would cut in and drive them to join the herd. Many of the cattle wore no brand, but many had brands she learned to identify. There was the Triple Sevens brand of the Peterson ranch, and she identified a few of the Double B of the Bloomberg ranch, father and son operating the biggest spread in the region. A variety of unknown brands adorned many of the cattle, brands of men who lost cattle moving them over the nearby Santa Fe Trail. These would be sold in Trinidad to the workers mess hall at the mine or to Bill's café.

The unbranded mavericks would be claimed by Kurt, and he planned a branding party when he got them to his home ranch, thirty miles outside of Trinidad.

Wendy pulled her slouch hat low and raced Shannon toward an incoming cow, relieving Kurt or Miguel of the mettlesome beast. The cattle hated being driven from their familiar ranges, and only great effort pushed them into the open where they were added to the swelling herd.

Shannon proved an excellent cutting horse. Fleet-footed and nimble, the quarrelsome horse had grown on Wendy. After a spirited battle of wills each morning, the mare would settle into a pattern of reliability and workmanship with noteworthy stamina. All day, Wendy and Shannon worked to keep the herd together, driving back any that attempted to return to the brush.

Wendy chased a cow back to the herd and reined beneath a pine tree, eyeing the cattle warily. Kurt couldn't say anything negative to her, and she knew it, proud of the job she'd performed. Her muscles ached and she felt exhausted, but she also experienced a great deal of pleasure, an unexpected emotion that startled her.

At the end of eight days, the herd was too large and difficult for one rider to manage. That afternoon, Kurt rode back to the bawling cluster without a single head of stock. An hour later, Miguel rode into camp with two trotting cattle.

"What do you think?" Kurt removed his hat and wiped his brow with his coat sleeve. A cloud of dust veiled the grassy meadow, and a sharp wind whistled from the high peaks. Shoved against the mountain range, a mass of dark clouds gathered ominously.

Miguel replied in Spanish, and Kurt nodded. "I don't think we can hold more either. Better sort the herd and deliver cattle to Peterson and Bloomberg before taking the strays to town." He glanced at Wendy where she sat on Shannon. "How many mavericks?"

Wendy tugged the small notebook from her coat pocket where she kept the tally. "Eighty-nine total. Thirteen for Triple Seven, eighteen for Double B, sixteen odd brands, and forty-two mavericks."

Wendy straightened in her saddle and lifted her chin. A week ago, she didn't know what a maverick was. Now, she rode a cutting horse all day, circling the herd and keeping the cattle from straying. Pride filled her, and she couldn't stop the smile that tugged at the corner of her mouth.

"Forty-two head," Kurt muttered with obvious disappointment. "How can I start a ranch with forty-two cows?"

Miguel snapped at him, and Kurt nodded. "I know I should be grateful. And I am. But that's not enough to start ranching on a big scale. Miss Marigold will never marry me with such a small ranch."

Miguel snapped again and Kurt scowled. "Well, I know if she loves me, it'll not matter. But she made it clear that she's only interested in a husband who can provide for her in a way she's accustomed to."

Wendy bit her lip. Marigold Peterson sounded awfully shallow. Yet, Wendy had her own problems, and she promised not to interfere where it didn't concern her.

The three riders spent the remainder of the day cutting the eighteen Double B cattle from the herd and pushing them eastward to their home range. Sunset found the cowboys seated around their tiny fire as wind scuttled the flames, an impending storm threatening. Kurt tossed another log on the fire and pulled up his coat collar. "Going to be cold tonight," he said as he leaned against his saddle and covered his legs with a blanket.

Wendy wrapped her blankets around her shoulders and nursed her third cup of hot coffee. She couldn't remember the last time she'd been warm. Was it back in Little Rock? The escape from the rundown plantation and the flight across the plains seemed so long ago now. Even the night in Trinidad where she and Aunt Lil had stayed in Mr. Hanson's stockroom seemed a lifetime ago.

Wind whistled from the high peaks, and the towering pines swayed. Wendy eyed the silent cowboys over the rim of her cup. Were they fools to be out on such a night as this? Yet the hard-working riders had accumulated a small herd of cattle, wrestling them from the thickets beside the river and from the small canyons that opened toward the swift moving water. Her wages from this expedition might help her and Aunt Lil make ends meet while they searched for a guide. The journey over the pass and into New Mexico Territory was always on her mind, and Wendy knew she must soon be moving on, pursuing the gold she hoped still lay hidden near the Mora River.

Without thinking, she retrieved the leather journal from her bedding and studied the faded pages by firelight, seeking any subtle clue she'd missed before.

"What are you reading?" Kurt's unexpected inquiry made Wendy tense. Previously, she'd only studied the book when she thought she was unobserved.

She closed the journal and returned the book to her gear. "Nothing," Wendy mumbled and lifted her mug once more.

"Can't be nothing," Kurt said with a sly grin. He glanced at Miguel. "I've seen Moylan looking at that book before. At first, I thought he was just reading a story, but now I suspect he's got a girl somewhere. Must be messages from a young lady. What do you think, Miguel?"

Miguel snorted and said something, then chuckled as Kurt turned to her, a twinkle in his eye. He put down his coffee cup and rubbed his hands together. "Now, that is interesting."

"I don't have a girl," Wendy mumbled and looked out into the stormy night. A shiver ran down her spine, and she knew the temperature had dropped, but her anxiety blossomed. Would they discover her deceit? Despite the cold, unexpected heat crept up her neck, and she could only guess the pink that stained her cheeks.

"Look, Miguel, we must've hit the target. Look at him blushing." Kurt chuckled. "Don't worry about it, kid. I understand. Love is a terrible thing."

Miguel laughed, but Wendy only drew her chin behind her collar, trying to hide from Kurt's scrutiny.

"What're you laughing at?" Kurt turned on his grinning companion, and Miguel scowled, suddenly uncomfortable. The young cowboy gestured to the silent Indian while he glanced at Wendy.

"Do you know who this is, Moylan? Miguel is a Yaqui, one of the last of a brave tribe located south of the border. First the Spanish and then the Mexicans systematically decimated his people. When the United States Army arrived to fight the Mexicans back in '46, Miguel here was a young boy, eager to serve the Americans as a scout. After the war, he guided the military and helped establish a few outposts on the frontier."

Kurt sipped his coffee, eyes still glittering in the ruddy firelight that played across his features. His unshaven face was grimy with dirt, and he needed a shave, but his firm jaw and high cheekbones were clearly outlined in the dim light.

"Yes, Wen, this old Yaqui is a warrior, strong and tested in battle." Kurt paused and Wendy glanced at Miguel where the Indian sat staring into the dancing flames. He didn't look old—barely ten years older than Kurt himself. And his chest swelled powerfully with muscles beneath his faded blue woolen military coat. But his face was set in stern lines, as if not enjoying Kurt's description.

Abruptly, Kurt snorted. "But he knows nothing of love. He's

got no girl, no wife stashed far away. He's been my partner and best friend for the past ten years, ever since I ran away from the orphanage in New Orleans. Yet he still feels he has the right to tell me about women, about love, and share his opinions of Miss Peterson."

Miguel looked up sharply, and a stream of words sliced across the campsite. Wendy could hear the attack in the sharp tone, and she watched Kurt, curious at his response.

The teasing grin vanished from the young cowboy's lean features, and he glared at his friend. "I could thrash you for saying that. And don't think I can't. I could wrap you up and deliver you like a Christmas package."

Miguel stood, arms limp by his side, but his gaze never left Kurt. Wendy read the invitation in his dark eyes and leaped to her feet, stepping between the two riders. "Nothing to prove here. You are both entitled to your opinions. As for me, I have no girl. You both probably know more than I do about love and such things."

She studied both men before gesturing to their former seats. "Take it easy. Nothing worth fighting over. We're all tired. This storm has got us keyed up."

As if by magic, tiny snowflakes swirled around them, and all three looked up at the night sky. The wind moaned through the trees, and the snow fell faster.

"See? We're going to be cold tonight. Everyone needs to do their bit to keep the fire going."

Miguel looked at her and then turned and stalked into the darkness. Wendy turned on Kurt. "You don't have to rub it in that you have a girl and Miguel doesn't. Sounds like his life has been filled with struggle and sacrifice. You should lay off."

Kurt's brow wrinkled and he almost said something, then stopped and nodded. "I know," he muttered, rubbing the back of his neck with one hand. "But he gets under my skin with all that patience advice he throws in my face. I *know* the Lord led me here. Miss Marigold is the only available girl in the region. Am I supposed to ignore God and not get married? I'm ready for a life of purpose."

Kurt paused and pointed at the dark place where Miguel had disappeared. "Maybe he can wander the world alone, but I'm called to find a mate, settle down, raise a Christian family, and serve the Lord by example. I plan on carving a home from this wilderness, and I'm not supposed to do it alone."

Wendy only stared, unsure what to say. Kurt knew what he wanted. She wished she could articulate what she felt God wanted for her. The problem was, she wasn't sure she knew.

CHAPTER TWENTY-ONE

Wendy felt the intense cold before she fully awakened. She shoved the canvas ground sheet back and peered into the bleak morning gray. The snow had stopped, leaving behind a thin layer of dusting across everything, bathing the world in a crisp white covering.

Teeth chattering, she pushed wood into the ring of stones, but only ashes lifted. She forced herself to stand and gather fuel. The sun had not risen above the eastern hills, and Wendy knew how much she'd appreciate hot coffee if someone else had gotten up before her.

When Miguel and Kurt emerged from beneath the layering of snow that hid their bedrolls, a cheerful blaze danced in the still air. Coffee simmered beside a skillet piled high with thick slices of venison and potatoes.

"Well, Wen, I take back whatever bad things I said about you," Kurt said as he leaned over the warm fire. Miguel seemed sullen, but his dark eyes softened when Kurt slapped his shoulder. "Sorry, old man. You know you get my back up sometimes. Forgive me. I didn't mean those things I said."

Miguel shrugged and reached for the coffee. Wendy watched as the Indian filled his cup and then Kurt's mug, steam rising from the hot black liquid as he poured.

The first time Wendy made coffee for the riders, they'd spit the weak concoction on the ground and lambasted her efforts.

Ever since, she'd refined the recipe, adding more coffee until the cowboys seemed satisfied with the dark drink.

She wondered at the silly endeavor, realizing she truly enjoyed the hard work of a rider and the severe test of her skills. She recalled that Lil had said she seemed happy, and Wendy mused at the remark. Since arriving in Trinidad, she'd worked harder than she knew was possible, yet she'd loved every moment.

"I was thinking," Kurt said, bringing Wendy from her thoughts. "Miguel, I think you should drive the odd brands to town. Set up a sell with Edmonds. He'll know who to get a hold of. And return Wen's nag to the livery. He can ride Shannon. Pay Mr. Hanson what we owe him and bring fresh supplies to the ranch house."

"What about me?" Wendy bent to pour herself a second cup of coffee.

Kurt gestured at her with his mug. "Me and Moylan can drive the mavericks and the Triple Sevens to the ranch and start the branding."

Miguel pointed at a nearby cow wearing the Triple Seven brand. Kurt nodded.

"After the branding, I'd like to personally deliver those thirteen head to the Peterson ranch."

Miguel pursed his lips into a thin line but said nothing. Two hours later, the Indian pushed the sixteen odd brands toward Trinidad, Wendy's borrowed horse among them. The slow-moving cattle lowed as they walked from the snow-covered meadow toward town.

"These fifty-five will be easy for two riders," Kurt said as he swung behind the herd and started them moving. He glanced at Wendy. "Ever drive cattle?"

She shook her head.

"Just do what I do. Keep them pointed in the right direction and don't let any of them run into the brush."

Yesterday's wind had disappeared, leaving behind a white world of crisp snow where sound traveled clearly in the still air. Wendy wrapped her scarf around her neck and pulled the material over her mouth, concealing much of her face. Only her eyes peeked from under the brim of her hat, and she felt safe from Kurt's piercing scrutiny. His gaze roamed restlessly as he searched for straying cattle or lost stock. She felt secure behind her cover of a thick coat, gloves, hat, and scarf. Thank God she'd be gone before summer when she would not be able to wear so much clothing.

She sighed as she moved to push the small herd toward Kurt's ranch house. She'd be gone by summer, but where would she be? Would she find the hidden treasure? Would she return to Little Rock? So much had changed so quickly. Would anything of her former life still remain by summer?

She glanced at Kurt from under her hat brim, watching the young cowboy move so easily through the scattered brush and rocks. The horse and rider seemed to glide, to turn so quickly behind darting strays. Wendy felt she was an accomplished rider, yet these western cowboys made riding a horse seem like an art form. Determined to hold her own, she nudged Shannon forward, eager to do her part.

"Well, Moylan, we've never had much time to talk, to get acquainted." Kurt's call surprised her, and Wendy stiffened, not wanting him to learn too much about her.

"We've talked every night around the campfire," Wendy retorted, hoping to quell his interest.

"Nope," Kurt replied as he darted after a stray and drove the cow back into line. "We've been working, too tired at night to talk much. I figure you've shown yourself a man to stick to a job. I might as well get to know you, you being a part of the Slash J now."

Wendy's eyebrows arched, a glimmer of happiness swelling unexpectedly. "Am I really part of the Slash J?" Wendy had always been different. Riding alone in the woods had created more gossip than she cared to recall. Would she ever belong anywhere?

"Of course," Kurt nodded. He grinned at her and his white teeth flashed in the morning sun. "Besides, it's a long day's drive to home. It'll help pass the time."

Wendy shrugged, surprised she liked his interest, although she didn't want him to learn her secrets. At her apparent indifference, Kurt continued.

"You're from Arkansas, too young to serve in the war. What's happening back there? We don't hear much out here about the fighting."

Ironically, the war seemed a safe subject, and Wendy explained about the Northern invasion into Southern lands, the naval blockade that sealed off Southern ports, the recent reelection of President Lincoln, and the final holdout of the Confederates outside of Richmond and in the Shenandoah Valley.

"When the Yankees captured New Orleans and bottled the ports, supplies became difficult to obtain," she explained, recalling many of her father's letters or things she'd heard from neighbors in town. "Then General Grant captured Vicksburg, closing the Mississippi to Confederate travel, and Lee was turned back at Gettysburg. When Sherman burned Atlanta, most southerners knew the end was near. The Confederacy can't hold out much longer."

Kurt chased another stray and then returned to her side, the two riders walking their mounts through the frigid morning. Sunlight glittered brightly across the snow-covered plains, and the high peaks of the nearby Rockies shone with white crowns.

"So, the war is almost over," Kurt spit. "Who could've guessed it would last this long? And what's the purpose? All that death and loss."

Wendy tilted her head. "Purpose?"

He gestured a gloved hand at her. "Take you and me, two young men out in the world. We're searching for purpose, what to do with our lives. The Lord has guided me to Trinidad, to a life I feel he wants for me. A life of freedom and love, and yet something more. To build, to shape the land. And hopefully have a lot of kids."

He whooped and then laughed at his own remark. Wendy felt the heat rise to her cheeks beneath her scarf. His candor made her feel uncomfortable with all his talk about marrying and children.

Randall Whitmore's proposal only intensified her desires to be left alone. Soon she would have her treasure and return to Little Rock, melt into the woods of the dilapidated Moylan estate, and hide from the world. Peace and quiet were what she craved. Then she thought of returning to Little Rock ... to her now empty home. She felt a wave of great loneliness then. Did she really want to go back to the way things were?

"My folks are gone," Kurt continued. "At least, I expect they are. I never knew them, and the orphanage is all I remember." He shot her a quizzical look. "How about you? Any family?"

Wendy sagged in her saddle, the memory of her mother flooding over her. A sudden need to share, to unburden her overwhelming anxieties surged and she blinked, angry at the emotion the simple question invoked. She felt surprised how natural it seemed to talk with Kurt. His easy manner relaxed her, and she wondered if she would tell him too much about herself. "Mother died when I was twelve, just when I really needed her. Life and all of its problems seemed to avalanche on me that summer, and Father was no help. I still miss her."

The cowboy's unexpected snicker brought her from her reverie and Wendy scowled as she fixed him with an icy stare. "What's so funny?"

"Nothing, I guess," he said with a shrug. "But that sure explains a lot. You're a mama's boy, huh, Moylan?"

A sad smile crept to her lips and Wendy nodded. "Yes, I guess I am."

Kurt dashed off to pursue a wayward cow and Wendy squinted up at the light blue sky. Wisps of clouds splashed across the heavens, and she wondered why God forced her to conjure up painful memories. Didn't he know she only wanted to find peace, to be alone but not feel so alone? She wanted to complete this quest and return to ... oh, she didn't know what she wanted.

She shook her head, confused at her own lack of decision. Of course, she would return home. That was the reason she'd come west.

She chewed her lip. It *was* what she wanted ... right?

Wendy glanced to the towering peaks. The hard work of helping the cowboys round up lost stock had temporarily allowed her mind to relax, but she was no closer to her goal. Time was running out. She needed to locate a guide to take her south to the Mora River country. If the Apache hadn't killed Kurt Jordan, perhaps she could sneak into the Indian lands and search for Grandfather Sean's gold, alone and without a guide. Perhaps Kurt would provide a better map of the region if Wendy asked.

Regardless, if she went with a guide or alone, she would need supplies. Her only chance of purchasing provisions was the money Kurt promised for her work with the cattle. After the branding and the delivery to the Triple Sevens Ranch, she vowed she'd return to Trinidad and outfit for an expedition into New Mexico Territory, with or without a guide.

She angled her horse away from Kurt, wanting space between them. She needed to think of her own problems and not simply enjoy the cowboy's pointless talking. Their conversation had felt easy, as if they'd known each other longer than a mere week, yet she knew the connection they shared would have little effect on her mission into Apache country. Kurt's desire to find a wife and build a Christian home seemed foreign, almost exotic to her. What would such a dream be like? Wendy had always known the companionship of other Christian women, but an entire family dedicated to the love and worship of Christ made her mind spin. Were such families real?

She shook her head, irritated she wasted more time on Kurt's ideas. She needed to concentrate.

A tan and white cow darted for the brush, and Wendy nudged Shannon. The fleet cutting horse shot like an arrow after the escaping animal and effortlessly brought the violator back to the herd.

"Moylan," Kurt called, and Wendy turned, following the cowboy's outstretched arm to see another cow heading for the brush.

"I got him," she waved and took pursuit of the fleeing cow.

Slowly, the small herd made its way down the valley. By nightfall, the group of cattle clustered below the summit of a tall hill, the sound of gurgling water tinkling merrily nearby. The tired cattle spread out and fell to grazing the scant winter grass or nibbling on leafless branches of thickets that ringed the rocky meadow. Hooves pounded, and Wendy peered into the gloom, barely recognizing Kurt as the cowboy rode up to her.

"We're here," he panted excitedly. "Home."

Home? Wendy peered all around, searching for any indication of buildings or barns or corrals. As if sensing her doubts, Kurt gestured toward a dark outline nestled at the far end of the plain, barely distinguishable in the faded light.

"My cabin is yonder. I'll circle the herd while you get a fire started. I'd tackle a grizzly bear for a cup of your coffee. It took you long enough, but you've finally learned how to make good coffee."

Wendy knew Kurt couldn't see her grin in the descending darkness, and she walked Shannon toward the end of the wide meadow, letting the mare pick her way around rocks in the frozen land.

Her fingers were frozen despite her gloves and cold settled in her bones, yet she felt an unexpected warmth at Kurt's praise. Pleased by his compliment, she nudged Shannon to a quicker pace, wanting to hurry and get coffee on for the weary cowboy.

A cabin loomed out of the darkness, and Wendy drew rein, peering at the empty doorway and the hollow windows that looked back at her. Starlight gleamed dully, and she dismounted, taking tentative steps toward the obscure building. A black gulf extended beyond the threshold, and Wendy retrieved matches from her saddlebags before venturing farther. By the glow of a match, she located the stack of kindling and started a blaze in the stone fireplace.

As the hungry flames licked at the dry wood, she stood and studied the cabin, her back to the warming fire. The room was spacious, and another dark doorway indicated an adjoining room. Her boots left no tracks upon the frozen dirt floor, but the walls seemed solid, the bottom half were cleverly fitted stones, the top half peeled, squared logs. A small loft extended half the length of the rafters, and Wendy peered at the ladder tacked to one wall, wondering what gear might be in the storage place. A wooden bench sat against one wall, and a box of matches and a few candles sat on the roughhewn mantel over the big stone fireplace.

Crude, but a huge improvement over the rustic campsites she'd shared with the cowboys this past week. At least the roof seemed solid.

"Not much to look at." Kurt's voice startled her, and Wendy turned to see him leaning in the door frame. "Miguel helped lift the logs into place, and I knew a sheep herder who's a good stonemason. The fireplace draws smoke perfectly."

Wendy shrugged. "Seems well built. A good start to your ranch."

He seemed pleased by her comment and hooked a thumb over his shoulder. "I've started a barn, and there's a hot spring a hundred yards down the trail, nice for baths. The pool was shaped long before I found the place, probably by Indians."

He paused, and Wendy watched as his gaze roamed the shadowed interior of the cabin, his eyes glowing with pride. Would she ever help build something permanent or lasting? A desire to *do* came over her. She wanted to head south and search for the treasure, to actually try and find the gold that might enable her to … to what?

If only she knew exactly what she wanted. Her former contentment at riding the Moylan Plantation had passed, and she knew she wanted something more, *needed* something more. No longer could she appreciate an empty life that served no one except herself. Leisure and ease had lost their luster. Her grief and sorrow at the struggles of life had been replaced with a longing to work, to build, to accomplish something.

Suddenly, Wendy knew that if she found Grandfather Sean's gold, she would not use the money to rebuild the Moylan estate. She wasn't even sure if she wanted to return to the dilapidated plantation where Randall Whitmore waited. She'd seen so many new things this past few weeks. The vast plains that stretched as far as the eye could see. The majestic Rocky Mountains that she'd only read about in books. And something more that touched Wendy in ways she'd never expected. The sight of dust rising thickly over a herd of cattle, like a moving veil. The feel of a horse beneath her as the animal tensed, prepared to plunge into the brush in pursuit of a fleeing cow. A glorious sunrise, the gray sky turning to pink and then blue as the clouds reflected the shafts of early rays.

All of these marvels spoke to her, and she knew she loved the west. Unexpectedly, the western lands filled her with a sense of wonder and adventure that she'd lacked all of her life.

Kurt shifted, and Wendy came out of her reverie. "I'll take a bath first, then you can go after dinner. We're both a couple of filthy pigs."

He chuckled easily, but Wendy tensed. Surely, she could not take a bath. She felt disgusting, covered in dried sweat and dirt, but she'd taken great pains to conceal her true identity. She thought of the big coat and the gloves over her small hands and her hat pulled low, the scarf across her face. As long as the cowboys believed she was a boy, she could work and think and prepare for the journey south. No one would guide a girl into Indian lands.

"I don't need a bath," she said in what Wendy hoped was a gruff voice that would not allow argument.

Kurt dragged his saddle and gear into the cabin and dropped the load against the wall. "Suit yourself. You stink, Moylan, but none of my affair."

He rummaged among his gear and gathered a towel and a clean shirt before disappearing down the trail beside the cabin, lifting one of the candles high as he strode into the dark.

CHAPTER TWENTY-TWO

"Come on, sleepy head," Kurt growled as he kicked Wendy's boots. "Pile out. We've got work to do."

She stretched lazily in her blankets, enjoying the warmer than usual morning air. Crisp and cold, it nevertheless felt much less frigid this morning.

She opened her eyes when the sharp crack of breaking kindling filled the cabin, and she remembered where she was— the cowboys, cattle, the rustic cabin in the wilderness, her trip west to find gold, her unfulfilled life, the unfamiliar work of a ranch rider. She felt a sense of accomplishment she was not used to, a sense of belonging as the cowboys taught her how to work cattle, to push a herd. Today she would learn to brand.

"Is the coffee ready yet?" Wendy yawned, reluctant to give up her warm blankets before she had to.

Kurt rattled the simmering pans over the fire, his back to Wendy. "Get up, Moylan. Coffee will be ready soon, but I want you to get another deer. There's usually a few grazing in the meadow when the sun rises. Get my rifle and get ready."

Wendy pushed back her covers, pleased they weren't covered in snow this morning. Despite the open doorway and the empty windows, the cabin had afforded some shelter from the cold night. Teeth chattering, she shrugged hurriedly into her big coat while Kurt's back was still turned. Her braided hair itched, and she desperately wanted a bath, but she stuffed the tight coils beneath her hat and slipped her hands into her gloves.

"Be back soon," she mumbled as she lifted Kurt's rifle and walked out the open door. She could hear the horses grazing down near the creek but could not see clearly where they were stabled. A dark mass of lounging bodies revealed the silent herd scattered around the rock-strewn meadow, a faint glow of light announcing the coming dawn.

Her boots crunched on the frozen ground as Wendy made her way past the horses to a point above the cattle, watching the sun rise slowly over the plains to the east. She scanned the surrounding region, picking out individual cows as night fled from the land. She shivered in the cold and rubbed her hand across her nose, but her heart swelled as the dark morning lighted. Slowly, shadows receded, and Wendy watched as God displayed his glory in the beauty of a new day dawning.

"Oh, Lord, you are amazing. Is a new day dawning for me too?"

A sense of expectancy fluttered in her belly, as if something were happening, something impending. She wanted to explore the unfamiliar feeling further, but a pair of deer stepped from the thickets along the nearby stream. A distant rumble drifted to her ears, and Wendy knew the Purgatory River lay farther along, the little stream that meandered across Kurt's homestead, wending a path toward the bigger river.

Lifting the rifle to her shoulder and feeling the faint chill of breeze on her cheek, Wendy factored windage as she aimed at the deer, taking up the slack on the trigger until the weapon leaped in her hands.

The sudden boom startled the herd, but the cattle merely peered all around, looking for the cause of the racket before returning to sleep or nibbling at the scant grass of the high plains. An hour later, she returned to the cabin, laden with the fresh meat packed in the deerskin.

"I only heard one shot," Kurt remarked appreciatively as he handed her a steaming cup of coffee. She dropped the load from her shoulder and accepted the hot mug. A low fire burned brightly a short distance from the cabin, and Wendy pointed at the blaze with her cup.

"Branding fire," Kurt explained as he began cutting the venison into manageable pieces. "Miguel will like the fresh meat. He can eat enough deer for two men," he added with a chuckle.

Wendy washed her hands in the wash basin Kurt had set beside the door, and she watched him over her shoulder as he cut the meat. His clear profile was outlined by the rising sun and his brown hair shone. She thought again of the bath she'd refused last night. A rank, dirty smell lifted to her nose when her coat gapped, and she knew she was way overdue.

"I'll rope a cow and drag it over to you. You be by the fire, branding iron in the coals. When I throw the cow, you hold the beast with one boot while you brand the flank with the iron."

Wendy nodded as she finished her breakfast. Tossing her dirty dishes beside the wash basin, she followed Kurt to the horses and saddled Shannon.

"You won't need to ride at first," Kurt went on as he mounted his gelding. "Just keep Shannon tethered nearby. You'll do your work on foot today."

"When will Miguel return?"

Kurt tugged on his hat brim. "Maybe today, probably tomorrow. We'll get a jump on the branding before he helps us finish. Then we'll push the Triple Seven cattle to the Peterson Ranch. I want to deliver them personally."

A gleam came to his eye at mention of the Peterson Ranch, and Wendy knew he thought of Marigold Peterson. She clenched her teeth, disgusted at his preoccupation, then she shook her head. The matter with Marigold was none of her concern. Wendy needed a guide, nothing more. Kurt Jordan could love whomever he wanted.

Yet Miguel's disdain for the young ranch princess came to her, and Wendy knew she wasn't wrong in disliking the snobby, rude girl.

Kurt rode out to the herd and spent a few minutes riding among the cattle as Wendy stood beside the little fire in the yard. She studied the metal running iron as the tool lay thrust into the coals, the design the blacksmith in Trinidad had shaped with his hammer. The angled arm and the crude J designated the Slash J, Kurt's recognized brand.

"Remember," Kurt called as he shook out a loop and twirled the rope over his head. "I'll drag a cow to you, and you'll have to be quick and strong. You're a little thin, Moylan, not much meat in your shoulders, but your weight will have to do to hold the cow while you press the iron to the flank."

Wendy lifted her chin, anger rising. "Didn't I shoot the deer? Don't I ride Shannon?" Her accolades made him grin, and Kurt chuckled.

"You're a wiry, tough lad. No one doubts your mettle. But I need you to hold the squirming beast while you burn the brand. This is no time to be a milksop."

A fiery retort bubbled on her lips, but Kurt's whistling rope stilled her comment as the cowboy dragged the captured animal toward the branding fire. His horse held the bawling cow with a taut rope as Kurt leaped from the saddle and raced forward, grappling the cow to the ground in a wrestler's move that startled Wendy.

"Hurry, Wen," Kurt shouted as he held the cow's head to the ground while the beast's legs thrashed in the air.

Wendy caught up the red-hot iron and ran to the cow. Placing her boot on the heaving stomach, she pressed the glowing branding iron against the cow's flank.

With a lunge, the animal kicked and howled. "Hurry up, Moylan, I can't hold her forever," Kurt yelled, and Wendy pressed her boot against the cow again and pushed the searing hot metal against the cow.

Smoke rose from the flank, the foul acrid smell of burning hair wafting, and Wendy wanted to cough and pull away. Yet she held the branding iron in place until Kurt nodded and released the animal.

The cow sprang to her feet and trotted away, merging into the nearby herd. Wendy wrinkled her nose, but Kurt grinned. "That's one. I thought you were going to throw up. You should see the look on your face." He laughed as he coiled his rope and mounted his horse.

"I did it, didn't I?" Wendy growled, but Kurt only laughed harder.

"We'll make a cowboy of you yet, Wen."

For the rest of the morning, Kurt hauled cattle one at a time to Wendy's fire, piled them into a heap, and held them down while she branded the cattle before releasing them to join the herd once more. "This would go a lot faster if I had more riders," he said after Wendy threw an armload of firewood on the little fire. "I wish Miguel were here."

"Me too," Wendy said with obvious revulsion in her tone. The sickening smell of the burning hides made her stomach pitch with nausea, and she wanted to be through with the gruesome task. But they'd branded barely a dozen mavericks, and the day stretched endlessly before them. Another thirty head of stock remained to receive the Slash J brand before they were finished.

"Fetch coffee," Kurt ordered while he threw his loop around another cow. "I'll bet you're not hungry."

"I couldn't eat if I were starving," Wendy admitted as she retrieved two steaming mugs of coffee from the cabin. She handed one up to Kurt where he sat on his saddle. Together, silently, they sipped their drinks while the roped cow stood stiff legged, watching the two riders.

Kurt's gaze roamed the herd and the distant hills and then on to the high peaks of the Rockies. The cattle lowed and milled, restless now with dust circling from the wrestled cows. They eyed the riders suspiciously, and Wendy wondered if the beasts were as stupid as Kurt claimed.

"I love it here," Kurt said in a faraway voice. "The high mountains speak to me. I love the prairie and the rivers and the wooded hills. This land is mine, and I know the Lord called me here."

Wendy sipped her drink, eyes scanning the area above the rim of her mug. The land seemed so peaceful, as if the war in the east didn't exist. And the rolling hills and the rocks peeking through the prairie appealed to her, as if this unfamiliar land held something hidden for her. Something special? She wasn't sure.

She grinned into her mug, surprised at her thoughts. This land was certainly unfamiliar, but not special. She felt Kurt's admiration of his ranch had kindled a desire within herself, a desire for a new home or a safe place or a land she could call her own. This was Kurt's land, not hers, but she wondered if Little Rock still held a significant place in her heart. Surely the Moylan Plantation could never be as before, a refuge from her grief, an escape from her sorrow. Her parents were dead, and she had no siblings, no family except Aunt Lil. Even Mary and Jasmine were gone. Once again, a feeling of loneliness washed over her.

Although she missed her aunt, Wendy felt pleased she'd arranged to be gone from her for a while. Somehow, she wasn't ready to depart from the cowboys.

She said nothing to Kurt's declaration, and the cowboy squinted at her. "You really want to find your grandpa's treasure, don't you?"

Wendy felt her back stiffen. "I didn't say it was treasure."

Kurt shrugged. "You didn't have to. No one goes into Apache country unless they believe great wealth awaits them. Nine out of ten times, you'll die within a day. It's suicide to go there."

"You went there," Wendy challenged.

"I worked for the ranch. My job was to chase cows. I wouldn't go there on my own," he argued.

Wendy said nothing to this, thinking she needed to be preparing for her expedition south. Soon, she'd get paid from Kurt and have the money to outfit her journey into New Mexico Territory.

"What if you don't find what you're looking for?"

His unexpected question startled her, and Wendy peered up at him.

"I mean, will you go back to Arkansas? Isn't the war back there? I could sure use another rider on the Slash J, although you're a scrawny boy. But beggars can't be choosy."

She scowled at his stinging speech. She would certainly not be a cowboy for Kurt Jordan if she could do otherwise. She needed money for supplies and then she would venture into the Apache lands south of Raton Pass.

"I'm working for you until I can buy supplies. I need to go to the Mora River country." She wanted to scream or shout. Wendy knew she was wasting time working for Kurt, yet what else could she do?

"You'll get paid," he snapped as he straightened in his saddle. "Let's get back to work."

Whether the cattle were wise now to the mounted cowboy or the chill of the afternoon breeze from the mountains or a sense of foreboding of an impending storm, the herd would not cooperate, and Kurt found it almost impossible to move through the clustered bodies and cut a maverick from the others.

"You want to trade places?" Wendy's taunt only served to make Kurt angrier.

"You can't rope. Besides, you're not as good a rider as me. You could do no better," he retorted with a sneer.

He was right, she knew. She couldn't ride as well as Kurt, but the cattle avoided his swirling rope adeptly and she grinned, pleased to watch his frustration grow as the afternoon progressed.

Finally, as the sun leaned against the mountains to the west, Miguel rode into the meadow. "We'll get some work done now," Kurt said with an accusing tone Wendy didn't appreciate. Was he blaming her for not finishing the branding?

Miguel drew up near the little fire in the yard and slowly dismounted, his gaze taking in the bawling cattle, the disgusted look on Kurt's grimy face, and the metal branding iron resting in the coals. A small stack of kindling and firewood stood ready beside the small blaze and Wendy knelt beside the flickering flames, warming her hands. The cold day had chilled her to the bone, making her reluctant to step far from the fire. And Kurt's constant nagging about the unfinished job had irritated her until she wanted to quit and return to the relative comfort of the cabin.

She tugged her hat low, refusing to give in to the stubborn cowboy. She could stand the interminable day if he could. She vowed to stick it out, ready to slap a brand on any maverick he dragged to the fire.

Kurt spurred his horse and cantered from the herd, coming to join Wendy and Miguel near the fire. "It's about time," he shouted at his friend. He climbed stiff legged from his saddle and reached for the coffeepot resting on the coals.

Miguel patted his pocket and said something in Spanish.

"Good," Kurt nodded as he knelt beside the blaze and sipped his coffee. Wendy noticed he didn't offer her or Miguel any. "I'll need the cash to pay this fool." He gestured at Wendy with his mug, a deep scowl creasing his dirty face.

"Wait a minute," Wendy interjected. "I've worked hard all day. No one can say I didn't do my share."

Kurt ignored her and eyed Miguel. "You paid Mr. Hanson? Good. We'll need your help to finish branding tomorrow and then I want to push the Triple Seven cattle to the Peterson Ranch."

Miguel mumbled and Kurt lifted his head. "Hey, don't talk that way about my girl. She's not mean."

The Indian hurriedly retorted, and Kurt leaped to his feet, throwing his coffee mug to the ground as he glared at his friend. "You take that back, Miguel, or I'll clobber you like you deserve."

Miguel frowned and shook his head as he crouched, inviting an attack. Wendy stepped back, sensing an altercation. But when Kurt rushed the Indian, she whooped, hoping to see Kurt thumped down. Suddenly, she felt angry at the young cowboy, angry at his slights against her and Miguel. And strangely angry at his interest in Marigold Peterson.

When the weary rider was knocked to the ground by Miguel's almost casual reprisal, Kurt scrambled to his feet, snarling as he lunged again at the grinning Indian.

Dirt and gravel scattered as the two cowboys fought. Wendy whooped again when Kurt fell in the dust, and she laughed when he lifted his dirt smudged face, eyes glaring at his antagonist. Miguel chuckled and shifted his feet, challenging Kurt to come at him again.

Kurt rushed, only to be tripped by the quick Indian. But when Wendy howled with delight, Kurt lifted himself from the dirt and glowered at her. "You think this is funny, huh, Moylan? I don't fight children, but maybe a good spanking will teach you some manners."

She gasped when she saw the serious glint in his eyes, and she backed from the fire. "Kurt, I only laughed because you looked so silly in the dirt. I wasn't really laughing at how Miguel gave you a beating, even though you deserve it."

Miguel snorted and Kurt clenched his teeth as Wendy turned to run. But Kurt gave chase and swiftly caught her by her coat and dragged her back to the fire.

Kicking and squealing, Wendy bucked in his arms as Kurt hugged her tightly until he dropped her on the ground and reached for a stick from the kindling pile. He scowled down at her through narrowed eyes. "A youngster like you should have respect for your elders. I think I need to teach you a lesson."

She could read the malicious intent in his taut features, but he moved so quickly, catching her by the boot as she tried to scramble away. He rolled the thrashing Wendy over and brought the stick down on her backside.

Wendy howled, tears springing to her eyes as Kurt railed with the stick. The suddenness of the assault hurt her more than the actual spanking, but Wendy felt embarrassed at Kurt's handling of her, and she protested loudly.

"You don't think it's so funny now, do you?" he panted as he brought the stick down again and again on her bottom. Hot tears of indignation rolled down her cheeks as her hat spilled from her and her tightly coiled braids tumbled free.

CHAPTER TWENTY-THREE

Kurt fell back as if he'd touched a hot stove. He stared at Wendy and then glanced at Miguel before gazing at her once more. "You're ... you're a girl."

Wendy scrambled to her feet and snatched her hat. "Of course, I'm a girl," she rasped defiantly. She pulled her hat down low and glowered at the two cowboys. "It sure wasn't hard to fool you two."

"To fool us?" Kurt bellowed and glanced again at Miguel. "Why would you want to fool us?"

"I needed the job. I need money for supplies to go to the Mora River. There's little work available here."

"I would never hire a girl," Kurt said with a ring of finality.

"You hired me," Wendy countered, trying to grin victoriously at him as she wiped the tears from her cheeks. She succeeded only in smearing the dirt on her face and Kurt handed her his scarf.

She snatched the rag from him and wiped her face. "I still need the work. I need supplies."

"I can't have a girl working for me," Kurt protested.

Wendy dropped her hands to her waist and squinted. "Didn't I do the work? Didn't I shoot and dress the deer and ride all day and brand your cattle?"

The two cowboys exchanged sheepish looks. "Yes, you did," Kurt admitted. "But girls shouldn't be doing men's work."

"Is there an alternative? You need help and I need the money. With Miguel back from town, we can finish the branding tomorrow and drive the Triple Seven cattle to the Peterson Ranch. It looks like your plan is still working out, despite me being a girl, so why don't you shut up and leave me alone."

The setting sun hesitated above the western mountains as Wendy stomped into the cabin. Shadows filled the dark room, but she rummaged through her pack and retrieved her towel and clean shirt. Grabbing a candle from the mantel, she retraced her steps to the silent cowboys where they stood beside the dying fire in the meadow.

"Where's this hot spring you mentioned?"

Kurt pointed to the dim trail beside the cabin, leading down the slope and toward the river. "Follow the trail for a hundred yards."

She bent to light her candle from the glowing embers, and without another word, marched into the gathering dusk.

Her whirling thoughts darted too swiftly across her mind to bring into order, so she concentrated on following the narrow trail around rocks and through gullies until she finally came to the bank of the roaring river. She paused and studied the white capped waters as they scuttled around submerged obstacles and leaped into the air, crashing once more to the flowing waves as the river rushed to join the Arkansas River farther to the north.

She could barely hear the moan of the twilight breeze moving through the pines and long shadows covered everything with a dull mantle. Peacefulness surrounded her, yet her emotions, like the turbulent river, jumbled and tossed within. What was she doing here? Why had she come west? What purpose was there in helping Kurt Jordan work cattle and build his fledgling ranch?

She drew a deep breath and turned away from the rolling river, walking slower now as she made her way along the rock-strewn bank to a clearing beneath a tall, dead pine tree. The pungent odor of minerals filled her nostrils, and Wendy knew she'd found the hot spring.

Water bubbled from the underground spring where large rocks had been removed and pushed to the edge. The final light of the fading day gleamed dully in the rippling water where a thin, welcoming wisp of steam beckoned, inviting a respite from the cold Wendy had endured for more than a week. Placing the flickering candle on a flat stone, she cast a worried glance back up the trail before undressing and plunging into the shallow pool.

Her teeth chattered from the freezing air, but soon the warm water comforted her, allowing her to relax and think clearly once again.

She'd laughed when Kurt championed Marigold Peterson, laughing harder when Miguel mirrored her own estimation of the ranch princess. She'd cheered when Miguel knocked Kurt to the ground, hoping the Indian would knock some sense into the stubborn cowboy. Kurt Jordan seemed too confident, too sure of himself. He'd chosen Marigold Peterson to be his wife with an assurance that nettled Wendy. Why couldn't she discover her purpose and direction with such sureness? What was Jesus doing with her?

She shrugged a bare shoulder, reminding herself that Kurt Jordan's choices were none of her concern. Yet she couldn't help but bristle when she remembered the rude behavior of Marigold at the livery in town. Still, it was none of her business. She'd be gone from Trinidad soon enough, never to return.

Wendy reclined against a large boulder, leaning her head back as she stretched her legs in front of her, enjoying the buoyancy of her body floating in the warm water. She felt filthy. Her fingers fumbled with the tight coils around her head, allowing her dirty hair to tumble down her back, greasy and smelling unwashed.

Ducking her head beneath the water, Wendy dragged her fingers through her tangled hair and then scrubbed her body with handfuls of sand she lifted from the bottom of the pool as her thoughts continued to search for answers.

But why had she laughed at Kurt? At least he was fulfilling his dreams. He was building something for the future, his future, something he felt the Lord had led him to. What had God led her to?

With a frown creasing her wet features, she glanced at the little candle and the sputtering fire as the flickering flame whispered in the faint wind. "Are you with me, Lord? Do you care what happens to me? Did you guide me here, or did I simply flee to the west to search for gold that probably doesn't exist? Am I putting off the inevitable by filling my days with hard work and hoping something will suddenly appear, suddenly lead me where I'm supposed to go?"

Only the faint groan of the deepening twilight answered her desperate questions. Tree branches rubbed softly above her while the evening wind played among the towering pines. A pinecone thudded to the ground. The gurgling of the nearby river reminded her she was not at home in Little Rock. No, she was far from home, all the way to the Rocky Mountains, where the endless prairie joins the foothills of the imposing mountains. What had brought her here?

She sighed when she recalled the leather books in her pack and Aunt Lil back in Trinidad, the faithful woman trying to locate a guide to lead Wendy to the Mora River country south of the Colorado Territory. How could she overlook her all-important quest?

Working with Kurt and Miguel had made her temporarily forget her more pressing need to locate wealth that might help alleviate her impending problems. Yes, that was it. Her land back in Arkansas, Randall Whitmore's scandalous proposal, the heritage of the Moylan estate. These concerns came flooding over her once again, reminding her that her problems could not be forgotten for long. She needed the money she earned from working with Kurt to purchase supplies for her expedition south. With or without a guide, she must venture into Apache lands to search for the hidden gold. Perhaps Kurt would help her construct a more accurate map of the region if he wouldn't go with her.

The thought of Kurt Jordan made her remember she didn't have time to waste. Hopefully, the young cowboy would allow her to help finish the branding and drive the small group of cattle to the Peterson Ranch. Then Wendy could return to Trinidad where Aunt Lil might've located a guide. With luck, her quest had only been postponed, and soon she'd be riding into the New Mexico plains.

Reluctantly, she rose from the warm pool, water dripping from her as she stepped onto large stones and retrieved her clothes. Only the blouse was clean, yet she quickly dressed before she shivered from the cold.

She wrung her long hair and squeezed water from the ends. Shoving her feet into her boots, she stood and shrugged into her coat. The cool wind teased her wet hair, but she ignored the chilling effect and lifted the candle, lighting her path back to the cabin.

Kurt looked up when she entered the snugly built house. Miguel lay huddled near the fire, asleep with his back to the dancing flames. But Kurt sat propped against the wall, eyes glowing in the dim light, an empty mug gripped in one hand.

Wendy mumbled a greeting as she stowed her gear in her pack and retrieved the leather-bound journal. She straightened and faced him.

"Am I still working for you?"

He nodded, a resigned look on his unshaven face. "I need the help."

A smile tugged at the corner of her lips. "I need you, and you need me," she said softly.

He blinked but said nothing. Crossing to his side, she handed the book to him, open to the carefully drawn map of the Mora River joining the larger Canadian River.

"What's this?" He squinted as she took his mug from him and strode to the fireplace.

"It's the map I was given. Do you know the place? Can you add any details?"

She filled her mug and Kurt's cup before tossing more fuel on the blaze. A glance revealed Miguel slept soundly, no doubt exhausted from pushing the small herd of cattle to town alone and then buying supplies before hurrying back to Kurt's ranch.

She held his cup and sipped her own while he studied the drawing by the bright firelight. He reached for his cup and took a sip before he spoke. "Yes, I know the place. Usually, the Apache don't like to range that far to the east, too close to the Santa Fe Trail. They usually stay west of the Rio Grande. But sometimes they venture into that region, hoping to find unsuspecting wagons or stranded pioneers."

Wendy leaned against the door frame. Her wet hair hung down her back and she shivered, lifting the warming drink to her mouth. "So, there might not be any Apache when I go there. Perhaps I can slip in and out before they suspect I'm even on their land."

Kurt arched an eyebrow. "I don't think you can do anything that the Apache will not know about. They're the fiercest warriors and almighty canny when it comes to desert fighting. Only the large numbers of wagons in a caravan ensure the safety of folks traveling near the Indian lands—sometimes even that doesn't protect them from Apache raids."

He paused and lifted his gaze from the journal to peer at her where she stood near the door. "Who are you? Is your name really Wen Moylan?"

She bit her lip, unwilling to divulge such information. She hated she was so needy. She and Aunt Lil had nothing, and the Moylan Plantation was as good as worthless. With the war ending, no one would be willing to purchase the valueless farm, and she owed Mr. Whitmore so much money. But although deceived, Kurt had been kind to her. He'd been rough too, allowing her to ride a half-broken mare like Shannon and having her work like a dog all day in the dust and cold, yet he'd been fair.

She frowned when she considered the past week, and then, she smiled,—grateful she'd had a break from her troubles. "Wendy Moylan. I'm from Little Rock, like I said, and I do need the money. I'm hoping I can still find the treasure my grandfather told me about in that little book."

She gestured at the journal he held, using her coffee cup as a pointer. "That book is all I have that will help me locate the treasure. But you've been there, Kurt, and you could help me."

The pleading in her voice rang in her ears, and she tensed. Would this stranger have any sympathy on her?

He shook his head as he handed the journal back to her. "Forget it. It's too dangerous, and I wouldn't go with you for all of the tea in China. Besides, I've got my hands full here."

He glanced around the room and her gaze followed, studying the rustic cabin with open windows and the dark doorway that led into the other room she hadn't yet explored. At her back, the doorway held not a plank door, nothing to keep out the cold or weather, but the structure was well built, strong and solid against the elements. The stone fireplace held a cheerful blaze that crackled and glowed. With some effort, glass windows could be installed, and a strong door fitted to the frame. Perhaps a plank or flagstone floor could be laid. She'd seen many flat stones around the countryside. There was a good stream near at hand and the river only a short distance farther. The pleasant hot spring was delightful, and Wendy knew anyone would appreciate such comforts on the homestead. Although he owned only forty-two head of stock, Wendy knew Kurt could build this place into a working, producing ranch.

For a brief instant, she hoped Marigold Peterson would appreciate all of this man's hard work, but she doubted the range princess would.

As she studied the cabin's interior, her gaze fell upon the roughhewn mantel, a thick length of oak fitted over the stone fireplace. On the beam's smooth face, three crosses had been carved.

"Why three crosses in the mantel?"

At her question, Kurt glanced to the fireplace and then looked up at her as a smile teased around his mouth. "Well, that's kind of embarrassing. It's really just a reminder to me."

"A reminder? Of God?"

He nodded and took another sip of coffee. "Kind of. When I ran away from the orphanage, I trusted no one. I had no friends and surely didn't think of God. I stowed away on a wagon train bound for the western lands. Miguel found me when I was starving, digging for scraps in a trash heap in Santa Fe. He fed me and told me about Jesus, but I only laughed at him and scoffed at his stories. Then, as time passed and we became friends, I listened and slowly turned my heart to the Lord. Now I live by the Spirit, hoping to walk everyday with Christ, giving him my heart and my dreams. But I'm a hardheaded cuss, like the boy who ran away from that orphanage so many years ago."

"And the three crosses?" Wendy liked his story but wondered at the wood carving in the mantel.

"It reminds me of Christ on Mount Calvary with the thieves on either side of him. They both scoffed at first, then one repented and turned to Jesus. That's me, a scoffer, impulsive and quick to do something stupid. Then I think and want to do what God wants me to do. When Jesus died on that hilltop outside of Jerusalem, he died for me and all the scoffers in the world, but we have to turn to him and repent, put aside our fears and stubborn ideas. Jesus forgives me, even though Miguel says I'm often too quick. He says I try God's patience, that I'm impulsive and throw my heart into a project without taking the time to pray for guidance."

"Is that what this is?" Wendy indicated the cabin and glanced at the sleeping Indian as she pondered Kurt's words.

He chuckled softly. "No, no. This is right from the Lord. I feel it. He saved me from the Apache and guided me here, to a ranch of my own, a home, a family. Marigold Peterson is an answer to my prayers."

She tucked the leather book under her arm. "But Miguel doesn't agree."

Wendy's statement brought a hard look to Kurt's face. He drew a deep breath. "Miguel says I'm not allowing the Lord to work, that I'm moving too quickly like I always do. But I've grown so much since I've become a Christian. I've prayed unceasingly about settling down, finding a Christian wife, raising a family with God's guidance. I know God led me here, to Trinidad, and Miss Marigold is the only available girl in hundreds of miles."

He grinned abruptly and Wendy saw a faraway gleam in his eye. "She's beautiful. Her pa is the owner of the biggest ranch in the region. I'm getting quite a catch."

Wendy shifted. "And she's madly in love with you?"

His grin fled as he stared into the flickering flames, and Wendy guessed he tried to ignore her jab. "Well, love comes in time for some people. She's wanting to get married and isn't afraid to let all the men know her intentions. I have some competition, but I'm not afraid. The Lord led me here. I'm sure she'll be my wife."

Wendy tilted her head. "You mean she isn't promised to just you? She's keeping her options open?" She was trying to be funny, for the idea of allowing every man in the area to court a woman upset Wendy's Southern sense of decorum. Was the young lady so bold as to invite several suitors at once? Certainly, the war had done much to destroy manners and proper behavior—surely the destruction left in the wake of the Union Army could not be denied—but to encourage numerous men at the same time flabbergasted her sense of propriety.

Kurt licked his lips and frowned. "I don't feel comfortable discussing this with you, Wendy Moylan."

"Because I'm a girl?" Wendy grinned. "You didn't have any difficulty discussing this with me all week. In fact, you've assaulted me with talk of Marigold Peterson. I'd think you feel even more comfortable talking to me about this, now that you know I'm a woman like Miss Marigold and would know the way she must feel and think. Surely you want my insight into the situation. I know how wily a courting woman can be."

She chuckled with a taunting note, but Kurt only stared into the fire, ignoring her challenge, and she moved to her bedroll. As she stretched out in her blankets, she glanced a final time at Kurt, where he still reclined against the wall. The thought of this simple, yet thoughtful, cowboy with the likes of Marigold Peterson annoyed her somehow, and she reminded herself it was none of her concern. She had major issues to contemplate, and they certainly did not include the intentions of this lovesick fool and the way he believed God was leading him.

She stared up at the dark rafters. "Good luck, Kurt," she said aloud before yawning. "I heartily believe the two of you might actually deserve one another."

CHAPTER TWENTY-FOUR

The next day, despite the cold weather and the slate gray sky, the branding continued and went smoothly.

Kurt kept one doubtful eye on Wendy as she pressed the hot branding iron on each maverick, but she did her job without having to be told. With the aid of the additional rider, the number of unbranded stock dwindled as the day progressed.

Wendy caught both cowboys peering at her throughout the task, as if unsure she was the same rider they'd teased and yelled at when they were gathering lost stock beside the river. Wendy shook her long ponytail and grinned each time she caught their perusal, letting them know she was indeed the same rider who'd shared lonely campfires with them and the grueling work of rounding up loose cattle in the dead of winter.

As the cowboys circled the herd, ropes swirling above their heads, she tossed more wood on the fire and nudged the battered coffeepot deeper into the coals. A bitter wind blustered from the nearby mountains, and Wendy removed her slouch hat and drew her coat sleeve across her face. She glanced at the branding iron where the metal tool lay in the fire, making sure the end glowed red.

The cattle bawled loudly as the cowboys nudged their mounts forward, the cutting horses slicing into the herd. With shouts, the two riders targeted a cow and their ropes sailed through the air, dropping effortlessly around the specific horns.

They dragged the thrashing animal to the fire, wrestled the beast to the ground, and held their ropes taut as Wendy burned the Slash J on the animal's flank. Kicking and wailing, the cow struggled to its feet and trotted back to the herd as the cowboys coiled their ropes.

"Any coffee left?" Kurt squinted at her as if expecting a challenge. But Wendy lifted the blackened pot and filled two mugs.

"Fresh pot," Wendy said as she handed the steaming mugs to the riders.

As they drank their coffee, Kurt eyed the milling herd. "Only a few head left unbranded. We'll finish this job and maybe have time to work on the stable a bit before dark. We'll have to wait for sunup to drive to Peterson's."

He gestured to the end of the wide plain where the half-finished stone barn squatted at the side of the cabin. Miguel grunted, but Wendy said nothing. Her thoughts had shifted to the remaining work. After the delivery of the Triple Seven cattle to the Peterson Ranch tomorrow, her job with Kurt and Miguel would be over, and she would have to consider her next move. She hoped Aunt Lil had located a guide, but with or without a guide, she must prepare for the journey south through Raton Pass and into the Apache lands to the west of the Old Trail.

That evening, after the branding was completed, Wendy prepared dinner with the supplies Miguel had purchased while the cowboys worked on the stone barn. The open cabin filled with the smell of beans and bacon simmering in a skillet. Her mouth watered at the aroma of fresh coffee and sourdough biscuits.

Wendy glanced at the three crosses carved into the mantel and wondered about Kurt Jordan. He said he was like the thief who recognized Christ after wasting time. Was she wasting time? Hadn't the Lord brought her west to find her treasure?

The sound of thumping boots made her come back to her surroundings, and she filled two mugs with coffee as the cowboys trooped inside. She scooped beans and bacon onto plates and handed each man a biscuit. They ate quietly, in the manner of tired men who worked hard all day, leaning against the walls or squatting near the fire.

"Miguel says he'll cut the deerskin into squares and tack them into the windows, help keep out the cold. They weren't tanned properly, so they won't last long, but surely into springtime." Kurt dropped his empty plate beside the fireplace and filled his mug again.

Wendy turned to Miguel. "And the door? What can we do?"

The Indian explained in Spanish and Kurt rose to take his place against the wall once more. The sun had set behind the western mountains and his face shone ruddy in the shadowed firelight. He nodded at Miguel's reply.

"He says he'll work on that while we deliver the cattle to Peterson's."

"You're not going with us?" She felt her brow furrow as she looked at the stoic Indian. Miguel shook his head and grinned before he replied.

Kurt shifted and sighed loudly. "He says he doesn't want to see Miss Marigold. Says his efforts are better served around the ranch. And I agree," Kurt concluded with a snort.

Wendy shrugged, still eyeing the smiling Indian. "We could use your help with the cattle. You'll be missed."

A gleam darted across his dark eyes, and Wendy suspected he appreciated her remark. Yet even she was surprised when he said something with a note of command that made Kurt scowl. Wendy turned inquisitively to the young cowboy, waiting an explanation.

"He says we should go with you to the Mora River country," he said softly, his eyes boring into his friend. The two men had quarreled and fought only yesterday, but the matter had passed quickly and their long-lasting friendship healed any rift between the two riders. Yet Kurt stared at the Indian with a piercing gaze that revealed his astonishment at Miguel's assertion.

A sense of wonder and elation welled within Wendy, and she smiled at Miguel. "You know much of that area too, don't you?"

Miguel nodded, but Kurt stepped forward shaking his head. "Oh, no, you don't. I'm building a ranch and need your help. Miss Marigold and I are to be married. You don't have any time to parade this girl in Apache country. And I don't want to hear any more about honor or what God would have you do. I'm your friend and I need you here."

Miguel's jaw tensed as a dark look came into his features. He retrieved the dirty dishes from the hearth and went outside.

"Well, thanks a lot," Kurt grumbled under his breath as the Indian disappeared into the darkness.

"What'd I do?" Wendy faced him, an anger she didn't understand replacing her earlier joy. She'd been pleased when Miguel offered to go south with her, but Kurt's plans demanded immediate results and the young cowboy would entertain no opposition to his desires.

"Miguel and I are busy building this place," he said, gesturing around the cabin and the surrounding region. "I've homesteaded a good piece of land and there's nothing holding me back from a prosperous future except you and your wild ideas of hidden treasure. It's probably not even real."

Wendy frowned, irritated at the selfish cowboy. "You're being silly. I'm not the one chasing a fool's errand. You've gotten the notion you can convince an undecided girl to marry you. She's not even in love with you. Don't blame your failure on me. Miguel was only being kind."

"He is kind," Kurt agreed, "but his loyalty is misplaced. He's with me, not a slip of a girl who appears out of nowhere and demands he risk his life to travel unnecessarily in Apache lands. You're going to get yourself killed, which is none of my business, but you'd get him killed too, and that is my concern."

Wendy pursed her lips into a thin line, suddenly alert to the danger her expedition south posed for her and anyone who accompanied her. She might lose her life—her need to acquire fast money was too great not to risk—but she would not, could not risk someone else.

She drew a deep breath. "I'm sorry, Kurt. I wasn't thinking."

"You were thinking. Thinking of yourself."

Anger flared anew and she felt her eyes widen. "How dare you accuse me of not thinking of others? Miguel has told you to be patient and wait for guidance, but you dive in with both boots, hoping the Lord will follow you into whatever mess you create. I think you're being more selfish than I am."

With a whirl, she raced for the door, escaping his hateful presence and stalking into the gloom. Behind her, she heard Miguel's return and the heated words exchanged between the two friends, but she was soon out of hearing and marching into the deeper gloom of the wide meadow.

Bellowing cattle guided her around the herd, and Wendy slowed, finding her way toward the hillside where she'd shot the deer. Panting, she climbed to the summit and looked down on the little ranch, a dim glow indicating where the distant cabin stood at the edge of the rocky plain, a column of dark blue smoke lifting lazily from the chimney. A coyote howled and she shivered, but she felt too angry to be cold. Upset and irritated, she stood with her arms across her chest, staring out over the low hills and the prairie beyond as the moon rose above the high mountains.

"Oh, Lord, what have you gotten me into?"

CHAPTER TWENTY-FIVE

Her saddle creaked loudly in the cold morning as Wendy mounted Shannon. She kicked the mare into a run across the meadow before the little devil could perform her tricks and attempt to unseat Wendy.

She circled the herd and peered all around, appreciating the dim gray hovering on the eastern horizon and the twin puffs of steam that emitted from her and the wily mare. But she thrilled at the sensations that filled her. The small ranch was coming along nicely. The stone barn would be finished soon, and Wendy already imagined her next visit to the hot spring for a comforting bath. The tiny herd of cattle pointed to a bright future, and she could only dream of such permanence and promise for herself.

Would she ever know the feeling of contentment that Kurt must possess? He had the promise of tomorrow, an obvious and clear foundation to the structure he kept busy building. But what about her? Randall Whitmore awaited her return to Little Rock so he could either receive his payment or her hand in marriage. Would she ever enjoy the security of a safe haven?

Her gaze roamed the wide plain as she rode, allowing the brisk action to thwart Shannon's daily routine. Wendy had learned to begin each morning with the regimen of a fast ride, and then the taciturn mare would settle down for industrial labor. She was an excellent cutting horse, and Wendy had learned a lot about herding cattle from the wise mount.

Slowly, the sky lightened, and a deep pale pink illuminated the still clouds overhead. Wendy loved this time, the time before a busy day crowded her ideas and dreams with the immediate demands of necessity. Right now, she could think clearly and put her plans into order.

First, she must receive her meager pay from Kurt. The cowboy promised to pay her when they reached town and squared debts with Hanson's store. Miguel had given the kindly shopkeeper all the money from the sale of the mixed breed cattle, and Mr. Hanson promised to hold the money until Kurt arrived in town.

Second, she would see if Aunt Lil had located a guide. Something told Wendy the possibility was small, but she resigned herself to purchase supplies and begin the journey south. Kurt was unable to add any helpful details to her map, although he had suggested she stop at Fort Union and see if a cavalry patrol was going near the vicinity of Mora River. The thought of asking Yankee soldiers for help made her wary, yet Mr. Whitmore's indecent proposal had taught her she must consider a new way of thinking. Surely God was the same yesterday, today, and tomorrow, but Southern culture and decorum had altered significantly since the war's beginning. No doubt the end of the war would result in even more dramatic results to her sense of propriety. Wendy vowed to gather her gumption and speak to the Yankees at Fort Union if the need arose.

Time was running out, and although much would be different back home, the plantation was her home, familiar and safe. Wendy decided she needed to move hastily now. The search for the hidden gold could take weeks, and she still needed to return to Little Rock before the end of April. She imagined the look on the old pirate's face when she handed the gold to

Mr. Whitmore and refused his request. She couldn't marry the scoundrel anyway.

A deep niggling fluttered within her whenever she lifted her head high and piously vowed she could never marry an unbeliever. But if the allotted time passed and she hadn't located the gold, what would she *really* do? Oh, Wendy hated her indecision, her flip flop of faith. She knew what was right, yet feared the outcome of such a solution. She and Aunt Lil had nowhere to go. They had no money. Where would two desperate women go when they had no choice?

She winced at the thought of marrying Randall Whitmore, and a profound terror settled in her belly, icy fingers clenching her vitals. She'd always wanted to marry for love, a man she desperately loved, not a man she married out of desperation.

She glanced again at Kurt's ranch and smiled. He was building for his wife. Foolish as he was over Marigold Peterson, the intent was sincere, and Wendy couldn't help but wish him well as he put his heart and soul into preparing a place for his family.

Would anyone ever perform such Herculean efforts for her? The lonely existence she pursued so fervently back in Arkansas had turned to ash in her mouth, revealing a longing to belong somewhere, to someone. Although she'd worked only a little over a week with Kurt and Miguel, she'd come to thoroughly enjoy the comradery of the range riders, enjoying their company and talking with them about building and cattle and hunting and horses. She'd never had casual friends, and the sensation delighted her. If she were to stay long term in the area, she would've enjoyed a growing friendship with the cowboys.

She sighed, knowing that wasn't possible, and she guided Shannon toward the cabin at the end of the meadow. Kurt packed gear behind his saddle as Miguel watched. When she neared, the young cowboy turned to her, his clean shaven face caught the rising sun, and his high cheekbones appeared in startling clarity. The strong jaw that had been concealed by days of dark growth now cut sharply in the morning light, and Wendy drew in her breath, suddenly surprised a handsome man stood where a hairy range rider had been. She looked away quickly as she drew rein before the staring cowboys.

"You've figured her out," Kurt greeted, indicating the blowing mare as Shannon rested in front of the cabin.

Wendy hoped Kurt didn't detect her unexpected assessment and patted the mare's neck. "She's a good horse."

They hadn't said anything to each other after the altercation of the previous evening. Silently, the three riders had eaten breakfast before Wendy saddled and rode Shannon around the perimeter of the large plain. Kurt's courteous words startled her. She had feared they would part under a cloudy sky. After delivering the Peterson cattle toward the distant ranch, Kurt would accompany her into Trinidad to pay her wages, and then, they'd likely never see one another again.

She lifted a gloved hand to Miguel. "Thanks for everything. I've enjoyed working with you."

The silent Indian only nodded, but Wendy thought she detected a gleam in his dark eyes.

"Come on," Kurt growled as he stepped into the saddle and swung his horse's head toward the herd. "Let's roundup those thirteen head and push them east. I can't stand to see the two of you cry."

Miguel grinned, and Wendy tried to smile. She waved again and followed Kurt. In less than an hour, they had the Triple Seven cattle separated from Kurt's stock and walking toward the Peterson Ranch.

Miguel watched their departure from where he stood beside the half completed stone barn, his eyes narrowed as Wendy trotted behind the group of cattle. She felt he studied her, pondering as she topped a rise and descended the other side, cutting her off from his view. She edged closer to Kurt. "Miguel thinks deep things. I feel he can understand more than he lets on."

Kurt snorted. "He's like a hound dog on a scent. He can sense things I can't even see. He surely knows me better than I know myself. Sometimes I feel he's an old mother hen, watching over her brood, and other times he's like a warrior, fighting hard to complete a task or accomplish something great."

He scanned the rocky ground and the trees and the faded grass before he spoke again. "I love this land. I know the Lord led me here. The Spirit helps guide me, but I feel the Lord speaks directly to Miguel. I hope to be like that one day."

He paused and glanced at the rising sun where the bright orange ball hovered over the distant, frozen plains. "He's like a brother to me, and I thank God every day that Miguel found me, took me in."

He paused again and then chuckled. "It's his fault I'm up here, chasing Marigold Peterson like a maverick in the thickets. He's the one who taught me to be intentional." He glanced sharply at Wendy. "A purpose, you called it. I agree. I crave purpose. I don't want to waste my life pursuing the wind."

With a whoop, he kicked his gelding and gave chase to a fleeing cow. "And today I'm going to see my lady love," he shouted over his shoulder as he rounded the stray and pushed the animal back into the little herd. It was then Wendy realized why Kurt had shaved. His smooth cheeks and dancing eyes gave proof to his motivation, and Wendy felt her shoulders hunch beneath her thick hunter's coat. He'd bathed and dusted his dirty clothes because he would see Marigold Peterson today.

With a kick, she nudged Shannon to the opposite side of the trotting cattle. So what? It was none of her business why Kurt took a bath. She'd certainly needed one the night she'd visited the hot spring. Sadness swept over her as she realized she'd never go to the perfect bathing pool or see Miguel or Kurt's blossoming ranch again.

She shook her head and sat straighter in the saddle. She must focus. The journey south would require all her strength, all her cleverness. She had her own problems to think about, and Kurt Jordan's love life was not one of them.

She felt her brow furrow under her slouch hat as she considered the spoiled daughter of one of the wealthiest ranchers in the region. Marigold Peterson was not good enough for Kurt Jordan—she knew that after only one encounter with the rich woman. He seemed so dedicated to the Lord and wanted only to serve God. Could the ill-mannered young woman Wendy met briefly at the livery in Trinidad make Kurt happy?

Wendy chuckled softly. Was she tired? Did the impending expedition into Apache lands make her nervous or anxious that she should worry so much about a cowboy she'd barely met? She laughed again, louder this time, letting her misguided concerns slip away. She needed a guide and supplies. Shannon was a good horse. Perhaps Kurt would sell her to Wendy. She would have to plan carefully before she attempted the journey south.

As if he could read her thoughts, the cowboy pulled his horse alongside Wendy, matching Shannon's gait. They rode silently for a moment and Wendy studied Kurt from the corner of her eye, appreciating the easy way he sat his saddle.

"I was thinking," he began, his gaze on the walking cattle. "Tell me your plans of travel, and I can give suggestions."

Wendy considered his idea, still annoyed he wasn't going with her and yet willing to help in some small measure. For the hundredth time, she wished he'd lead the expedition.

"I'm leaving here and going over Raton Pass. I'll drop into New Mexico, and well, uh, I expect to pass Fort Union ..." She trailed off, trying to remember the map in the leather journal her grandfather had penned decades ago.

Kurt huffed. "You'll go through Raton Pass and into New Mexico. At Fort Union, ask if any patrols are going your way. The fort is on the Cimarron River. Angle to the southwest and you'll strike the Canadian River. Follow the river south until you locate the Mora flowing into the Canadian from the west."

He paused while Wendy made mental notes, comparing his information with the drawing in the journal. "And the Mora River? How big is it? How will I know I'm where I should be?"

A long sigh escaped him, and he peered at her, a disgusted look in his eyes. "Why are you doing this? You have no idea what you're getting yourself into. The Apache don't joke around. This sounds like a suicide trip if you ask me."

Wendy thought about his comment for a moment, then shook her head. "I don't think so. I feel God has led me here, like he did you. I feel safe somehow, although the expedition does make me nervous. I think I'm supposed to do this."

Kurt didn't reply and she went on. "Aunt Lil dreamed of this journey from her youth, but she never followed the map. Now I feel I'm doing this for the both of us."

Again, when he didn't say anything, she decided to divulge more. After all, he wasn't a threat to her treasure hunting. "I need money, Kurt. A lot of money. The treasure is the only way I can save my home back in Little Rock."

He turned and stared at her. "I think you're a fool to go there, but I have my own troubles," he said in a flat tone, then shrugged. "Your funeral."

He kicked his horse and drifted to the other side of the herd. Wendy knew he was right, and she was risking her life but felt she'd already dealt with that possibility. She would serve God with her life, her love, her marriage, whomever that might be with one day. If she didn't find the hidden gold, she couldn't marry Randall Whitmore. Better to lose everything than to knowingly accept a sinful situation.

Yet she had Aunt Lil to consider, and Mr. Whitmore had promised to only visit the plantation sparingly. How much time remained before she had to return to Little Rock and pay Randall Whitmore? Would she pay with gold or with herself?

The disturbing thought made her gasp, the tempting solution choking in her throat. She couldn't marry Mr. Whitmore, no matter how badly Wendy needed security. He was not even a believer. Surely God would never have her disregard sound guidance found in Scripture. Wendy loved Jesus and trusted his ways were best. The Lord knew what would content Wendy's restless heart. She would lean into the Lord, pray for direction, and trust God had a plan for her.

She glanced up at the scattered clouds that drifted across the dull, blue sky. Cold wind buffeted her back, pushing her toward the prairies that stretched endlessly to the east. Behind her, the mountains towered, and Wendy felt their majesty, the handiwork of the Creator, and she peered over her shoulder at the high peaks, glistening with fresh snow. "Help me, Jesus. You know I need help. I want to trust you and your holy Word, but I'm so worried. What if there is no gold? What will Aunt Lil and I do?"

Nothing called to her, and she didn't see any sudden streaks of lightning or peals of thunder, yet a sense of not being alone came over her, and Wendy knew the Lord was with her.

"All right, I'll be patient," she whispered.

CHAPTER TWENTY-SIX

A half mile from the Peterson ranch house, the two riders left the small herd and cantered up the hill. A large house perched atop the ridge loomed in the late morning sunlight, and Wendy squinted at the observers watching their approach from the wide porch that ran the length of the sprawling house. She made out a tall, ruggedly built older man beside Miss Marigold and a younger man in range attire. She stayed close beside Kurt as they drew rein before the trio, gravel scattering as the two horses pranced.

"Howdy, Jordan," the older man remarked with a nod.

"Howdy, Mr. Peterson," Kurt said and then tipped his hat at Marigold. "Morning, Miss Marigold." He barely turned his head to glance at the third member on the porch. "Howdy, Webb."

Wendy remembered Kurt's comment that Webb Larson, foreman on the Triple Seven, shared an interest in Miss Marigold. She studied the powerfully built rider, admitting a rough strength clung to the ranch foreman. He seemed to be a man with authority who exuded confidence. Wendy shifted her gaze to Miss Peterson, her ire rising when she saw the pinched looks of the finely dressed girl. Wendy frowned and tightened her grip on her reins.

"What you doing over this way?" Larson's gruff question didn't allow further pleasantries.

Kurt gestured to the cluster of cattle out on the plains. "We delivered some Triple Seven cattle we rounded up when we were beating the brush for mavericks, hiding in the brush along the Purgatory."

Mr. Peterson snorted. "Way over there? No telling how far my cattle have strayed." He turned to his foreman. "Larson, take the boys over to flush the brakes of the river, find any of my stock, and drive them this way. I don't want my cattle drifting that far away from my land."

Larson's jaw tensed, and Wendy could see he did not appreciate the rebuke Kurt's unexpected arrival had provoked.

"I'll get right on it, Mr. Peterson," Larson growled, not taking his eyes from Kurt.

"Well, do it now," Peterson said shortly and turned to his daughter. "Marigold, are you going to invite your guest to stay for lunch?"

Marigold ignored her father and stared at Wendy. "Who are you?"

Kurt cleared his throat before Wendy could reply. "This is Wendy Moylan. She's, uh, passing through. I hired her to help me round up and brand loose stock, but now she's done and is moving on."

"You hired her? A girl?" Marigold's tone simmered with suspicion.

Kurt shrugged. "I couldn't find any other riders. She did a good job."

Wendy sat up in her saddle, grateful for Kurt's praise under Marigold's sharp scrutiny, but Mr. Peterson grunted abruptly.

"There are no riders to be found on this range. Or women. What with that infernal war back east and the Indians out here along with the tough land and harsh weather, it's no wonder we can't find riders."

Wendy wanted to grin at the older man's assessment. Surely the War Between the States had kept a lot of men busy these past years, but she wondered what the rancher would say if she told him she was only in the west long enough to locate hidden gold and then planned on returning east once more. The scarcity of women and riders on the range didn't concern her, and she knew she must concentrate on preparations for her upcoming journey.

"Well, since you're a rider, you can eat with the cowboys." Marigold pointed to a low building near the barn and turned to Kurt, a sudden smile spreading across her smooth face. "And Kurt, we'd be honored to have you dine with father and me."

Webb Larson grumbled as he stalked from the porch, but Marigold clung to Kurt's arm and smiled up at him as they walked into the house. Wendy dismounted, and leading Shannon, followed Larson to the bunkhouse.

"I'd like to punch your boss in the nose," he muttered as he pushed the door open, a wave of heat drifting from the long room. "Boys, eat some grub and saddle up. We're heading for the Purgatory to find strays."

His call made three men seated at the table look up from a card game. "Boss," an old man with thick gray beard eyed Larson. "It's cold out there. Too cold to go riding to the river."

"If Kurt Jordan can round up stock in this weather, we can too." Larson paused and moved aside, revealing Wendy where she stood behind the ranch foreman. The three cowboys gaped.

"Why, it's a girl," the old man said in an astonished tone.

"She's wearing britches," a young boy of about fifteen squeaked. The third boy of maybe thirteen or so said nothing, his gaze glued to Wendy where she shifted uneasily.

"Hello," she ventured softly.

"Eat up," Larson growled. The range riders ate in silence, stealing not so covert glances at Wendy where she sat alone at the end of the long table. Finally, the meal finished, they shrugged into coats and shuffled from the warm bunkhouse, heading for the barn. A gust of icy wind blew in the open door, reminding Wendy how cold the weather truly was outside.

Larson hesitated at the door and peered at Wendy. "Kurt Jordan doesn't have a chance with Miss Marigold. I'm taking her to the dance Saturday night."

Wendy shrugged. "I'm just passing through," she said in a meek voice. She had no intention of getting between the two lovesick fools. Wendy didn't care which of them netted the haughty ranch girl.

Larson scowled at her and slammed the door behind him. Soon, she caught sight of the quartet of riders heading away from the barn, heads bowed to the frigid wind. Wendy loitered at the window, watching for Kurt. When the cowboy finally appeared on the porch, Wendy hurried to join him.

"Tell your pa thanks again," Kurt said as he stood before Marigold, his hat twirling in his hands. Wendy hunched her shoulders against the cold as she stood nearby, trying hard to be inconspicuous as Kurt shifted and glanced at Wendy before he turned back to Marigold. "You know there's the dance at the sawmill this Saturday night."

Marigold tilted her head as her smile widened. "Well, yes, Mr. Jordan. I do recall hearing something about that dance," she said in a coy tone that sickened Wendy. Hadn't Webb Larson already confessed he was taking the little flirt? Wendy ground her teeth.

"Well, uh, I was thinking that maybe you would go with me, if you don't have other plans," he stammered, and Wendy rolled her eyes. What a pathetic sounding invitation.

"I would love to dance with you this Saturday night. Unfortunately, pa insists he drive me to town, so I'll have to meet you there."

Kurt nodded eagerly. "That's all right with me. I can't wait to see you there, and ..." he hesitated, glancing sharply at Wendy where she stood holding Shannon's reins, "I'm thinking I'll be needing to talk to your pa real soon, about ... about ... you know, about—"

"About my future," Marigold finished, her eyes shining brightly.

"About *our* future," Kurt agreed with a grin. He straightened his shoulders. "I'm glad we have an understanding. Well, I need to be getting on. I'll see you Saturday."

Marigold mumbled her farewell as Kurt strode off the porch, boots thumping down the stairs. Wendy couldn't help but notice the radiant glow on his clean-shaven cheeks as he passed her on his way to the barn where his gelding had been tethered out of the wind.

Wendy patted Shannon's neck and spoke softly to the horse, trying to ignore the other girl's presence.

"I have more suitors than you can shake a stick at," Marigold crowed when Kurt had walked out of earshot. Wendy squinted up at her.

"Yes, Webb Larson told me you're going to the dance with him."

Marigold giggled merrily. "With him, with Kurt, and with Reggie Bloomberg. Everyone thinks he's sweet on Jenny Blair, but he's already promised the first dance with me."

Wendy arched an eyebrow. "Three men?"

Marigold waved an indifferent hand. "Oh, more than that. Two miners from the coal mine have asked me too, and I told them I'd meet them at the dance."

Wendy bit her tongue as a harsh lashing choked her throat. She didn't intend to interfere where these silly romancers were concerned, but Kurt didn't deserve to be treated badly by this shallow girl. But something niggled in Wendy's mind, reminding her she had other business to attend to. Surely, she couldn't waste time meddling where she wasn't wanted. Didn't Kurt and Miguel almost fight over similar attitudes about Miss Marigold?

Wendy shook her head. "None of my business," she said from between clenched teeth.

Marigold glanced toward the barn as she crossed her arms over her chest. "Well, you can't expect me to wait for just any man to marry me. I hate this horrid land and can't wait to get away. The world awaits me. New York, Philadelphia, perhaps even Paris. I'm not cut out to be a rancher's wife."

"Then you have no intentions of staying out west?" Wendy frowned at her unexpected query. Where had that come from? Surely she didn't really care, she told herself quickly.

Marigold lifted her chin as she gestured to the distant prairie. "Look at this bleak place. Empty as far as the eye can see. Not a city for hundreds of miles. And I'm stuck here. I figure to let all the men give me their best shot, and I'll take the one who has the best promise of getting me out of here. A girl can't gamble on love when she might get stuck slaving away for a dirty cowboy in a filthy cabin up in the hills, a passel of kids underfoot. Not me, no sir. I want more out of life."

Wendy thought of Kurt's spacious cabin, rustic and unfinished, but she thrilled at the potential. And children? Wendy hoped she'd find a man one day to have children with, to raise a Christian family. She bit her lip as she studied Marigold.

"Does Kurt know you allow every man to chase you, or does he think he's the only one? Does he know you intend on leaving Trinidad?"

The ranch girl scowled at Wendy, shooting daggers with her piercing eyes. "What affair is it of yours? You said you're just passing through."

Wendy nodded, her lips pursing into a thin line as Kurt led his gelding to the porch. Suddenly all smiles and dancing eyes, Marigold waved as Kurt and Wendy rode from the ranch yard. But Wendy scowled as she noticed the radiant look on the cowboy's smooth face.

CHAPTER TWENTY-SEVEN

Wendy watched as Kurt dropped the coins and crumpled bills into her hand. "There you go, Moylan. Er, well, I mean Miss Moylan." He looked away quickly.

Wendy grinned and nudged him with her elbow. "Call me Moylan or Wendy or even Wen. We've worked hard together, Kurt, and I feel we're friends."

He nodded. "Friends," he agreed. "Although I'll never forget that night, uh, well, never mind."

"The night you discovered I wasn't a young boy," she finished for him, wondering why he struggled to say the words aloud. Then the heat crept up her neck as she recalled he spanked her, and she understood why Kurt felt uncomfortable. "Forget it," she went on. "I deceived you. It wasn't fair. I should've told you."

"Well, you're a good hand. I'd let you work my ranch anytime."

A warmth filled her chest at the high tribute. "Thanks," she murmured. Kurt shrugged and turned to settle accounts with the storekeeper. As Wendy looked around the store, she noticed a pretty girl with a downcast face, moving mechanically as she shelved cans. Wendy remembered Jenny Blair from her initial visit to Hanson's General Store, and what Marigold had said about her. Wendy wondered at the girl's obvious sadness.

Abruptly, Aunt Lil bustled in from the back room, arms full of folded blankets.

"Aunt Lil," Wendy called as she rushed upon her aunt. They embraced as the older woman beamed. Wendy noticed her aunt seemed particularly bright, an unfamiliar rosy glow staining both cheeks, making her seem younger somehow.

She stepped back and eyed Lil. "Why, you look great. I can't remember when I've seen you so fit."

"Fit as a fiddle," Aunt Lil said with a smile. She peered over Wendy's shoulder and her eyes gleamed with excitement. Wendy followed her aunt's gaze, her jaw dropping when she saw Mr. Hanson talking with Kurt.

She faced Lil. "What are you doing here?"

Lil shifted, her smile slipping. "Well, I got lonely sitting in that old drafty stockroom, waiting for you to return. Mr. Hanson seemed so kind and always had a cheerful greeting for me, so I started helping in the store. Gives me something to do."

"You work here?"

"No, no," Lil explained hurriedly. "Jenny works here part time. I just lend a hand and help where I can. It's been good to have someone to talk with and things to do."

Wendy stared at her. Aunt Lil had never looked better. Her face held a glow Wendy didn't remember. And she'd looked at Mr. Hanson with a twinkle in her eye.

"Welcome back, Wendy," Lil went on, placing the stack of blankets on a table. "I gather you found Kurt Jordan's camp. Miguel came in when he sold the cattle to the mine. Fresh beef in town! The miners have been talking about it for days."

"Yes, I worked with the cowboys," Wendy said with a ring of pride in her words that surprised her. She'd worked hard and had done a good job. She could ride and shoot and wasn't afraid of getting dirty. She felt grateful Kurt agreed with her. His compliment had meant much.

Lil leaned close, lowering her voice. "Will he guide you to the Mora River country?"

Wendy shook her head, disappointment washing over her. If anyone were to guide her south, she wished it'd be Kurt. "He's busy chasing a wife."

She hadn't expected to sound so bitter, but her brow furrowed beneath her hat, and she glanced to where Kurt and Mr. Hanson still talked.

Aunt Lil laughed as she tugged on Wendy's ponytail. "I see the charade is over. Did the sham work?"

Wendy wanted to say something about hiding her true identity and Kurt respecting her efforts and him discovering she was a girl. She wanted to tell Lil about hunting deer and skinning the meat they ate for meals, the half-broken mustang she'd ridden each day, what a maverick was, and how to brand cattle. Instead, she nodded. "Yes, it worked."

She looked to where Kurt had been, but the cowboy was gone. She missed him as if they'd known one another longer than a week and a half. "I need a bath," Wendy said as she led the way to the back door. Lil waved to Mr. Hanson and followed Wendy through the alley to the stockroom.

Cold wind whistled from the mountains, and Wendy peered out the small window to the prairie beyond while Lil prepared a bath. The older woman kept a running monologue as she poured heated buckets of water she retrieved from Bill's Café. As the tub filled, Wendy wondered what her next move should be.

"Did you locate a guide?"

Lil paused. "What did you say?"

Wendy frowned as she slipped into the hot bath. "I asked if you located a guide. I need to find Grandfather's treasure."

Lil shook her head. "Well, no, dear. I didn't find a guide. But I had Bill and Carl and Michael looking everywhere for one."

Wendy arched an eyebrow, letting the heat steal through her chilled body. "Carl? Michael?"

Lil giggled, a blush blossoming across her cheeks. Her aunt actually *giggled*, just like a schoolgirl. "Carl at the store,

Michael at the livery, and, of course, Bill at the café," Lil explained as she waved a hand casually.

Wendy leaned back and sighed. "This feels good," she muttered. Her eyelids drooped as she felt herself relax. The drafty stockroom was a step above the open prairie or the windowless cabin of Kurt Jordan. Wendy could imagine a good night's sleep here.

Startled, her eyes opened, and Wendy leaned forward, her gaze locking on her aunt. "We're not supposed to be getting comfortable here," she snapped, and her voice held an accusing tone for Lil and herself.

Her aunt nodded, a repentant look on her face. "I know, Wendy. But it's been so nice to not hear about the war or to worry about food, the Yankees, or how we're going to pay Mr. Whitmore. It's been good to just work and enjoy making new friends."

Wendy leaned back again, the water encircling her neck. She thought of the cattle, the open plains, the high mountains, and the cowboys. Her mind drifted to the half-finished stone barn and the intended corrals. She bit her lip as she thought of Marigold Peterson, the spoiled ranch princess, living at Kurt's cabin.

But would she? Hadn't she admitted she would allow any man to provide the wealth that would ensure her escape from the frontier? Did Kurt even have a chance?

Kurt and Marigold didn't belong together. She was not right for him. Kurt was handsome and owned land. He was building for the future and would never leave the west. Most importantly, he was a believer, sharing Wendy's faith.

Her faith? Wendy's eyes fluttered wide. Her faith didn't matter to Kurt. He was looking for a wife while she was looking for hidden gold. He'd given his heart to Marigold Peterson, and Wendy would be going back to Arkansas soon enough. It was true what Kurt had said about her, she was only passing through.

"What are you thinking?"

Lil's sudden question broke into Wendy's thoughts, and she sighed again. "Nothing," she said, pleased to be brought back to reality once more. She needed a guide and then she'd be off, the journey south sure to take weeks of travel. With any luck, she could gather her gear and be ready to ride in a few days, with or without a guide. She had her map and the road lay clear before her. She'd have to be careful to not attract unwanted attention at Fort Union. Surely the Yankee soldiers would not allow a single woman to venture into Indian lands. Perhaps she could slip by the fort unseen.

The gold, she reminded herself with a reprimand. Stay the course and stay attentive. How dare she forget her mission and allow her mind to wander into unfamiliar territory—territory Wendy had no business being in. She wasn't here to find new friends. Her father had died, and her family estate was in danger. She was here to pursue a lifelong dream of her aunt to locate lost treasure, treasure that would save both Wendy and Aunt Lil. Wendy could not afford to spend any time thinking or worrying about Kurt or Marigold. Nor the beautiful mountains that loomed to the west. Or the way the fading sunsets splashed the snowy heights in splendor and painted the thick pine forests along their ramparts in shadow as the sun dipped behind those impressive peaks. No, she was a Southern girl from Arkansas, and she belonged in the South. She would go home and figure out how to navigate poverty or a sorrowful marriage, whichever she was forced to endure.

"Aunt Lil," she said suddenly, glancing to the small window which revealed the unchanging faded, weary light of late afternoon that hovered above the foothills on this cold winter day. Her aunt stopped fussing over Wendy's stained and soiled range costume and lifted her eyes.

"Yes?"

"I want you to talk with Mr. Hanson," she began, and then grinned and started again. "I want you to talk with Carl and start putting supplies together for my trip south."

"Your trip?" Aunt Lil's voice held a note of concern.

"Yes, my trip. I can travel faster without you, and I can handle a journey in winter weather. I've slept in the snow."

"Snow?" Lil repeated Wendy's words like a frightened parrot, and Wendy nodded, silently confident she was making the right decision to go alone.

"I will need a horse, a pack animal, bedding, and food for two weeks. If I need more than that, I will be forced to visit Fort Union and resupply, but I hope to hurry and not need a trip to the fort."

"You think you can find the treasure on your own?" Aunt Lil's tone held a hint of doubt that nettled Wendy.

"In the past two weeks, I herded cattle and worked a branding iron. I can ride, shoot, and hunt."

"Will you need a gun? What about the Indians?"

Wendy scowled. She'd thought about that but decided she couldn't shoot a man even if she had a gun. "No. I'll not hunt. The rifle will bring attention I can avoid if I'm quiet. That goes for the Indians too. I'll move very carefully and hopefully will not even see the brutes. Kurt says they often do not venture far from their homes in winter. Perhaps I can slip into the country and out again before they know I'm there."

Lil tossed Wendy's stinking, rumpled clothes aside and came to sit on a keg of nails beside the little potbellied stove, a frantic look on her face. "Wendy, what are we doing here? We're two women in a strange place, sending you alone into Indian lands. Are we stupid? You could get killed."

Suddenly, the bath water had turned cold. Wendy pursed her lips and thought of Lil's words. She was afraid, she admitted to herself, but there was nothing else to do. She didn't want to go north and live among the crowded cities full of strangers.

She had no wealthy relatives who would take her in or a skill that would enable her to make a living, and she had no desire to marry Mr. Whitmore. All she had was her faith and an old journal with the tale of a lost gold pack from a mule train many decades ago. The account might not even be true, or the gold might've been discovered by others. There was no telling how many men Colonel Gomez had repeated the story to.

Wendy squinted up at her aunt's terrified scrutiny and drew a deep breath. "I won't be alone," Wendy whispered, unable to keep a note of bitterness from her words. "Jesus is with me, right?"

"Don't be so melodramatic," Lil snapped, her eyes narrowing. "I'm serious, Wendy. Are we doing the right thing?"

Wendy nodded slowly, less sure of herself than ever, as she prayed silently. *Jesus, you're with me, right?*

CHAPTER TWENTY-EIGHT

The next day, Wendy rented a sturdy-looking horse from Michael Edmonds at the livery, but the pack animal he suggested was the same old nag she'd ridden to Kurt's camp nearly two weeks ago.

"I guess, if it's the best you can do," she said doubtfully as she smacked the animal on the rump and walked from the gloomy barn into the dull sunlight of the street.

"I'll keep my eyes peeled for a better horse," Edmonds promised. "But there's slim chance of that. There's little travel on the road this time of year."

Wendy nodded. "Thanks, Mr. Edmonds." She turned to go when the hostler stopped her.

"Is your aunt going to the dance tomorrow night?"

Wendy blinked. Dance? Tomorrow night? She'd been far too preoccupied to remember the dance at the sawmill was only a day away. "I don't know," she admitted, amused by his sudden interest.

He wiped his hands on his coat and shifted. "Well, I'm going," he said, as if that simple statement conveyed his desire to take Lil to the town's event.

"All right," Wendy said and walked away. She wasn't about to get involved with these silly men fluttering around her aunt. Just like the younger men buzzing around Marigold like honey seeking bees, it appeared Aunt Lil had acquired some ardent admirers of her own in Wendy's brief absence. Mr. Peterson's claim of the scarcity of women out west came to her, and Wendy smirked, secretly pleased to see Lil enjoying herself and making new friends, albeit temporary ones. With any luck, they would be on the stage east within a month.

She joined Lil at the café and shared her news. "The horses are as good as I can find. They'll have to do."

Lil nodded, but her gaze followed Bill as the man hustled around the room, his stained apron protruding over his ample belly. When he visited their table and poured coffee, he noticed Wendy's furtive assessment of his round torso.

"Never trust a skinny cook. If they don't eat their own cooking, you know the food's no good."

Lil chortled like she'd never heard anything wittier in her life as she watched the café owner walk away.

"You know, Mr. Edmonds over at the livery asked if you were going to the dance," Wendy remarked as she sipped her coffee. She smiled when she realized her camp coffee tasted as good.

"Michael?" Aunt Lil shifted on the bench as a slow grin spread across her face. "I confess I've considered going. No one has asked me, but I feel the town's invitation extends to travelers. What do you think?"

Wendy hesitated. She didn't want to go and had no intention of making the effort at socializing with the town folk, people she never expected to see again. But it was obvious Lil wanted to attend. And Wendy felt there'd been so few opportunities for enjoyment in the last few years. The war, destruction, and then Yankee occupation had limited gatherings among the locals of Little Rock. Lil deserved a diversion.

"I think you should go. You'll have fun."

Lil's eyes sparkled with excitement. "But I won't go without you," she said hurriedly.

Wendy shook her head. "Don't make me go. You know I don't like dances, parties, or festivities. I'm the proverbial wall flower, and no one knows me here. I'll end up watching you dance the night away with your new friends."

Lil sipped her coffee. "Michael will be there, and Bill mentioned the gathering. I heard Mr. Hanson ask Jenny if she would attend with Reggie Bloomberg."

Wendy recalled Marigold's claim that Reggie promised her the first dance, and she wondered about Mr. Hanson's dispirited clerk. "This Jenny Blair," Wendy began. "She seems so sad."

Lil nodded. "The poor girl is all alone in the world, no family except a brother fighting in the war. And she hasn't heard from him in months."

They were silent for a moment before Lil continued, bringing the conversation back to the upcoming dance. "Come on, Wendy. All of the men are so kind to me, and I do love the smell of Carl's pipe smoke, although I know that's coarse."

She paused and took another sip, eyeing Wendy over the rim of her mug. "Won't Kurt Jordan be there?"

"Oh, yes," Wendy snorted. "He's courting Marigold Peterson. He'll be there."

Aunt Lil placed a hand on Wendy's arm. "Please go with me. I can't go alone, and I so want to attend."

Wendy sighed. "All right, but only for a short while. I'll probably slip out and go to bed early. I want to leave Sunday morning for New Mexico Territory."

Lil glanced up sharply. "So soon? Without a guide?"

"We came all this way. We've spent our last dollar on this venture, this gamble," Wendy said bitterly. "I'm not going home without trying. We've prayed for guidance, and I have to trust the Lord is with me. Other than that, I have nothing. I don't hear the Lord saying not to try. God bless me or not, I'm heading south Sunday morning."

"Thank God you're here," Kurt breathed in her ear as the cowboy sidled beside Wendy at the dance. Men and women moved around the sawmill, fetching drinks for partners or eyeing prospective ones. A fire burned in the large fireplace at the end of the great room.

She felt her eyes widen at his unexpected presence. "What's that?" She wasn't surprised to see him, but she wondered at the way her heart lurched at his clean clothes and dark suit coat. His neatly combed hair impressed her, and she realized she'd rarely seen him without his hat. A scowl touched her mouth when she also realized she'd been waiting for him, knowing he'd be present this evening.

He leaned against the wall and acted casual, but she sensed his unease as he whispered from the corner of his mouth. "I don't know how to dance."

Wendy shrugged. "So what? Don't dance. I'm certainly not going to."

He huffed and glared at her from the corner of his eye. "I can't not dance. Marigold is here, and she's dancing with every man in Colorado Territory tonight. I need to be present, make my intentions obvious."

"You need to mark your territory like a dog," Wendy summarized.

"Not funny." His gaze roamed over her lithe form. "Hey, you look real nice in a dress, Wendy."

"Thanks," she mumbled at the surprised compliment. She felt suddenly pleased Lil had told her to pack a dress. Clearly, he had not expected her to look like anything other than a girl in boy's garb, chasing cattle and riding a wild mustang.

She scanned the lantern-lit sawmill, taking in the smooth plank floor and the benches lining the walls. Couples paraded across the room, showing off their finest clothes, and Wendy smiled when she saw Lil surrounded by a half dozen men, her aunt appearing younger than ever with a wide smile and eyes glowing, her face beaming.

"I need your help," Kurt persisted. Without waiting for a rebuttal, he grasped her hand and led her from the bright room and into an office. A scarred file cabinet stood against one wall and a large desk filled a corner, the surface covered in scattered papers and deep scratches. The small room lay in shadows as only a faint light streamed through the open door.

"What's this?" Wendy pulled her hand from the cowboy's grip and glowered.

"Settle down, Wen," he soothed as he wiped his palms on his pants. "I don't know how to dance, and you've got to show me now."

"What makes you think I can dance?" She eyed him coolly, suddenly angry he wanted to learn so he could dance with Marigold.

He lifted his arms. "Come on. Show me," he pleaded.

A scowl settled on her face, and Wendy felt the pinch as her brow wrinkled. She didn't want to show him how to dance with *her*. But Kurt had been nice to Wendy and given her a job, a chance many men wouldn't have allowed. Besides, she was leaving in the morning and would likely never see Kurt again. It was the least she could do to repay him. With a huff, she stepped forward.

"All right. Take my hand here," she indicated, waving. "And rest your other hand on my waist."

He took her hand and stepped forward, his eyes widening as he gently placed a hand on her slim waist. "Like this?" he whispered.

"Yes, but a bit more firm. I won't break. Now this is the easy part. The hard part is keeping your feet moving correctly with the music. You must listen for the tempo."

"Tempo?"

"Yes." Wendy stood very near him. She could smell bath soap, leather, and a faint scent of pipe smoke lingered about him, as if he'd spent time recently with Mr. Hanson.

Had Carl Hanson suggested Kurt seek Wendy out and learn dance moves?

Kurt gulped. "Look, I'm sorry about that little joke I played on you."

"Joke?" The single word sounded sharp in her own ears. "That was no little joke. You took a switch to my backside."

"Well, I'm sorry. I didn't know. Can we just forget it?"

"Can you?"

He nodded. "I need to learn to dance. Help me, Wendy."

His imploring tone wrung consent from her, and she pursed her lips. "Move your feet like this," she said as she slid across the floor. "No, don't let go of my waist. Now move this way and listen while I count the steps."

She guided him around the cramped room as she counted. She pointed with her chin at the nearby room where couples swayed around the dance floor. "There. Hear that melody? That's a waltz. Now follow me."

The couple danced in the shadowed office as the music played, Wendy trying to recall the proper dance moves while trying to ignore Kurt's touch.

"How am I doing?"

She tensed at his question, confused by her whirling emotions. She wondered at the unfamiliar sensations washing over her, wondering why she enjoyed the cowboy's nearness.

"You're as graceful as a bull," she teased as he stepped on her foot for the third time.

"Oh, I'll never get the hang of it." He stepped back, releasing her.

Wendy stood still, suddenly feeling very alone. When her father was still alive, she'd danced countless times with various men at all the balls in Little Rock. But none had the effect on her as this cowboy with the scuffed boots.

"Wendy? Are you all right?"

His concerned query brought her back to the moment and she felt pleased she could hide behind a swift, fabricated smile.

"I'm fine. And don't worry about how you dance. All of the men look like they haven't a clue what dancing is. Do your best and be confident. Miss Marigold will not notice your clumsy ox feet."

He nodded, but his sharp gaze still studied her.

"I'm leaving in the morning," she said without warning.

Kurt's eyebrows arched. "Without a guide?"

"We both have things we need to do. I need to do this. You need to marry Marigold Peterson."

Kurt grinned sheepishly. "Have you seen her? She's beautiful, Wendy."

An ache pierced her chest that annoyed her. Why should she care what Marigold Peterson looked like or what Kurt Jordan thought of her?

He tilted his head. "Am I ready?"

She stared at the handsome cowboy. Tall and broad shouldered, Kurt Jordan ignited an interest she couldn't comprehend. Confused, she crossed her arms over her chest and nodded. She worried he could hear the throb of her heart, and heat raced to her cheeks as she felt her stomach clench.

"Wendy?" He narrowed his eyes, studying her in the dim light.

Her tongue clove to the roof of her mouth and she couldn't speak for a moment. Then she found her voice and pointed to the spacious room where the dance continued. "Go," she rasped hoarsely.

His grin split his face and he winked. "Thanks," he said as he strode from the room.

Wendy watched the cowboy go. "Goodbye, Kurt," she whispered.

CHAPTER TWENTY-NINE

Kurt fled the small room, and Wendy leaned against the wooden desk, catching her breath and putting her thoughts in order. She had prepared for the journey south. Countless hours and all of her and Aunt Lil's last dollars had gone into their flight from Little Rock and the impending trip to the Mora River. Secret gold awaited her search, and yet she didn't care. What had come over her?

Wendy left the little office in a daze and reentered the large room where couples danced. The lively music had no effect on her now, and she watched the surrounding laughter and brightly colored gowns as if she were a ghost, observing something not real.

Across the room, Aunt Lil sat on a bench surrounded by men as she fanned her heated cheeks. No doubt she'd just finished a reel. Wendy frowned when Lil pointed at her and said something to her listeners. Carl Hanson left the group and hurried to Wendy's side.

"Dance with me, Miss Moylan," he called as he took her hand and pulled her onto the dance floor.

"I'm sorry, Mr. Hanson, but I had no intention of dancing," she said above the music.

The storekeeper grinned. "Lil said you would say that." He whirled her around and Wendy surrendered to the situation, frowning even more when she saw Kurt glide by with Marigold in his arms.

"He thinks he's in love," Mr. Hanson said suddenly. Wendy looked up at him.

"What does that mean?"

"It means he doesn't know what real love is yet," the storekeeper went on, twirling easily. Wendy felt surprised at his graceful movement. "It means he's got his heart in the right spot, but wrong horse."

"Wrong horse?"

"The Lord's brought him to Trinidad to find his future. He's homesteaded land and made friends. He feels God wants him to settle down, but that little filly is a fast one. She would never be content on Kurt's lonely ranch. She wants glitter and bright lights and noisy crowds."

Wendy inhaled the comforting smell of pipe smoke and peered at Mr. Hanson. "Why are you telling me this?"

He smiled as the final chords of the music came together in a crescendo, signaling the end of the dance. "He's chasing the wrong horse."

Wendy couldn't understand anything the storekeeper said. Perhaps his interest in Aunt Lil had made him dotty. But Wendy appreciated the older man's ability to dance and the faint smell of pipe smoke that clung to his shirt.

She thanked him for the dance and hurried to a side door, eager to disappear before anyone else demanded a dance. She stepped through the door and leaned against the wall, hidden by deep shadows. Sawdust littered the floor in this room, and stacks of lumber lined the walls. The heady smell of fresh cut lumber filled the air, but Wendy paid little attention to her surroundings, suddenly wishing it were morning and she was on her way to Raton Pass. A thump on the other side of the wall made her shrink into the corner. She leaned closer and pressed an ear to a knothole when she recognized Marigold Peterson's muffled voice coming through the thin board.

"What do you mean dragging me over here, Webb? I want some refreshments."

"In a minute," the ranch foreman growled. "Is it true what Reggie Bloomberg said?"

Marigold laughed merrily. "It sure is. I told all the men they needed money if they wanted to marry me."

"Reggie said he never intended on marrying you. He's with Jenny Blair, but admitted he played fast and loose with you."

"Well, I'm getting tired of waiting. I want to get married and leave this place. I want to see the world. Whoever can give me what I want, I'm theirs."

"You shallow flirt," Larson went on in a disgusted tone. "And I suppose you said this to Kurt Jordan too."

"Sure I did. All of you, including those miners. Let's see who can dig up the money first." Marigold laughed again, and Wendy felt her stomach coil in knots. Was Kurt aware of this girl's desire to marry the first rich man she found?

"But you told me you loved me."

Marigold's laughter stopped, and for a moment, Wendy felt sorry for Webb Larson. "Love you? Well, maybe, if you win the game. I like you best of all, Webb. You have to know that. But Kurt Jordan is a handsome man, and I'd be a fool not to cast a wide net. There's more than one fish in the sea, my father tells me."

"Your father doesn't like me. He'll have me as foreman, but not as son-in-law."

Marigold's laugh returned, and Wendy almost stepped from her hiding place, disdaining the covert role she played. Kurt Jordan wanted this silly girl, and the affair was none of her business. Yet he was a friend of hers, wasn't he?

She made up her mind to walk from her concealed position when Webb spoke again. "I guess that explains why Jordan fled out of here like his tail was on fire."

"Kurt's left?" Marigold's sudden interest angered Wendy. Could this range princess have any decency left in her?

"Yes," Larson replied gruffly. "He left after your last dance with him. What did he say?"

"He said something mysterious," Marigold said so low that Wendy strained to catch her words. "He said he had an idea where to get the money."

"Well, he isn't going to get it taking the time to build his small ranch. It'll be years before he can sell to the cattle buyers."

Wendy had heard enough. With a whirl of her dress, she stomped from the shadowed recess and marched across the crowded dance floor, weaving among twirling couples as she made her way toward the door. A hurried glance over her shoulder revealed Marigold and Webb gazing after her, but she didn't care. Anger propelled her through the door to the moonlit glade before the sawmill. Wagons and buggies and lone horses stood around the clearing, but she noticed none of them. She'd ridden with Mr. Hanson and Aunt Lil in a buggy, but she wasn't afraid of the cold that enveloped her as she strode onto the road to town. Not more than a mile lay between the mill and Trinidad, and Wendy needed the time to consider.

Her shoes crunched gravel, and she slowed, realizing she was nearly running. What was Kurt thinking? He was so good and honorable and hard working. Why would he settle for this little snippet of a conceited girl? He tried so hard to please her, all to no avail. She didn't even love him.

Wendy kicked at a stone and began to question her wisdom. The cold night descended, and she shivered, suddenly aware she hadn't even brought a coat. She'd left her shawl at the dance and hoped Lil would retrieve the garment, but the walk would do her good, allow her to clear her mind.

She picked up her step, knowing the brisk pace would warm her. Could Kurt Jordan be such a fool? Miguel had seen through Marigold Peterson, seen her for what she was— shallow, disloyal, not to be trusted. Yet the impatient cowboy had thrown his heart at her with a suddenness that threatened to destroy him.

Would God intercede? Would the Lord allow Kurt to make such a mistake? Wendy slowed, her mind spinning with possibilities. If he saw soon enough, perhaps Kurt would refuse to marry Marigold. But if his stupid, misguided heart persisted, he would be subjected to exactly what he deserved, his impatience leading to sorrowful consequences.

Wendy shook her head. This was none of her business. She needed to concentrate. Her expedition began in less than twelve hours. She'd come west for a task, a mission, ordained by God with an incredible opportunity at great wealth. Surely the Lord had brought her here for this important chance. Grandfather Sean's journal cried out to her and announced the answers to her problems. *Focus*, she told herself as she peered at the towering pines that lined each side of the narrow road. A sliver of moon glittered above, filtering light through dense branches of evergreens that created shadows across the road and in the depths of the nearby forest. The cold seemed more apparent now, her slow gait and the lonely night making her want to run for shelter. The drafty stockroom behind Mr. Hanson's store suddenly seemed a welcome haven after the freezing night air that held her in its grip. Did the anger she suffered from or the irritation at Kurt's foolishness have anything to do with her mounting annoyance? Marigold was a scheming cat, and Kurt was a sucker.

She kicked at another stone, reminding herself she wasn't wearing boots and stone kicking wasn't advisable in dance slippers.

Finally, the lights of Trinidad loomed, and Wendy hurried on, eager to arrive at the room she shared with Lil. Her teeth chattered uncontrollably now, and she hoped she wouldn't catch a cold. She would need all her strength for the trip into Apache lands.

She crossed the bridge over the Purgatory River and then passed the livery. Hanson's General Store was dark now, but she glanced at the silent store. Lil seemed to be enjoying the company of both Michael Edmonds and Carl Hanson and even chubby Bill from the café. She didn't seem worried about the journey into Indian lands or Wendy going without a guide near as much as she had been a couple weeks ago. In fact, Lil's preoccupation with new friends startled Wendy, and yet pleased her too. Lil deserved friends.

She made her way in the dark to the alley behind the store and then stood shivering in the cold as her numb fingers fumbled with the door. For long minutes, Wendy hovered around the potbellied stove, red embers glowing through the grate. She fed sticks into the fire and watched the blaze brighten as flames licked the dry kindling. Soon, her shivering stopped, and warmth crept into her frozen bones. But her heart still felt cold in her chest.

Later, when Lil entered the room with a hushed whisper from Mr. Hanson before she said goodnight and closed the door on the storekeeper, Wendy hadn't yet warmed thoroughly. Her nice dress concealed beneath her blankets, she pretended to be asleep as Lil prepared for bed.

And even after that, Wendy listened to the even breathing of her aunt and wondered why she thought so much about Kurt and Marigold and the frontier town of Trinidad instead of the impending journey only hours away.

CHAPTER THIRTY

"Wendy?" Lil's drowsy call in the dark startled her, and Wendy tensed, her nerves taut as she gathered her gear.

"Go back to sleep, Aunt Lil. I'll saddle my horses and pack my supplies and then I'll stop by on my way out of town."

Lil said nothing to this, and Wendy wondered if the older woman was wrought with emotions too intense to allow speech. Either way, Wendy pulled her slouch hat low and buttoned her coat before pulling the door open. She stepped into the alley and peered back into the dark room, but nothing stirred. Only the fire crackled merrily in the stove, Wendy's parting gift, an armload of fresh fuel.

Her boots crunched loudly in the road as she made her way to the shadowy livery. Not even a single lamp burned in any of the saloons farther down the street, nor a light shone in the mine office at the east end of town. She felt all alone, on a trip void of any interest or concern from others. Wendy wondered if this was true or if her imagination were running wild.

The big barn door creaked on strained hinges, and she stepped inside. Mr. Edmonds had shown her where the candles were stored and where the water bucket stood for discarded matches, the fear of fire always a distress for the liveryman and his barn full of dry hay.

The bright match hissed when she dropped the stick into the water and lifted the glowing candle. The barn felt warm and safe after the outside cold, and she saddled slowly, making sure she did everything right. Even the knots on her packs she checked and checked again, making certain the supplies were packed correctly before she led the two animals from the barn and blew out the candle.

Moonlight gleamed drearily in the early dawn, the slivered orb barely above the mountains to the west. In the east, a faint tinge of gray hung low over the plains. For a moment, Wendy wondered what was happening back in Arkansas. How did the Confederates fare? They could not last much longer, Lee's army was besieged around Richmond and the Shenandoah Valley was overrun with Yankees, cutting off the South's final food supply.

And Randall Whitmore? Did he still wait for her return, or did he take possession of the Moylan estate the moment he learned she'd given his watchdogs the slip?

Now, the impending expedition loomed large in her mind as she realized she was about to embark on the adventure of her life. Could she follow the sketchy map in her grandfather's journal? Could she find the hidden treasure?

She leaned against the saddle of the rented horse and peered up at the towering peaks, studying the jagged teeth of the high ridges in the fading moonlight. Dark clouds whirled ominously, pressing against the front of the Rockies. A storm brewed, but Wendy felt more concerned with the storm that raged within her. Could she do this? Could she single handedly travel into unknown lands, evade hostile Indians, and search for the gold in the dead of winter?

"Lord, am I stupid? Is this what you want me to do?" Her whisper broke the suspended stillness and then the horse stamped, and Wendy nodded. "I feel I need to get going too. I guess this is it," she concluded softly, trying to ignore the anxiety that threatened to overwhelm her.

She tried to repeat encouraging Scripture, only to lose her train of thought for a moment before she could concentrate. *Be strong and courageous. Do not be afraid.*

LASTING TREASURE

Grasping the reins of her horse and the lead rope of the pack horse, she led the two animals down the alley behind Mr. Hanson's store, pausing before the dark stockroom. A single flake of snow fluttered silently, then another, lighting on her gloved hand as she reached for the door. Aunt Lil handed Wendy a steaming cup of coffee, messy hair spilling over the quilt she wrapped tightly around herself.

"Do you want to wait an hour and have breakfast at Bill's? He's closed on Sundays, but last night, he offered to open early just for you."

Wendy shook her head and sipped the hot drink. "I think he offered to open for you," she said with a teasing note. Lil beamed at the remark, and again, Wendy noticed how well her aunt appeared. Despite the pre-dawn hour, the quilt draped over her nightgown, and her untidy hair, a look of happiness filled her rosy countenance.

"They are all so nice to me," Lil whispered wistfully.

"You like Trinidad." The statement wasn't a question, and Wendy realized the truth as she said the comment. Lil had never seemed more content.

Aunt Lil tilted her head. "Do you have to go, Wendy? I mean, can we do things a different way?"

"No, Lil. You've had this dream for decades. Here we are, on the edge of knowing the truth about Grandfather's treasure. You deserve this. Besides, Mr. Whitmore has claim to our land. We'll never know if we did the right thing unless we try."

Lil nodded slowly. "I guess," she muttered. A smile crept to her lips, and Wendy felt encouraged by the gleam in her eyes. "You're right, Wendy. Here we are. We must believe the Lord made this happen, brought us here for this moment in time. Let the adventure continue. We're so close."

She paused a moment longer as Wendy drained her cup and handed the empty mug to her aunt. "You still think you can do this alone?"

219

Wendy grinned as she shoved a boot into the stirrup and pulled herself into the saddle. She glanced down at Lil as a sudden wave of excitement swept over her. "I'm not alone. But pray for me. I'll need Jesus to ride with me the whole way if I expect to make it back in one piece."

"I love you, dear," Lil said.

Wendy ignored the glistening tears that quivered in the older woman's eyes.

"See you soon, Aunt Lil." Wendy nudged the horse, and they left the alley behind, their hooves making little sound on the frozen dirt of the road as the snow continued.

Hanson's General Store lay behind her, and Wendy passed the livery barn before crossing the Purgatory. The tall pines stood as silent sentinels on either side of the road, the only observers to her departure as she made her way up the mountain to the south, passing the sawmill where she'd been only last night. A dim memory of Kurt holding her in his arms as they danced alone in the little office filled her mind, and Wendy smirked, erasing the image from her mind. She was on the final leg of her journey, and she would need to concentrate. Silly notions of handsome cowboys and unexpected friends could not be allowed to distract her from her goal. Not only her future or Lil's future, but the outcome of her family land was now at stake. Wendy knew she risked her very life to attempt this foolhardy expedition alone. But the Lord was with her, right? Surely God would not bring her all the way out here only to abandon her now.

Yet fear niggled at her thoughts as the snow fell, swirling thicker the higher she climbed toward the pass. She peered ahead, wondering why the morning sun had not appeared. Instead, a dark cloud surrounded her, smothering her in wispy folds as she climbed, making it difficult to locate and follow the road.

She pulled her scarf high on her face and tugged her hat low. Her ponytail helped keep the back of her neck warm against the rising wind that blustered down from the heights, and Wendy worried she'd attempted the crossing of Raton Pass on the wrong day. She hadn't counted on the snowstorm blowing so fiercely. Should she turn back? Would the road vanish beneath the snow?

She plodded on, and the horses seemed to trust her confident manner. If they guessed her true misgivings, they might balk and demand to return to Trinidad. But the hours passed slowly, and Wendy guessed she must be approaching the summit, although she didn't know exactly where she was. New Mexico Territory stretched on the other side of these smaller mountains, the Raton Range extending from the Rockies directly east for a hundred miles. She hoped soon she would cross the pass and drop into lower elevations. Perhaps if things got much worse, she could head for the dreaded Fort Union where the Yankees were sure to question her about her errand that could not wait for more favorable weather.

She wiped a gloved hand across her eyes and squinted at the fading trail. She slipped from her saddle and hurriedly tied the lead rope of her pack animal to the stirrup and then gripped the reins of her horse and started walking. At first, the road seemed easier to follow on foot, but as the storm increased, Wendy struggled to find any indication of the dimming road. She worried she couldn't find her way in the storm and now it was too late to turn back. Her tracks would be covered by snow and hours of travel lay behind her. Perhaps she was quite near the summit, at least she hoped she was. If she kept on, surely she would cross the mountains and enter New Mexico.

Snow blinded her and Wendy couldn't tell where she was going. Her boots dragged through the piling drifts, but she didn't feel the hard packed road anymore. Howling wind assaulted her and she tugged on her already low hat. The relentless storm bullied her and shoved her around as the ceaseless cold refused to give up its grip on her.

Despite her resolve, the piercing freeze penetrated to her bones. Her teeth chattered and she stuffed one gloved hand into her pocket as she gripped the reins with the other. Shivering uncontrollably, she stumbled on.

"Lord, don't bring me out here only to die," she shouted into the wind. Her toes seemed numb in her boots, and she bent her chin into the top of her coat as she struggled to drag the horses on. They'd sensed her unease, or the storm frightened them, for they pulled back, knowing safety and warmth lie behind.

"Help me, Christ," Wendy whimpered as she tugged on the reins. Her whole body felt like a block of ice now, and she wanted to let the horses go and run, try and save herself. The summit must be nearby, and she could flee the mountains, flee the storm, and reach safety somewhere ahead.

"Oh, Lord, why did you bring me here?" The painful ache of freezing feet and hands and face now was replaced with a growing numbness that reached all her limbs and pierced her chest. She was freezing to death as she still staggered on, trying to leave the storm behind.

"I'm going to die," she told herself, fear leaving her as she accepted the inevitable. The intense ache in her limbs had disappeared and only a numb resolve remained as she took another step, wondering how many more she might manage before she succumbed to the fatigue that weighed her down. A fallen tree caught her eye and she considered releasing the horses to find their way home as she huddled beside the dead pine tree and went to sleep. She would go to heaven, she knew, but images of a cowboy in hat and boots with sharp eyes and unshaven jaw made her squint even harder, peering into the falling snow.

"Kurt? Kurt?"

An arm caught her as she tumbled to the ground, and someone pulled her into a tight embrace. "I'm here, Wendy," Kurt said above the roaring wind. As if carrying a child, he held her close to his chest and trudged off the trail, following another shadowy figure that pointed the way. She snuggled into him, relinquishing control and worry and the despair that had threatened to overtake her. A sense of safety overwhelmed her, and she slept.

CHAPTER THIRTY-ONE

Wendy's eyelids fluttered, and she blinked at the roaring fire that blazed beside her. Like a mummy, she lay wrapped in piles of blankets, unable to move. A familiar battered coffeepot simmered in the coals, steam wafting from the spout.

"Don't move, Wendy," Kurt ordered when she tried to untangle herself from the woolen cocoon. "I'll pour coffee and then you can talk after we get your insides nice and warm."

He filled a mug and held her as she sipped the scalding drink. Heat and pinpricks of fiery needles stabbed her toes and fingers. But his soothing words and self-assured manner made her trust him, and she sipped the coffee, ignoring the acute agony as she looked up into his worried face.

"You're crazy," he finally said as he leaned her back to the ground once more.

"Crazy?" Her voice croaked and she swallowed, indicating with her chin that she wanted more coffee.

This time, Miguel hastened to fill her cup. He smiled at her as she struggled to a sitting position and freed one arm from the tangled blankets.

"Thank you, and thanks for finding me." Her voice sounded stronger after she drank a little more. "What are you two doing up here?" She peered around at the cheerful blaze and the rock wall at one side of the camp and the whipping canvas tarp at the other.

Kurt filled a mug for himself and leaned back on his haunches, his eyes boring into her. "Thank God there's lots of wood up here, seasoned and dry. And thank the Lord that Miguel remembered this little cavern from when we came over the pass last summer."

He used his mug to point at the canvas shield. "We leaned poles against this rock face and secured the tarp. The horses are safe, and we can wait out the storm in relative comfort, although it's colder than a miser's heart."

Wendy grinned at his imagery, and then she scowled. "Kurt, what are you and Miguel doing up here?"

He shifted and glanced at the Indian, but Miguel's smile had fled also. The cowboy pushed his hat back and nodded, a look of acceptance settling on his features. "I need money. I tried to round up loose stock and start a ranch, but it's not enough. I need money right now."

Wendy shivered, pleased to notice her teeth had stopped chattering. She eyed Kurt over the rim of her cup and wondered how much to share. She'd heard everything last night at the dance. Marigold Peterson wanted wealth and didn't worry who provided. Should she tell Kurt? Was it any of her business?

Before she could decide, he frowned at Miguel and spoke. "Although not everyone shares my estimation of Miss Peterson, I am in love and want to get married. If money is to be the test of that desire, then I will do my best to locate the expected wealth. Since I have no money, I figure the Lord brought me to Trinidad to find Marigold and then you."

"Me?" Her voice sounded more like a squeak.

Kurt swung his gaze back to Wendy, turning a shoulder to Miguel where the Indian sat with a deepening scowl on his taut features. "Yes, you. The Lord led me to Marigold and then brought you to show me where to find treasure. If gold is essential for winning the heart of my fair maiden, then let's hunt treasure."

She narrowed her eyes. "Let me get this straight. You followed me to join my expedition into Apache lands? You'll guide me?"

A sense of relief and gratitude poured into her at the thought of these two capable men traveling with her. She didn't feel so vulnerable with the cowboys along, and a sudden thrill assailed her. God *was* with her. He'd delivered her from the storm and brought men she could trust to guide her through the danger that lurked all around. Danger in the harsh weather, the inquisitive Yankees at Fort Union, and the Apache that roamed the river where she would search for the hidden gold.

Then his words sank in, and she frowned. Gold? How had Kurt known the treasure was gold? She hadn't told him that detail.

Her gaze went to her pack. Had Kurt read her grandfather's journal when she wasn't looking? She looked at him warily.

"How did you know the treasure is gold?"

Kurt shrugged. "I didn't. Well, not for sure. But Miguel and I have heard countless lost gold stories in the desert or the mountains. Gold discovered by the ancient Spanish conquistadors and hidden while trying to evade pursuing Indians or the testimony of the lone survivor of an attack."

He chuckled and glanced at Miguel. When the Indian nodded, Wendy felt something cave inside. Perhaps her story was one of innumerable rumors of lost gold stories that persisted in the desert. If Kurt had heard such legends, there must be many such lost treasures, false tales of great wealth or incredible amounts of piled gold. Was her tale one of these? Was she on a wild goose chase?

"Then why would my story be any different from the rumors you've heard before? Why chase *my* gold?"

Kurt reached for a blanket and draped the cover around his shoulders. He pondered her question as wind howled along the ridge and snow drifted through the gaps in the canvas shield.

"I don't have any other option. I thought I'd find lost cattle along the river to start my ranch, and I did, although the number of cattle isn't enough. But not bad for free. Miguel and I think we can find even more along the Arkansas River, and we intend to try in the spring. But I need money now."

"Did Marigold tell you she wanted a man with money? A man who can provide all her heart desires?" Wendy had determined not to tell what she'd heard between Miss Peterson and Webb Larson, but Kurt's unexpected presence and his willingness to join her adventure upset her equilibrium. She couldn't hold her tongue any longer.

He narrowed his eyes. "How do you know that?"

"I heard it from Webb Larson."

"You danced with that skunk?" He stood abruptly, the blanket slipping from his broad shoulders. "I can't believe you would dance with him."

She wanted to tell Kurt she would never dance with Webb, but his apparent jealousy made her check her words. With a coquettish shrug, she glanced into the blustering storm. "I danced with you, didn't I?"

Miguel chuckled, and Kurt pouted as he dropped to his haunches once more, draping the blanket around his own shoulders. "I can dance with whomever I want," Kurt muttered as he took a sip from his mug.

"So can I," Wendy replied tartly. She wasn't used to these exchanges with a man, yet she suddenly realized how much she enjoyed seeing the care in Kurt's face. He'd shaved yesterday for the dance at the sawmill, but a dark line of stubble covered his jaw now, and she had to look away lest he see her studying him. She still reeled from being saved from freezing to death and the news he expected to join her search for the gold. All in the twinkling of an eye, everything had changed. Where before she felt very alone, now she felt invincible, as if the three of them could handle anything that came their way. Kurt and Miguel were strong men, smart men, and she was ready now for the journey into the southern lands.

"Well," she said and changed topics. "I doubt you're taking me into the Apache land for free. What do you expect to get for your pains?"

Kurt arched an eyebrow and looked at Miguel. At the Indian's pinched features, she guessed they'd argued over the amount he intended to ask for.

"Half," he said at last, but Wendy heard the unsure note in his declaration, and she laughed.

"Of course, you would never receive half. I need the money more than you do. Besides, it's my money. I know where the loot is, and you don't."

"That's another thing," Kurt interjected. "You'll have to show me the journal entry, not just the map. I need to know exactly where we're going."

"Of course, partner," Wendy smiled. "But you don't get half."

Miguel snorted and gestured at Wendy with his mug while he said something. She saw the frown flit across Kurt's face, and she grinned. "What did he say?"

"He says you'd make a good horse trader." He paused and then shifted beneath the blanket. "All right, I'll take a third."

"For you and Miguel to split?" She winked at the Indian when she saw the way his bushy eyebrows bunched, and she wanted to let him know she hadn't forgotten him. Miguel nodded solemnly, but Wendy read the gratitude in his dark eyes.

"Yes, yes," Kurt mumbled. "Now let me see the journal."

Wendy dug the leather book from her pack and handed the ledger to Kurt, indicating the dog-eared page with the map and the specific entry he requested.

For the next half hour, Kurt read the page in the journal with the description of the hidden gold's location and studied the map again. Finally, he looked up, tapping the leather-bound book with a gloved finger. "I think I know where this is."

Wendy grinned. "Then we have nothing to do but go and get it."

CHAPTER THIRTY-TWO

The fresh snow blanketed the summit in drifts the horses floundered through. The top of the newly fallen snow resembled waves of creamy white butter or piles of sugar, and Wendy remembered Mary's cooking with longing. She wondered when she would savor another home cooked meal.

The road down the mountain lay open before them, occasional drifts barring their way. But the horses struggled on and worked their way to the bottom of the ridge where a vast, endless plain stretched before them.

Wendy drew rein and pulled her scarf low, leaning to pat Shannon on the neck. Wendy had been surprised when she learned the cowboys had delivered the stubborn, tough little mare for her to ride. Her rented horse had been relegated to travel with the pack horse. Now, with the favorite horse beneath her and the two cowboys beside her, Wendy felt ready for anything.

As the horses took a breather, she gazed far to the south. Unlike the higher pass behind them, only a scant dusting of snow coated the bleak landscape, and she felt pleased the storm had passed. With luck, they could cover many miles in the frigid cold if no more storms arose.

As if reading her mind, Kurt pointed south. "As long as the weather holds, we can move at a good pace. We'll send Miguel into Fort Union for supplies and to sniff around. He used to ride dispatch for the army, and they know him. I raced home from the dance, and we rode all day to catch up with you. We didn't take the time to properly prepare." He cast a sidelong glance at her.

"Good thing." Wendy nodded, her mind filled with images of Kurt lifting her from the snow and carrying her to the shelter. A blush crept up her neck at the thought of pressing against him, her head on his shoulder. With a jerk, she covered her face with her scarf.

"Time to move on?" Kurt frowned when she lifted her scarf, a signal to keep moving. He nudged his gelding and the cavalcade started on.

She eyed Kurt's rifle he carried in his saddle sheath and thought about the old horse pistol Miguel always carried on his saddle. She knew she couldn't shoot a man but felt pleased her companions came prepared.

As the trio rode southward, Wendy's thoughts turned to herself, Aunt Lil, and the war. A series of events seemed to hover at the edge of her mind, drifting like fog. As the war progressed, Wendy had pulled away even more, her loneliness blossoming with grief as her constant companion. Yet her father's death had forced her to face her uncertain future. God had always been her friend, quiet and forgiving, but now he seemed to want something from her. Something Wendy wasn't sure she could produce.

Jesus had proven faithful. She chewed her lip, disappointed in herself for thinking he might be anything other than faithful. Hadn't he guided her thus far? Sure, his ways were not the path she would've chosen, yet a realization the Lord rode with her comforted her.

A grin teased behind her scarf as she remembered Jimmy's boat trip in the rain, the stage ride across the barren plains, and the work on Kurt's ranch. Certainly, she would never have considered such a devious route to her plans. Yet here she was, with unexpected friends beside her. Despite her worries, the Lord had been at work all along.

She shot Kurt a quizzical glance. Had the Lord provided such companions? Her whole world had turned upside down in such a short amount of time. If they found gold, her life would change again. She felt she was being pushed into some kind of action—but what? Perhaps Jesus wanted more of her, maybe more than she could give.

The cold winds blew from the mountains behind her, pushing her across the plains to Fort Union, yet that was nothing compared to the uncomfortable feeling that overwhelmed her. She felt pushed to think, to do, to act. She'd always been left to roam quietly, undisturbed by the events around her. Now she wondered why God had not allowed her to remain unseen, as if isolation was no longer an option.

Wendy glanced at her two silent cowboy companions. Hadn't the Lord done so much with her already? Along with her sundry list of accomplishments in the past few weeks, she'd survived a snowstorm thanks to these new friends.

A shiver raced down her spine as she tried to blot out the memory of the intense cold and how she'd felt so lost in the swirling whiteness. The storm had almost killed her, yet Kurt and Miguel had found her, saved her.

She clenched her teeth, amazed at everything Jesus had pushed in her path. Was he trying to crush her? Was he committed to throwing obstacles in her way she must learn to navigate?

She drew a deep breath and sat straighter in the saddle. Already she'd made new friends and learned a lot, stretching her faith and the boundaries of her knowledge. And Aunt Lil? Wendy loved how alive the older woman had seemed these recent weeks.

Her gaze locked on Kurt, watching him from beneath the low brim of her hat. He'd seemed so cantankerous at first, self-absorbed and focused solely on his own plans. Yet a kinship had sprung between them. They both needed direction, purpose, a place to belong.

Maybe he could feel her eyes on him, for Kurt turned, catching her perusal. Wendy looked away quickly, but not before she read the startled expression on his face.

That night, they camped below the rim of a dry creek bed. Their small fire didn't scuttle in the wind down here, although Kurt demanded they keep the blaze to a minimum. "The Apache usually don't range this far north, and with the cold, they should be home. But you never can figure an Apache."

Miguel said nothing, his eyes always shifting, peering all around as if he expected an attack at any moment. Although he watched constantly, Wendy felt her anxiety grow, instead of lessen, at his vigilance. When she said this to Kurt, the cowboy nodded.

"Good. Always be prepared when you're in Indian lands. They appear when you least expect them, so expect them at any time."

They passed a quiet night, although none of them slept well. In the morning, they continued.

Snow covered grasslands stretched on either side of the endless road. The Santa Fe Trail showed signs of recent travel. Wagon wheels cut narrow paths through the dusting of snow and Miguel pointed and grunted.

"Stage," Kurt said as if he could read his partner's query.

"In winter?" Wendy felt amazed the stagecoach would risk traveling in this cold land with storms that could sweep down on unsuspecting folks.

"If the driver thinks he can make the next station, they often try, weather permitting," Kurt explained as they drew rein on a low summit. He pointed with his chin to a cluster of buildings in the distance. "Fort Union."

Wendy squinted at the row of squat buildings. A few naked trees marked a parade ground, and a few additional buildings lay to one side of the military structures, indicating saloons or stores for all travelers.

"Miguel will go for supplies. We'll ride past the fort and stop at a place we know of farther on."

The two cowboys exchanged a look, and Kurt handed the Indian a scrap of paper his list was written on and a few crumpled bills.

As Miguel galloped for the fort, Kurt and Wendy trotted their horses on the trail. Glancing over her shoulder, she saw soldiers in blue uniforms crossing the empty parade ground, and Wendy grimaced, remembering the Yankees that occupied Arkansas.

"You don't like the Union soldiers?"

Kurt's question made her scowl at the little army outpost. "I don't know. I shouldn't have any personal feelings against the Yankees. They did nothing to me. But they have assaulted the South. No doubt things will be different when I return."

He shifted, his cold saddle leather creaking. "So, you'll go back? I wondered if you might stay out west."

She felt surprised and pleased at his interest, and then her scowl deepened. "Why? You have plans you're pursuing, so do I."

"Really?" He grinned, and Wendy felt her heart flip flop at the twinkle in his eyes. "I wondered what you intended after your trip to the Mora River. You've been secretive, as if you don't want me to know what you need the money for."

He glanced at her with a questioning look, but she ignored him. "All you need to know is we are looking for a treasure that is decades old. Like I told you, I need the money to save my family's land."

He shrugged and went silent, but Wendy fumed. Why hadn't she just told him the whole truth? Her apprehension over Mr. Whitmore and her father's debt to the smuggler annoyed her still, and she'd been forced to depart the only peaceful place she'd ever known. Now, with the freezing cold wind whistling around her, she wondered if she'd ever be warm again.

As they rode on, she glanced once more at Kurt, wondering if his ranch would satisfy Marigold Peterson. The sturdy cabin with the adjoining stone room and the three crosses carved into the mantel over the immense fireplace. The endless hills and prairie that promised the most ideal grazing land for cattle, even though Kurt's small herd would take years to build up. And the half-finished stone barn where the cowboy wanted fine horses. Would the rustic homestead bring Marigold the joy she longed for?

Something made Wendy think the snooty ranch royalty would not enjoy or appreciate the hard work Kurt had initiated, and Wendy smiled behind her scarf. For some reason she couldn't name, it pleased her to think Marigold would not be happy with Kurt.

CHAPTER THIRTY-THREE

Kurt stood beside the small fire in the dry streambed and peered above the bank to the north, restless and agitated as he looked for Miguel. Wendy smiled faintly, appreciating the cowboy's concern for his friend. Did anyone care about her whereabouts? Certainly, Lil did but Wendy couldn't shake the feeling of loneliness that assailed her, and she felt grateful for Kurt's presence.

"Miguel is all right, Kurt," Wendy soothed as she poked the little blaze with a stick. "He'll be back soon."

Kurt nodded and drew a deep breath, never taking his eyes from the direction of the distant army outpost. "I know. He's used to being in tough spots, but I worry, nonetheless. Will this search bring us the money we need?"

Wendy shrugged, knowing she'd asked herself the same question a thousand times. "We hope so, right? Aunt Lil's favorite Scripture is 'Be joyful in hope, patient in affliction, faithful in prayer'. We need to wait on the Lord, see what he has to say about our mission."

Kurt dropped his gaze and studied her. "I like that Bible verse. Which Scripture speaks to you, your favorite?"

Wendy blinked. "My favorite? Well, I don't know."

Kurt turned suddenly as the sound of pounding hooves drifted on the wind. Wendy arched an eyebrow when she saw him reach for his rifle, something he hadn't done since crossing Raton Pass and descending into New Mexico Territory.

"It's Miguel," he said over his shoulder as he scanned the surrounding plains, the hair below his hat waving gently in the twilight's breeze.

The dull sun had not peeked through the canopy of gray clouds all day, but the storm seemed to have passed. Only the relentless cold remained as they hunched over the tiny flames, soaking up whatever heat they could.

Miguel drew rein and said something in Spanish. Kurt craned his neck and peered farther back up the trail while Miguel dismounted his heaving horse.

"He says two men followed him from Fort Union. They just hang back, not trying to catch up."

Wendy narrowed her eyes and studied the land to the north. Low bushes and darker shadows clung to the plains, but she couldn't see any riders.

"Why follow Miguel?"

"That's the question," Kurt replied as he kicked dirt over the small fire. Coals hissed while Wendy filled a cup with coffee before turning to help Kurt pack their gear.

While Miguel sipped his drink, he relayed the particulars of his visit to the fort. Kurt nodded as he tightened the cinch on his saddle. "He says he spoke to a few men he knew. The Apache are reported to be laying low, staying close to home during the winter, but you cannot ever predict what an Apache will do. The two men watched him at the general store, asked a few questions about him traveling in the cold, but Miguel bought supplies and left the fort quickly. Still, the two men followed him."

The cowboy swung into the saddle and turned to face Wendy. "We're in Indian lands now, and we'll have to be clever. We'll always move after dinner to hide our camp. No fires at night."

"And these two riders on our trail?" Wendy mounted and gripped the lead rope to the pack horse as Miguel led the way into deepening dusk. She pulled her scarf high and hunched her shoulders against the increasing cold.

"Until we know they are really after us, we ignore them and focus on our mission." Kurt turned into the trail behind Miguel. "We're looking for the Mora River. When we strike the Canadian at Willow Springs, we'll follow the river down to where the Mora intersects, farther to the south. I know that country probably better than most, but few men have ventured into Apache country and lived to tell about their journey. We'll have to go slow and be almighty careful."

Two hours later, Miguel turned off the trail, pulling up behind a thicket of mesquite a hundred yards from the road. Silently, the three riders stripped saddles from weary horses and picketed the animals on ropes. Working slowly in the dark, Wendy tried to make no sound. If what Kurt said was true, wild Indians were all about them, simply waiting for unsuspecting travelers to pass.

By the dim light of a single star in the black night, she watched the cowboys spread their blankets and roll in them, not making any sound as they went to sleep, ignoring the bitter cold. Wendy sought her own bed with chattering teeth, not bothering to remove coat or boots. She gripped her blankets to her throat as she stared up at the lone star. Shudders raced through her body, and she slowly warmed, her teeth clenched together to stop their racket.

"Lord, what am I doing out here?" Her whisper broke the deep silence. Not even the wind stirred, and Wendy hoped that only Jesus heard her prayer.

"I was safe at home just a month ago. Now father is dead, my family home is threatened, and I'm chasing fairy tales in the desert." She paused and searched the black covering above, searching for … for what? Did she really believe the gold existed? What had made her trust these two men and the journal entry in her grandfather's diary? Was she a fool?

"Father, I only want to do the right thing. I'm not sure I'll find the treasure, but I know you wanted me to try. This adventure is no accident. And I hope you achieve the results you want. Grow me, stretch my faith, help me learn to trust you more. You have a plan for me, but I can't figure it out. Yet I know whatever happens on this journey will bring me closer to you if I allow it."

The black sky revealed nothing to her heartfelt plea, and Wendy sighed, wiggling her toes in her boots. "All right, Jesus. Your will, not mine. Do with me as you want."

The next day they struck the Canadian River. Wendy gazed at a stand of willow trees, their bare white branches stretching like bones to the steel-gray sky. Rocky outcroppings rose from every hillock, and there didn't seem to be a flat, level place anywhere in sight.

Kurt gestured at the rough terrain. "Willow Springs. Good water. The river is difficult to approach with wagons. The teamsters on the Old Trail prefer this watering hole to the Canadian yonder."

He scanned the region while Miguel studied their back trail. The former army scout reported only a glimpse of riders in the distance, too far away to tell if they were the pair from the fort. He added something to his remark, and Kurt chuckled.

"What's so funny?" Wendy didn't like the desert that stretched all around them. Even the roaring river seemed less impressive than the Arkansas River or even the Purgatory where Kurt's ranch was located.

Kurt hooked a thumb at the Indian. "Miguel says one of the men had half an ear, a big gold hoop in the other. Sounds like a pirate."

LASTING TREASURE

Wendy felt the cold shiver travel down her back but wasn't sure the sensation was from the frigid weather around her. Didn't one of Randall Whitmore's watchdogs have only half an ear and a gold hoop?

"Shouldn't we get going?" She glanced at their back trail as a sense of apprehension mounted.

Kurt and Miguel took turns leading and locating a winding route through the hills between the Santa Fe Trail and the Canadian River, always heading to the south. When Wendy asked why they couldn't simply follow the easier road, Kurt pressed his lips into a tight line. "For a few reasons. We're being followed. If they don't really want us, they'll pass on the road. Also, Indians watching the trail won't expect us moving through the brush and hills. And we want to find the Mora. Even though its miles ahead, we cannot afford to pass the river."

The hills worked to shield the trio from the ceaseless wind, and Wendy didn't mind the slower pace. A weak sun broke through the gray canopy, and a faint suggestion of the coming spring teased their long day. By late afternoon, they'd only covered twenty miles.

"Will we ever get there at this rate?" Wendy grumbled as she picked up sticks. Miguel looked after the horses while Kurt prepared a meal.

"I'm as anxious as you to go faster," he growled as he struck a match. The dry wood gave off very little smoke, but Kurt kept the blaze small, tucked into the bottom of a hole he dug. "I need to hurry to beat those other fools if I hope to marry Marigold. She won't wait forever."

"Will she wait at all?" Wendy muttered to herself as she gathered more firewood, but Kurt heard her anyway.

"What's that? You think she won't wait for me?" He stared with angry eyes as Wendy approached the fire.

The sticks clattered to the ground beside Kurt and Wendy wiped her hands. "I don't know. I do know I saw her dance with more than a few men Saturday night."

"She's very popular," Kurt snapped, glaring at Wendy.

She bit her tongue and poured coffee into three mugs. The riders ate in silence until the meal was finished, Kurt glowering as he kicked dirt on the small fire. "And she told me she would marry me," he blurted as he packed gear and handed the packs to Miguel to load on the horses. "I haven't asked her pa for her hand yet, but we're as good as engaged."

Wendy arched an eyebrow. "But she danced with a lot of men."

Kurt threw up his hands and stalked to his horse. He mounted and settled into the saddle, his eyes locked on Wendy. "I said she's popular. All the men want to marry her. But she chose me. She loves me."

Wendy mounted and tugged on the reins, following behind Miguel as the Indian led the way. She could hear Kurt muttering under his breath behind her, but she ignored him, angry at herself for speaking her mind. What business was it of hers? She didn't care who Kurt Jordan married.

Miguel turned in his saddle and narrowed his dark eyes as he studied her silently. She felt he could see through her and read her thoughts, and she shifted uneasily. The Yaqui seemed to want to say something, to tell her something, but then he scowled and turned around, his back as stiff as a ramrod.

Somehow, she felt reprimanded, as if Miguel were telling her to be patient. Or to speak her mind again and not allow Kurt to share his silly ideas about Marigold Peterson. Of course, she had no idea what he was thinking. The quiet man rarely even spoke to Kurt in his rough Spanish, and Wendy tilted her head, suddenly curious.

She tugged on her reins and waited while Kurt came alongside her. He wouldn't look at her and for a while, they rode beside one another in silence.

"How well do you know him?" At his glance, she motioned

toward Miguel. "He only speaks Spanish, and he used to work for the army. He saved you from starvation and gave you a home, but what do you know about him?"

His downcast face altered with her question, and he grinned, lifting his head as he pushed his hat back. The dark stubble that surrounded his mouth could not conceal his firm jaw, and Wendy admired his high cheekbones and the nose that looked as if it might've been broken in the past. Despite his unruly hair and soiled clothing, a boyish glow radiated from him as he spoke of his hero.

"He's kind. I guess I'll say that first. He didn't have to lend me a hand when he found me, but he did. Of course, he loves the Lord, and he shared his faith with me. I accepted Christ when I was seventeen."

He chuckled and pulled his hat low again, shaking his head. "Not that I didn't give him a fight first. Oh, we would argue. But the Lord called me to him, and I eventually submitted, accepting his sacrifice on the cross and his promise of eternal life."

"I know that," Wendy said with an impatient ring in her voice. "But what does he want from life? He used to work with the army, and he followed you to Trinidad where you started your ranch. But where does he fit in?"

Kurt shrugged, adopting an air of indifference. "Wherever he wants. He's like my big brother. He goes where I want to go, and I go where he wants to go. We're a team."

"But your ranch doesn't include him," Wendy persisted. "The Slash J is for Jordan."

Kurt scratched his chin. "Well, no, not at all. Like I said, we're together. For always. Family. But he won't put his name on anything. Says it's not right to claim things. He says you can claim a horse or a gun or personal belongings, but the land and ownership of large things scares him. The Yaqui believe the land should not be owned by anyone. The Spanish, the

Mexicans, and now the Americans do things that way, and he doesn't like the idea. But the ranch is half his, of course. What I have belongs to him and t'other way around."

He paused as Wendy processed this information. For a moment, they both watched Miguel as the Indian rode around a clump of leafless bushes. "And as for Spanish," Kurt went on suddenly. "He can speak English pretty well but prefers Spanish. I learned the language working the docks around New Orleans when I was young, running messages for ship captains or asking Spanish ships for work."

He paused again and smiled at Wendy. "I speak French too. I can read, write, and speak a few different languages, but I only went to school for a couple of years when I was at the orphanage."

"No other family?"

He shook his head, his smile never faltering. "I have Miguel. He's my brother." He squinted at her, and she tensed, wondering if he were going to turn the curiosity around. "And your family? I know your ma is gone. But you have Aunt Lil."

A frown creased her face, but she hoped he couldn't see her sorrow behind her scarf. "Just me and Aunt Lil. My mother died when I was young, and Father died last month."

"Last month?" He seemed to ponder for a minute and then nodded. "Now I think I'm beginning to understand the need for hurry to find the treasure. Your pa must have left you in a fix."

Wendy didn't reply, her thoughts drifting to the rundown Moylan Plantation. Although a large garden remained, there would be no one but her and Lil to tend the great home if they returned. And how would they fix up the broken down exterior after repaying Whitmore? Could they make a go of it? Would the local society she had shunned embrace them still?

Reluctantly, Wendy had learned how to dance and mingle among the elite of Little Rock. As a member of the old class of wealthy citizens, she was expected to participate in many situations she dreaded and eventually dodged. Her grief had at first knotted within her, making it difficult for her to cope with the loss of a strong and independent mother. Wendy could barely breathe after her mother died, her love and comfort and guidance gone forever. Aunt Lil's arrival had helped tremendously, yet even now, Wendy wondered where her place was. Did she belong anywhere?

"So, the gold will solve your problems."

Kurt's unexpected remark brought Wendy back to the present. The gold. That's what she was doing out here, she reminded herself quickly, finding an anchor to cling to. She had a job to complete, a task that stretched her strength, her faith, and her abilities. Yet would the gold solve all of her problems?

She looked at Kurt, suddenly envious of his friends, his rustic ranch, and even his pursuit of Marigold Peterson. Kurt knew what he wanted, and he went after it with vigor. Perhaps a little foolishly and without the patience Wendy would have applied, but he got things done. Part of her admired his tenacity.

"The gold might help," she admitted. Her words sounded unsure even to her own ears.

CHAPTER THIRTY-FOUR

"That's not very big or impressive." Wendy frowned when she saw the Mora River, the smaller waterway pouring into the Canadian with a lack of ferocity she'd hoped to find in such an important landmark.

"It'll grow when snow melts on the higher mountains," Kurt assured her. He gestured to the tall peaks to the west. "On the other side of this range is the Rio Grande that flows from Colorado down through New Mexico to turn east and forms the border between Texas and Mexico."

Wendy recalled the image of the map in the leather journal and nodded. She was precisely where she needed to be to begin the search for the hidden gold. A cold wind blew from the nearby mountains, and she shivered, hunkering down into her coat.

"When will that be? It feels like spring will never arrive," she muttered.

Kurt laughed, and even Miguel smiled. "Out here, you need to be patient. And then, when you believe spring will never come, the trees bud, green leaves unfold as if overnight, the prairie grass grows, and the cold retreats until next winter."

Miguel said something, and Kurt nodded. "Yes, March is almost over. I'm sure April is soon upon us."

"I left Arkansas on March first," Wendy volunteered as she considered how many days remained for her to search before she needed to return to Little Rock. Her brow wrinkled as she recalled the riverboat trip in the rain from her home, the interminable stagecoach ride to Trinidad, the unexpectedly rewarding work on Kurt and Miguel's ranch, and the hurried preparations for the journey to the Mora River. Could it be that almost four weeks had passed?

She remembered her father's funeral at the end of February and knew it was true. How swiftly time had flown! With a shock, she realized that unlike her mother's death that had led to such intense grief and sorrow—a sense of loss that overwhelmed her, her father's untimely death had prompted her into quick action she now appreciated. Having something to do, to think about, and prepare for had kept her moving forward, kept her planning.

Wendy peered at the little river and smiled. A cold wind buffeted her, but something felt different about the breeze, and she pointed her nose to the sky, inhaling deeply.

Miguel grunted, and she peered at the Indian. He smiled and gestured all around, saying something in Spanish.

"He says you have sharp senses, like an Indian. He's proud of your ability to smell the coming spring," Kurt explained as he dismounted and started gathering sticks.

Wendy felt her eyes widen, and she looked at Miguel. "Really? Spring is in the air?"

He nodded, but held up a hand, signaling patience.

They made dinner on the high banks of the Canadian, their tiny fire shielded by a large boulder and a clump of mesquite. "After dinner, we'll cross the river and make camp in Apache country tonight," Kurt said in an excited whisper as his gaze swept the land to the west. "This will be the last of the fires and coffee for a while," he announced, lifting his steaming cup for emphasis.

As Miguel kicked sand over the glowing coals and Kurt packed their gear, they discussed the leather-bound journal and the entry that outlined the directions to the hidden gold. Twilight descended over the desert as they splashed across the Canadian River to locate a suitable camp and begin the probe. Yet after three days of searching, they had found nothing. As each stream that poured into the river was explored, Wendy thrilled, believing they'd found the lost treasure. But each fruitless search netted nothing but skinned hands and knees as they crouched and crawled to investigate every crevice and hole.

"You know Gomez said the particular stream joined the Mora from the north," Kurt advised for the third time after searching yet another small rivulet of water that dribbled into the Mora River.

"I know that," Wendy snapped as she sat on a rocky ledge and leaned her face up to the sunlight. Back in these narrow gullies, the chill wind had difficulty finding them, and the dull sun often warmed them, a little heat reflected from the rocks close by on either side. Her scarf sagged around her throat, and Wendy could feel a trickle of sweat rolling down her back beneath her unbuttoned coat.

"Come on," Kurt said as he heaved himself to his feet. "Miguel will be worrying about us."

Long shadows stretched across the desert, and Wendy felt surprised at the late hour. The sun that had followed their progress all day now leaned far to the west. The narrow gully lay shrouded in shadow as the rock walls narrowed. Wendy and Kurt stole stealthily down the small canyon where it opened upon the Mora River and the water leaped and splashed noisily around submerged boulders. Yet the little river seemed so tame compared to her mighty Arkansas River from back home, nearly a mile wide near town.

Kurt paused and studied the river for ten minutes before venturing out of their narrow chasm and onto the riverbank. Slowly, they made their way downriver to their concealed camp.

Miguel handed each of them a biscuit and a piece of jerked meat. The defeated looks they wore must have been enough information for the silent Indian. No one spoke while they ate, the twilight deepening all around as Wendy leaned against a rock and chewed her simple fare. Fatigue nagged at her, but she could feel they must be close. *Tomorrow. Tomorrow we will find the gold.*

She hated when her mind reminded her she had thought these same words the last three days. Disappointment threatened, and Wendy pursed her lips, resolved to keep searching. Surely, there could not be so many streams that poured into the Mora that they couldn't find the right one.

"Gomez wrote it was the third stream that poured into the Mora from the north. We've searched the second stream and the third and the fourth and the fifth. Then we went back to the third one again and searched the stream thoroughly for a second time."

The two riders seemed to ignore her complaint and Wendy narrowed her eyes, squinting at Kurt as if the cowboy had something to do with their failure. "Well?" Her icy demand made him look up from his meager meal.

"Well, what?" His challenging tone made her bristle.

"Well, you're the guide. Guide us to the gold."

Kurt glanced at Miguel and the Indian shrugged. "There's no way of telling if the streams we're searching are the same ones from forty years ago. Trees fall and block streams. Landslides alter a stream's course. Springs dry up. Any number of things could've happened to create a different route or an entirely different stream than the ones that were here forty years ago." Kurt picked up a small stone and tossed the pebble at a bigger rock.

"So, you're giving up?"

Wendy's query made him look at her in the dim light. "No, Wendy, I'm not giving up. We will continue to be patient and search every stream we find, but we may never find that lost gold."

He hesitated and then sighed. "We have no idea how many men Gomez told this story to. Perhaps the gold was found and taken away years ago."

Wendy shook her head, her heart feeling heavy in her ribs. "No, I can't believe that. I won't believe that. The Lord led me here. The wild trip from Little Rock and the hard work I've done, it all points to some deeper meaning, as if Jesus is with me but wants me to keep digging, keep looking. I know it must be here. It *has to* be. God wouldn't drag me out here for nothing, right?"

Miguel interjected, and Wendy scowled as she turned to Kurt for interpretation. "God will do anything that brings the results he wants. If he wants to grow your faith or teach you a lesson, he will do anything to get your attention."

A faraway look came over him, and Kurt smiled wryly. "Lonely orphanages, starvation, tragedy, and sorrow. God will use everything to bring folks to him."

Her selfish demands made her feel ashamed, and Wendy placed a hand on his arm. "I'm sorry, Kurt. I'm worrying only about myself, and I forgot you have a stake in this too. Forgive me. We'll try again tomorrow."

He stared down at her hand and then nodded. "Get some sleep. I'm tired, and it'll get cold tonight."

Despite the early hour, they rolled in their blankets. They'd not enjoyed an evening fire for days and the threat of Indian attacks loomed over them like a spring storm, hovering on the horizon, waiting to unload its ferocity when least expected.

Wendy stretched her weary muscles and looked at the unbelievably clear night sky. Countless stars glittered overhead, and Wendy relaxed, allowing her mind to release her frightening anxieties and cling to the sensation that God had truly brought her out here for some reason.

"Let me surrender, Jesus. Let me trust that you have a purpose for this journey, whatever it may be. I don't understand what you want from me, but I will obey, I will trust you. I am here because you walk with me. Do with me as you wish."

Early the next day, Miguel joined them as the searchers crept through the dim light of dawn. Painstakingly, they counted each of the streams that entered the Mora from the north and spent hours seeking a crevice below rock ledges, a scrap of leather or fragment of bone that indicated a rotted pack saddle or the sun-bleached bones of a pack mule.

"Perhaps Gomez said the wrong stream, or your grandfather wrote it down all wrong," Kurt suggested that evening as they grouped around their fireless campsite.

"What do you mean?" Wendy stared at the fading sun as the orange sphere dropped behind a distant peak. The sunsets were surprisingly beautiful in the desert, and Wendy found herself looking forward to each one as they combed the countryside for the lost treasure. Although she dearly missed hot coffee and a warm meal, she couldn't say she was having a horrible time. Miguel and Kurt had become friends she felt comfortable with, and the cowboys discussed things with her easily, as if they accepted her presence without question. At first, she felt a little annoyed they didn't treat her like a girl, but then reveled in the newfound freedom that wearing boy's britches had provided. Still, sometimes she wished Kurt would say something kind to her or make an observation about her ponytail or even the inappropriate clothing she wore. Any indication that he remembered she was a girl. Hadn't they danced together at the sawmill? The memory of being in his arms never failed to make the heat steal up her neck, yet Kurt seemed oblivious and informal around her, never letting on if he recalled the night they'd danced together.

The cowboy shifted and reached for another strip of jerked meat. "I'll be ready soon for coffee and a real meal," he grumbled as he bit a piece from the tough meat. He chewed for a minute before he explained.

"Maybe Gomez panicked when he ran down the creek and joined the other soldiers on the Mora. Perhaps he incorrectly remembered which side of the river the little stream joined the river. If a bunch of Apache were chasing me, I might not recall exact details."

Miguel nodded and said something. Kurt nodded. "I think we'll check the other side of the river tomorrow, make sure we're not missing anything. If we don't find any sign, then we go farther up the river and try more of the small streams that feed the Mora."

Wendy agreed and they all climbed into their blankets. In the morning light, they ate cold biscuits and drank colder water before they picked up their weapons and started for the nearby river. Wendy tagged behind Miguel and Kurt as the trio left their hiding place among the rocks and she bumped into the Indian when he stopped abruptly in the trail. As she peered over his shoulder, she saw two men sitting on their horses, guns pointed at the cowboys as the strangers smiled, their dirty faces dully reflecting the morning sun.

CHAPTER THIRTY-FIVE

Wendy stared at the two men, comprehension dawning. She knew these men, the ripped ear and the golden hoop of the one confirming her suspicions.

"Kincaid and Brewer," she breathed loud enough for Kurt and Miguel to hear.

Miguel spoke, and Kurt sighed. "You've known these two men were on our trail from Fort Union. Why didn't you say so?" His words held a stinging accusation Wendy didn't like, yet she knew he was right. Why hadn't she said something? Certainly, Miguel and Kurt had the right to know they were being followed, that she was being followed. The long arm of Randall Whitmore had reached into the frontier and found Wendy, despite her efforts to give him the slip.

As the two spies walked their horses closer, Wendy whispered. "I couldn't believe Randall would send them all the way out here to keep an eye on me."

"Randall?" Kurt hissed, and then, the two louts were upon them. Kincaid pointed with his rifle barrel, a sneer plastered across his dirty face.

"Well, well, Brewer, look what we found."

Brewer smiled and Wendy noticed again the wide gap in his teeth. "You were right, Kincaid. You said we had only to wait at Fort Union, and they'd show up."

Wendy felt her chest tighten, but she fought off the apprehension and fear that writhed within her. Her friends were in danger, and an unfamiliar courage spurred her forward. She brushed past the two cowboys to face her accusers. "How did you know I'd be here?"

Kurt shifted behind her, and Brewer lifted the muzzle of his rifle. "Stay put, you and the Indian. This is between Miss Moylan and us. Stay out of it and no one gets hurt."

"We're only here to, well, encourage you," Kincaid interjected with a malicious smile Wendy didn't trust. "Mr. Whitmore told us your pa said something long ago about a hidden treasure on the Mora River that the family considered chasing. When you disappeared and the trail led west, he told us to come to Fort Union and hang around the Mora River country. We waited weeks, and Brewer thought you'd gone somewhere else, but I told him to be patient."

The two men chuckled, and Wendy felt her palms moisten, despite the cold. These were dangerous men, and she worried for herself and her friends. Then she remembered they were in Apache lands, and she lifted her chin. They were all in danger, these two idiots from Little Rock as well as her small party of explorers.

She glanced over her shoulder and took in the angry looks on Miguel and Kurt's faces before she scanned the surrounding area. The sun had just risen over the eastern plains, and she knew they must get moving if they intended to search the small streams that entered the Mora from the south. She faced the newcomers and placed her hands on her hips.

"So, what now? You found me, but we haven't discovered the treasure."

Kincaid nodded, his smile replaced by a sudden scowl. "Our orders are clear. You haven't much time to find the money you owe Mr. Whitmore. You have to return to Little Rock by the end of April."

"Don't tell me my business," Wendy snapped.

Kincaid chuckled again and licked his lips. "Brewer, ain't she pretty when she gets riled?"

Miguel stepped to one side and reached for his horse pistol, but Brewer pulled the hammer back on his rifle and the sharp sound stilled everyone. "Don't move," Brewer warned, and Kincaid started backing his horse.

"We're just making sure you're searching for the treasure, Miss Moylan. And we wish you luck," he called over his shoulder as he tugged the reins and guided his horse from the sandy bench beside the river. Brewer followed his partner, and they spurred their horses, the two men galloping away, a cloud of dust lingering behind them.

Kurt turned slowly, glowering at Wendy. "You have a lot of explaining to do, Miss Moylan," he spat as Miguel herded them back into the narrow ravine where they camped. Despite her mounting anger and apprehension, she remembered where they were, and she appreciated Miguel's caution. The Apache would hear loud voices or running horses if they were not careful. Though unseen, Kurt had assured her the hostile Indians lurked everywhere and anywhere, ready to attack unsuspecting travelers without warning.

When they reached camp, Miguel drew his big pistol and stretched on the rim of the ravine to watch, peering all around sharply. Kurt glared, his brows bunching as he studied her. "Randall Whitmore? And who were those two thugs?"

Wendy shifted and wrung her hands. How much to share? Her family estate was in danger and only the lost gold could save her now. Surely her and Lil's very existence depended on them discovering the treasure and slipping out of Apache lands before the Indians learned of their presence.

Before she could reply, Kurt went on. "Is it even true about your parents passing away? Did your pa really die last month?"

Kurt's doubts made her wince, and Wendy nodded hurriedly. "Oh, yes, my father died. At his funeral, Mr. Whitmore, my father's business partner, told me Father owed him a great deal of money. If I don't find this gold and pay him back, I will lose my family's property. I have nothing else. Although the plantation is almost worthless, Aunt Lil and I have nowhere else to go."

Kurt turned to pace the confines of the sandy ravine, a scowl darkening his features as he marched up and down. He glanced at Miguel and said something in Spanish. When Miguel responded, Wendy stepped forward. "What? What are you planning?"

Kurt squinted and faced her. "I'm planning on doing what I came here for. My future depends on this lost treasure, but now we're in more danger than before. With those two raising dust and making noise, we'll have to move almighty careful. We can't afford for the Apache to find us."

He tapped Miguel's boot and led the way toward the mouth of the ravine as Miguel shimmied to the sandy trail and joined them. Kurt scouted the silent terrain, and then turned on Wendy. "We're all doing our best. This gold could mean a lot to all of us." His tone was brusque, almost icy. Then his voice lowered and his scowl softened. "I need you to be honest with us, Wendy. I can't stress enough how much we're risking here. Please don't hold anything back from us. It's not fair to me and Miguel."

"I know. I'm sorry. I never thought that Whitmore's men would come this far. I truly believed Aunt Lil and I left them in Arkansas." Wendy smarted beneath his piercing stare. Something made her feel worse about hurting Kurt than the danger of the invisible Apache or the two henchmen from Randall Whitmore. She tried to smile, to reassure Kurt of her sincerity. He nodded but didn't smile in return.

LASTING TREASURE

For the next five days, the trio continued to explore every small stream that poured into the Mora from the south. Although this was contradictory to Gomez's instructions to Sean Moylan, the northern streams had netted nothing of value.

As the weather slowly warmed and spring arrived in tiny measure upon the New Mexico plains, Wendy, Kurt, and Miguel spent the days searching every rivulet and creek, regardless of size or their number from the mouth of the Mora. None of the streams from either side of the river revealed any sign of previous travelers.

Wendy began to wonder if they were wasting their efforts. She searched every crevice and narrow gap between rock ledges. Any space where a few leather sacks of gold could be hidden or concealed.

They found nothing as they went from ravine to streambed to creek. Her feet ached and the taste of the cold jerked meat and sourdough biscuits now turned to sawdust in her mouth. She craved a hot meal with steaming coffee and fresh meat. Their bland diet, the hard ground she slept on each night, and the cold winds that blew down from the nearby mountains grated on her nerves. Her cheeks and lips had chapped from the relentless wind, and her stomach growled incessantly. Her body ached from the constant hiking and crawling, and she wished they'd find the elusive treasure and leave New Mexico forever.

What if they never found the loot? Her thoughts turned to this disappointing concept more and more as the days passed. They might find nothing. Then what?

Wendy glanced at Kurt where he searched a rocky crevice, his gloved hand snaking between the stone walls. He'd searched just as thoroughly as she did. His marriage to Marigold Peterson depended on locating the gold that would provide the wealth Marigold demanded. Something sour poisoned her guts at the memory of the haughty ranch girl with Kurt, but Wendy pushed the image aside. She needed the money too.

Kincaid and Brewer had vanished. Miguel reported seeing the two sentinels only once, riding their horses across the Canadian River, far to the east, along the Santa Fe Trail. But they all knew Whitmore's henchmen hovered, keeping an eye on Wendy as the trio continued to seek the lost treasure.

Kurt kept his distance from Wendy. Whether he felt driven to locate the lost gold or worried he could no longer trust her, he avoided Wendy. His absence pierced her, making her miss him in ways she didn't want to explore. Yet their fledgling friendship had blossomed with such promise. She'd never had friends she enjoyed. After countless rebuffs to the young people of Little Rock, they had finally left her strictly alone. At first, she appreciated the space as she grieved for her mother. Later—too late—she'd realized Aunt Lil's concerns were well founded, and she became desperately lonely. Only Mary and Jasmine broke the social isolation Wendy had exiled herself into.

"Except for you, Jesus," she muttered as she paused to push rocks from a narrow crack between two boulders. "Mother and Lil and Mary were right. You never leave me or forsake me."

Her boots grated on gravel as she moved up the winding streambed to explore other possible hiding places. She glanced over her shoulder to see where Kurt and Miguel silently searched other crevices in the same waterway.

"You are always with me, Lord. You've become my constant companion. I can always count on you to know me, to walk with me, wherever I go. But what am I doing here?"

She paused again and stretched her aching back, her face lifting to the warming sun. Little of the chilled wind from the open plains swept down into these narrow watercourses that drained the mountainous terrain into the nearby Mora River. A hint of spring teased in the vibrant blue sky overhead and the small trickle of sweat that rolled down her back. Wendy unbuttoned her heavy hunter's coat and wiped a hand across her brow as she studied the pair of drifting clouds that seemed to float just out of reach, like fluffy sheep ready to shear.

"Why did you bring me all the way out here to find nothing? Could you be so cruel to lead me on a wild goose chase?"

Her gaze shifted to Kurt, and Wendy dropped her eyes, ashamed of her lack of attention while she spoke with God. She recalled Kurt asking her about her favorite Scripture verse and that she couldn't think of one, always relying before on her mother's or Lil's training rather than developing her own spiritual ideas. Had her faith always been so shallow?

"Forgive me, Father. I don't want to be distracted from your purpose. You brought me west to find treasure, to save me and Aunt Lil, right? I have no doubt that you are intentional in all that you do. Kurt is only a friend, yet I care for him. It's good to have friends again, like when I was a little girl. He's kind to me, or at least he was before he learned about Mr. Whitmore. I didn't mean to hurt him, Jesus."

She shook her head and turned away, striding slowly up the steep ravine, looking for more hiding places. "Oh, Lord, what am I doing here and why does my heart feel so confused? Help me know your will and give me the strength to follow you, to not give in to the fear that nags at me. I know you would not have me marry an unbeliever, so let me submit to you, whatever you choose for me. Whether poverty or loneliness or even death, I want to obey you. I give you my willing heart and pray I may find favor in your sight."

CHAPTER THIRTY-SIX

The next morning, while the sun still hid below the eastern horizon, Miguel stirred in his blankets. Wendy awakened and stared up at the deep blue of dawn as the night sky prepared to change color.

She loved this time of morning, when the dark night passed and the promise of a new day lingered just beyond. Everything was new, fresh, and Wendy could hope this might be the day they discovered the lost treasure.

Miguel sat up and tugged on his boots before shrugging into his worn blue army coat. Wendy lay still and listened as he moved stealthily up the narrow ravine to where the horses were picketed on a patch of grass beside a small spring.

His footsteps died away, and she stretched beneath her warm covers. The thought of more hard biscuits and the tough jerked meat made her grimace, and she wished they could risk a fire and make a warm meal. The memory of hot coffee made her mouth water, but she sat up and dressed hurriedly, stomping into her boots as a gray light tinged the eastern sky. She shivered and wrapped a blanket around her shoulders as she glanced toward the still sleeping Kurt and dragged her fingers through her tangled hair, securing the bunched mess into a tight ponytail. What she wouldn't give for a hot bath.

She smiled when she recalled the night of the dance at the sawmill and the simple dress she'd worn. Her smile trembled when she remembered the way this handsome cowboy had held her in his arms, firm and yet courteously, confident yet respectful.

A wave of heat spread across her cheeks, burning her with embarrassment, and she turned away, pulling the blanket tighter around her. She was here to find gold, to return home with the money to pay her father's debt. The old plantation would still be hers and Aunt Lil would always have a place to live.

A scowl creased her features and Wendy felt her eyes narrow as she glanced up at the dark peaks. Aunt Lil would be safe, comfortable, taken care of, but what about Wendy? Something had stirred within her these past weeks, calling to her, beckoning her to ... what? The challenging trip to the frontier and the hard work with the cowboys had awakened something unfamiliar in her, and a smile tugged at her lips. The wide-open plains and the towering peaks of the Rocky Mountains made her realize there was so much of America she'd never thought of. Her little corner of Little Rock with its low hills and fallow fields surrounded by dense undergrowth had been enough for her. Her isolation had allowed her to grieve and mourn for her mother, producing an unexpected loneliness she had at first reveled in. Now she loathed being alone, and the new sensations of making friends and riding unexplored lands and new experiences thrilled her in ways she'd never dreamed. Like a flower blossoming in springtime, opening its petals to the warm sun, Wendy felt opened to unknown experiences for the first time in her life.

Her gaze drifted again to where the young cowboy slept, and she knew it wasn't only new lands and new experiences that called her west. But he was an engaged man. Her chest tightened when she remembered she might be an engaged woman.

She rummaged in the canvas pack for the boring food stores, but her smile didn't fade. She'd come alive on this journey west. Her lungs felt filled with fresh, intoxicating air, and her soul wanted to sing. Despite her concerns about Mr. Whitmore and the responsibilities she felt for Aunt Lil, Wendy felt an exhilaration that surprised her.

Kurt stirred and rolled on his side, propping on an elbow as he watched her pull food from the bag.

"Good morning, sunshine," he whispered lazily, keeping his voice low. He yawned and scratched his chin as his gaze swept the dark little campsite.

Wendy handed him a chunk of hard as rock sourdough biscuit. He wrinkled his nose and popped the tidbit into his mouth, chewing slowly. "I want coffee and pancakes and bacon with about a dozen eggs and more coffee."

Wendy chuckled, pleased to be speaking casually with Kurt once more, like before. He'd been distant since Kincaid and Brewer had confronted them last week, but now he seemed more like his old self.

"Your hair looks longer," he observed as he kicked back his blankets and stepped into his boots. Shrugging into his coat, he tugged his hat low and accepted the tin cup of cold water Wendy handed him.

"And you need a shave more than ever," she replied, not able to keep the teasing lilt from her words. His nearness never ceased to affect her, and today she wanted to be close to him, to enjoy his company, talk to him about the fruitless search and the warming spring days, and listen to his plans for his ranch. She wanted to forget the deadline Randall Whitmore had given her and the not knowing what she and Lil were going to do if they didn't find the gold. She wanted to forget her responsibilities and the nagging anxieties that wouldn't leave her alone.

"Is Miguel with the horses?"

Wendy nodded, breaking off a piece of jerked meat and handing the chunk to Kurt. "He always tucks that big horse pistol in his pocket and disappears into the night. I wonder how he knows it's time to get up," she said as she took a bite of a cold biscuit. "Like a clock, he just seems to know when dawn is near."

"El reloj de los Yaquis," Kurt said, pointing his tin cup at a dimming star in the sky. "The clock of the Yaquis, the big dipper, tells him what time it is. His people have used the stars for centuries."

She glanced at the sky but watched Kurt from the corner of her eye. He stood tall in the early light, and Wendy felt safe in his presence. Was this how friendship with men was supposed to feel?

She wiped her hands on her pants. "I need to wash up. Seems like it might be warm today. Maybe I'll leave my coat in camp." She hugged herself and smiled. "But still too cold right now."

Wendy bent to retrieve her towel and started for the river, slinging the thin cotton cloth over her shoulder.

Kurt tucked a towel under his arm as he buttoned his coat, following her to the river.

She felt uneasy as he walked behind her, as if she should look a certain way or wear her hair a special style. She shook her head as she remembered they soon would resume their search up another creek bed or small stream Miguel scouted for them and her appearance meant nothing. Nonetheless, she appreciated his proximity in ways she didn't like to consider. Her emotions had been so flustered since arriving in Trinidad, and Wendy wondered if the altitude had anything to do with her unbalanced feelings.

They paused at the opening to the ravine and peered up and down the river but saw nothing to worry them. Their boots made no sound on the sand as they crossed the open shelf to the rim of the riverbank, sliding down the steep side before skidding to a halt at the edge of the flowing water.

Wendy handed her blanket to Kurt and knelt, washing her face and hands, conscious that he watched. A thin crust of ice caressed the sandy bank, and a huge pile of driftwood lay only a dozen yards upriver, collected in a bend of the waterway. After her brief bathing, he draped the blanket around her shoulders before he washed his face, spluttering at the cold water.

She laughed, suddenly aware they were having fun together. Shyly, she stepped away, wondering if he would follow as she led the way back to camp. Kurt took her elbow and lifted her to the river's rim as Wendy mumbled her thanks, drawing the blanket tightly around her. She watched him scramble up the bank and stood beside him for a moment before they started on for camp, side by side. As if an unspoken truce had descended, Wendy thrilled anew at his presence, his nearness, his friendship. She'd missed Kurt when they sparred, and she didn't want any trouble between them.

They both stopped at the same instant, Wendy's eyes widening as she recognized the two riders in the dim, gray light. The sound of their hooves had been masked by the river, and now Kincaid and Brewer sat on their horses a dozen yards away, grinning at Wendy and Kurt.

"Isn't that sweet, Brewer. The cowboy puts a blanket around her like she's a queen. And she's engaged to another man."

Brewer chuckled. "Doesn't matter now. She'll never see Mr. Whitmore again."

Wendy straightened, glaring at the louts. "What do you want? We haven't found the treasure yet."

The riders scowled as they exchanged glances and Brewer leaned and spat a dark stream of tobacco. The sun was just rising behind them, outlining their profile in the morning dim. "Well, that answers our question. You see, we talked it over on the ride west, and we decided to give you a chance to find that treasure. But we never figured on letting you go home, with or without the loot."

Wendy tensed and she sensed Kurt stiffen beside her. They were in danger and they both knew it.

Kincaid lifted his rifle and pointed the barrel at Kurt. "The war is almost over, and we're tired of the lack of food and the constant scratching out a living. We're both deserters and don't want to go back. The North will have bigger pickings for men like us. We've been waiting for you to find the gold, but you haven't, and we're done waiting. No one will miss you, and no one will find you out here."

He paused and licked his lips as his gaze devoured her, and Wendy read the malicious intent in his beady eyes.

"The cowboy will die first, and we'll have a little fun with you before you die. Then we'll take your gear and scat," Brewer explained with a casualness that sickened Wendy. She knew they were right. No one would ever find their bodies out here. No doubt, wild animals would tear their flesh and scatter their bones. With a rush of dread, Wendy realized she was about to die.

She glanced at Kurt, wanting to say something, but he squinted at the shadows beyond the two horses and leaned closer to Wendy. "Get ready to run," he whispered out of the corner of his mouth.

"I hope you said goodbye," Kincaid said as he cocked his rifle, the sound ringing loudly in the still morning.

Wendy squeezed her eyes shut, unable to see what was going to happen. They would kill Kurt and assault her, but she was wondering at her anger at Kurt's death. They'd been friends, but suddenly she wished he could live and build his ranch and accomplish all of the things the Lord had for him. She wasn't worried about herself, knowing where she would go after death mercifully found her. Yet a sense of missing Kurt assailed her in a way that surprised her.

Kurt groped for her hand as she heard the two riders snicker. Eyes still closed, she imagined Kincaid lifting the rifle to his shoulder. She held her breath, waiting for the shot, squeezing Kurt's hand tightly.

LASTING TREASURE

A sudden gasp and then Brewer's scream split the morning calm. Kurt pulled on her arm. "Run!"

CHAPTER THIRTY-SEVEN

Wendy's eyes fluttered open in time to see bronzed men leaping atop Kincaid and Brewer's prancing horses, black hair streaming as their knives gleamed in the dim morning light. At least four Indians vaulted silently and overpowered the pair of mounted men. The blanket slipped from her shoulders as Wendy found her footing and raced after Kurt, the heavy booms of Miguel's horse pistol filling the air as the screams died away behind her.

Sunlight dappled the ripples of the dark river and Kurt splashed into the water, dragging Wendy downriver. He ran to the east, legs pumping furiously through the water as Wendy struggled to follow.

As if in a frenzy, Kurt spun and raced upstream, and Wendy saw the look of concentration etched into his features as he plowed the river, making way toward the pile of driftwood she'd seen earlier.

"Kurt?" Her call was lost in the leaping water, and she allowed him to maneuver her against the log jam, the wild scene on the bank above lost to her sight.

"In here," he hissed as he forced her between two logs and into the shadowed recesses of the pile of driftwood.

She scrambled farther into the darkness and lay prone atop a bleached tree trunk, various limbs and branches all around her, concealing her from any observer. Kurt crouched next to her, panting as he peered back the way they'd come. River water flowed murkily below the pile of logs and Wendy scowled, wondering why they hadn't continued running from the Indian attack.

"Kurt?"

"Shhh," he said quietly, still watching the high bank. He gripped her arm, and she looked at his hand, thankful for his company.

"Did ... did the Indians get them?"

Kurt nodded, not meeting her searching gaze.

"Why aren't we trying to get away, run downriver?"

"You can't run fast enough from Apache," he said grimly. "We left prints on the bank showing we went to the east, but I'm only trying to fool them. We can't move, Wendy. We must be quiet and hope they don't find us."

Wendy gritted her teeth and peered through the tangled underbrush and branches to the silent riverbank. Her heart pounded in her chest, and she tried to inhale slowly to calm her rattled nerves. But apprehension riveted her, and she felt taut, like a bent sapling ready to snap.

A horse snorted and Wendy saw the animal milling restlessly at the edge of the high bank, a splash of red across its saddle. She cringed. Surely Kincaid and Brewer were dead.

The lone horse drifted from sight. Nothing more stirred on the riverbank. As if the Indian attack had never occurred, silence fell all around them. A bird call from a nearby bush made Wendy wonder where Miguel had gone. Were the Apache still lurking along the river or had they discovered their camp and rummaged through their gear?

She was about to ask Kurt about Miguel when a pair of Indians stepped over the rim and slid down the bank, studying the boot tracks in the mud. Wendy held her breath and watched the pair lift their gaze from the ground to the east, obviously looking for signs of Kurt and Wendy.

LASTING TREASURE

She let her pent breath out when the two Apache walked along the bank, moving downriver, scanning the far bank. A moment later, two more Indians mounted on horses rode into the water and splashed across the noisy river. Leaning from their makeshift saddles, they looked for tracks on the opposite bank, never speaking, eyes darting everywhere.

Kurt's hand squeezed her arm, as if he were telling her to be quiet. But she couldn't speak even if she wanted to with her heart lodged in her throat. The Apache seemed to move with a methodical style as they silently searched both sides of the river, their bodies gleaming like dull copper in the rising sun. Their loose black hair blew gently in the breeze, and Wendy wondered where they'd come from. Had they been watching her and the cowboys? Did they know the three intruders searched for something in the little canyons that intersected the river? When had their camp been discovered by the Apache?

Her gaze shifted to the nearby rim of the riverbank where her blanket lay in a crumpled heap on the sand. Surely Kincaid and Brewer were there, their bodies lying on the sand as the sun shone down upon them. Could they have guessed today was their last day of life? Had they prepared in any way for life's end? Would anyone mourn them?

A shudder raced down her frame and Wendy thought of herself. Had she even begun to live? Hidden in the brush of the Arkansas River as she grieved her mother, had she allowed herself to heal? Sorrow and loneliness had become her constant companions, a familiar routine she'd gotten used to. But was that what the Lord wished for her? Grief was one of those things no one could tell you how to handle. Death and loss are inevitable, but everyone copes with the pain in different ways. Yet something whispered to Wendy the time had come to move on. She would always miss her vivacious mother and her love and support, but Wendy felt ready to begin again. Lil had said so, and Wendy suddenly agreed wholeheartedly. She wanted to live, to enjoy the days on earth God had given her.

Was this why the Lord brought her west? What other lessons had she learned from her journey to the frontier?

She gripped a dead branch in front of her. Had she learned her lesson too late? Now the Apache searched for her, and death hung in the morning air. Sunlight filtered around her through the jumble of broken branches, and Wendy wondered again if she were too late.

She glanced at Kurt. The cowboy squatted beside her in the gloom, intently scanning the river and the nearby bank and the distant hills. His lips trembled, and she realized his teeth chattered. Looking down, she saw he knelt in water up to his hips.

"Kurt, you're freezing," she whispered.

"I'm all right. Stay quiet."

"Do you want the blanket?" She pointed with her chin to the wrinkled material on the distant shore.

He shook his head. "Don't move."

She hesitated and then blurted, "Kincaid and Brewer. They're dead?"

He sighed, and Wendy could barely make out the scowl on his taut features. "The schemes of the wicked," he muttered, and she pressed him no further.

For the remainder of the day, they didn't move. The sun warmed the log pile, and Wendy even dozed as the hours passed. There was no sign of the Apache, and Wendy speculated if they'd successfully given them the slip. But where was Miguel? Her worry mounted as the day progressed.

Late in the day, a rider rode swiftly up the opposite bank. Wendy watched as the Indian shouted, hair streaming in the wind as he drove his ragged mustang toward their hiding place. Sheets of water splashed as the Indian continued to shout and plow the darkening waves, looking all around as he raced up the shallows on the other side of the river.

Kurt gripped her arm again and leaned close. "He's trying to flush anyone hiding. They don't know where we are."

His warm breath tickled her ear and Wendy tensed, but not from fear of the searching Indians.

"I'm glad you're with me."

"Shhh," he cautioned, still peering out through cracks between the heaped logs.

Shadows stretched across the river, the glittering sunlight that had danced on the waves all day finally dimming as twilight descended. Wendy shivered as the shadows deepened. She felt stiff from not moving and worried Kurt would freeze from kneeling in the cold water. But he didn't complain, and she marveled at his strength.

"What will we do when it gets dark?"

Her whispered query broke the extended silence as the pair hadn't spoken for hours. He shifted in the water and looked at her, squinting in the fading light.

"I have an idea," was all he'd say. She remembered he'd been near here before and pondered how he'd escaped the Apache the first time.

Darkness fell. Soon, only the rippling gurgles of the ceaseless river disturbed the night. Wendy arched her back, grateful for the thick coat she'd considered leaving back at camp today. How long ago that seemed now. Kurt lifted himself from the murky water, drips scattering as he leaned across the log where Wendy lay. He sighed as he stretched beside her on the huge tree trunk.

"You must be freezing and exhausted," Wendy whispered. "Can we stay here and let you sleep?"

"No," Kurt said to the mass of tangled roots and branches woven above him as he lay on his back. "The Apache will work their way downriver, knowing we must go that way to escape. The Old Trail is our best chance where traffic is heaviest."

"Something tells me we're not going that way." She couldn't hide the disappointment in her voice, but Wendy knew whatever Kurt decided, his plan would be the right way. She trusted him and after spending a day in constant prayer, she knew God was with them too.

"We can't go that way," he agreed. She could hear the fatigue in his words. Sighing, she propped her head on her arm and peered at him, unable to make him out in the darkness. She waited, knowing he'd share his idea when he was ready.

"We need to go the way they don't expect, deeper into Apache land. If we can find the rocky ledge I remember from last time, we can hide there."

"And if we can't find the same place?"

Kurt didn't reply and Wendy shifted, trying to ignore her rising apprehension. She took a deep breath and reminded herself she wasn't alone. Jesus and Kurt were here. By all accounts, they should've been discovered long ago, but they remained unseen, and she had to believe the Lord had something to do with that.

"Are you ready to move?"

His question cut into her thoughts and Wendy feared they would leave this relative safe haven in search of another that didn't promise to be found.

"Are you?"

He nodded in the gloom, not saying anything, but she could tell he was ready to depart. She fisted her hands and resolved to be stealthy, observant, careful, and helpful. They risked their lives, and every step they made could be their last. She thought of Kincaid and Brewer, dead on the riverbank above them, and she thought again of Aunt Lil's claim that the journey west would be an adventure she would never forget.

"All right, Kurt. Let's go."

CHAPTER THIRTY-EIGHT

"We'll stay in the water," Kurt whispered as they slid from beneath the pile of driftwood. "They can't track us if we leave no tracks."

Moonlight shimmered on the river's ripples, and Wendy crouched beside the heap of snarled debris. Kurt stepped near her and faced west, then hesitated and glanced over his shoulder.

"Stay here." He waded downriver and retrieved the rumpled blanket from the sandy shore. He returned and wrapped the rolled material around her neck. Facing upriver, he began wading in the shallow water closest to shore, attempting to move as quietly as he could.

She placed a hand on his shoulder, and he halted, leaning back to catch her whispered words. "Won't the Apache see us traveling at night?"

He shook his head, his hat shifting in the dull light. "They don't like to travel at night. Those who die at night are forever destined to wander the afterlife in darkness. They will only find us tonight if we pass closely to their camp."

Wendy glanced at the nearby riverbank, hoping the Apache had gone far away in the hours since she'd seen them last. Kurt continued, his body leaving a small wake in the water as he pushed ahead.

Keeping a few yards from shore, they waded on for what seemed like hours. Occasionally, Kurt would take a break beneath the deep shadows of a towering pine tree that leaned over the river and blocked the moon. They would drink and stand perfectly still while Kurt listened into the night.

After a while, Wendy quit scanning the riverbanks for glowing campfires or straining her ears for the sound of horses. A scattering of stars gleamed dimly above, and a half moon glowed over the distant mountains, but here in the ceaseless water, Wendy could see little on the dark riverbanks.

The cold water numbed her feet, and her teeth chattered loudly. She didn't dare unfold the blanket around her neck and risk the woolen material might show from a distance. In time, she plodded wearily behind Kurt, barely aware of her surroundings. No doubt they'd traveled miles, and she felt dog-tired. He could've led her off a cliff and she wouldn't have cared.

Kurt motioned to a dark place in the shadow of a huge boulder, and Wendy plodded after him. They cupped their hands and drank, but Wendy felt exhausted and wanted only to climb up the bank and fall asleep on the dry ground.

"How are you doing?" Kurt whispered into her ear, and she nodded, not wanting him to learn of her extreme weariness. Surely, he was tired too.

"Fine. How much farther?"

His grin surprised her, and she stared as his teeth gleamed dully in the faint light. "We're there." He gestured across the river and indicated a rock ledge that protruded all the way to the water's edge. "We have to cross the river and step onto that rock outcropping."

She sensed his concern and tilted her head, suddenly wide awake. "What's wrong?"

"I don't know how deep the river is here."

"Can we go farther upstream and swim across?"

"Yes, but we'll get soaked and I'm afraid we'll freeze to death. If we don't get out of this water soon, I'm afraid we'll freeze anyway."

Wendy peered into the gloom and measured the distance across the small river. Not far, but possibly deep. Glancing around, she saw a long stick with withered branches, leafless and sodden, floating in an eddy along the bank.

Stepping to the branch, she stripped twigs from the shaft and held the slender limb out to Kurt.

He leaned close as he gripped the pole. "Don't let go."

Wendy wrapped the rolled blanket tighter around her neck and grasped the other end of the long stick. Kurt took a step toward the opposite bank and Wendy watched as the water rose to his waist.

Anxiety swirled inside her and she wished there was another way. But their journey seemed to take the most difficult route, and she stepped hesitantly after Kurt, seeking purchase with her heavy boots before trusting her weight. Slowly they inched across the river.

At midpoint, Kurt stepped onto a low rock and pulled Wendy after him. They stood there a moment while they caught their breath, cold wind piercing their frozen pants.

She leaned against him while he wrapped his arms around her, any pretense of decorum long forgotten as he held her close. She remembered the feel of his arms around her at the dance, but this felt completely different. There, her heart had thudded so hard against her chest, and she still recalled the confusing emotions that raged. Now, she felt only safe and protected in his arms, as if she needed protection and craved the safety of his embrace.

Wendy looked up at him, wanting to see his face. His head leaned away, and his gaze scanned the far bank. She could see his unshaven jaw outlined boldly in the moonlight and his sharp profile defined by the scattered stars that accompanied them on their night trek.

He stepped from the rock and Wendy saw the water rise once more to his waist. He pulled his coat high and took another step, one hand still gripping the pole Wendy held.

She let him go another yard before she followed, the water swirling around her with renewed strength. Her boot slipped on the rocky bottom, and she staggered, dropping the long stick. With a lunge, Kurt snatched at her and dragged her the remaining distance to the rocky ledge. Lifting her bodily from the river, he placed her on the stone outcropping and stepped beside her as water dripped from them in puddles.

Shivering and teeth chattering uncontrollably, Wendy could only stare as Kurt unwrapped the blanket from her neck and draped the material around her shoulders.

"The water puddles will dry before the Apache can find them, I hope," Kurt explained as he led her to a fallen tree trunk that leaned against an immense boulder as large as a house.

"Wh—wh—where are we go—go—going?"

He frowned at her stuttering query but pointed up the angled tree toward the rim of the giant boulder. "You'll see."

Large pieces of peeled bark lay scattered over the level stone. Pinecones and shattered sections of wood piled all around, amidst broken branches. With a faint graying in the eastern sky, Kurt took the blanket from her and led the way carefully up the slanted tree trunk, moving slowly and using branches as footholds.

Winding and twisting around the profusion of limbs, she made her way cautiously to the top of the tree where the trunk leaned farther over the rim of the boulder. Kurt released her hand and stepped to the side of the tree in what appeared to be a hidden recess carved into the huge boulder. The concealed cleft was unseen from below, but as Wendy stepped from the tree onto the stone floor of the tiny enclosure, she could vaguely see the shape of the stone retreat.

Barely seven feet long, the space was maybe four feet high, covered from above by an overhanging rock shelf.

"I climbed that tree to get to the top of the boulder, trying to get away from the pursuing Apache." He gestured at the small cavern. "I found this and stayed put, hoping they didn't know about the little hollow."

Wendy nodded, teeth still chattering. "Is this wh—where we're stay—staying?"

Kurt led her to the farthest corner of the hidden notch. She slid to the stone floor, her back to the wall, and Kurt spread the blanket over her and tucked in the edges. As she huddled against the cold rock, Wendy peered up at him and tried to grin. "We're safe, right?"

He smiled down at her as the morning sun burst above the eastern horizon, golden shafts shining on his unshaven chin. He looked so tall, so strong, and Wendy thanked God she wasn't alone.

"We are for now. Get some sleep."

She didn't even try to nod. Her teeth chattered so violently, and shivers racked her frozen body, but she felt her eyes droop closed as if they had a mind of their own.

Sunlight warmed her cheeks and Wendy stirred. Without opening her eyes, she stretched her legs out, her wet boots reaching beyond the blanket's edge. Her damp pants felt stiff and heavy, yet she soaked in an unexpected warmth. Despite her wet legs, she didn't feel cold, and shadows dappled behind her shut eyelids. She knew exactly where she was, yet sensed they were still undiscovered. The blanket wrapped tightly around her, and she reveled in the warm sunlight on her cheeks. Eyelids fluttering, Wendy looked around her.

She recognized the stone cleft in the massive boulder, the top of the windblown tree leaning against the rim like a giant ladder, but something else caught her attention and she froze. Kurt sat beside her, nestled against her under the blanket, his head on her shoulder. She looked down at his worn features and enjoyed being needed.

Not wishing to disturb his sleep, she remained still and peered all around. The nearby river roared dully, and tall pine trees stood beyond the stone outcropping they occupied. A gentle wind hummed through the evergreen boughs and a blue jay called while the hammering of a woodpecker sounded far away. Wendy smiled, basking in the peaceful setting and nature's melody. So deceptive, so unreal. Her smile faded as she remembered their plight. The Apache had located their camp and searched for them even now.

Her stomach growled fiercely, and she felt her brow furrow. What time was it? The flight from yesterday morning's Apache attack seemed long ago, but that had been the last time she'd eaten anything. Her stomach growled again, and she felt starved.

Her tongue resembled a dry stick as she licked dry lips, and she worried at her thirst. The pleasant sound of the river drifted on the breeze, but she knew she wouldn't risk going for water.

In her mind, she ticked off their lack of supplies. No food, no water, no matches. Thank God Kurt had brought the blanket. Without the warm cover, would they have survived the night?

Her frown deepened when she recalled she'd almost left her hunter's coat in camp yesterday. The arrival of Kincaid and Brewer had happened so suddenly. The Apache rising from the shadows without a sound had occurred as swiftly and unexpected. Whitmore's men were dead, and the hostile Indians were on Kurt's and her trail. Would they find the hidden niche in the boulder?

Her gaze dropped to the sleeping cowboy, and another smile tugged at her mouth. He'd given the Apache the slip before. Could he do it again? Of course, he'd been alone that time and now he was saddled with her.

Her chin lifted, not liking the negative light she'd cast on herself. Hadn't she fled Little Rock at night, in the rain? Hadn't she endured a rough stagecoach ride across the plains? Hadn't she ridden a half-broken mustang and herded wild cattle?

An unexpected sensation of excitement and anticipation filled her, and Wendy thrilled to be in her current predicament. As if prepared for hardship and struggles, she accepted her situation and hoped she'd face the challenge as a Christian, faithful and strong.

Her smile widened at the thoughts of her many accomplishments, and she realized Lil had been right. The journey had been all that Aunt Lil predicted. An adventure. *Her* adventure.

She thought of Lil and how the older woman enjoyed being needed at Hanson's store. She also remembered how all the men in town paid her aunt such attention, and Wendy tilted her head, wistful at the memory. Perhaps her adventure included Lil as well. Perhaps they both needed a change of scenery.

Her eyes went to the few puffy clouds that drifted overhead. The long slanting shadows revealed the early twilight hour. She'd slept all day. Her stomach growled again with demanding ferocity, and she dearly wanted a drink of water. Yet she studied the blue sky as the sunlight faded and shadows thickened around her.

"Thanks, Jesus," she breathed, inhaling deeply of the fresh air scented with pine. "I had no idea what you held for me, what's in store for me. Trinidad, Shannon, the Mora River, and … and …"

She paused, not looking at the cowboy as her whispered prayer continued. "And Kurt. You knew I needed something to jar me from myself. My grief and loss are real, but so are your tender mercies, new each day. Teach me, stretch me, grow my faith, that I may know you in deep ways. Let me praise you for the good and the bad as you shape me and develop me into the woman of God you desire. Let me be your servant and trust you in all things."

Her gaze swept the sky, the distant mountains, and the towering pines and she nodded. "Let me trust you have me here, right now, for a purpose. You have a plan for me, and I want to walk in obedience, trusting you through the fire. You know our needs, my fear, my great anxieties. But you are my rock, my redeemer. You are the strength of my soul. I pray I may please you as I look to you for guidance and help."

An overwhelming peace settled upon her, and Wendy closed her eyes and soaked in the Lord's presence. They were not alone. She knew Jesus was with them, and she inhaled again, drinking in the unseen companionship she sensed.

As she opened her eyes to the gathering dusk, Wendy glanced down at Kurt where he leaned against her shoulder. Her brows arched when she saw him staring up at her, a soft glow in his gaze she didn't recognize.

CHAPTER THIRTY-NINE

Kurt shifted beside Wendy and leaned against the rock wall, their shoulders touching beneath the blanket. He stared out at the darkening landscape and swallowed. "That was a beautiful prayer."

Embarrassed, Wendy said nothing, her gaze locked on the distant horizon where she could see undulating hills that led downriver toward the plains and the Canadian River, perhaps a dozen miles away.

"Do you always pray like that?"

She puckered her lips. "Like what?"

Kurt shifted again. "You know. Putting your heart into your words. I'll bet God smiles when his people pray with such ... honesty."

Her embarrassment mounted, and Wendy laughed with a nervous twitter. "I just talk to Jesus with my thoughts. Whatever I'm going through, I know he's with me."

Kurt nodded. "I'm thirsty." He paused and then drew a deep breath. "I'm starving too, but I can't do anything about that. When it gets real dark, we'll go down to the river."

"Then what?"

He flexed his shoulders and stretched his legs out in front of him, his boots resting beside Wendy's. "I'm not sure," he mumbled.

Wendy cocked an eyebrow. "Not sure?"

"Well, we can run for it and see how far we get. No doubt the Apache are watching every trail and combing all avenues to the Canadian River. I'm sure they've realized by now we didn't go east toward the Old Trail and are right now searching all over these hills. But we have no food, and the longer we wait, the weaker we become."

"Why do I feel another boot is about to drop? Something tells me you don't think we should try and get away tonight."

He sighed, glancing at her from the corner of his eyes. "No, I don't, but I'm worried."

Wendy chuckled. "You're worried. About Apache Indians searching for us? Or about the long walk across hostile lands that lay before us? Or worried about starving to death while we hide from them?"

Kurt smiled grimly. "All of it, I guess."

She squinted at him, sensing something more. "No, you're not worried about escaping the Apache. You've done that before. You're worried about escaping with me tagging along."

He sighed again and removed his hat, thrusting a hand through his thick mane. "Wendy, I won't lie. I have to weigh all options, take every detail into consideration before I make a decision."

"Before *we* make a decision," she corrected with an icy tone to her words. "I'm in this too."

He nodded but didn't reply. She cooled her heels and leaned her head back, the stone wall unmoving and solid behind her. Unmoving and solid. Strong, like her faith, or the faith she longed for. She took a deep breath.

"All right, I get it. I'm the weak link. You're trying to figure out how long I can last. You think your decision has to be based on what is best for me."

Kurt laughed shortly. "You're clever. I guess I can't fool you. We need to go before we're weakened by our lack of food, but we shouldn't attempt the journey until the Apache have scattered their search and left this region. In time, they'll have no choice but believe we're somewhere else if we don't move or make tracks they can find."

Wendy gritted her teeth, realizing what he was saying. "So, if we stay put a little while, our chances of escape are better, but we'll be half starved. And you wonder how much I can take?"

He didn't reply and she chewed her lip. How much could she take? She'd been hungry before, but never starved on purpose. Could she endure as long as Kurt and still retain the necessary strength required to walk out of here? The night trek would demand stamina and reserves she might not have if they waited too long.

She lifted her eyes to the deepening twilight, searching for guidance. Was God asking her to believe he would take care of her? Would he give her the strength she needed? And not just for her, but the strength she would require to help Kurt escape. This situation might spell the destruction of her friend as well as for her. They were in this together.

She shot a silent prayer skyward, resolving to give her best. To endure, to persevere, whatever God asked of her so they might get away and pursue the lives the Lord had for them. Death lurked nearby, threatening and ominous, yet Wendy felt an inner power rise to meet the heavy challenge that weighed upon her. Assurance swelled within her, and she felt God testing her. She chose to meet that test with faith and acceptance. Whatever happened, Jesus was with her.

She nudged Kurt with an elbow. "So, what's your problem?"

"Huh?" he looked at her sharply.

"I can take anything you can handle," she boasted with a casualness she didn't feel.

He cocked an eyebrow. "This isn't going to be a game. We're talking life and death."

Wendy nodded. "I'm well aware of the gravity of our situation." She paused and then smiled. "God is with us, right? He knows exactly what we face."

She thought she sounded like Lil, always pointing to the Lord's intervention. Her aunt's favorite verse came to her again, and Wendy frowned, not wanting to lean on Lil's faith, but to grow her own. Was the Lord shaping Wendy's faith, growing her through trials?

"Trust God?" Kurt chuckled low. "You sound like Miguel. Well, we don't have any other choice, do we?"

Her eyebrows bunched. "I'm not saying trust God because we have no other choice. I'm saying to trust him because he is God, our first choice. He can do anything, even what we think is impossible. Let's lean into him and see what he does."

He grinned, and Wendy felt her heart flip flop. "You definitely sound like Miguel. He would agree with you. He'd turn to Jesus first."

"An adventure, Aunt Lil would call it. Let's see what God does with our hunger and the Apache and our escape."

In the vague light, she saw Kurt's eyes soften. "God forgive me for my lack of faith." He studied her and nodded. "Thanks, Wendy, for reminding me of who I am. I'm a child of the living God. I laugh at fear and stare death in the face."

"Now you're talking." Wendy tugged the blanket higher. "Now, when do we go for water?"

The raucous river flowed under a silver band as the rising moon glowed upon the rippled surface. Kurt stood and watched as Wendy knelt and eagerly gulped water from her cupped hands. After a minute, she stood sentinel while Kurt drank.

"No tracks on the rock." He gestured at the evaporated puddles where they had exited the river the day before. "With luck, they won't find any trace of our passing," he whispered as he led the way back to the leaning tree.

"I wish we had a canteen," she complained as they worked their way up the tree trunk, grasping branches and pulling themselves higher.

"We'll drink again before dawn, before sunrise." He turned to help her step onto the rock ledge, the deeper dark of the hidden notch making it difficult to see details. They settled onto the floor, their backs to the stone wall, as Kurt fitted the blanket around them. Wendy wanted to say she was hungry, to declare aloud how starved she felt, but she bit her tongue, dedicated to their cause.

"My pants are still damp," she grumbled instead.

Kurt was silent for a long while and Wendy frowned, wanting to hear him complain about something as she had done. They were a team, right? He should complain to let her know she didn't suffer alone.

"So, you're engaged." His remark surprised her, and she shifted, uneasy at the unexpected remark.

"Not really," she said quickly.

"Not really?" His repeat made her bristle.

"Look, you're engaged, aren't you? Can't others be engaged too?" She bit her tongue again, angry at herself for vomiting her disapproval. She wasn't really engaged, but he was, and to a conceited girl Wendy didn't like.

She puckered her lips. That wasn't fair to Marigold Peterson. Wendy sighed. "I'm sorry. What I mean to say is I'm not engaged in that I didn't accept Mr. Whitmore's proposal of marriage."

She could sense his piercing gaze on her in the darkness. "You didn't? Then why did those men say you were going to marry Mr. Whitmore?"

She knew she didn't have to explain, but she closed her eyes and continued. "Randall Whitmore is my father's business partner. Or *was* his partner, until he died. Father owed him money and Randall demanded the debt be paid, or I marry him."

Kurt remained quiet for a long moment. "Is that why you came here looking for the treasure? You don't want to marry him?"

"He's almost twice my age." Wendy chuckled sourly. "He's not a Christian, and I don't like him. We have nothing in common."

"Then why did those men think you might marry him?"

Wendy could taste the bitter sensation in her mouth. She hated to confess her sin, her anxiety over being left penniless in an uncertain world. Especially after crowing about trusting God and leaning on their faith. She felt like such a hypocrite.

"I have nothing. We have no money to pay the debt, and Aunt Lil and I would have nowhere to go, with nothing to start again. Arkansas has been destroyed by the war, and well, fear filled me."

"And you made me feel small," he accused slowly. "Like my faith was nothing."

"I know," she almost wailed. "I'm sorry, Kurt. I want to do great things for the Lord, but I feel inadequate, like I can't do it. I'm ashamed I considered Mr. Whitmore's proposal, but I'm afraid for the future. For me and Aunt Lil."

Silence hung like a damp fog, chilling Wendy to her bones. She eyed his dark shadow where he sat silently beside her. Wouldn't he say something? Would he understand or forgive her? She felt surprised how badly she craved his kindness.

"I guess I understand. At least as much as a man can understand what a single girl has to face in the world." He paused. "Tough choice. No relatives or other options?"

Wendy shook her head in the darkness. "No. Stay and marry Mr. Whitmore, or flee somewhere else and begin again with nothing, with thousands more like me who lost everything in the war. The roads back home are choked with refugees, looking for a better life somewhere else. What chance do Aunt Lil and I have?"

"The treasure," he whispered between clenched teeth, and she felt he comprehended a bit of her overwhelming anxiety.

"Yes," she replied. "The hidden gold would solve all my problems. But we haven't found any clue. Every stream on both the north and south side of the Mora leads to nothing. I fear we will never find the gold, especially now with the Apache on our trail."

"Any chance you could return and try again?"

His question astonished her. "You'd come back with me again and look for the gold?" Her whispered query sounded ridiculous in her own ears, but she felt grateful he would even consider the dangerous expedition twice.

"You've proven yourself a good friend," he said with a casualness that didn't fool Wendy. She fully understood the danger he was willing to endure for her, and her heart warmed. "I'd try again if you wanted to."

"Don't worry about it," she said with a sigh. "I'm on a deadline. I have only sixty days to accept his proposal or pay the debt. Or refuse him and vacate the old house."

"You said you left Little Rock on March first."

"Time's running out," Wendy agreed. "I figure at least the first week of April has already passed."

"Why didn't you tell me?" The angry note in his voice startled her.

"Tell you what?"

He stirred beneath the blanket. "We don't have time to hide from the Apache. We need to be searching for the gold."

"Don't be silly. They would find us and kill us if we continue traipsing over the hills, looking for treasure in every stream and side canyon that touches the river. We're lucky to still be alive."

He settled back and tugged the blanket higher. Stars dotted the heavens, and a cool wind blew from the high up mountains to the west. Despite their damp pants and wet boots, they were warm in their big coats, huddled together beneath the woolen blanket, and Wendy knew they wouldn't freeze to death.

She peered at him in the gloom, unable to see him in the deep shadows of the narrow notch. He'd befriended her when she had no friends. He'd agreed to help search for the treasure, her treasure. Of course, he expected to be compensated if they discovered the gold, but he would deserve all of the loot if they escaped this place alive.

A warmth for him glowed within her, and she thanked the Lord he was here. But his sudden silence concerned her. What was he thinking? Where was Miguel? Would they ever eat food again?

Her worries and questions darted across her mind, and she fidgeted, wanting him to speak, to allay her fears, to give some kind of solace or guidance.

"Well, what's on your mind?"

"Shhh," Kurt whispered. "I'm praying."

Wendy smiled as she closed her eyes and went to sleep.

CHAPTER FORTY

Before a light gray showed on the eastern horizon, they left their hidden retreat and drank thirstily at the river.

"I'm not tired now that I've slept all night," Wendy said in a low voice that was swept away by the noisy river at their feet. She peered anxiously to the east, watching for the first hint of sunrise, the time they needed to be safely in their hideaway. "What'll we do to pass the time? I wish—"

She was going to say she wished they had a fire and a hot meal, but she held her tongue, remembering her promise. She would not discuss food, despite the hunger pangs that gnawed at her insides.

Although far from weakened by lack of food, she imagined she was dying of starvation and barely able to stand. Surely the night flight from this place would demand all of her remaining strength. Worry and fear gripped her. Would she be able to withstand the ordeal?

As she'd done a hundred times since the attack of the Apache, she lifted her eyes to the heavens and prayed. God had a purpose. God had a plan. God was with them. God would help them.

She felt better after seeking the Lord, but her belly still felt just as empty.

Kurt stepped beside her and followed her gaze eastward. "We'll do what Miguel and I always did when we needed to kill time or at night around the campfire before we went to sleep. We'll talk about our dreams and what we hope the future holds."

Wendy scowled but said nothing. They knelt at the river again, Wendy taking time to drink all she could hold, as this was the last opportunity for water until this evening after the sun had disappeared. After wending their way carefully back up the slanted pine tree, they hunkered down where they couldn't be seen from below and leaned against the cold rock wall as the sun peeked over the eastern hills.

Shafts of golden rays speared through the trees and lighted the shadows beneath the forest and around the rocks. Slowly, as if by magic, the sun rose and the darkness retreated.

Wendy stared, watching the glory of God revealed anew, as she had done thousands of times before. But as always, her heart beat faster and a lump lodged in her throat. To worship, to sing, to praise, bubbled within her until she couldn't contain the overwhelming emotion. As a tear brimmed in her eyes, she began to whisper.

"Praise the Lord, you his servants, praise the name of the Lord. Let the name of the Lord be praised, both now and forever. From the rising of the sun to the place where it sets, the name of the Lord is to be praised."

Wendy dropped her face and sniffled. Lifting her chin, she watched as the colors changed around her, the vivid green of spring making splashes among the trees and bushes she hadn't noticed before. Spring heralded the end of her time in the west, and she held her breath, feeling both wonderfully alive at worshipping Christ and with a sadness niggling at her as she realized she would miss the glorious mountain lands and high plains she'd unexpectedly come to love.

She shot a quick glance at Kurt, as if to assure herself he still sat beside her. He peered to the east, an intense gleam in his eyes.

"I love psalms," he whispered softly, then cleared his throat. "I will extol you, my God the King, I will praise your name for ever and ever. Every day I will praise you and extol your name for ever and ever."

He smiled and looked at Wendy. "Miguel told me memorizing Scripture would come in handy. Like everything else, he was right. God's Holy Word speaks to my soul, especially now when I feel I desperately need him."

She nodded as a tear rolled down her cheek. "Jesus is with us, Kurt. We need to trust him."

The cowboy's smile faded as he lifted a hand and brushed the tear from her. Startled and yet somehow comfortable with the intimate gesture during the emotional moment, she closed her eyes and leaned into his warm palm.

They sat there an instant longer, and then Kurt shifted, taking his hand away. An awkward moment followed as they both looked away. Confusion swept over her, and Wendy couldn't think straight. What did she feel? She couldn't name the unfamiliar sensation that overwhelmed her, but she knew the powerful sentiment must be wrong. Kurt was engaged to Marigold Peterson. He was merely Wendy's friend, nothing more. Yet the unexpected touch had touched more than her cheek. She leaned farther away, pulling the blanket after her as she pretended to go to sleep.

Hours passed before she could manage to sit up and endure his nearness. Their shoulders rubbed and Kurt pushed the blanket back as the warming noon sun filled the little notch in the massive boulder.

He shot her a halfhearted smile, testing and unsure. "Feel better?"

She nodded, not sure he meant what she thought. She would refuse to think of him, about her feelings, and what lay ahead for her. Instead, she resolved to think only about staying alive and figuring out a way to escape. No doubt the Apache still lurked in the region, searching for them.

"I feel good," she lied as her stomach growled violently. Kurt ignored the loud rumble and indicated his boots propped neatly together in the pool of bright sunlight along the opposite wall.

"Put your boots in the sun," he ordered and wiggled his toes in his dirty socks for emphasis. "Let your feet dry."

Wendy complied and leaned back again, unbuttoning her thick coat. Sunlight reflected off the rocks and warmed the narrow niche where they sat. For the first time in days, Wendy didn't need so many layers. A foul odor of unwashed body and stale sweat rose from her as she pulled the coat open.

"Whew." She made a face and Kurt laughed.

"We both could use a bath," he commented as he opened his coat to the sun.

Wendy wondered if he would ask her about the wonderful worship time they'd shared earlier, but worried about her response. What would she say? Did he feel the electricity she experienced at the vulnerable moment? Worship always unlocked her to intense emotions as she drew near to Jesus. The Lord was always with her, but to seek him in praise seemed to release her love in ways she couldn't articulate. Did he feel anything similar?

She shook her head, clearing her muddled thoughts. But she tensed when he faced her, a look on his face as if he wanted to say something important.

Ducks quacked noisily as they flew overhead, their wings flapping violently as if pursued by unseen predators. Kurt frowned and pressed a finger to his lips. He stretched on his belly and snaked to the edge of the stone notch where he peered over the rim.

A voice drifted on the breeze and Wendy froze. Another voice lifted from the river and Wendy closed her eyes as her heart sank. They'd been found. The Apache would kill them both, after tormenting her in ways she didn't want to think about. They'd tried to flee the Indians and failed.

When Kurt placed a hand on her arm, Wendy jumped, almost screaming in fright. He narrowed his eyes and held his finger against his lips as before. For a long time, they stared at one another, ears straining to hear anything more from below.

Finally, Kurt leaned toward her and whispered. "A pair of Apache walked the river searching for tracks. They're close, but they haven't found us yet."

"How long can we hold out here?"

Her panicked query made him squint even harder. "We can't last long. We need food, and every day that passes, we get weaker. I suggest we leave tonight."

"Tonight?" Wendy squeaked as her eyebrows arched in shock. They had no supplies and she felt faint. Could they manage an arduous night trek with Apache roaming the vicinity?

She leaned against the stone wall, her body aching from the relentlessly hard rock behind and below her. Her dream of locating the lost gold vanished with Kurt's words. She wasn't surprised at his idea to flee while they still possessed strength, but they had sealed her fate with a finality she'd avoided until she was certain they couldn't find the treasure. That time had come, and Wendy winced, knowing she had only two options— marriage to a man she didn't love or extreme poverty.

"We're not going to last here much longer," Kurt explained with a frankness Wendy understood. To stay was to starve. "I think we can move at night. We don't have to travel in the river because we'll leave tracks but should be out of the area by morning."

They sat silent for a long moment and then Kurt glanced at her. "You all right?"

Wendy pursed her lips, her shoulders slumping as she wiggled her damp socks in the warm sunlight. "I guess we didn't find the treasure," she whispered.

Kurt sighed. "There was never much chance we were going to find it anyway. Colonel Gomez could've lied to your grandfather for the fast horse. Or he could've told countless other men about the gold. And we looked up each stream, each little ravine, each side canyon on the north and south side of the Mora. The Mexican army could have the wrong river, or the event never actually happened. Any variety of things could make this a wild goose chase. But we tried."

She nodded, grateful for his solicitous words. He'd been kind the entire time, and Wendy appreciated he'd made the effort. Suddenly, she realized what not finding the gold meant to Kurt.

"Oh, no," she said as she studied him. "I've been so selfish, only thinking of how this affects me. But Marigold—will she marry a man who doesn't have great wealth?"

Kurt stiffened and his features darkened. "She said she'd marry me. We're engaged. I have my own ranch, and it'll take time to build the herd, but we can work together to make a good home. I'm convinced the Lord led me to Trinidad to find a Christian mate and start a life together. I do not doubt the power of God."

His pious words made her bristle and Wendy swelled with indignation. "Don't give me that 'holier than thou' attitude," she snapped. "I'm sensitive to the Holy Spirit too and want to serve God, wherever that may be."

"Well, it's not with an unbelieving husband," Kurt retorted. "Whitmore sounds like a real winner. He doesn't value your faith or your ideals."

She glared at him and pressed her lips into a tight line. "Are you going to preach to me about Christian virtue? Miguel says you're impulsive, and I've seen your impatience for myself. What makes you think Marigold is the wife for you?"

He shook his head and looked away. "I'm not going to debate this with you," he countered over his shoulder. "Be ready to move after the sun goes down."

LASTING TREASURE

The sudden argument ended as quickly as it had begun. Wendy crossed her arms over her chest and studied the distant mountains, her thoughts whirling. Yet two thoughts stuck out to her—there was no gold, and she wasn't certain what she was going to do.

Wendy refused to look at Kurt, although he sat beside her, unable to get any farther from her. Yet the heated exchange of words had not gone the way she'd hoped. She wanted to tell him how grateful she was that he'd come out here and tried to find the treasure. She wanted to thank him for saving her life.

The mountains were so tall and massive, bigger than any other mountains she'd ever seen in her life. And the hills and the trees were suddenly covered in splashes of green that decorated the wild landscape in verdant swaths. The crisp air felt like spring water to her lungs, and she breathed deeply, trying to calm her rapid heartbeat.

Their argument had made her furious, but not because of anything Kurt had done. With great clarity, she saw she had allowed her emotions to have free rein, and now she regretted the imprudence. She was supposed to come out here and find hidden treasure, but now her heart ached from betrayal, and she wished she'd never met this special cowboy who touched her soul. Anger, frustration, and envy warred within her, and she knew why but feared to put a name to the strange sensation that assailed her.

With a shudder, she stifled a sob and blinked through wet eyes as the mountains dimmed in her sight. Her anger had turned to sadness, a sensation she'd known for years, and she slumped against the rock wall, wondering what God wanted from her. Had he really brought her out here to suffer? Were her raw emotions from her youth to only magnify with additional grief after this exceptional trip to the west? Why bring her such great joy only to rip it away again?

Danger was all around them. Starving and weak, they would have to flee this lofty haven tonight. But Wendy realized the real danger was the struggle within her own heart.

CHAPTER FORTY-ONE

"Wendy?"

Kurt's whispered call brought her to her feet. She'd already pulled on her boots and rolled the lone blanket. Now she buttoned her coat and stepped to the rim of the little notch, preparing to depart, eager to get away from him.

Yet her fear doubled as he stepped from the stone rim to the leaning tree. He turned and reached for her, but Wendy froze when they grasped hands. He peered at her in the dim light, and she leaned closer. "Are you sure about this? We're safe here. Perhaps we should wait another day or two."

Kurt shook his head. "We need to go now, Wendy." He paused and squinted, studying her. "So do not fear, for I am with you. Do not be dismayed, for I am your God. I will help you and strengthen you, I will uphold you with my righteous right hand."

The familiar Scripture verse washed over her like a comforting wave of security, and she nodded, smiling faintly as she released his arm and followed him down the dead pine tree. He was right. Trust God, she reminded herself as she slowly descended the precarious ladder. God was with them, he was doing something, although she felt she didn't like the way the Lord did things right now. Her nerves strained as she stepped to the rocky ground beside Kurt.

She didn't look at him as she waited for him to lead off. His encouraging recital of the passage from Isaiah didn't allow her to forget their earlier argument. She pretended to survey the surrounding darkness, avoiding eye contact with Kurt. They hadn't spoken all afternoon and the silence had drained her. Images of Randall Whitmore and the broken down old plantation swirled in her mind along with pictures of wild cattle with long horns and tricky mustangs that knew how to throw unsuspecting riders. She thought of Aunt Lil and helping her tend the immense garden now that Jasmine and Mary had left the Moylan estate. Somehow, the old place had lost its significance and appeal with the loss of people Wendy loved.

Now, in her mind's eye, the falling down farm seemed to be just that—falling down. The value she'd attributed to her parents' land seemed suddenly misplaced, with everyone gone. Her favorite haunts and trails beside the Arkansas River didn't call to her or make her want to visit them again. They were corridors of sorrow and grief where she had spent countless hours as she worked through her pain. But now, she didn't feel an urgency to return.

Her lack of eagerness to depart New Mexico surprised her, and Wendy clenched her fists. Without the gold, she wasn't sure which direction to go, only she knew she must get away from Kurt. The unexpected pain that overwhelmed her threatened to crush her like she'd never been crushed before.

A touch on her shoulder made her jump. Kurt nodded and together they moved eastward, stopping only for a moment to slake their thirst at the noisy river.

As far as she could figure, they were no more than ten or twelve miles from the Canadian River, the eastern border of the Apache lands. Beyond and bordering the distant river ran the Santa Fe Trail where they hoped to locate a caravan of freight wagons or a wagon train of settlers moving west. The thought of hot food made her stomach snarl loudly, and Wendy pressed a hand to her empty belly as she followed Kurt, careful to watch her footing. To step on a dry branch or to kick a rock could make noise that would travel in the cool night air.

Her hunger annoyed her, bullying obsessively with its need for sustenance. But she resolved to take every thought captive, to discipline her mind to trust the Lord. She would not allow her complaining belly to master her focus. She vowed to keep her eyes fixed on Jesus, silently whispering prayers skyward as they trudged along the riverbank.

A sliver of moon topped the mountains, and Wendy marveled at their rate of travel. Angling downhill, they made good time, the miles slipping behind them as they wound around boulders and deadfalls and leaping small ravines. After an hour, Kurt paused in the shadow of a steep ridge.

"How are you doing?" He peered intently at her, searching for clues to her condition, but Wendy nodded easily.

"Good. I feel we're moving quicker than I expected."

Kurt glanced at the surrounding landscape and Wendy studied his sharp profile in the moonlight. She shook her head when she thought of how handsome and strong he was.

None of that, she reprimanded herself and took a deep breath. Better to think of her gnawing hunger than about Kurt Jordan. He was an engaged man, and she would be returning to Arkansas soon.

A wave of disappointment crashed over her, and Wendy shook her head again. *Steady*, she coached. *You have a task to complete. Stay focused.*

But she didn't want to think of her future, her return to Little Rock, or a life without her new friend. Kurt embodied everything she'd experienced in the west. The arduous expedition, rugged exploits, and unexpected sensations that thrilled her, had been an adventure of a lifetime.

He spoke, and his words brought her from her reverie. She stared at him. "What?"

A frown creased his features as he leaned closer. "Are you all right?"

She read the concern in his gaze and her heart warmed. It felt good to be worried about. "I'm fine," she mumbled. "What did you say?"

"I said we are making really good time. We're not far from our old campsite where the Apache found us. We need to angle north and avoid a possible ambush at the mouth of the river where it strikes the Canadian. They might be waiting for us there, knowing we need to reach the Old Trail."

Wendy nodded. "I'm with you. Lead on."

He turned and led the way from the shadowed recess and into the moonlit trail, wending a path beside the river. Another hour passed before Kurt suddenly stopped, pulling Wendy into the deeper darkness behind the screen of a mesquite thicket.

She peered through the foliage, confused at the abrupt halt. Then something niggled within her brain, and she recognized the familiar pile of driftwood in the bend of the river. Her glance lifted to the far riverbank where two motionless forms sprawled on the ground, dark in the dim light.

Brewer and Kincaid. The two rascals had intended to double cross their employer and flee the South, fearing the end of the war would make it too hot for them in Arkansas. What reception could she expect upon her return to Little Rock if the war's conclusion occurred soon? Already the economy had collapsed, inflated prices making life difficult. What would the future hold for her and Aunt Lil?

She was about to point out the lifeless forms to Kurt when two dog shadows slunk to the dead bodies. Low growls rose above the din of the little river and Wendy blanched, knowing coyotes feasted on the corpses.

Kurt touched her shoulder. "Those coyotes indicate the Apache are far from here, but we won't risk a scouting trip to camp. It might mean they've left the region or they're waiting for us down at the Canadian, but we'll go round and head north, avoid the intersection of the rivers." He hesitated and then whispered again. "No doubt the Apache took everything they valued, but there might be camp utensils they didn't want. That gear was all of the stuff I own in the world, except the ranch I'm building. God surely knows how to remind a man that nothing is as important as faith in Christ, the only thing that lasts. Thank God we're still alive."

Wendy felt her eyes widen as she stared at this honest man. With a shrug, he rose and tramped down the river for another hundred yards before turning up a dry wash, the sandy ground choked with brush.

Wendy followed in a daze, still angry at God. Having lost nearly everything, Kurt still retained his faith. Could God be so cruel as to strip a man of all that he'd acquired, everything he'd worked so hard for? But hadn't God done the same thing to her?

Grumbling quietly to herself, Wendy blamed Jesus for hard times as she trailed Kurt through the scant foliage and up the ancient streambed. God had led her to the west. He'd joined her to this good man only to watch her quest for hidden treasure go up in smoke and Kurt lose everything he owned. Together, they'd gambled and lost.

She scowled at their combined dismal futures and pondered the Lord's intent as Kurt rounded a huge boulder and slowed, his steps faltering as he tilted his head and studied the narrow ravine they traversed. Wendy halted and blinked, surprised she didn't recognize the dry streambed. Hadn't they explored them all in the region?

He leaned and spoke into her ear. "This streambed isn't visible from the river. We must've missed this wash. I think it might lead up and over this ridge to the north. Could be a good way to avoid the Apache."

She nodded, not bothering to reply. They'd become so comfortable with one another in the past weeks and Wendy knew he understood her silent acceptance of his suggestion. Without another word, they strode cautiously up the little chasm that showed signs of early water runoff, the sandy floor masking the sound of their boots as they worked their way higher up the hill and away from the boisterous river.

Wendy panted as they climbed, maneuvering around fallen trees and jumbled rocks. Despite her resolve to remain faithful, disappointment dogged at her heels. Wendy wondered if she could blame the cold or her mounting hunger or her extreme fatigue for her lack of discipline. She loved Jesus and wanted to live for her Savior, but something whispered he'd let her down. As she trudged up the sandy wash, she couldn't help but feel melancholy. She'd tried so hard and prayed continuously. She'd been so sure God had led her west to search for the hidden treasure, but now she only felt cheated, as if Christ had sent her on a wild goose chase when he knew all along he wasn't going to allow her to succeed.

Her shoulders slumped as she plodded on, the heavy sand weighing her down as she plowed after Kurt. God had tricked her. The excitement she and Lil shared seemed a distant dream now, a ghost of the reality she now faced. Heartsick, lonely, desperate, Wendy knew what awaited her back in Arkansas and her despair swelled. Why had God lifted her hopes only to dash them to the ground?

She narrowed her eyes as she navigated another pile of stones and plodded after the steadfast cowboy. He'd touched her life, and she'd allowed emotions she hadn't expected to come alive. But he was promised to another, and Wendy knew she'd been cheated again. Besides, she didn't deserve happiness. Her lot in life felt heavier than she could bear, but she vowed to stay true to Jesus, even if the Lord had only difficulties in store for her.

Kurt halted abruptly and Wendy almost stumbled into him. She appreciated the break, her lungs heaving to get enough air, but she still felt confused at the Lord's will for her. He was too silent, always asking her to remain faithful as he maneuvered her through the maze she called her life. Yet she resolved to place one foot in front of another, always hoping, always seeking God.

She shoved her hat back and wiped her sweaty brow. Angrily, she unbuttoned her coat, the cold night no longer a concern after miles of challenging travel.

"Wendy?" Kurt hissed, and she froze, expecting the shouts of attacking Apache to come from the surrounding rocks. Her gaze swept the high bank and the deep, shadowed recesses of the rock wall beside the ancient streambed. Stunted cedars leaned in the moonlight, casting eerie fingers of darkness all around them. Bright moonlight splashed and dappled the open spaces between the towering pines and the giant boulders that loomed all around, yet she heard no wild Indian cries.

"Wendy?" Kurt's whisper seemed more urgent now and Wendy leaned on his shoulder to peer around him to where he stared.

At first, she saw nothing out of the ordinary. Small clumps of brush and a few scattered weeds and countless rocks of every size. Then she saw it, the bleached jawbone of a mule gleaming dully in the moonlight, the skull partially covered by sand.

CHAPTER FORTY-TWO

Her heartbeat slowed, and Wendy felt time pause. Not a sound broke the quiet night and even the bright rays of the moon seemed to still, as if nothing moved on the planet. Shadows filled the crevices of the nearby rock wall as Wendy slowly turned her gaze to inspect the area. More bones lay scattered along the sandy shelf, and Wendy could see where a leg joint had been gnawed by long ago teeth. The mule had clearly died years ago—perhaps decades—and Wendy felt her heart beat faster as realization swept over her.

The ancient streambed led to the Mora River on the north side of the waterway. Perhaps Colonel Gomez had traveled here in early summer when melting snow created temporary runoff streams. Regardless, Wendy stared at the various bones that protruded from the ground and then squinted at the dark crevices in the rocky ledge above the wash.

Kurt moved carefully to the rock wall and dropped to his haunches as his hands reached into several fissures. "The gold's got to be here, Wendy," he said over his shoulder as he searched more of the cracks and splits in the wall. She could hear the excitement in his voice, and she moved beside him, her hands probing the cracks in the rocky shelf.

She cried aloud when her fingers located a ragged and rotting empty leather bag, something old that certainly held the gold they sought. Kurt grinned, his teeth gleaming amid his dark unshaven face. She wanted to shout, to laugh and give the cowboy a fierce hug. But she worked furiously, her hands darting over the rock wall and into the black cracks where more of the ancient bags might be hidden.

Kurt held aloft another empty leather bag and Wendy grunted. They were getting close. Surely the treasure was here. Her heart raced like a locomotive, pushing her to delve into every niche and fissure. The treasure was here, she could feel it, God had not let her down.

Guilt and remorse assailed her, and she wondered if the Lord would forgive her doubting him. He was God after all, promising to forgive those who confess their sins, but Wendy wouldn't worry about that now. She felt frantic and shoved her fingers roughly into each crack as she moved down the rock wall, searching for the hidden gold.

Ignoring her scraped fingers and ripped nails, she went on, scrambling farther down the dry wash until the rock ledge gave out. Returning to the other end of the stony outcropping, she hesitated when she saw Kurt staring at his feet. There, at his boots, lay a pile of discarded, ragged leather sacks.

Panting, she straightened, unwilling to believe the disappointing proof lying on the sand, the moonlight shining upon their failure.

"Empty?" Her query disturbed the silent night and Wendy felt her heart sink as Kurt nodded, still studying the worthless bags.

"It was here, Wendy," he said softly. "The hidden gold was real, but someone got here before you and loaded the gold into other containers. Nothing left but empty sacks."

He nudged the limp bags at his feet and looked up at her. Wendy's legs wobbled and she stumbled to the edge of the dry streambed and leaned against the rim. Cheated. Her brain latched on the single word, and she grimaced, feeling duped. Her gaze traveled to the few clouds that hovered among the stars as a lump rose in her throat.

"I thought I was doing everything correctly. I prayed and felt God lead me west. Aunt Lil told me the story of Father and her pouring over Grandfather's journal, and I felt the doors were opening, leading me here."

She kicked at the sand, watching the grains pelt a small cedar tree. Tears brimmed her eyes and then slid slowly down her grimy cheeks. "I have no money. I don't want to go home. I have nothing. But I really believed Jesus wanted me to come west. I felt I was on a great adventure, that something big awaited me. Now I know I've wasted my time. If I don't return to Little Rock by the end of April, my family's land will be taken from me as well."

She slumped against the dirt bank and closed her eyes, fighting the tears that threatened to develop into sobs. Could life get any worse? Had God truly taunted her, teasing her to come all the way out here for nothing?

"Your home is going to be taken away anyway, unless you marry Whitmore."

Her head snapped up at his unexpected words, and Wendy glowered at Kurt, suddenly realizing he hadn't gotten his part of the treasure either. Her lips turned up as a faint smile tugged at her mouth, and she also realized Marigold Peterson would never marry a poor cowboy, no matter how handsome he was.

Elated, Wendy's anguish vanished, and she felt better. She could endure the loss of wealth, but she could not endure the thought of Kurt marrying anyone else.

She blinked and her elation dissolved. How dare she wish bad things on Kurt, just because she couldn't have him? Who was she? Wendy had nothing, even less than Kurt. But she still had her faith, and she knew it was wrong to withhold success, victory, and joy from others. Ashamed, she lowered her head once more. "God forgive me," she whispered, smearing mud across her cheeks as she swiped at her tears. "Forgive my covetous and wicked heart. I sincerely thought you wanted me to come west, but I see now you have revealed how sinful I am. Am I all about me? Forgive me, Jesus. I pray a blessing over Kurt and Marigold and Aunt Lil. May my shortcomings not interfere with your plans for these others."

"What's that?" Kurt queried from a dozen yards away.

Wendy snorted and cleared her throat, wiping a final tear from her eyes. She looked up at Kurt and tried to smile. "God has tested me, and I've been found wanting," she confessed quietly as he walked closer. Moonlight shone all around them like a searchlight from heaven, exposing her guilt and corrupt nature. Despite all of her prayers, Wendy felt appalled that she was nonetheless still a selfish sinner.

"Thank God I know Jesus," she breathed as Kurt studied her.

"Well, of course, we all need Jesus," he agreed. "But what are you talking about? What do you mean you've been tested?"

"God tested Abraham and God tested Job. They were found faithful men, but I am weak. I am no great woman of faith." She giggled, suddenly giddy at her disclosure. There was no use trying to hide her defects from this sharp-eyed cowboy. "You know me, Kurt. I'm not an adventurer. I'm a simple girl, lonely and full of sorrow. My parents are dead, and I'm left almost entirely alone in a changing world I cannot navigate. I used to hide in the woods while others worked around me. My grief became my banner, the crutch I leaned on, and I held it high for all to see. Now, as I begin to feel ready for something more, something different, God wants to test me, to see what I'm made of. Sad to admit, he has found me sorely lacking."

Kurt shifted on the sand. "Has your hunger made you soft?"

Wendy's eyebrows arched. "Huh?"

He shook his head slowly. "You are the toughest girl I know. You share your faith openly, like a Christian should. I felt a kinship with you from the first, and I could tell the Spirit is with you. You're not wrong to walk through open doors and see if the Lord might close them in your face or use them to guide you somewhere you didn't expect."

He paused, and Wendy dragged her sleeve across her eyes. Kurt's kind words made her want to cry again, but she bit her lip and held them in check as he went on.

"And God does test his children. The testing of your faith produces endurance," he quoted, and Wendy grinned despite herself, enjoying the reminder of the familiar verse. "Testing sharpens your faith, develops your faith. God is the potter, and you are the clay. He slowly shapes you into the woman of God he wants you to become. Miguel says the Lord uses fire and flood to shape a piece of land and he does the same with us."

He paused again and straightened, eyeing Wendy sharply as he folded his arms over his chest.

"Now, he doesn't say it'll be easy. In fact, he says it won't. But he promises he will never leave you. Jesus is always with us, Wendy, even when we don't feel his presence."

She sniffled and lifted her chin, feeling refreshed from his encouraging speech. She nodded, but he wasn't through yet.

"Is God testing you? You better hope he's testing you. Hope that he finds you worthy of testing and not one of those who slips away when things get tough. Lean into him as he squeezes the stuffing out of you. As you endure and persevere, he builds and shapes your character. He molds you and develops your faith. This"—he gestured at the empty sacks on the sand and the wilderness all around—"this is not a test you've failed. You have not been found wanting. You are a warrior, Wendy, a soldier of Jesus. This is all part of your adventure, and I'm proud to be a part of it with you."

He nodded once, a wide grin on his dirty face, and Wendy's vision blurred as the dam burst and tears streamed down her face.

"I don't see anything," Wendy whispered as they crouched on the shore of the Canadian River. Dawn still lay an hour away and the pair of travelers hunkered down behind a clump of mesquite. Kurt's powerful speech still resonated in her mind, but Wendy felt weaker than ever, faint from hunger and fatigue despite the kind and supportive words he'd said to her at the sandy streambed. She'd floated on a cloud for hours after that, but now her spirit waned and she wasn't sure how much farther she could go.

Kurt peered downriver before he spoke. "We're miles above the Mora River. I doubt if the Apache would come this way seeking us, especially at night. I think we should chance crossing. We need to get to the Old Trail by sunrise."

Wendy yawned, feeling her remaining strength ebb away. She'd give anything to curl up behind this bush and go to sleep, cover the two of them with the blanket and sleep for hours. She'd gotten used to sleeping beside Kurt and found him comfortable, a deep sense of security enveloping her as she nestled close to him.

A wave of heat rose up her neck and Wendy frowned, startled at the unladylike thoughts. She had no business thinking of Kurt in any fashion. Soon, she'd be on her way east and would never see the likeable cowboy again. Sadness loomed, threatening to overwhelm her, but she brushed the hateful idea aside. Her adventure was not over yet, and Kurt had certainly played a significant role. She'd be grateful for the time they'd shared.

"Thank you, Lord," she whispered as she studied the watchful man beside her. Kurt peered up and down the wide river again and then stood.

"Come on, Wendy. Let's get across while we can." He led the way to the sandy riverbank and Wendy followed, her muscles aching as she staggered after him. They stood on the shore as water lapped at their boots. The river widened at this point, and Wendy frowned at Kurt's insistence that a river was shallowest at its widest point. The placid water seemed safe enough as she couldn't detect any big waves or tall ripples where the current went around submerged rocks.

"You look like you're about to fall over," he said, eyeing her dubiously.

Wendy nodded dumbly, then shook her head. "I'm all right. Let's go."

He scowled and handed her the folded blanket before he shrugged out of his coat. "Hold this," he ordered as he tossed the coat on the blanket and swept her into his arms.

"What are you doing?" She felt imprisoned by his strong grip and her heart leaped into her throat.

"Put an arm around my neck," he commanded and stepped into the river.

She complied meekly, secretly pleased to be in his arms. She pressed into him as he waded farther into the current, the river swirling around his legs as he moved away from the shore.

"Hold that blanket higher if we go in," he said as the water rose to his waist. "We're going to need it to stay warm after this."

Wendy wrapped her arm tighter around his neck and held on. Foot by foot, Kurt navigated the treacherous crossing, angling downriver as the current pushed him. He slipped only once and Wendy wanted to scream, but she bit her tongue, not allowing her fear to break his concentration.

Finally, the water seemed to lower about him, and Wendy could see they neared the opposite bank. Beyond lay the Santa Fe Trail. By dawn, they hoped to be walking north toward Fort Union. With any luck, a caravan would discover them today.

The thought of a warm meal and a hot cup of coffee made her almost cry again, and Wendy closed her eyes, afraid to let Kurt see her extreme helplessness. She'd asked God repeatedly—no, she'd begged him—to reveal her purpose, why she'd been led west. What skills did she possess? What direction could her life take? But the Lord had been all too silent, never speaking, never disclosing his intent for her. As if he wanted her to be unaware, to be completely dependent on him, he'd remained quiet. She felt Jesus was a soundless observer, testing her, patiently watching her to see if she leaned on him or on her own understanding. And, of course, she'd failed. Her faith was so small, so weak. She wanted him to speak, to shout at her *exactly* what he wanted her to do.

Wendy snuggled deeper into Kurt's hold. He'd been a good friend. He'd saved her life up on the mountain when the snowstorm almost did her in. He'd allowed her to work on his ranch and had finally agreed to guide her into Indian lands for the hidden treasure, although there was no guarantee they'd find the gold. And now he carried her across the Canadian River to safety.

She squeezed her eyes shut tight, so tight they hurt. Oh, why did God have to be so punishing?

Deflated by her troubles and her physical condition, Wendy sighed loudly, air escaping her lungs along with any hope she might have had for her life. Everything had fallen apart and had come to nothing. She was broke, and there was no gold. Dejected, she sighed again, allowing despair to replace the last ounce of strength she retained.

"Wendy?" Kurt paused and her eyelids flickered open. Water rushed around his knees as he stood staring down at her, studying her in the fading moonlight. She read the concern on his face and something more, something she'd already discovered within herself. Perhaps he reflected what he read in her own eyes for she knew she could no longer deny her feelings for him.

An intensity glowed in his gaze and a sad smile touched her lips, trying to reassure him that she understood the turmoil he seemed to wrestle. She'd accepted her love for him back at the notch in the rock, their secret hiding place that would hold a special place in her heart forever. But she knew they could not be, and in that moment, Kurt's eyebrows arched, as if he also realized they were never to be together.

Yet he tensed, and Wendy felt him hold her tighter as his arms pulled her to his chest.

"What's wrong?" He squinted down at her.

Wendy wanted to laugh and tell him nothing was wrong, that he needed a shave or she wanted something hot to drink, but she couldn't speak. A glimmer of the joy they could have shared made her throat tighten, and she closed her eyes again, unable to look at him as her heart splintered into a hundred pieces.

Like a lightning streak that illuminates the darkest night, she saw that God had not been silent at all.

CHAPTER FORTY-THREE

Wendy loved him. Finally, she admitted the truth. All of her worries, all of her cares, all of them had been delivered to this man, and he'd proven reliable, capable, durable. Kurt helped carry her load.

She saw how he'd given her a job and allowed her to become essential in his plans to build his ranch. He was strong and hardworking, but her limited abilities were required for his success, and she felt needed. In his presence, her loneliness had vanished. Her ancient sorrow and grief had disappeared as she grew to love his company and his leadership. She'd grown to love *him,* and she knew her time of testing was not over yet.

God had brought her west to find a treasure, and she'd succeeded. Kurt was a treasure more valuable than gold.

"Wendy?"

His query held a note of panic she couldn't ignore, yet she shook her head, still unable to speak, her eyes still shut tight.

When he shook her gently, her eyelids fluttered. Stars hovered over his shoulder and a sliver of moon glowed. Amidst the earthly beauty all around, she vowed to keep her secret.

Abruptly, his eyes gleamed and she held her breath as his gaze drifted to her lips. Anticipation swept over her, and she stared up at him, waiting. But he blinked and pulled away.

"I can't," he mumbled, and he blinked again. In the twinkling of an eye, the powerful moment passed, and a frightened look darkened his features. With a lunge, he plunged on the remaining distance to shore. Staggering, he raced up the dry bank to drop to his knees, peering intently at Wendy.

"I can't," he said again and set her on her feet. He handed the blanket to her, and she draped the covering around her shoulders, still looking down at him where he knelt with a look of great longing mixed with sorrow on his grimy face.

She patted his shoulder as his gaze shifted to the western mountains, as if searching for an unseen strength from the immense peaks. "I know," she whispered, choking on the lump in her throat.

Embarrassment brimmed and she shifted, suddenly finding her tongue. "Kurt, I'm all right. Put on your coat. You'll freeze to death."

She coaxed him until he finally labored to his feet and wrestled into his coat, his eyes never meeting hers. He shivered but didn't complain as he buttoned his coat and turned to walk north, toward Fort Union and Colorado and back to his former life.

"Hold my hand." Wendy hated herself for the ruse, but she still felt faint. Was her weakness from hunger alone? She loved a man who was spoken for, and her heart broke with the pain she endured. Perhaps he shared her pain, for his gaze never wavered from his northward trek, unwilling to deviate in any way from what he'd promised. Wendy prayed Marigold could deserve him.

Kurt gripped her hand tightly and she wound her fingers around his. She wished there was a way to start a fire and dry Kurt's wet clothing, but she knew walking would help keep him warm. She peered ahead, studying the rutted trail they followed.

"The Old Trail?" She indicated the road they walked, and Kurt nodded.

"There's still a chance the Apache are around, but we hope they're farther south, waiting for us at the mouth of the Mora

River." He grinned and Wendy felt her heart betray her again. "I think we fooled them."

She held the hand of the man she loved, and the confusing emotions seemed to weigh her down. This was Marigold's soon-to-be husband, and Wendy knew she couldn't have him, but she didn't release his hand. *Not yet, Lord.*

She'd found love, and the unfamiliar sensation burned like a fire in her chest, filling her with both an indescribable joy and a deep chasm of horror at losing the precious discovery.

She glanced at the cowboy as they walked hand in hand. They both loved the Lord, they'd become friends, and Wendy's few attributes seemed to compliment his rugged life on the frontier. She could hunt and herd cattle and ride wild horses. Who could've guessed she'd find such a perfect fit for her unorthodox skills here in the west? Of course, Jesus did.

As if in a dream, Wendy squeezed his hand tighter, not wanting to ever let go. Wouldn't it be nice to have someone to be with, someone to lean on, someone to serve? Her burdens had been so heavy. She'd suffered grief from her mother's death and then the loneliness and the never-ending sadness that filled her. Now she saw the Lord wanted something different for her. He'd truly brought her on an adventure of a lifetime, but was she not to get anything she wanted? With just a word of encouragement from Kurt, she knew she'd never return to Little Rock.

Kurt helped her across a deep ravine in the trail, and Wendy feigned needing his support. She admitted it wasn't a complete deception, as hunger and weariness had made her faint. Yet the truth was she refused to let go of Kurt's hand. Until absolutely necessary, she wanted to keep hold of him and believe there might've been something between them, although she knew it couldn't happen.

As the eastern sky turned from black to dark blue to a faint gray, a clatter of hooves sounded behind them. Kurt led her off the trail where they crouched behind a row of low bushes.

She recognized the rider's cavalry hat and the faded blue military jacket. Kurt stepped into the road, waving until Miguel slowed. Wendy stumbled into the road and stared at the mounted Indian and the three horses behind him. Within minutes, a fire blazed and coffee simmered in the familiar blackened pot while bacon sizzled in a skillet. Miguel said something, and Kurt laughed.

Wendy looked up from the hard biscuit she nibbled, savoring the flavorless bread more than she could've believed possible. "What?"

Miguel had been filling in details to Kurt while Wendy sat shivering beside the fire. Whether from cold or from hunger or from the realization that their ordeal had come to an end, she felt a sudden release of emotions that drained her. Her taut nerves had been stretched too far, and now she only wanted to be warm, eat food, and rest.

Kurt dropped to the ground beside her and placed an impatient hand on the barely bubbling coffeepot. "He says he heard Brewer and Kincaid riding close that morning, but he didn't know the Apache were there too. He slipped away with three of the horses but was forced to leave our gear. After the attack, he opened up with his horse pistol and that's when we made our break. Later, at night, he came back to camp and gathered what was left of our gear."

He paused to toss another stick on the flames and touch the coffeepot again. Frowning, he looked at Wendy where she sat huddled beneath a blanket. "They took my rifle and the other horses. But Shannon came to him a day later, after apparently escaping the Apache."

Wendy smiled and glanced at the mare where she munched green leaves from the mesquite bush. As if by magic, green foliage now dotted the bleak landscape. The desert seemed to have blossomed overnight. Spring had come to the high plains, but Wendy didn't want to consider the implications for herself. Soon she would have to leave the west and Kurt Jordan.

"He found this on the two dead men," Kurt added as he showed a handful of crumpled bills to her before stuffing the cash into his pocket. He narrowed his eyes as he studied Wendy. "Apparently it was worth quite a bit of money to keep an eye on you."

He lifted the blackened pot from the blaze and filled three cups, steam rising into the morning air as the sun topped the eastern horizon. No one spoke as they ate and drank coffee, Wendy struggling to remember Kurt's admonition to eat slowly and only a little at a time. Her stomach had shriveled over the past few days, and she could only eat a small portion, but she relished every bite.

Eyes drooping and her belly satisfied, Wendy struggled to stay awake as Kurt and Miguel performed the necessary camp chores.

"Get some sleep," Kurt urged. She tried not to think of him as she snuggled deeper into the blanket. They had decided to stay here a day longer to allow Kurt and Wendy to recuperate, but she suspected it was on her account alone. Kurt seemed fit as a fiddle after some hot coffee, but Wendy felt exhausted and couldn't rouse herself to pitch in and help around camp, to gather firewood, or attend to the horses. Despite her desire to assist, she went to sleep, a broken heart reminding her she needed to go back to Arkansas.

The afternoon sun leaned far to the west when Wendy awoke. She wanted more coffee yet felt reluctant to leave her warm blankets. She knew food and drink were now readily available, waiting for her when she rose, and her thoughts drifted lazily.

Her love for Kurt had spoiled the treasure hunt, and she wanted now only to be away. A shadow of something significant lurked beyond the edges of her mind, and she knew God was working, doing something, yet she couldn't comprehend. Sadly, she'd found herself content with sorrow back in Little Rock. The familiar emotion had consumed her, and she'd fallen into a rut, a routine of hiding from society and embracing her grief as an old friend. But this form of diseased life had become a bad habit, making her life empty.

Randall Whitmore's illicit proposal had been the catalyst to move her west, but her adventure had ended in failure. She found no gold and had fallen hopelessly in love with a penniless cowboy. How could this be God's will? Yet a sense of anticipation lingered, as if the Lord were not done with her, her adventure unfinished.

She squirmed under her covers. What now? It seemed Kurt would marry Marigold Peterson, and Wendy would return to Arkansas, taking her broken heart with her. Back in Little Rock, she faced abject poverty and no alternatives. The war was surely to end soon, and the South would be overrun with returning soldiers facing worse predicaments than hers.

She'd already come to the conclusion she couldn't marry Mr. Whitmore. Not just because she wasn't to be unequally yoked, as Scripture commanded, but because she didn't love him. He wasn't a man who shared her faith, and her heart belonged to another.

She peered over the edge of the blanket to where Kurt and Miguel sat beside the little fire, flames barely leaping above the ring of stones one of the men had placed around the blaze. They seemed in earnest conversation, whispers of Spanish language drifting to her on the gentle, spring breeze. They'd become her friends and she would miss them.

Her spirit felt heavy, weighted like a stone that crushed her. She would miss these friends, but she loved Kurt, and for the first time in her life, an unfamiliar joy crouched at the fringe of her heart, threatening to explode into full bloom happiness if she wasn't careful. And she must be careful. Grief had defined her entire life. She'd clung to her sorrow like a drowning man clings to a rope tossed from shore. She'd believed only sadness lay before her, that her future would only include bad things. Aunt Lil's suggestion to go west and pursue something out of her realm had frightened her, because she wasn't sure how to live again. And now Jesus teased her with both failure and hope. Wendy had changed on this journey. She'd followed her aunt's advice and discovered wonderful things out here. New friends, new experiences, a new love. And now she would leave them all behind as she returned to a life of suffering. As a martyr marching to the gallows, she accepted her fate. Good things and happiness and handsome cowboys were not for someone like Wendy, yet the truth of the trip west remained, and she knew she was being unfair to the Lord.

She drew a deep breath and nodded, resolved to do what Jesus asked of her.

"Wendy?" Kurt's call made her hesitate, forgetting for a moment where she was. Spring had come to the desert, and vibrant green danced across the plains, splashing the gray and brown landscape with a profusion of color. Yellow and orange and pink wildflowers swayed in the breeze, and Wendy squinted up at the azure sky as a pair of fluffy clouds hovered lazily overhead while birds chirped merrily in the mesquite thickets.

She turned her head and met his searching gaze. He seemed concerned, a look of worry filling his features, but she smiled, allaying his fears. Her worries need not be his.

"Any coffee left?" She struggled to a sitting position and pushed the blanket from her as she reached for her boots. The boots were dry now, and Wendy wondered who had thoughtfully removed them from her while she slept and placed them in the sun.

Despite the afternoon warmth, a chilled breeze blew from the high mountains, and she shrugged into her coat, leaving the buttons undone as she moved toward the little blaze. Her heart flip flopped when Kurt smiled and handed a steaming mug to her. Then a sharp pain like a knife pierced her chest at the memory he would marry Marigold soon and she would be alone forever.

"Miguel and I were talking," Kurt said as he indicated a log for her.

Wendy took a seat, blowing on her coffee as she studied the two riders over the rim of her mug. She felt disgustingly filthy, and her hair resembled a rat's nest, but she would miss this—the comradery, the feeling she was an equal among tough riders who performed tough jobs. They respected her riding skills, and they all knew she was the best shot with a rifle. She'd found a place among these men, and she wondered why God would take her from something, from some place she'd come to feel she belonged.

"Miguel found at least fifty mavericks along the river when he was scouting for us. With the money he took from those two skunks, we can buy another rifle and supplies to make a play for them. No one else seems interested in the strays along the rivers, and whatever isn't branded belongs to anyone."

"Sounds good," Wendy said softly, wishing she could join them. "But you'll need a third rider to hold the cattle while you drive strays from the brush."

He narrowed his eyes and nodded. "I know that. I figured you'd come with us. We could sure use you."

Wendy pursed her lips and shook her head. "I'll be returning to Arkansas. There's no gold, and my time has about run out. I'll be leaving as soon as we reach Trinidad."

A scowl darkened Kurt's features and he scratched at his unshaven chin. Miguel frowned and poked at the fire with a stick as Kurt shifted. "But you can't go back to marry that scoundrel. I thought—"

"You're engaged, Kurt," Wendy snapped, no longer able to hold her tongue. "You will build your ranch with Marigold at your side. Perhaps she can ride with you."

He chuckled sourly and kicked at the stone fire ring. "I don't want Marigold to ride with us. I want you."

She stood, staring down at him. "Well, you can't have us both." Not waiting for a reply, she stalked into the brush.

CHAPTER FORTY-FOUR

Fort Union lay quiet under a bright sun as Wendy shifted on her saddle, leather creaking as she watched Miguel trot toward the sprawling military buildings. From the corner of her eye, she could still read the disappointed and confused look on Kurt's face.

"You don't want to go with him?"

Her question seemed to bring him out of a lethargy, as if he'd been pondering deep things. He scowled. "No, he doesn't need my help. He knows plenty of those soldiers."

They remained silent as Miguel disappeared among the shops and outbuildings of the frontier post, before Kurt nudged his horse into motion. "Come on. We'll set up camp."

He led the way to the banks of the nearby Cimarron River where a strong current of melting snow muddied the shallow water. Without a word to Wendy, he unsaddled his horse and the pack animal and began gathering firewood as she threw her gear behind a tree, rummaging among the packs until she found a towel and a blanket.

"I need a bath," she mumbled as she marched upriver, not bothering to look at him. She walked for almost a quarter of a mile before she searched for a suitable swimming pool. The dirty river didn't allow many options and Wendy tossed her coat and boots under the spreading branches of a huge cottonwood tree before undressing. With a furtive glance all around, she carried her filthy clothes into the river and scrubbed them clean while she shivered in the cold water.

Wringing her clothes, she removed all the water she could before spreading them on the bank and washing her hair. Her teeth chattered, but she bathed anyway, grateful to shed a layer of dirt and grime.

Later, as she sat with the blanket wrapped around her, she prayed while her clothes dried in the sun. Her resignation to her plight had not resulted in the peace she thought her obedience to the Lord would bring. She felt like crying as she thought of leaving Trinidad and her new friends, especially Kurt, but she'd do all that was expected of her if she could only know what the Lord wanted from her. Surely a sense of joy or happiness would come as she submitted to God's guidance.

"Am I to always feel miserable? I'd gotten used to grief and loss back in Little Rock, and then I thought you wanted me to come west and find gold to pay Father's debts. Aunt Lil said it would be an adventure, but I never expected to find Kurt. And now that I've found love, you lead me back to the same sad place I came from." She sighed and arched an eyebrow as she studied the blue sky and the pine tree covered mountains to the west. A triangle of ducks flapped overhead, quacking noisily on their trek north. "What do you want from me?"

Wendy hung her head and waited, hoping Jesus would say something, answer her plea in a way she could comprehend. But only the gentle moan of the wind through the tree branches and the cry of a hunting hawk broke the still day.

Green grass carpeted every aisle between the trees and rocks. Small colorful wildflowers dotted the sandy soil, and Wendy knew winter had retreated for another year. Snow might still fall in the high peaks, but spring had come to the prairies, and she knew the time Randall Whitmore had given her had almost passed. She would need to head for home soon, and she hated it. Something called to her here. A feeling, a sensation she didn't recognize filled her as she peered up at the towering mountain heights. A fragrant pine scent drifted on the wind, and she inhaled, drinking the aromatic air into her lungs, savoring the intoxicating smell. She loved being here and wondered why God would have her leave. What awaited her back home? Surely only pain, heartache, and poverty loomed in her future. But Wendy wanted to trust, to obey the Lord. Life wasn't supposed to be easy. The Lord tests those he loves, Kurt had said.

But, did she have to go home? Were there no other options?

Kurt. Her heart swelled as a lump rose in her throat. She never dreamed she'd find love. And a cowboy? A grin tugged at her lips as she thought of the rugged outdoorsman. They made a good team, she believed. Why did God have to bring her west after Kurt had met Marigold Peterson? If she'd come last summer or perhaps even in the autumn, she might've convinced him to consider her. But not now.

She pulled her hair into a messy ponytail before dressing slowly as she continued to argue her case with the Lord. It would've been better if he had left her hiding in the forest along the Arkansas River back home. There she was safe, and her dull routine had been established and accepted by everyone, except God. He was the only one who wanted something different for her. And look where that had gotten her.

She tossed her still damp coat over her shoulder and started back to camp. Her stomach growled as she walked, and she knew supper awaited.

A curious idea niggled in her mind, and she scowled up at the lone cloud that dotted the sky. Did she truly regret the trip west? The journey had proven to be the adventure Lil claimed. Wendy knew she would never forget the thrills and fears that plagued her as she navigated hostile lands while they searched for hidden treasure. She'd worshipped with Kurt and shared Scripture, spending precious time she'd never have again. Although she'd starved in the wilderness with Kurt and almost died from the Apache and the snowstorm, she wouldn't have missed the experience for any amount of money.

"Why go back?" Kurt's query cut into the deepening twilight as Wendy climbed the riverbank where she'd cleaned dirty dishes. The two riders sat beside a bright fire, hats pushed back to reveal their consternation as Wendy approached. She packed the dishes in the canvas sack and faced them, hating this final confrontation with the two cowboys.

"You already know. I have to meet with Mr. Whitmore before the end of April. It's over, Kurt. My time out here has come to an end. I'll gather Aunt Lil and head home after we reach Trinidad tomorrow."

Miguel said something, and Kurt nodded. "He says it's a long ride. Might take a day or two."

Wendy smiled faintly at the Indian, knowing he was trying to extend their time together. But she felt convinced there was no reason to drag out her departure any longer. Her heart ached more each day. "You know we can make the trip in one day if we get an early start."

She met Miguel's dark eyes over the fire, and she nodded, trying to tell him how much she'd come to appreciate him. He pressed his lips into a thin line and glowered at her, but she knew he would miss her too.

"We've got gear again," Kurt went on, gesturing to the used rifle that leaned on a pack and the two sacks of food stores Miguel had purchased at the fort. "We could start right now. Turn around and begin beating the brush for strays. I'll bet we can drive a hundred head of stock from the rivers and build our herd all the quicker."

Wendy shook her head, her chest tightening like a vice. "You know we can't start right now. The Apache are around, and Marigold is probably waiting for your return. And I need to go home."

She paused and then pointed her chin at Miguel. "What did you learn in Fort Union about the war?"

He spoke briefly, and then, Kurt arched an eyebrow. "Dispatch riders have reported Lee has retreated from Richmond, General Grant on his heels. The Confederacy is collapsing."

No one said anything for a long time and Wendy felt the Confederacy was out of time as she was. She completed her chores, making sure things were ready for an early departure. She straightened from the camp gear and leaned against a rock while she studied the familiar sight that she'd only recently come to know. Dancing flames cast a ruddy glow on the riders' faces, and Wendy wanted to etch this scene forever in her mind. Deepening shadow stretched to where the horses cropped grass. The crackling fire brightened the camp circle where the leaping flames lighted the thrown packs, saddles, and cooking utensils. She wanted to never forget the blackened coffeepot that simmered in the glowing coals. She wished to always remember the vivid night sky with countless stars that never ceased to thrill her and reveal God's presence and artistry. Jesus had given her the delight of a lifetime. Even with a broken heart, she realized she'd enjoyed her time out west. Although she'd doubted God's plans for her, Kurt's words returned to remind her she'd stepped out in faith and experienced more of life than she'd expected. Wendy would remember her journey west forever.

As Miguel and Kurt sulked by the campfire, she backed into the shadows, eager to say a proper goodbye to Shannon. The mare bent to graze, nibbling at the fresh leaves that decorated the tree branches and bushes. She lifted her head as Wendy approached, nuzzling into the girl's shoulder as Wendy encircled her neck.

"I'll miss you, girl, and your shenanigans. You taught me a lot about perseverance and grit. I needed to learn that. Life is tough, and you have to get back up after you've been knocked down."

She frowned at her words, pondering them, seeing them anew. With a jerk, she glanced up at the night sky. "Is that why you brought me out here? Are you teaching me lessons?"

As if her memories were strung on a rope, they darted across her mind in a series of scenes overlapping one another. The great sorrow at her mother's death. The years of riding in the forest where she tried to hide from everyone. Father's death that ended his corrupt career and Mr. Whitmore's indecent proposal that drove her west. The hard work on Kurt's ranch as she attempted to get him to guide her to Indian lands. The beautiful dance with Kurt in the sawmill office. The fruitless search for gold and her falling in love with the misguided cowboy. Kurt was no more in love with Marigold Peterson than Wendy was, but his impulsive quest had led him to the spoiled ranch princess, and he was convinced he'd been brought to her by the Holy Spirit. Who was Wendy to argue with divine intervention? She had enough problems of her own.

She searched the night sky, wanting answers. "Why? Why bring me here to break my heart? I appreciate the adventure and the exciting expedition, but I still have nothing. I've lost my family's land and don't have a skill I can use back home. Where am I to go?"

Nothing but the gentle sound of the horses cropping grass disturbed the silent night, and then a shooting star rocketed across the expanse. Wendy nodded. "Yes, Lord, I know. You are God, I am not. Let me trust you. Let me believe you are not through with me yet. Help me know I can lean into you, and you want good things for me. With your help, let me accept whatever happens to me."

She thrust her hands into her coat pockets and bit her lip as Kurt's face gleamed in her mind. God tested her and she knew it. Like Kurt had said in the wilderness, God tested those he loved, to shape them, to build their faith, to develop their character. Struggles come for a purpose. Valuable lessons lurked in every trial. She was being shaped more into the image of Christ and she hated it. Why couldn't she have what she wanted? And she wanted Kurt Jordan.

Yet Jesus meant more to her than life itself. Tears brimmed her eyes, and she blinked several times. "He's not mine, Lord," she whispered into the night. "I accept and will not interfere. Your will be done."

Wendy vowed to submit to the Lord. Yet she felt certain of two things. She would not marry Randall Whitmore, and she could not stay in Trinidad.

CHAPTER FORTY-FIVE

The trio of riders trotted their horses down the narrow road that led past the sawmill. Men hurried around the structure like an army of ants, moving stacks of lumber and preparing logs for cutting, but the threesome didn't stop or even wave at the bustling crew of lumbermen. Heavy thoughts rode with them, and silence shrouded their passage.

They drew rein beside the river where the bridge led into town. Alongside the river wound a trail to the distant range where Wendy knew the Peterson ranch perched atop a low knoll.

"Well," Kurt said as he held his horse steady, eyes locking on Wendy. "Is there anything I can say to persuade you to stay?"

Her lips trembled as she peered at him, then her gaze lifted to the high peaks beyond, unable to look at him any longer. *Where does my strength come from? Does it come from the mountains? No, it comes from God, maker of heaven and earth and the mountains.*

She sighed and met his piercing gaze. He seemed reluctant to leave, and she could tell he wrestled with similar struggles as they stared at one another. Shannon pranced sideways beneath her, and Wendy tugged on the reins with a firm hand.

"We both have things to do. You have your path, and I have mine. May the Lord bless you, Kurt, and thanks for letting me tag along with you and Miguel."

Her eyes shifted to the somber Indian, and she tried to smile, but he only squinted at her in return.

Kurt pressed some crumpled bills into her palm. "You'll need a stage ticket," he mumbled.

Wendy appreciated the miserable expression on his unshaven face.

"Well, so long, Wen Moylan. I've enjoyed knowing you."

"Say hello to Marigold," Wendy whispered. "Good luck to the both of you."

He stiffened in his saddle and narrowed his eyes. With a determined look plastered on his features, he tugged his hat low and spurred his gelding away.

She watched him go, a sharp pain stabbing her heart. She wanted to cry, but lifted her chin, resolved to trust God. She'd come west for adventure, and she'd had an exciting time. She should've died more than once, and she remembered riding the wild mustang, stumbling in the snowstorm, and being pursued by Apaches. She nodded, realizing God had done exactly what she wanted. She'd experienced life in ways she couldn't have dreamed.

"You love him."

Miguel's comment wasn't a question, and his words caught her off guard. "I know," she whispered as she watched Kurt vanish over a rise and disappear from view. Then her eyes widened as she realized she understood the Yaqui.

"You speak English," she accused, staring in astonishment.

A frown puckered his mouth. "Kurt is a fool and doesn't know his own heart. The Lord is working on him."

"He is not for me." She placed a hand on Miguel's arm. "I cannot make this about me. The Lord knows my heart, and I trust he has a plan. A plan to help me and not harm me. But I will always love Kurt."

Miguel gestured at the nearby river. "Long ago, Spanish soldiers died here, and the place became known as the River of

Lost Souls. French trappers called it *Purgatoire,* and it became the Purgatory. But I feel you have found your soul here. I think you have discovered something important about yourself."

Wendy nodded and tried to smile as tears rimmed her eyes. The wise Indian looked at her, and she nodded again, unable to articulate all she wanted to say to him. "I thought he felt something for me."

"I believe he loves you in return, but he is engaged to another. His honor will not allow him to speak of his feelings. Would you have him be less than honorable?"

A tear slid down her cheek and her smile trembled as she brushed the wetness away. "Of course not. Thank you, Miguel. Thank you."

She slipped from Shannon's back, tossed the reins to the Indian and hurried away, crossing the bridge and entering Trinidad.

A bell tinkled above her head as she walked into Hanson's General Store. Lil was there, bustling about the crowded store while Jenny Blair waited on customers at the long counter.

"Wendy?" Lil's greeting held all the uncertainty Wendy felt as the two women embraced. Aunt Lil held her at arm's length, studying her critically. "How are you? You look like something the cat dragged in." A wide smile creased the older woman's face, and Wendy wanted to tell her everything—about being lost in the wilderness and almost dying in the snow. But something checked her story, and Wendy squinted, seeing for the first time the joyful glow on her aunt's cheeks.

"What's happened since I've been gone? You look different."

Aunt Lil beamed, and Wendy worried even more, something telling her everything had changed.

"Oh, Wendy, I'm so happy."

Wendy stared, not comprehending. She needed to depart Trinidad if she were to meet Mr. Whitmore's deadline. And she planned on leaving Trinidad at the earliest opportunity.

"What's happened?" She considered Lil, knowing she wasn't going to like what she heard.

"Mr. Hanson has hired me to help Jenny with the store. He is such a busy man, and his business is booming as the mine expands. Also, I work half a day for Mr. Bracken."

"Mr. Bracken?" Wendy could feel her stomach tighten, fearing what was coming.

"Mr. Bracken is the mine manager. I work in his office, filing and writing correspondence." She paused and looked away, a crimson blush rising up her neck. She glanced again at Wendy, her eyes glowing. "Oh, I love it here. I love my work and all of the men are so nice to me."

"Men?" Wendy whispered, her heart sinking.

"Well, Mr. Hanson of course, and then Mr. Bracken, and Mr. Edmonds at the livery, and certainly Bill at the café. They're all so nice to me and I never dine alone."

Wendy swallowed her surprise and grasped her aunt's elbow, propelling her out of the aisle and into a quiet corner. "I need to leave here immediately."

Lil blanched, her smile fleeing. "But Wendy, I don't want to go. I'm happy here, happier than I've ever been in my life. This adventure has been the best thing for me."

"Well, not for me," Wendy snapped. "I didn't find the gold, and I need to go home. Now."

"The gold?" Lil narrowed her eyes and nodded. "Oh, yes, of course. Well, no matter. We can stay out here and find work for you. There's nothing at home for us now."

"There's nothing out here for me," Wendy almost wailed. Her heart felt like a blacksmith's anvil in her chest. Wouldn't God help her? Why would he not lift his heavy yoke from her neck? If she stayed in Trinidad another hour, she felt she might lose her mind.

Lil crossed her arms over her chest and scowled. "I'm not going. For the first time in my life, I'm appreciated and feel I have a place in Trinidad. There's nothing for me back in Arkansas. I'm staying."

Wendy knew this was all part of her ordeal. More weight landed on her shoulders, and she sagged beneath the load. But she realized she wasn't through being tested. Clenching her teeth, she nodded again. "I'll write you from Little Rock."

CHAPTER FORTY-SIX

The stagecoach bumped roughly over the rutted road, but Wendy didn't feel the jarring. Her aunt had begged Wendy to reconsider, but she knew she had to leave immediately. Kurt's image haunted her, and she knew his marriage to Marigold Peterson would torment her forever. Without shedding a tear, she mounted the wooden box into the stagecoach and waved listlessly to Lil as she departed the frontier town.

Sunlight faded, and shadows filled the corners of the stagecoach, but Wendy hardly noticed. Her mind whirled with accusation and memories of the past few weeks. Why would Jesus do this to her? As if her ancient grief were not enough, now she felt overwhelmed with a broken heart that God brought upon her. Hadn't the Lord guided her to Trinidad?

"Why, Lord?" Her whispered plea went unanswered as the miles sped by, the jostling coach following the Santa Fe Trail along the Arkansas River. A tiny measure of relief washed over her when the driver announced they'd left Colorado Territory and entered Kansas. She smoothed her dress, the only clean clothes she possessed. Everything was happening too quickly, and she felt a headache coming on as the interior of the coach darkened with twilight descending over the plains.

God's adventure to the western lands had not been what Wendy expected. Danger, starvation, and freezing cold had exploded all around her, blasting her out of the comforts of her sedate existence back in Little Rock. Yet she had weathered each situation. Despite misgivings at the results of her expedition into New Mexico, she knew Jesus was with her. He walked with her through each storm, providing strength as she navigated new and exciting challenges. Although her faith lagged at times, she knew she would lean into the Lord.

Wendy gritted her teeth, allowing perhaps God had done a little to build her confidence. Surely, she wasn't afraid of hardships anymore. And she could travel in wild lands and not fear deprivations. The Lord had taught her many lessons and had certainly stretched her faith. But Kurt had come along and knocked her heart catawampus.

Wendy leaned her head back on the seat cushion, closing her eyes to the maddening thoughts darting across her mind. Love had surprised her, coming when least expected, and upsetting all of her ideas. And now she needed a plan.

Sometime after midnight, she formulated a loose strategy. After informing Mr. Whitmore that he now owned the dilapidated Moylan Plantation, she would spend the last of the money Kurt had given her on a steamer ticket upriver, following the Mississippi northward. Perhaps the rumors of employment opportunities in urban factories were true, and Wendy could find work. If not, she didn't know what to expect. She had nothing and didn't care. Her future seemed precarious at best. Yet, with the Lord beside her, she resolved to give moving north a try and see what happened.

"Buffalo Wallow," the stage driver bellowed as the coach slowed. Wendy recalled a few weeks ago when she and Lil had stopped here on their way west. Then, she'd been so filled with a sense of adventure and hope, starting on a journey that was supposed to impact her life forever. Then, they had feasted at the little café on the main street. Now, she'd be lucky if she could afford a cup of coffee, her meager funds hoarded for her unknown future. Sad and heavy hearted, she was returning to Arkansas with nothing.

Yet, the expedition had impacted her life as predicted. Surely, she would never be the same again, and her faith had been stretched, refined, developed. Although her heart ached, she felt stronger and more confident after the struggles she'd endured. Reluctantly, Wendy had to admit God worked through her pain.

The stage came to a stop and dust rolled over them in a thick wave as Wendy stepped from the vehicle. She blinked in the morning light and accepted the steaming bowl of soup a serving girl thrust into her hands. At Wendy's hesitant look, the girl smiled. "Your ticket pays for the soup, miss."

Wendy inhaled the rich aroma and smiled. Was God taking care of her? Why couldn't she just trust Jesus? Hadn't he always taken care of her?

"We'll be here about twenty minutes," the stage driver shouted from his high perch as the girl handed a bowl up to him. "Eat quick and be ready to go."

Fresh teams of horses were walked to their places in the harness as the spent teams were led away. "What's news, Danny boy?"

The driver's question made the hostler scratch an ear as he pushed horses into position. Wendy watched the horse exchange as she ate, her ears pricking at the suggestion of information.

"You haven't heard, Lew?" The hostler draped the leather harness over the horse and started buckling straps, his hands moving deftly as he scowled up at the driver.

"Haven't heard a thing," Lew replied around a mouthful of stew.

Danny nodded, still working. "Figured as much, or you wouldn't just be sitting there stuffing your face. The war's over. General Lee surrendered outside of Richmond. Got the news over the wire."

A stunned silence fell over the onlookers as people digested the startling information. Wendy saw a man begin to cry, and the serving girl dropped her head, pretending not to notice as she moved among the small crowd and gathered empty bowls.

Wendy didn't hear Lew's response as she turned away and walked a few steps from the others. The war was over. Suddenly, she knew she wasn't going back to Little Rock. The derelict plantation and empty house held no appeal for her at all. There was no reason to meet with Mr. Whitmore and tell him she wouldn't marry him, and he could have the rundown farm. He'd probably already taken possession. She chewed her lip and peered all around, searching for clues as to possible employment opportunities or a stage schedule nailed to a wall, telling of departures to the north. Perhaps the serving girl needed help.

The crowd of agitated passengers parted, and she saw him. She wondered if her eyes were playing tricks on her as she watched Kurt ride into the station, Shannon trotting beside him.

Her heart leaped, but she drew a deep breath, forcing calm. She needed to think of herself now, and he was not hers.

She walked toward him, unable to stay away, somehow drawn to him as he halted a few yards from her. He scanned the crowd and then squinted when he found her, their eyes locking as her hands clutched the folds in her dress. Why was he here?

Without greeting or questions, she blurted. "The war's over."

A scowl creased his weary face, and then, he nodded. "I figured the war would end soon."

They stood silent for a long moment in the dusty street, and then Kurt shoved his hat back and peered down at her. "Are you going back?"

She wrinkled her nose. "No reason to now. I think I'll go north or see what I can find along the stage route." Wendy felt surprised when the fear she'd wrestled slipped away, leaving only a resolved obedience behind. Come what may, she'd put God first. She studied Kurt and tilted her head, her curiosity getting the better of her. "What are you doing here?" She glanced at the pair of lathered horses and noticed the sweat streaks on both animals. "And why do you have Shannon?"

Kurt pressed his lips into a thin line and sighed, then he stepped stiffly from the saddle. He gripped the gelding's reins and stepped closer to Wendy. "I'm a fool."

Wendy tried to smile. "I know, but answer my question. Why are you here?"

A faint grin hovered around his mouth as he shifted uneasily, still looking at her. "I think I love you."

She gasped as the breath sucked from her lungs. She'd hungered for these very words and now that she heard them, she didn't know how to respond. "You *think* you love me?"

His skeptical grin spread wide into a real smile as he nodded. "Uh-huh. Miguel says I'm impulsive, but he also says I'm right this time."

"This time?"

He chuckled, and Wendy thought his laughter sounded like music. "Are you going to repeat everything I say? Yes, Miguel says he thinks I'm right this time, but he says I have to be sure. That's why I'm here."

Wendy crossed her arms over her chest. "Why are you here?"

Kurt straightened. "Miss Wendy Moylan, I wish to court you."

Her brows arched even higher and then furrowed as she squinted at him, confused. "But ... but what about Marigold?"

His smile twitched. "She ran away with Webb Larson while we were down in New Mexico."

Her laughter rang out, and a few people glanced their way. His smirk made her grin.

"Don't laugh. It's not funny. We were engaged, you know."

"Yes, I do remember some details about such an arrangement." She giggled, happiness bubbling inside her like the hot springs near Kurt's cabin. Could this be real? Could God be giving her the desire of her heart?

The Lord had brought her west to challenge her, Wendy knew, but now things came clearly into focus as she saw her faith deepen through the trials she faced out here. As if Christ had maneuvered events to shape her, crush her, grow her, she now saw he was building her faith.

"I love to worship God with you, to work with you, to struggle with you. But I didn't know I loved you until the river, when I carried you across the Canadian."

Wendy recalled the moment when he'd stared down at her, love shining in his eyes. She thought he'd been about to kiss her, and she blushed, remembering the fading moonlight and the way the night's final stars shimmered above him.

"But I was promised to another girl," he rushed on. "The wrong girl, it seems. The Lord was testing me too, Wendy. My impatience has caused me more troubles than I can count, but now I want to do things the right way."

"What does that mean?"

"If you agree to allow me to court you, I'm to bring you home."

"Home?" she echoed.

Kurt shook his head. "You'll have to stop repeating everything I say. Yes, home. Miguel says to bring you home so we can plan our trip to the Canadian River. Lots of strays down that way. Slowly, with patience, with your help, I aim to build my ranch."

Wendy smiled, her heart bursting. "Our ranch," she whispered as she stepped nearer, peering up at him. Pleasure radiated from her, and she believed he must know how she felt, just from her excited words as she raced on.

"I'll sew curtains for the windows, and you can put in a floor, perhaps a plank floor or flagstones. I love the fireplace with the three crosses, and we'll raise our children with Christ at the center of our family."

"Hold on." He laughed as he wrapped his hands around her waist and drew her near. Her arms slid around his neck. "Who's the impulsive one now?" He paused and studied her for a long moment. "I want to do things right this time, Wendy. I want to go slow and pray often and court you the right way, waiting for the Lord to guide us."

She nodded and bit her lip, hoping her tears wouldn't spoil the magic moment. Her broken heart had healed in the twinkling of an eye, and she couldn't believe she deserved such happiness. Why was God so good to her?

Kurt studied her intently. "May I kiss you?"

Wendy's eyelids flickered closed as she pressed her lips to his.

"We're moving on, folks," the stage driver shouted as passengers boarded the coach, but Kurt's arms tightened around Wendy, and they didn't move as the driver's whip cracked and harness jingled as the stage left town.

When she stepped from him, she looked away, embarrassed. She lifted a trembling hand to her warm lips and glanced at the bright morning sky, then nodded. "I thought I was out here to find gold, a hidden treasure. Instead, I found you, Lord, a lasting treasure. Thank you." Her gaze shifted to the dusty cowboy who beamed down at her. "And you. We found each other."

Kurt nodded. "Well, I guess God's testing will produce results, one way or another. It's best to trust him when you walk through the fires."

Contentment washed over Wendy, and she smiled, knowing her trials had grown her faith and drawn her closer to Christ.

Wendy nodded. "Trust Jesus," she whispered as she melted into Kurt's embrace again.

ABOUT THE AUTHOR

ANDREW ROTH taught American History for twenty-two years at the middle school level before beginning his literary career. He lives in Bakersfield, California, with his wife and is a proud father and grandfather. A native of Kansas, Andrew was raised with a deep love and appreciation for history, particularly the Old West. Andrew has been a Christian for more than three decades, and his hope is that his writing will encourage readers and rebuild lives. The passage he feels is his guiding verse is Jeremiah 31:4, "I will build you up again and you will be rebuilt." Andrew's website is: http://andrewrothbooks.com.

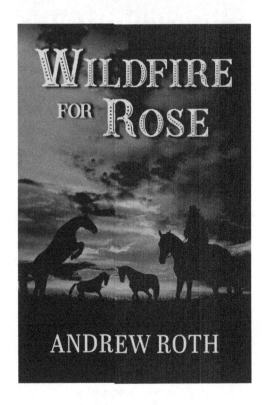

For information about Andrew or his books, check out his website, https://www.andrewrothbooks.com, or https://ElkLakePublishingInc.com. Andrew's books are found on Amazon in both Kindle and paperback.

Made in the USA
Coppell, TX
02 September 2023